KEEP CLOSE

Kristen Wade

ISBN (Paperback): 979-8-9919658-1-1
ISBN (Hardback): 979-8-9919658-2-8
ISBN (eBook): 979-8-9919658-0-4

For Charlie, Nicholas, Rosemary, and Chris

The yearning to protect those we love is
the most noble virtue we all have in common.
When humanity is threatened,
let it not be this truth that destroys us.

The Haley Family
Jim Haley "Pop"
Claire Haley "Mom"
Dr. Nick Haley "Dad"
Siblings
Lauren Haley "Ren"
Peter Haley
Elizabeth Haley "Lizzie"

The Keller Family
Mr. Greg Keller "Dad"
Siblings
Fitz Keller (married to Mae)
Lee Keller
Caleb Keller
Penny Keller
Will Keller
Ozzie Keller
Karen Keller

PROLOGUE

September 20th, 2015 - The North Sentinel Island in the Andaman Sea. Home to the uncontacted Sentinelese natives.
12 years until.

W hen the village hunters went searching for the three missing children, they found the oddity lodged deep in the sand on the northern cove. At first, they mistook it for a sea turtle. The men gazed at the mysterious crimson rock in fear and wonder; it was crystallized, speckled, and uneven, with two rodent-sized holes bored into its surface. Without any outside trade or influence, the Sentinelese had never encountered anything so strange. Certain of its malevolence and too afraid to touch it, the men argued over what to do. Until a piercing screech rang out from the forest.

CHAPTER 1

REN

R en gripped her phone tighter, tapping incessantly on the cracked screen that had destroyed her life, rejecting every memorable tune. Skip... Skip... Her eyes glazed as she stared at the moonlit Pacific from her grandfather's sailboat. Skip...

In a rush of anger, Ren cocked her arm and hurled the phone overboard. She pictured it sinking into the abyss and wondered what it would feel like to helplessly fall deeper and deeper.

Ren shuddered and pulled her sweater sleeve over the scar that stretched across the top of her forearm.

The night was crisp, clear, and windless. The ocean lay as still as she'd ever seen—like another night sky spread out below her.

Pop had insisted this family cruise would improve things between Ren and her siblings. But after another awkward dinner, Ren was happy to have the *Bethie* to herself. She exhaled and

2

gazed across the mirror-like sea, searching for her favorite constellations.

Scorpius... Corona Borealis... Ursa Major.

Then, a change in the water woke her from her daze.

The reflection of stars had become a wavering cascade of lights, shooting across the surface. Ren looked up to see hundreds—no, *thousands*—of falling meteors, giant and bright, leaving trails stretched behind them like a cat's whiskers across the sky. She stood dumbfounded as they descended above her. One meteor rivaled the moon in its size and brightness. It thundered overhead like a low-flying plane, plummeting through blaze and smoke.

Could it be that close? Am I hallucinating?

The boat rattled, and the blast of wind nearly knocked Ren off her feet. She held tight to the railing and gripped her bare feet to the deck. Her brown hair thrashed behind her as she watched the pulsing ball of light scream toward the ocean. She laughed out loud in shock and exhilaration, marveling at the awesome spectacle until it disappeared in the distance.

No way that just happened!

She wished Dad had been there to see it.

A moment passed.

BOOM!

The colossal sound of the impact surged through the deck and up her spine.

Ren's heart clenched as she stared at the horizon. In the moonlight, she could see it starting to churn and swell.

The shockwave.

Growing. Rushing. Coming toward them like a throbbing

fifty-foot wall.

"Pop! Peter!" she yelled.

Ren's heart pounded as she threw open the bench lid and grabbed an armful of life jackets.

She slid down the stairs, twisting her ankle and cracking her forearm. Her younger brother and grandfather were already out in the galley.

"Ren! What was that?" Pop asked, pulling her up.

"Jackets...Go above! Lizzie..." was all she managed to sputter as she shoved two vests at them and slid the other two up her shoulder.

Slowly, the boat tilted, an ominous lean as if being pulled by a hungry sea creature.

"Lizzie!" Ren cried to her little sister as she pushed past Peter, clambering toward the bunk room at the bow. She could hear the millions of gallons of Pacific water sucking skyward from the surface, just outside the hull. Through the skylight, Ren watched in terror as the moon disappeared behind the foaming monster towering above them.

"No!"

Then, it crashed.

The ferocious wave pummeled the *Bethie* into a violent death roll, ricocheting Peter, Ren, and Pop around the cabin. Broken dishes, pans, and equipment projected around them like cubes in a blender as freezing water fought its way through the walls.

Ren scrambled and flailed as the gushing water washed her down the narrow hall toward Lizzie's screams. It was up to Ren's waist in seconds, mounting pressure against the bunk door.

4

Ren fought the violent rocking to stay upright.

"Lizzie! Stand back!" But she could barely hear her own voice. Ren turned the knob. The fierce current flung the door from her hands and rushed into the bunkroom, pummeling eight-year-old Lizzie with the force of a firehose. Ren was sucked through and slammed into the wall above the bed— just inches from her sister. They turned and twisted in the small room as the water swirled higher.

The *Bethie* finally settled upside down, and the two girls climbed to the remaining air pocket in the cabin; their foreheads pressed to the floor-turned ceiling. Ren could hear the sea washing into Lizzie's mouth between her pleas for help, for Pop, for Peter.

Ren knew they couldn't fight the incoming flood to get out. They'd have to wait until the cabin was fully submerged and then swim to the surface.

On one breath.

Ren trembled as she pulled the life vests from her shoulder and pushed them away.

"Lizzie, we'll have to hold our breath and swim out, okay?" Ren instructed.

"I can't. It's too far, Ren!"

"I'm right here with you, Liz. Just hold tight to my belt."

The water crept toward Ren's neck, and Ren wondered how well she'd see through the night water. She tried to picture the route and what she could hold on to.

Okay, down the hall, through the galley...I can reach the cabinets...Up the stairs...no, they'd be below me. What if the galley door is jammed?

Ren couldn't think as she watched the water swell to Lizzie's chin. A slosh of foam smacked Ren's face, and she spat out her last words.

"Now, take a deep breath!"

Lizzie nodded and gasped. Ren took one last gulp of air and pulled them both to the middle of the cabin. As the current waned, Ren sprang her legs off the back wall and kicked toward the bunk door. Her injured foot ached with every jolt. She had imagined herself drowning just minutes ago, totally naïve to how terrifying it would be. The water was angry, dark, and freezing, and she didn't want to die in it. In fact, she'd never wanted to live so badly.

C'mon, Lizzie, kick harder!

Lizzie felt like an anchor around her waist, and at this pace, they'd never make it beyond the galley. The salt burned Ren's eyes as she reached blindly along the hallway. The darkness was overwhelming. Ren tugged and stretched, her gut clenching in panic.

Peter's long arm shot through the dark and grabbed Ren's hand, yanking the two girls into the kitchen. Peter gripped Lizzie's shirt. Then, the three of them swam hard through the debris toward the light of the stairwell.

Pop's torso appeared through the glowing door hatch, and Ren flung Lizzie at him. Pop yanked her down the stairwell and out of sight. Ren and Peter followed his lead, crouching out through the passageway to the deck. The wide upside-down vessel loomed above them.

Ren's lungs started cramping. Still barely able to see, she

tried to stay in Peter's wake, clawing and kicking toward the light beyond the edge of the boat. Peter cleared the railing and shot upward into the moonlight. Ren pulled herself past the metal bar into the open water. As she shot upwards, a sinking cabinet door cracked the side of her skull. Stunned, Ren coughed out the rest of her breath. Her senses clouded, and her limbs felt like lead. She forgot how to swim.

The blur of Pop's body dove toward her in what seemed like a dream. He pressed a clump of her shirt in his teeth and then flew skyward, one powerful stroke at a time, like a gator dragging a puppy. Ren had gone limp. She didn't even feel cold anymore. Above them, the shadow of the life raft drew nearer. Her lungs were collapsing. She wanted to help swim, but couldn't move.

At last, Pop pushed her through the surface, and Ren's head slumped backward. Blinking up at the sky, she drank in the glorious air. She took three huge gasps before convulsing bile back into the water.

Peter and Pop heaved Ren into the inflated boat and laid her next to a small, shivering body.

Lizzie.

They were alive. Ren panted and spat as warm liquid rolled down her face. When it hit her lips, she tasted the blood.

"Ren! Ren! Are you okay? Can you hear..." Pop's voice seemed to fall down a well. As her vision went black, she thought of Mom's voice.

Will I ever hear it again?

CHAPTER 2

LEE

September 3rd, 2027 - Gladys, Oregon.
30 minutes until.

"Lee, come pick 'em up," was all the voice said. Lee grunted and rubbed his eyes awake. He didn't need to ask who was calling or who he was picking up. He already knew.

Twenty minutes later, Lee sat in Dad's old Jeep, watching his older brother, Fitz, exit the police station.

Fitz climbed into the front seat with the smell of whiskey and cigarettes. "Thanks for comin', man. I knew Mae would be real sore 'bout gettin' up."

Fitz's hands were bloody, and he had a swollen eye. His University of Washington T-shirt was ripped and stained with reddish-brown blotches from his injuries or someone else's. At least Fitz's fingertips didn't have the inky stain of an official arrest.

Another catch and release.

Fitz scratched at the beard he'd been neglecting to shave. Without it, he and Lee looked very similar—charred olive skin, dark eyes, and saddle-brown wavy hair. At twenty-four, Fitz was only six years older, but his jagged features, smoker's voice, and battle-scarred complexion made him look almost thirty. Lee was a broad six-foot-two, but Fitz had an inch and thirty more pounds on him.

"No problem. You okay?" Lee asked as Fitz sprawled his meaty arm across the console. Lee shifted to the left. His rough hands sat loose on the wheel. He wasn't angry, just dog-tired and thankful that he was too young to get into the bar. Three years from now, Lee will either have to talk Fitz down or fight alongside him.

"Yeah, I'm good." Fitz clicked on the radio. He twisted the knob until he found a clear tune. Then he pulled the Marlboro from his ear and lit it, flexing the hawk tattoo on his forearm. "Dennis was bein' a pain. He'd have been taken in with me if I didn't mess him up so bad."

Lee exhaled through his teeth. He knew what the fight was about. The Mariners lost again, and Fitz didn't have the cash to settle his debt. The day before, Fitz had only given Lee a couple hundred bucks for rent, far less than was needed. His contributions to the family had been light for weeks.

But Dennis should have known better than to challenge Fitz, who'd been compared to a grizzly for his size, strength, and bite.

Lee gazed at the quiet street. The asphalt glistened from the recent shower. It was only 9:48 pm, but Gladys was a fishing town, so everyone got to bed early. Lee yawned, scrunching up his forehead to keep his eyelids open.

The country radio went to static. Fitz reached to change it as the street before them lit up. A blaring rumble surged above them, and the Jeep began shaking and shifting on the road.

"Ho, what's goin' on?!" Fitz yelled.

"I don't—"

Boom. Boom.

The ground rocked, split, and quaked as car alarms exploded up and down the street. An old pine tree to their left uprooted, toppling toward them.

"Watch it!" Fitz shouted.

Lee slammed the brakes and pulled a hard right. His bald tires hydroplaned, spinning the Jeep until it pounded flat against a minivan. Lee's shoulder plunged through the shattered window.

The falling tree ripped the electrical wires down to the road. Hot powerlines jumped and popped around the downed branches.

"Fitz, are you…?" Lee panted, his hands still tight on the wheel.

The crippled telephone pole gave a loud crack as its base buckled and split. The massive beam fell onto a house at the corner, its metal cross-arms and barrel crashing through the roof in a spray of sparks and shingles. The transformer exploded within the house, and a column of flames erupted into the sky.

"No!" Fitz shouted as he leaped from the car. "That's Coach Terry's house!"

"Wait, Fitz!" But Lee's door was pinned against the van. He stumbled over the passenger side, barely keeping his legs below him.

By the time he'd reached the lawn, Fitz had already run inside the burning home.

11

"Fitz!" Lee fumbled with his phone to call for help. No signal.

Lee hurdled the porch steps and crossed the billowing threshold. Smoke blasted into his eyes and throat.

"Fitz! Fitz, where are you?" Lee yelled through fits of coughing.

The den and kitchen had been crushed into a wall of rubble. At the top of the stairs, a cloudy glow churned from all directions. Clumps of the ceiling crackled onto Lee's shoulders and hair. He tucked his nose into his shirt and went further inside. Lee wanted to call out again, but was afraid to inhale.

His foot hit the stairs just as Fitz came around the banister above, with a quivering yellow lab in his arms.

Otis.

Halfway down the steps, Fitz stumbled and careened forward. Otis yelped as Lee lunged to catch the two of them in mid-air, like catching a cinderblock, then a dump truck. The blow knocked the wind from Lee's lungs. He gasped in a mouth full of smoke, which scorched back up his throat with violent wheezing.

Fitz remained heavy on Lee's shoulder, struggling to stand. Lee pivoted and slid down the stairs against the wall. The fumes and ash in his eyes burned like acid. Ceiling plaster continued to fall around them, and the walls trembled. Lee squinted at their exit. The front doorframe was tilted and faltering. Lee shifted Otis and thudded down the last steps with Fitz on his back.

A loud pop sounded above, and the foyer light fixture fell, striking Lee's elbow and knocking the brothers to their knees. Otis howled as he rolled across the floor, then froze, whimpering beneath the smoke. Lee pulled Fitz to his feet, then yanked on the dog's collar as Fitz shoved his rear through the imploding doorway.

They staggered to the grass. Otis ran from Lee's grasp to a woman in her nightgown across the street. Lee and Fitz stumbled behind him, taking their first slugs of clean air as they dropped to the curb at her feet.

Through his heaving, Lee watched the house as the rest of the roof collapsed in a booming cacophony of cracks and hisses.

"Are you alright?" the woman asked, holding Otis' collar. "I've been trying to call 911 but can't get a signal."

"Coach…" was all Fitz could rasp out.

"Terry's visiting his sister. There was no one home. I've been watching Otis for days," she said. "Thank you, boys, for getting him out."

At this, Lee and Fitz lay out flat on the sidewalk, hurling the smoke from their lungs. The cool air and cement soothed Lee's skin. Otis came and flopped between them, resting his snout on Lee's shoulder as sirens and alarms wailed across town.

———

Emergency services took Fitz to the hospital, but they cleared Lee to leave. He managed to get his busted Jeep started and rushed home to check on the kids. He burst through the front door only to find the house still and silent.

I can't believe they slept through it.

Lee exhaled and brushed some of the ash from his hair. He swiped a t-shirt from the stair railing and wiped his face, then trudged up to Caleb's bedroom.

His younger brother was hunched over his desk, studying

with a flashlight. He was wearing one of Dad's old Keller Ranch T-shirts. The worn cotton hung loosely on Caleb's lean frame. His long sandy bangs hung over the desk, revealing Caleb's protruding and functionless ears. Lee tapped his shoulder.

'Everything okay?' Lee signed.

'Yeah. The kids woke up, but I got them back down. The power went out,' Caleb signed back. Then he leaned forward, scrunching his nose. *'What happened to you? You smell terrible.'*

'I'll tell you tomorrow. Gotta get to bed. You should too, egghead.'

Caleb nodded and gave him a thumbs-up. *'Almost done.'*

Lee sighed. Caleb had to double his course load to graduate early. The school for deaf kids was expensive, and even with financial aid, they could only afford one more semester.

Lee did smell terrible, and his skin felt baked and filthy. After a cold shower by the light of his phone, Lee pulled on his sweats and flopped into bed. He had to be up in five hours for work.

There was a knock at his bedroom door.

"Lee?" came the small voice from the other side.

Lee winced. He pulled Dad's flashlight from the dresser, clicked it on, and opened the door.

There was his nine-year-old sister, Penny, holding baby Karen on her hip. His four and six-year-old brothers, Ozzie and Will, clung to Penny's nightgown.

"Hey, munchkins," Lee said, scooping Ozzie up in his arms. "You all want to come in here with me for a bit?"

They nodded, and Penny set the toddler down on the bed with as much care as Mom used to. Lee felt a pang of sadness in his chest. He missed Mom. He missed the ranch they lost to pay for her cancer care. Dad got a good job working on offshore wind turbines, but he was gone for months at a time. Fitz lived by the river with his wife, so for half the year, Lee was head of the household at just eighteen years old.

Penny, Will, Ozzie, and Karen cuddled around Lee in the king-sized bed that filled his room. Despite the ample mattress space, the kids snuggled together as if it were only a twin. Lee wiped his scorched eyes and yawned. He did his best to get comfortable against the wooden headboard. The shifting seemed to disturb Karen, so he gave up and accepted the wakeful night ahead of him.

"That was scary," Penny whispered. She nuzzled under Lee's arm and pulled the comforter over her knees. "What made that noise?"

"Probably just a little earthquake. It's over now. How about we go back to sleep?"

Ozzie climbed over Lee to lie in Penny's lap. She rubbed his back until he settled. Lee's head fell back, and his eyes had just started to close when Penny tugged his shirt.

"Mm, hmm?" he mumbled.

"What if it comes again?" she asked. Lee looked down into her bright eyes.

"Well, if it does, I'll be right here to keep you safe, okay?"

Penny smiled and nodded, then leaned her head against Lee's side.

"Hey, what do I love most in the world?" Lee whispered.

"A lucky Penny," she replied with a yawn.

"That's right…You're my lucky Penny."

CHAPTER 3

LEE

T he next morning, Lee blinked awake to find the kids out of bed and the room much brighter than it should have been.

Oh no! What time is it?

His phone was dead. He'd plugged it in last night, but the power never came back on.

Lee could dress as fast as a fireman when he needed to. Within seconds, he was down the stairs, stuffing his arms in his jacket. Caleb came in the front door with Karen and Ozzie, nearly knocking Lee over. Caleb motioned his hand, and the Hutch device wrapped around his forearm lit up.

"What are you doing here? I thought you'd left already," Hutch's robotic voice announced from his wrist. Caleb wasn't a candidate for cochlear implants, and hearing aids weren't working. Thankfully, Dad's new health insurance bought him the digital sleeve that allowed Caleb to communicate with anyone. But if Caleb signed too quickly, it would get tripped up. The kids found it hilarious, so he often did it intentionally for fun.

"I overslept. Phone died," Lee said, and the gadget lit and vibrated, transcribing the words across Caleb's forearm. Lee preferred to sign with his brother, but he was in too much of a hurry. "Please eat all the leftovers for breakfast before they go bad."

"Okay, we'll eat all the laundry for breakfast," Hutch translated.

Ozzie giggled.

"Okay, bye, guys," Lee smirked. Then he swiped his keys from the table and was out the door.

———

Lee prayed his crew hadn't left yet as he scooted into the harbor parking lot. Maybe the outage delayed everyone, and he wouldn't be the last to arrive.

Lee spotted Fitz and a few other fellow crewmen in an angry horde outside the harbor master's office. Lee's Jeep door, still crumpled shut, had him climbing out the passenger side, where he banged his head on the frame bar. He cursed, realizing he'd have to keep doing this until he had enough money to fix the darn thing, which would be no time soon.

Lee jogged up behind Fitz, who was barking at his father-in-law, their boat captain, Big John.

"Dag nam it, John, you still owe us for the past two days. You can't send us off with nothin', you pilferin' ole' coot!" Fitz hollered, pointing his finger in John's ruddy face. Fitz's hospital ID bracelet was still on his wrist.

"That right?! Why should I pay you when you've been having Lee here do all *your* work, Fitz? I should never have let

17

Mae convince me to take you on."

Lee flushed, and his body tensed, but Fitz didn't miss a beat.

"Don't turn this 'round. You're not payin' anyone. It's not just me. How can you live with yourself?" he countered.

Lee withdrew through the mob of riled fishermen and turned toward the water.

He gasped.

Half of the pier was gone, completely swallowed by the sea. The other half was nothing but a pile of splintered planks and pylons. And the boats...The boats were all capsized, sunken, crushed, or run aground, many buried in the oceanfront shops and restaurants. Every hull crippled and broken, every crane misshapen, every mast chopped down like a fallen tree.

Not one vessel remained intact.

Hells Canyon...What happened?

Fitz grasped Lee's shoulder.

"Lee, you gotta go talk to this stingy high-muck. The old man likes you more than me."

"Fitz, was all this from the earthquake?" Lee asked in disbelief.

Fitz shook his head, pulled a pack of nicotine gum from his pocket, and punched out a piece.

"It weren't no earthquake. It was a dang meteor shower. A few medium-sized ones landed in town, and they found a biggun' over on the beach by the lighthouse."

"Meteors? Seriously?"

"Yeah, well, another one must have hit right offshore and caused all this. Our boat's half-sunk around the bend."

Lee stood fixed with confusion. Why hadn't the news put out

a warning about it?

He tried to recall what had caused last night's accident. He only remembered the tree, the wreck, and the telephone pole.

"How are you doing? What did the doctors say?" Lee asked.

"I'm fine. I think I tweaked my bad leg when I fell down those stairs. They said it'll settle in the next few days."

Lee flinched at the reminder of Fitz's leg injury from years ago. Fitz looked over at Lee with the same reassuring big brother smile he always did. Never a hint of blame or resentment. Not once. Lee bit his lip.

"Did he…uh…give you a pain prescription for it?" Lee asked. He held his breath.

"Nah, Mae wouldn't let him. Don't worry, just Tylenol for old Fitzy. And I gotta take a break from the smokes."

Lee relaxed as Fitz popped another pellet of gum. His eyes were still bloodshot and watery.

Lee thought of Fitz running into that burning house. He hadn't seen his brother act like that in years, not since that night in the woods.

In a way, Lee regretted that their old football coach hadn't been there for him to rescue. The town would have gotten a precious glimpse of who his brother used to be. As it was, the neighbor never even asked for the name of the stranger who saved Otis.

"Hey, Melissa was here asking about cha, in them tight jeans she wears," Fitz said with a glint in his eye. "Man, when are you goin' do something about that? What do all these gals gotta do to git cha to notice 'em?"

Lee was sweating. He unzipped his jacket.

19

"Fitz, I don't have time for any of that. Dad just made a big payment on the hospital debt. There's barely any savings left, and the next deposit won't come until the end of the month. If we can't fish, we won't be able to buy groceries after a week."

"The power and phones will come back soon. When they do, we'll call Dad and see if he can rush us some money," Fitz said. "And you and me can try to pick up work somewhere in the meantime."

As Lee scanned the hundreds of fishermen now out of a job, he wasn't so sure that would be an option.

CHAPTER 4

REN

September 4th, 2027 - 415 nautical miles off the Seattle coast. 12 hours after.

R en's splitting headache and ringing ears woke her. She dragged her eyelids open to find herself on the life raft.

"Pop, she's moving!" came Lizzie's muffled voice.

Ren felt the grasp of her sister's hand.

She shielded her eyes from the sun and rolled to her side. Pop was quickly above her, casting a merciful shadow.

"Lauren! Oh, thank God. Lizzie, back up. Give her space." Pop pulled the matted hair from Ren's face as she tried to sit up, her arms too wobbly to support her. The bandage around her head loosened and drooped.

"No, don't get up. Take it slow," Pop cautioned.

But her stomach erupted through the back of her throat. In a surge, she pushed past him and hurled her torso over the water, then vomited her guts out. Pop kept her steady until she slumped back down, wiping her mouth. Her whole body ached.

Ren squinted over the glaring Pacific. The *Bethie* floated on her side a few dozen yards away. She'd never sail again, but the old girl hadn't sunk. Ren tried to remember the wreck and how they'd survived, but it was all a blur. Pop helped shift her back to a sitting position as Lizzie threw herself into Ren's arms.

"Ren, I was so scared you wouldn't wake up," she whimpered.

"I'm OK, bug." At least, she *thought* she was. Ren really had no idea. She could barely understand her own words. Ren feebly stroked Lizzie's back and kissed her head. "Are you okay?"

Lizzie nodded into Ren's chest, her fingers digging into Ren's shirt. Pop sighed. "You've been asleep for twelve hours now. We were worried about your concussion."

"Wait...I got knocked out?"

"Yes. You came to last night, but not for long. You don't remember?"

Ren groaned and shook her head. She'd had a concussion once before. After a track meet, she'd collapsed from exhaustion and hit her head on the pavement (or so they told her).

"Can you hold up two fingers?" Pop asked.

Ren raised her hand and wobbled two digits.

"Now, try following my finger with your eyes. Keep your head still."

No problem, she thought. *Wait, what did he say? Oh, he wants me to move my head.*

She slowly turned the throbbing boulder on top of her neck.

Pop held her chin as he moved his finger back and forth in front of her.

She strained to keep her eyes fixed on it despite the blinding light and blurred vision. Pop seemed satisfied and cupped the side

22

of her face with his hand. His palm was wet, cold, and shaky. Not at all like the warm, sturdy hand her grandfather usually offered.

She blinked until the far side of the raft came into focus, and she made out Peter's figure. His knees were pulled up to his chest, propping up his arms. His hands were resting on the top of his head.

He looks upset. Was he that worried about me?

She and Peter had barely spoken in years.

"Peter? Are you hurt?" Ren grunted in his direction.

He cleared his throat. "I'm ok. Pop, I can go get more supplies now. I've rested enough."

"You can't go alone, Pete. Just wait a minute."

"I'll be fine. We need to dry out more clothes before dark."

"In a minute, I said." Pop turned back to his patient. "Here, have some water. Just take little sips." He pulled Ren up and held the plastic bottle to her lips. It was warm but salt-free at least. Ren clutched the container for more, nearly spilling it. Pop let her have another small sip, then pulled it away.

"What happened?" she asked.

"We're not sure," Pop said. "What do you remember?"

Think, Ren.

But it was all blank. They could have been attacked by pirates, for all she knew.

"I can't remember anything. Was it a storm?"

"No. It could have been a rogue wave, but I'm just guessing. We're very lucky the *Bethie* stayed afloat so Pete and I could salvage some supplies."

"What about the radio? Or the beacon?" she asked.

"The radio is busted, but I found the beacon, and it seems to

23

be functional. Anyone within seventy miles will pick up on our location. We are due back home three days from now, so that's when your mom will report us missing."

Mom. Thank goodness she didn't come.

"It may take up to a week for them to find us, but they will," Pop insisted. "We'll just hold on until then."

Ren twitched as she realized they'd be on that life raft for at least a week. She surveyed the meager food and water they'd collected thus far. They wouldn't last more than a few days.

"Do we have enough?" she asked.

"There's plenty more in the *Bethie*. Peter and I just had to stop and rest, but we'll go back now for another round." He squeezed her shoulder. "We'll be just fine."

Three minutes later, Ren watched Peter and Pop swim to the capsized vessel still sleeping beside them. They had tied a rope from the deck railing to the raft to keep the two crafts from drifting apart. When the swimmers reached the sailboat, they pulled themselves to the galley opening, which was bobbing just a few feet above the water line, then disappeared inside.

Ren loved the *Bethie,* and losing her was a punch in the gut. She had so many memories with her father on that boat, memories that flooded back to her whenever she boarded it. Ren worried those memories would fade now that the *Bethie* was gone. She tried to conjure a shared moment with him, but her head was pulsing, and concentrating hurt. She rubbed her neck.

It was bare.

My necklace!

Ren groped at her clothes and body until she felt the soft gold chain tangled in her hair. She gently pulled it free and examined the broken clasp. At least she hadn't lost it. Ren rubbed her thumb over the round pendant with the words *Ad Astra per Aspera* on it, a gift from her dad on their first trip to NASA. She slid the necklace into the zipped pocket of her pants.

Lizzie leaned her head against Ren's shoulder, her blond curls wisping against Ren's arm in the breeze. She was still in her pajamas—blue with funny-faced clouds all over them. Ren checked to make sure Lizzie's life jacket was buckled and realized how quiet she was being. Ren longed for one of her absurd questions or made-up jokes. Lizzie's cheerful presence had been the last remaining tie between Ren, Peter, and Mom lately.

Ren gazed back out toward the *Bethie*. Within minutes, Pop and Peter emerged from the galley with a full open cooler tied to life jackets. The two plunged into the water and carefully ferried the goods back to the raft. Ren and Lizzie emptied the cooler while the swimmers held onto the raft's handles. Canned food, wet crackers, Tupperware of leftovers, orange juice, water jugs, blankets—maybe they would be okay. They'd definitely need more, but it was enough to make Ren hopeful.

"There's another load," Pop said, reaching for the cooler. "We're heading back."

Before the last word left his lips, the *Bethie* gave out a loud, creaking moan.

"No…Come on, Peter! She's going down!" Ren threw the bin back in the water, and he and Peter raced back toward the *Bethie*. When Pop reached the railing, he untied the rope, freeing the life raft from the faltering sailboat.

"Ren, don't let the raft get any closer!" he called. "The *Bethie* could topple it, and we'll lose everything."

"Okay!" Ren replied, feeling ridiculously unhelpful. But she'd probably sink like a stone if she tried to swim.

Peter tied the raft's tether to his waist and pulled the cooler from the water as Pop crawled through the sideways galley stairs, now closer to the waves. Once the water reached that opening, they would have only seconds to get clear. Ren watched Pop duck in and out of the galley with armfuls of boxes, cans, and bottles as Peter struggled to fit them all in.

Ren scanned the water. She pictured how worried Mom would be when they didn't return. She squeezed her eyes tight, trying to block the image from her mind.

At least Mom's instant panic mode will have her alerting the Coast Guard by sunset. We shouldn't be too hard to find if the current stays weak. One more load of goods and we'll be fine.

Ren noticed movement in the water, just beyond the *Bethie*. She shaded her eyes with her hand. It was probably a weird-looking wave.

But then, the sharp fin re-emerged.

It was a shark.

A *big* one.

CHAPTER 5

REN

"**S**hark! Peter, there's a shark over there!" Ren hollered.

"*Where*?! I don't see anything!" Peter hoisted himself up on the boat, but his weight dropped the *Bethie* faster, so he jumped off.

"Out there behind the hull! Off the bow!" Ren cried.

Peter yelled something into the galley. Ren saw Pop's arms sling the last items in the cooler and crawl out into the water.

Ren couldn't believe this was happening.

Aren't sharks endangered? The Pacific Ocean is enormous. What are the chances we'd run into one? You're more likely to get struck by lightning than attacked by a shark, right?!

She recalled Pop recently celebrating an article about a rise in the Northern Pacific Great White population. Then she caught sight of the blood stains all over the raft—the blood from her head injury that any shark could smell from almost a mile away. Between that and the clunking noises from Pop and Peter all morning, they may as well have held up a buffet sign.

Perfect.

The shark surfaced again, angling its dorsal fin toward the

raft.

"Ren! It's getting closer!" Lizzie screamed. Ren gripped her hand.

"Don't move, Lizzie," Ren said. "Don't make a sound. Sharks are drawn to noise and movement, so you have to stay still."

At this point, Pop and Peter were clinging to the boat deck with the full cooler floating in front of them.

If the *Bethie* sank with them so close, they could be sucked underwater. The life vests would surface them, but they'd lose the supplies and be left flailing in open water like a pair of delicious-looking sea lions.

But Pop and Peter couldn't leave the safety of the hull now. The swim back to the raft was too far. The kicking would only draw the shark in. There's no way they'd make it.

Ren could see the two murmuring to each other as the boat sank lower. She wished she could hear them.

What can I do? How can I help them?

She cursed herself for always rolling her eyes at shark movies. Maybe if she'd paid closer attention, she'd know what to do.

Ren decided to paddle to them and just prayed they'd be able to get away before the *Bethie* submerged and flipped their raft.

Ren yanked on the cord connected to Peter. As it tightened, her brother looked to Pop. Their grandfather grabbed Peter's shirt to anchor him to the boat, and Peter began pulling, too. They had a plan.

The *Bethie* just had to hold on a little longer.

The sailboat groaned again like an ominous death rattle. Now, the galley entrance bobbed right at the water line, waves sloshing onto the stairs. Ren searched the glaring water for the shark, but it hadn't resurfaced.

Just keep pulling. Just keep pulling.

Hand over hand, arm over arm, Ren drew the life raft nearer to the wreck.

Almost there.

Then she saw it.

The shark was passing just below them like a fifteen-foot ghost in the water. Ren and Peter froze as it idled between them. Ren could feel Lizzie's fingers clawing into her back.

The water reached the galley opening—rushing into the belly of the *Bethie*. She was drowning.

They were out of time.

Pop shimmied along the railing and pulled a lifesaver loose. He hurled the ring over the backside of the boat. It smacked the far water like a pancake, and the shark jerked toward the sound. Ren and Peter resumed pulling as the *Bethie* continued to flounder, more of the hull disappearing below the surface. Pop and Peter let go of the boat deck, quietly pulling themselves along the outstretched sail, still lying flat on the water. Ren yanked harder and faster with each length of rope.

I'm almost there.

The *Bethie's* body began to succumb just as the two reached the top of her floating mast. The shark made another close sweep, and they huddled against the sail. Pop held up his hand for Ren to stop pulling, until it passed once more to the other side of the wreck. Pop untethered Peter and fastened Ren's rope to the cooler.

29

Then he nodded to Peter.

The two of them abandoned the *Bethie* and dove into the open water.

Pop and Peter swam, kicked, and pulled through the choppy waves. Now they'd revealed themselves, and the shark surfaced, its fin turning toward their wake.

"It's coming! Swim! Swim harder!" Ren yelled as she tugged the cooler onward.

The shark was gaining, but Pop and Peter were nearly there. They threw their arms over the lip of the raft and surged up from the water. Ren reached out to help just as the shark dove beneath their feet. Gasping for breath, Pop and Peter tackled the raft paddles and dug them into the ocean, thrusting away from the drag of the sinking ship. Ren kept reeling in the cooler as it staggered against the waves.

Come on...come on...almost got it...

The shark torpedoed their raft from below, pushing it into the air and knocking the rowers off balance. Lizzie shrieked, nearly bouncing over the side.

"Peter!" she screamed. Ren lunged for Lizzie's arm and secured her to a hold on the boat.

"Hang on tight and crouch low," she directed, then took up the tether again and kept pulling.

After just a few tugs, the shark emerged again. The slash of its tail sprayed foam into Ren's eyes and snatched the cord from her hands, knocking the container askew. Handfuls of its precious cargo flew out. Now tilted, the cooler was dangerously close to toppling. Ren and her family definitely wouldn't last the week without that last pack of goods.

"Stop! I lost the cord!" Ren shouted. "Paddle back!"

By now, the raft had made it clear of the *Bethie's* pull. The shark circled below them, methodically nudging and jostling the raft from all sides. The beast could easily overturn them but seemed to enjoy taunting its quarry. It reminded Ren of those nature shows where the sharks toss around doomed sea lions for fun before the kill.

The cooler floated further away.

"Paddle back, or we'll lose it!" Ren stressed again.

Pop and Peter turned around, plunged their paddles into the surf, and pumped back as Ren scrambled to find something to grab the bin with. She tore through blankets and life jackets until she found Pop's docking hook, a seven-foot rod with a metal claw at the end. Ren grabbed the stick and thrust it out toward her target.

It's so close. A few more inches...

"Lizzie, come sit on my legs," she yelled. Her sister anchored Ren's calves as she pushed her whole torso out of the boat. She stretched over the water like meat on a shish kabob, bracing the rod with both arms toward the cooler. Her abs quivered. The buckle straps from her life vest skimmed the waves.

If the shark comes up now, its open jaws could chop me in half without chewing. And that's assuming I don't fall in on my own.

"Look out!" Pop yelled.

The shark seized Peter's paddle and jolted the boat. Ren knocked herself in the head with the rod and flopped sideways, nearly dropping the docking hook.

The blow had enraged her concussion, but Ren fought to stay

31

alert. Trembling, she reached back out over the water, her legs still secure under Lizzie. The cooler twirled on the surface just a few yards away. She held her breath and stretched further.

Almost there…almost…

The claw fell onto the mouth of the bin.

"You've got it!" Pop yelled. Ren reared back in the raft, drawing the rod in with her.

Just beyond the cooler, the shark's dorsal fin surfaced again.

"It's coming back!" Ren yelled.

"We see it, Ren! Just get the cooler in the boat!" Peter shot back.

One last yank on the hook, and the cooler bounced against the raft. Pop and Peter lunged to fish it from the water. As they struggled with the load, Ren wondered why they were even bothering. Eventually, this shark would get bored and hungry, and that would be it. There's no way this floating baby pool would keep them safe for long.

Pop and Peter yanked the cooler sideways over the raft, spilling cans, boxes, and supplies at their feet. Ren could see the shark's fin charging toward them.

"Pop, what do we do?!" Peter screamed.

Pop searched for his paddle as Lizzie's cries rang in Ren's ears.

Her fist tightened around her rod.

Ren rolled to her feet and stared at the fin slicing closer and closer. She flipped the hook downwards and tightened her stance.

The animal burst from the water, battering the boat with its nose. Peter toppled forward, and the shark thrashed its jaws toward his arm.

Ren thrust the hook into the beast's eye. It bucked and jolted the raft. Ren fell flat on the tube, then bounced over the side.

"Ren!" Pop snatched her wrist as Ren plunged into the water up to her shoulders.

I'm dead. I'm dead. I'm dead. I'm dead.

She felt the shark's body jerking against her legs and imagined the coming pain of teeth on her flesh. Pop tightened his grip and ripped Ren upwards as she looked over her shoulder for the next attack.

But the shark was fleeing.

Disoriented and erratic, it swam toward the pull of the sinking shipwreck.

In a last act of courage, the *Bethie* dropped her colossal boom on its back as she descended. The shark writhed as her sail collapsed around its body, dragging it far beneath the surface and then out of sight.

Within seconds, their raft was floating in quiet solitude.

The cooler had lost a quarter of its contents, but the boat was now full of supplies. Out of breath, the survivors looked at each other. Ren felt an urge to hug them all, but held back. She couldn't remember the last time she'd reached out to anyone but Lizzie (and even that had been less frequent). Now the motions seemed difficult. Pop and Mom had always just come to her for occasional hugs these past few years, whether she welcomed it or not. Chests heaving, Peter and Ren made brief eye contact, then looked away.

It was Pop who finally embraced them all until their aftershock from the battle had passed.

They'd bested the shark and salvaged enough food for the

week.

Maybe they *would* make it home.

CHAPTER 6

LEE

September 9th, 2027 - Gladys, Oregon.
6 days after.

N early a week after the meteors hit, Gladys and the surrounding areas still had no power, phones, or internet. With the wrecked harbor and gas shortage, even fewer people than usual passed through town. Real news was hard to come by, and gossip was rampant. Meanwhile, Lee's meager funds had dried up, and there was still no contact with Dad. He spent most of his time looking for work, but with hundreds of other idle fishermen, jobs were scarce.

The meteorite that had struck the Gladys shoreline was the size of a dump truck. All the smaller ones had been claimed as souvenirs, so the big rock was the closest available for public viewing. Lee had taken the kids to look at it the day after it landed. The meteorite wasn't black but a shimmery, crystallized red. The smoother portions were nearly reflective with an illusion of moving shadows beneath the surface, quite beautiful to look at. He heard the whole West Coast was littered with these garnet rocks and boulders of all sizes. Some claimed they covered the entire country, but nothing could be confirmed.

That morning, chilly daylight flooded the foyer as Fitz and Mae let themselves in. Lee was buttoning up his last clean shirt—one of Dad's old flannels.

"This doorknob's gettin' loose again," Fitz announced as he wedged the door shut behind him.

"Hi, Fitz!" Will chimed. He and Ozzie tramped down the stairs and into Fitz's arms.

"Hey! There they are." Fitz grunted as he scooped the little boys up in a bear hug. "You two are gettin' enormous. Hey, Mae, I caught us a coupla' fat grouper here."

The kids laughed and wiggled, and Fitz gave them another squeeze before putting them down.

"Mornin', everybody," Mae said as she hung up her jacket. She flashed Lee a smile and followed the boys down the hallway.

"Fitz, did ya find work for today?" Lee asked.

Fitz took off his cap to scratch his greasy scalp. There was a run on the store, and now you couldn't buy soap or shampoo. Everyone had to ration.

"Naw, I ain't found nothin'."

"Caleb heard that the county might be paying people to clean up the beach," Lee offered as he grabbed a toy racecar from the stairs.

Fitz's eyes narrowed, and his grin fell.

"*Caleb heard*? Now that he's got that little gizmo on his

arm, I guess he feels like he runs the town. Just best friends with everybody," Fitz snarked. "At least now, he can't play dumb when I'm talkin' to him."

Lee hardened. "Fitz, don't start. On that note, have you and Kenny been messing with him again?"

Fitz rolled his eyes to the ceiling.

"Aww, man, what'd he tell you? Me and the boys was just playing 'round."

Fitz didn't have many friends, but the few in his circle found Caleb's condition a source of entertainment. Fitz seemed happy enough to go along with it.

"It's not funny, and it's really ticking me off. I know you two don't get along, but you gotta stop being so hateful towards him."

Fitz put his hands up in defense.

"Yeah, alright, alright…Jiminy." Fitz pulled his Swiss Army knife from his pocket. He peeled out the screwdriver and set to fixing the loose doorknob.

Fitz had been bitter toward Caleb for years. Almost since that night in the woods that no one ever talks about.

But after Dad started working offshore, Fitz had grown even more contemptuous toward their younger brother. The job offered good money, but Dad might have passed on it if it weren't for the health benefits for Caleb. Now, everything Caleb did seemed to get under Fitz's skin, and Caleb had come to despise Fitz in return.

"Okay, then, will you go talk to the harbor master about the cleanup?" Lee asked.

"Yeah, sure, I will."

Fitz tested the knob, then jerked the door open.

"Hey, I meant to tell ya," he said, looking back at Lee, "We saw the big meteor yesterday, and it looks real different—kinda melted, and there's big ole' foxholes all over it. You should go see it."

Lee scratched his jaw. He wanted to go check it out, but thought better of it. "No, we should probably stay away. If it's changing, there may be some kind of bacteria on it. The cops should rope it off."

"Ha, folks have been climbing all over it for days. What's the point now?" Fitz called from the front stoop. "See you all later."

"Yep."

Lee shut the door and headed into the kitchen, where everyone else was well into breakfast.

The sunlight beamed through the east windows. It cheerfully spotlighted every crack, dent, and rust patch on the furnishings and walls. Dad had planned to renovate the kitchen when he bought the house, but never found the time or money.

Lee glanced at the kids' artwork covering the pantry door as he poured hot water from the kettle into a mug. He added a spoonful of coffee grounds and winced as he took a sip.

Thankfully, the town's wells kept the family's faucets working, but getting enough food was becoming difficult. Their neighbor had been nice enough to share eggs from her coop. Caleb had hooked up the grill propane tank to the stove so that they could cook. Scrambles and granola kept the kids satisfied most of the day.

With how valuable eggs were now, Lee worried about when the neighbor would stop sharing them for free. Lee had been skipping breakfast for the past three days to save food for the kids.

He and Caleb were headed to the beach that day, hoping for a good catch to sell or trade.

Caleb leaned against the counter with his Lipton tea as the younger kids ate at the table. Mae sat next to the highchair, opening an applesauce cup for Karen. Ever since she'd married Fitz, Mae had been doing her seamstress work at the house so she could help with the kids. That morning, she wore one of Fitz's old T-shirts, which she'd cut into a V-neck. Her natural jet-black hair covered the top of her head, then turned into a Kool-Aid red dye job from her crown to her shoulders. Between the hairdo, penciled eyebrows, pale skin, and wiry frame, Mae had a pretty severe look for a babysitter.

Like a redneck Cruella de Vil.

Mae served herself the last eggs from the skillet and another cup of applesauce. She peeled off the top and licked the foil.

"You kids are quiet today," she remarked, squirting more honey into her coffee.

"Yeah, they're just extra hungry," Lee said. "They're too busy eating to holler like usual, right guys?"

"Roought," Will agreed, his mouth full of food.

"So, still no news on the power comin' back on? It's goin' on a whole week now." Mae scraped the last bite from her plate. "I just don't see how a few little meteors could have messed everythin' so bad."

"It's more than just a few," Lee said as he moved the empty plates to the sink. "They think there's thousands of them. Maybe more. I wouldn't count on it coming back this week."

Mae flicked ash in her empty mug.

"I know, I'm just sayin'…I miss my microwave," she muttered.

'What did she say?' Caleb signed to Lee. Hutch didn't work if people spoke too softly.

'She's sick of the power being out,' Lee signed back.

Mae side-eyed the two of them, then pursed her lips and wiped Karen's face.

Lee downed his last gulp of coffee.

"Okay, we're about ready to go. Mae, make sure you keep the door locked. There have been a lot of break-ins lately. And Karen needs to nap in an hour."

"I know, Lee. You don't gotta keep telling me."

Mae pulled out a creased Newport from her purse and lit it. Smoke wafted around the table, and the toddler coughed into her sippy.

"Mae…," Lee sighed.

"I know." She waved the air clear. "I'll smoke the rest of it out back."

Lee grabbed his hat and slapped his hands together. "Okay, who wants to come clamming with me and Caleb?"

The room lit up with smiles and hands. "Me! I want to come!" the kids cried as if Lee would choose only one.

"I'm gonna need Penny to stay and help with Karen today," Mae cut in.

Penny's face drooped, and she slumped in her chair. Lee forced his frustration into a smile and then squatted beside her.

"Thank you so much for helping. How about we go back to the beach tonight and watch the sunset? Does that sound good?"

"Yeah, okay." Penny leaned into his shoulder. She smelled like Mom's perfume.

"That's my lucky Penny." He picked her up in a hug, her bare feet dangling below her. "Gimme a good squeeze for the road."

Lee set her back down and rubbed her shoulder.

"We'll have fun, won't we, girl?" Mae chirped.

Penny gave a dutiful grin.

"Well, come on, boys. Thanks again, Mae. We'll see you, ladies, later."

Lee signed to Caleb: '*You ready?*'

Caleb nodded as he rinsed his mug.

Lee waved to Penny on his way out.

"Toodaloo, kangaroo."

"Take care, polar bear," she replied.

Caleb reached into his pocket and gave Penny his last piece of gum.

'*Thank you!*' she signed.

"*I'm welcome,*" Hutch replied.

Penny giggled, and Caleb tickled her neck. Then he took off the device and left it on the counter. He never brought Hutch to the beach.

CHAPTER 7

LEE

H igh cliffs towered above the Gladys cove. Usually, the coastline was well-maintained for tourists. Now, dead fish and debris littered the beach and shallows. The smell of rotting flesh, moldy seaweed, and scavenger poop was enough to keep anyone away.

It was only the first week of September, but the weather had already begun to turn.

"Watch out for nails and sharp stuff, guys," Lee called as the boys ran from the stairs to the wet sand.

The youngsters immediately found wooden boards for a sword fight. Lee smiled, remembering how he and Caleb used to play on this beach as kids. Born only thirteen months apart, they had always been inseparable.

Caleb gave Lee a pat on the shoulder; then, they lugged their bags toward the surf. Lee's wetsuit was well-worn and snug, better sized for a boy four inches shorter and twenty pounds lighter. Lee shimmied the zipper up as Caleb fastened his waders, then rooted through his tackle box.

Ozzie and Will had given up on dueling and rushed back to

claim their clam shovels. Lee promised a treat for a bucket full of clams. Lee would give them the old Easter candy, regardless, but having a 'paid job' seemed to make them feel important.

"Ok, here you go, guys. Don't lose the shovels this time," he reminded.

"We won't!" Ready for the hunt, the two scampered off.

'Think they'll find anything?' Caleb signed.

'Maybe a few, if we're lucky. There aren't many out here this season. I'm really hoping the crab traps worked.' Lee nodded toward the water. As he pulled the net strap over his shoulder, he heard a strange sound—a rumbling shriek carried on the wind. He scanned the beach and cloudy sky but saw nothing.

"*What's wrong?*" Caleb vocalized as he signed. He was pretty good at speaking short sentences, but only did it around family.

'I just heard a weird sound,' Lee signed back.

"*Like what?*"

Lee shrugged. *'I don't know. Some kind of animal, maybe.'*

Another call sounded in the distance.

'There it is again,' Lee signed, more perplexed.

'Maybe a wolf?' Caleb guessed.

'I guess it could be, but it doesn't sound like one to me.' In thirty years, only a handful of wolf sightings had been reported in the area.

'Maybe it's the sound of you losing your mind,' Caleb signed with a grin.

'Hilarious. You know, sometimes, your being deaf is very inconvenient for me.'

'Then it's totally worth it,' Caleb answered with a chuckle.

Lee grinned and shook his head.

'Awesome. Just watch the kids, okay? Can you do that, smart alec?'

Caleb looked over his shoulder at the boys flinging sand and gave Lee a thumbs-up. Lee waded out into the shallow water and cringed.

"Son of a gun, it's cold!" Lee turned his back to the waves, clenching his arms around him like a timid old lady. He looked up to see Caleb laughing at him. Lee was a sissy when it came to cold—not ideal for a North Pacific fisherman. Caleb never seemed to mind it and barely flinched as he followed Lee into the water, stopping to bait his hook once the water reached his calves.

Lee gritted his teeth and forced himself deeper. The few docks left standing after the meteor shower were overcrowded with traps, so Lee had had the idea to set his lines from a wrecked boat. The little craft was twenty yards offshore at low tide. Now, at high tide, it was more like sixty. Lee shivered through the choppy foam and thought about how irritated he would be if this didn't work.

The eerie sound interrupted his grumbling, and he turned back to his brother.

'There it is again,' he signed.

Caleb looked around and shrugged.

'Hey, I'm keeping an eye on you. The surf is rough today,' he cautioned.

Lee waved over his shoulder and kept moving, still surveying the gray skies for whatever made the noise. After stumbling over the rocks, the water got deep enough for Lee to swim with the strong current the rest of the way.

He climbed aboard the sunken pleasure cruiser, formerly one of Mike's tourist rentals. Now it was junk, already stripped for parts.

The wind and waves had started to pick up, the water's foamy peaks rising higher and faster.

A storm was coming in.

Lee waved to Caleb from the deck. Will and Ozzie were happily digging. They seemed unfazed by the piles of decaying fish. Lee paused to watch the two boys playing and laughing together, thinking how big they'd gotten.

Dad will barely recognize them when he gets home.

Caleb waved back, then recast his line.

Lee muttered a prayer, then peeled the wet trap rope off the ledge. Hand over hand, he hoisted the first crab trap, already worried that the load was too light.

Sure enough, he had only caught two.

He swore, put the scanty catch in his carry net, then dropped the cage. As much as he disliked the trek out to this boat, he had no better crabbing spots in mind. He pulled up the second cage and found only four tangled in the wire. Nothing to trade, but a little something to eat.

Lee pushed it back overboard as the same high-pitched warble echoed over the cove again, louder this time. It sounded like a growling whale call from overhead.

Then, again, it came.

He'd lived here his whole life and never heard anything like it.

Lee looked to the sky in every direction, along the clifftops, and up and down the coast. Nothing.

What the heck is that?

Just as Lee tried to signal the others, Caleb turned around to check the kids.

Lee tried calling Will.

"Hey, Will! Will!" he shouted, but the waves and wind drowned his voice.

As he affixed the net to his shoulder, the noise came again. Sharp and much closer now. Lee's heartbeat quickened, his curiosity shifting to panic.

Where is it coming from?!

Lee's stomach felt heavy and sour, like that night when he saw Bull's truck at the gas station. It felt *just* like that.

Lee jumped in the water, and a wave smacked him in the face. He sputtered and wiped his eyes, no longer aware of the cold. He just wanted to get back and get the kids off the beach.

He made it just a few strokes before the shrieking grew so loud that he could hear it underwater. He shot back up, frantically searching for its source, waves breaking hard on his shoulders. He could see Ozzie holding his ears. He and Will were looking for it now. Lee kept swimming. Too afraid to take his eyes off the beach, he kept his head above water. But as hard as he fought, he couldn't get closer to shore.

The strengthening undertow was pushing him back out. He'd have to swim in diagonally.

"Will! Ozzie!" Lee called again. His voice was straining, but they still didn't hear. The sound continued from all sides of the cove. Ozzie crouched down, hugging his knees.

Caleb looked up to check on Lee.

Thank God.

Lee waved and pointed toward the boys, but Caleb's attention jolted back toward the shallows as his rod lunged forward.

A fish. Not now!

Lee planted his foot on a high rock and pushed up.

"Will!" Lee screamed again, and Will looked out at him. "Get Caleb!"

Will obeyed, running through the wet sand to his big brother. Lee dove back in and kept swimming, trying to keep sight of the boys as he ricocheted through the mountainous surf.

Caleb was following the rod away from the boys, leaning in and reeling back. His graphite shaft curled hard, nearly bent in half. Lee could tell it was something huge—probably big enough to sustain the family for a week. He knew Caleb wouldn't risk losing it to check on Will.

A salty wave swallowed Lee's head. He gagged, wiping his face to see Will tugging on Caleb's shirt.

But Caleb stayed fixed on his line.

Lee cursed and kept racing. He was more than halfway, but the riptide felt like a brick wall pushing against him. He couldn't get around it.

The shrieking came again over the sound of falling stones from the cliff, as if dislodged by something descending the rock face, closing in around the beach.

Around Ozzie.

"Ozzie! Go to Will!" Lee hollered.

The boy lifted his gaze to Lee but wouldn't budge.

"Ozzie, run!" Lee pleaded again.

Ozzie stood and looked to the sky above him, his arms hugging the side of his head.

Caleb's line snapped, and he staggered backward, finally noticing Will's gestures toward Lee.

Caleb looked out at the water as a cluster of broken boards pounded against Lee's back, battering him underwater. Lee crashed and rolled through the current, bouncing against the rocky sand.

Disoriented beneath the tide, he couldn't break the surface without another surge hammering him below. A board bounced off his skull, and his vision darkened. His body turned to lead.

Something caught Lee's right arm, ripping him up from the water. Lee spit and gasped for a clean breath, unable to move his legs. Caleb hooked his brother's elbow over his shoulder and dragged him toward the beach as Lee fought to get his bearings.

Ozzie...Will...

Lee sharpened his focus on the beach, searching for the boys. He could only find Will.

"Ozzie! Ozzie!" he bellowed. He pushed free from Caleb and ran toward shore.

Ozzie was gone.

The screeching was now constant and blaring. Wet sand sprayed up from the beach in a cyclone behind Will, who was covering his ears and shielding his eyes.

"Will! Come to me!" Lee screamed, stumbling onward.

"Where's Ozzie?" Caleb yelled from behind him. "Ozzie!"

"I can't see!" Will called through the sandy whirlwind.

"Will, please!" Lee begged, racing toward him. "Come out here!"

"Ozzie! Ozzie!" Caleb screamed.

Lee whipped his legs above the water, barreling through the shallows. He was almost there.

"Will! Come to me!"

Lee twisted his foot on a rock and fell to his hands and knees. His hand sliced into a seashell. The sound wailed above them as Lee pushed himself up.

"Will!"

The shrieking went silent.

It was already too late.

———

After searching the beach for hours, Lee and Caleb staggered up the steps to the house, mad with shock and fear. Mae was crying as she rushed outside to meet them, followed by a neighbor.

"Lee! The girls! Karen was in her bed, and I can't find her now! Penny's missing, too."

"No! Please, no!!" Lee tore into the house, tripping on the threshold and knocking over a table.

Steps from the nursery, he grabbed the doorframe and pulled himself through. Karen's crib sat barren beneath an open window, Mom's pink curtains billowing above it. Lee's heart burst through his chest. He barely had breath to call for his other sister.

"Penny! Penny! Where are you?" he choked out, dashing from the room.

Everyone swarmed around the house. Lee flew up the stairs, taking them three at a time, and bounded into the kids' empty room. With his last prayer, he opened the closet and threw the clothes off the rack.

And there was Penny—sleeping peacefully in her favorite hiding spot, wearing her mother's old headphones. Lee lifted and held her tightly as tears of relief and sorrow swelled in his eyes. He was too confused and afraid to do anything but thank God for leaving her with him. Caleb and Mae ran into the room as Penny woke.

"Lee? What's wrong?" she asked.

Outside, sirens whined over the sound of people screaming for help.

CHAPTER 8

PETER

September 29th, 2027 - 500 nautical miles off the Seattle coast. 25 days after.

P eter and his family had now been at sea for three and a half weeks, eleven days past Pop's initial timeline for a rescue. Peter had been doubtful from the start; now, he'd completely lost hope of being rescued at all. But he'd never let Lizzie know that.

They needed a miracle at this point.

Once Pop put up the shelter tarp, their raft more resembled an orange rubber playhouse, bobbing alone in a vast sea of nothing. The stuffy, putrid stench inside was making them sick, so they took down half the tarp to allow fresh air. Now, with only partial covering, the sun had scorched them all. Peter's nose, cheeks, lips, and hands were blistered and peeling, just like the others.

He and Pop had also developed saltwater sores, and the first aid kit had long run out of pain meds and topical treatments.

The worst part of all was the hunger. Only two cans of

beans remained. Peter never thought he'd be counting how many individual beans he would get per day. He'd eaten a whole pizza by himself the week before they'd left. Now, it felt like his stomach was shriveling up inside him, his abdomen concave beneath his ribs. He could barely keep his pants up.

During the first week, the kids had fought with Pop over the meagerness of the rations. Had their grandfather given in, they'd probably all be dead by now.

The drinking water saved from the boat was long gone, but they had managed to catch rainwater in the tarp. Ren also knew how to make fresh water from seawater with a plastic water bottle and a tin can. A dozen of these evaporation projects collected tiny droplets all day long.

To Peter, however, they were only prolonging the inevitable. They were all going to die in this pumpkin coach from hell. He wondered what would happen if another shark came and how hard they would bother to fight it.

That afternoon, Peter and Pop sat with hooks in the water for another unsuccessful hour while Ren sat back against the tube. She said she still couldn't remember what had happened or what she'd been doing on the deck that night. Peter knew, though. She was probably up there enjoying her miserable solitude, as usual. Peter tugged at the shirt collar, itching his neck.

How did Pop ever expect me to 'reconnect' with her?

Ren put a dark towel over her eyes and started rubbing her forehead. Peter was reminded of her head injury and cringed. When he'd surfaced alone the night of the wreck, Pop had asked where she was, and Peter had just stared at him, still catching his breath. He'd thought she was right behind him.

52

Lizzie was inside the covering, still unable to sleep. She was too hungry, too sunburned, and too scared, and Peter couldn't do anything to help her. None of them could.

Lizzie started moaning a little.

"Ren," Peter muttered, "check on Lizzie."

Ren didn't respond—just continued soothing her eyes.

"Lauren!" Peter demanded.

"*What?*" Ren snapped in response.

"Don't you hear, Lizzie? Can you *please* check on her?"

Ren glared at him, then nodded and rubbed her eyes. She got up and crawled under the flap.

Peter shook his head and yanked up his sagging shorts for the millionth time that day. He needed to make himself a belt.

"Take it easy, pal," Pop murmured.

"Yeah, I know. Lizzie needs help, though. Ren was just sitting there."

"It's okay," Pop patted Peter's back, then offered him a little water. Even the tiny sip helped. Peter closed his eyes—a short reprieve from the piercing light. He took a deep breath.

He could hear Ren singing Lizzie a song. He recognized it as one that Dad had liked, but Peter didn't know what it was called or who sang it. Music was something Dad, Mom, and Ren had in common—concerts and stuff. That's where they had gone *that* night after Ren's last race.

———

Another day without a fish. The group squatted under the cover around the one remaining can of food. Pop had saved the most flavorful dinner for last—baked beans.

53

Like a last meal on death row.

Pop sawed into the top of the can, and Peter salivated at the smoky, sweet smell. Lizzie even smiled. As usual, they each took a turn having a spoonful, then Pop placed the lid back on the can and braced it amid empty food containers in the cooler.

"Well, now, how about we all wash it down? Pete, can you go check the water?" Pop suggested.

Peter crawled outside to examine each water vapor collector. From the fullest, Peter started to pour the few sips into their drinking cup, but stopped when he spotted a silhouette on the horizon.

Holy smokes. Am I dreaming?

Peter gagged on his breath, and his hands rattled. He dropped the bottle, spilling half a day's worth of water.

"Peter, what was that?" Pop called from inside.

Ren shot out from the flap.

"Peter, did you drop the water? How could you do that?!"

But then, she saw it, too…and froze.

An old fishing boat, five times the size of the *Bethie,* was less than two hundred yards away.

It was gliding right for them.

CHAPTER 9

REN

"Pop! Lizzie! It's a boat!" Ren could barely get the words out. "They're coming for us!" She grabbed an orange life vest and started swinging it overhead, praying they would see it.

Pop exploded from the cover, followed by Lizzie. With the last of their energy, they joined in Ren and Peter's cries for help, beckoning the fishing boat to save them. The decrepit fish-gut-stained vessel was the most beautiful thing Ren had ever seen. She and Pop looked at each other with teary eyes as someone tossed them a rope, a literal lifeline, and Peter pulled them toward the descending ladder. Lizzie was sent up first, followed by Peter, Pop, and Ren.

"Thank you so much!" Ren said as crewmen helped her over the guard railing.

The family collapsed with relief and exhaustion, gasping in the sweet smell of survival. The four beamed at their rescuers as they struggled back to their feet.

"Thank you, thank you," Pop said. "We've been out there for over three weeks. We were shipwrecked."

At that moment, Ren noticed that the whole crew looked

Japanese. They were standing back, cautiously withdrawn from the newcomers. Not at all the welcome Ren expected from their saviors. Some looked almost threatened. Ren scanned the crew and found four men with rifles slung over their shoulders. The youngest there appeared to be slightly older than Ren, maybe eighteen, and wearing an old yellow hoodie with an anime graphic. He handed her a water canteen.

It was the most heavenly full gulp of water she'd ever tasted. Ren, Peter, Lizzie, and Pop passed it between them until it was empty.

"Does anyone here speak English?" Pop asked, wiping his mouth.

The men stared blankly at them.

Ren instantly regretted not taking Japanese in high school. Instead, she'd taken French for the study-abroad program she never even applied for.

"English? Uh… *Eigo?*" Peter asked.

How Peter knew the Japanese word for English, Ren had no idea. He'd taken Latin, which was even more useless than French at this moment.

The men traded glances. Some shook their heads. The younger one reached for the empty canteen and gestured to himself.

"Kenji," he said. He repeated the word, and Ren guessed it was his name.

"Jim," Pop said, pointing to his chest, then to the kids, "Ren…Peter… Lizzie."

Kenji gave a polite smile.

"*Tanaka. Fujita*," said an older crewman in the center of the crowd. He nodded toward the family. Two men came at Jim and Peter, yanking their arms out, patting them down, and pulling out their pockets.

"Hey! Watch it." Peter's outburst prompted another man to pin his wrists back. Ren noticed that one in the crowd had pulled his rifle forward.

"Peter, stop," Pop insisted. "Just be still and let them search."

Peter bit his lip and relented until the men let him go. Next, it was Ren and Lizzie's turn.

"Why are they doing this?" Lizzie asked, looking up at Ren.

Ren just stared back in silence at the man, whom she deduced was the captain, locking his gaze. He was bearded with a sea-worn face, more formidable in build than most of the others.

The security detail stepped back, seemingly satisfied.

"Can we please use your radio?...uh...radio?" Pop pantomimed by cupping his hand up to his mouth and pressing an invisible button.

"*Rajio*?" another man with a ripped jacket mumbled to the captain, and he mimicked Pop's radio motions. The captain glared at Pop and shook his head.

"*Kanpan no shita ni motte iku,*" he directed. Ren hoped that it wasn't an order to toss them overboard.

Instead, Kenji gestured toward the metal cabin door. It seemed the captain wanted them taken below.

Perhaps to keep as kitchen slaves. At least we'll be with the food.

A man came up the ladder with three sacks full of gear from their lifeboat and carried them away. A crewmate followed him and signaled toward the bow.

"*Crane de hikiagete!*" he yelled, and the big metal arm groaned awake. Everyone watched as their raft lifted out of the water like an orange, harpooned marlin, who had long given up.

The captain turned away, and Ren reached for his arm to stop him. A guard shouted and raised his gun at her. The captain shot her a scornful look.

"Please… *rajio*?" Ren persisted. Her tone came out sharper than she had intended.

"*Kanpan no shita ni motte iku!*" the captain ordered again.

"Ok, ok, we'll go. It'll be ok, Ren," Pop said, pulling Ren back.

Kenji gestured again for the family to go with him, and Pop nudged them along, followed by a more forceful escort.

They clonked down steps into the galley kitchen. Kenji seated them at a large bench table. Japanese lettering was etched in the wood as you'd find on a grade school desk.

Kenji started preparing a fish and rice dish for them, and Ren's stomach twisted with hunger; nothing had ever smelled so delicious. He handed each of them a bowl.

"Thank you," Pop said.

"Okay," Kenji replied with a smile and bow of his head.

Kenji disappeared to the back, leaving the family with an older, sour-looking man with wire-rimmed glasses and a tiger-head tattoo on his bicep. He scowled at them as they ate.

Then, quite unexpectedly, he introduced himself.

"Riku," he said with his hand to his chest.

The family members blinked at each other and then said their names as Pop reached out to shake hands. Riku accepted without changing his expression.

"THIS IS DELICIOUS!" Lizzie said to him as if speaking louder would help. She rubbed her stomach.

"He doesn't understand," Peter chided.

Riku grinned back. "*Oishi. Hai,*" he said. He rubbed his stomach, too.

"See?" Lizzie snipped.

The meal was gone within seconds, and Kenji led them to a small cabin with two bunks. There, they found fresh clothes, towels, and soap on the mattress. Kenji pointed across the hall to the washroom, bowed, and left.

"I'm first in the bathroom!" called Lizzie as she dashed across and closed the door. The other three just stood there in awe.

"Uh, I guess we're saved," Peter said.

Pop laughed and hugged them both.

———

Once clean and changed, the family crawled into the bunkbeds. Pop and Peter lay end to end on the bottom, and Ren snuggled with Lizzie above. Ren felt her skin melt into the soft, dry sheets. So exhausted and comfy, she thought she could sleep for a week.

Ren reached over and tucked the covers around Lizzie's body. "There we go. All bundled in tight. The great thing about sleeping on a boat—it rocks you to sleep," Ren whispered.

"Dad used to say that," said Lizzie, then rubbed her nose. "Can you tell me something else about him?"

Ren pondered for a moment.

"Hmm…Dad used to say, 'It's cold out. I might need this jacket!' Then he'd sling you on his back and walk around pretending you were a coat. He'd ask us how it looked and rave about how warm and cozy it was. You'd nearly fall off from giggling so much."

"That's funny." Lizzie rolled toward Ren, nuzzling under her chin.

"Yep, Dad was hilarious." Ren brushed the hair from Lizzie's face. "He made everyone feel special."

"I want to marry someone like that," Lizzie said.

"Me too, kiddo. Now, get some sleep. We're finally going home."

She kissed Lizzie on the forehead, then Lizzie rolled deep into the covers and was out in seconds.

Ren lay on her back thinking of Dad as she touched the ten-inch scar on her arm. Her eyes got hot as she wished for him to suddenly appear. He would probably be the most popular person on the boat by now. *He* could have convinced the captain to let them use the radio.

Ren wasn't like that, though. She wasn't fun or warm or engaging like Dad. When she met people nowadays, it seemed like a race to see who could end the conversation first. *Everyone* loved Dad.

But he was gone.

Gone because of Ren.

CHAPTER 10

REN

R en woke to the smell of food, reigniting her hunger and thirst. She slipped her arm from beneath Lizzie's head and climbed down to find the bottom bunk already empty.

The t-shirt Kenji had given her was huge, but the drawstring pants fit well enough. Ren stepped out into the galley as Peter and Pop finished their breakfast alongside two other crewmen.

"Good morning," Pop greeted. "How'd ya sleep?"

"Best night's sleep in weeks!" Ren was trying to sound more chipper and thankful in front of their shipmates. No time like the present to make a better impression.

Peter paused and gaped at her with a stunned expression.

"Erm…how are your sores?" Ren asked. "You should show them to someone."

"The ship's medic dressed them this morning," Pop said. "He'll probably come back in a bit to check on you."

Ren exhaled—one less thing to worry about. Her stomach rumbled just as Pop stood to get her a plate of food. In the borrowed clothing, Pop looked like skin and bones. They all did.

"What's for breakfast?" Ren asked as she slid into the

booth.

"Miso and pickled fish," said Pop.

"Pickled fish?" Ren kept her smile fastened and her tone cheerful.

"It's delicious," Pop said with a wink as he handed her a set of chopsticks.

"Great!" she announced to the galley. Pop chuckled and patted her hand.

"Lizzie will for sure love it," Peter snarked into his bowl. Lizzie was a choosy eater and hated anything pickled.

"Hey, what's for breakfast?" Lizzie had emerged, holding her pants up to her chest.

"It's delicious," Ren, Pop, and Peter stressed in unison.

———

On the first day, Ren and her family did whatever they could to be useful. Ren was assigned to kitchen duty with Lizzie, prepping food and cleaning dishes. The space was cramped, but very clean. Blue plastic-covered cabinets supported steel countertops and an industrial sink. Silver pots and pans hung above the stove, and two wall hooks held aprons and hairnets that the girls were instructed to wear.

"Why can't we fish with Pop and Peter?" Lizzie asked.

"Look, squirt, we're guests on this boat, and I get the feeling these guys are old school. We should just be grateful to be cabin wenches...or whatever."

"What's a wench?" Lizzie asked.

"Uh, it's just an old pirate expression. Forget it," Ren answered, then grabbed a diversion. "Here, put on your apron."

The kitchen wasn't so bad. The cook was a joyful, heavyset man named Haruto. He seemed thrilled to have the girls' company. Haruto would go on and on, laughing hysterically at his own jokes. Neither Ren nor Lizzie understood a word but found him hilarious, nonetheless. Occasionally, Haruto entertained them by twirling a spatula above his head, then catching it behind his back. He even stuck toothpicks in potatoes to make a little man called *Jo*.

Haruto could peel six spuds to Ren's one and was able to pull every scrap of meat from a fish, while leaving the bones intact. Ren wasn't much of a cook, but she impressed Haruto when she opened a stuck jar for him. She took it in a towel and held the top upside down in a hot pot. In seconds, the top had loosened.

"How did you do that?" Lizzie asked.

"It's thermal expansion…um…physics. Most things get bigger when heated. It's how a thermometer works. As the temp goes up, the alcohol inside the tube expands. So, when I got the lid hot, it lengthened and relaxed around the glass," Ren said. "Dad showed me this trick."

"Cool."

At lunch, Haruto sent Ren to the deck to bang on a pot—the signal for lunch. She stepped outside and looked for the sun, hopeful for any sign of the boat's direction, but dense clouds covered the sky.

Ren clanged her instrument, and the men gave a jovial cheer as they headed inside. Ren found Pop and Peter sprawled out on a pile of nets.

"You two okay?" she asked.

"Just out of shape," Pop said. "It'll get easier."

Ren sat beside them, her body aching from the long morning. "There's a guard at the bow," she murmured, rubbing her sore hands. The dead skin from the sunburn rolled off on her fingertips.

"Yes, we know. Another one is above the bridge," Pop added.

"Why would they need armed men in the middle of the Pacific?" Ren asked.

Pop took another swig of water. He shook his head.

"I don't know, but I'm sure there's a good explanation. For now, just keep smiling and try not to worry."

CHAPTER 11

LEE

September 30th, 2027 - Gladys, Oregon
26 days after.

L ee sat hunched over the radio in the Coast Guard office. He
and Caleb had spent hours each day for a week waiting in
line to get a few precious minutes with it. It was the only real form
of communication left, although responses were sparse and
mostly unhelpful.

Lee's back hurt, and his head was pounding from the endless
sounds of beeps and static in the overcrowded room.

"Pan-Pan. This is the U.S. Coast Guard Office 122 calling
any vessels in range. Is anyone there? Over," Lee repeated into
the receiver.

He released the call button and said the same
prayer he'd been saying for weeks. The silver
whistle they'd been told to carry rested on the table in front of
him. He fiddled with it to calm his nerves and keep his voice
steady. The past week's events proved the whistle wasn't good
for much else.

"Pan-Pan. This is the U.S. Coast Guard. Is anyone in range? Over."

Please, God.

"Boys, your time's almost up," Lieutenant Mathers called from his desk across the room. He was one of only three officers still showing up for work.

Caleb turned and gestured toward Mathers.

"Just a few more minutes, please," Hutch said. Caleb was a lot more patient than Fitz. That is, before they banned Fitz from the building altogether.

Lee's shoulders slumped. He didn't know why today would be any different than yesterday or the day before.

"Pan-Pan. This is the U.S. Coast Guard looking for anyone who can hear us."

Nothing but sputtering white noise.

The crowd behind him was getting restless. Lee could feel them inching forward, eager for their turn.

Lee looked up to Caleb and shook his head. He pushed to his feet just as the radio came alive with a woman's voice.

"This is Captain Lunts of the Emerald Cruise Line responding. Go ahead. Over."

The whole office went silent as Lee jumped back on the microphone.

"Uh…yes, this is civilian Lee Keller, seeking information on the Tern Wind Farm Project off the coast of Shelter Cove, California. Have you passed the site? Over."

Please, God…Please.

"Mr. Keller, that's affirmative. Our vessel passed the site several days ago."

"Captain Lunts, was there anyone there? My father, Gerry Keller, was stationed at the hub. Did you see anything?"

Lee dug his nails into the chipped wooden table and held his breath.

"Mr. Keller, I'm sorry, but the site was mostly destroyed. We were unable to contact anyone at the facility. Structural damage prevented us from conducting a search, but there were no signs of life. Over."

Hutch vibrated and lit up with the captain's response. Lee's heart sank, and his mouth went dry.

Then, voices from behind them piped up.

"Ask her about San Francisco."

"What are the updates from the government?"

"Can they take anyone on board?"

But Lee couldn't focus. He wanted to throw up. The Lieutenant grabbed the microphone from the table and began asking the prioritized list of questions. Lee shuffled through the advancing crowd.

All of them praying for better news than I got.

If anyone offered him words of support, Lee didn't hear them. He was suffocating and had to get out of there. Lee pushed his way through to the exit door and thrust it ajar. He got only a quick taste of fresh air before Caleb yanked him back.

"Stop. We can't go out now," Hutch said. Caleb handed Lee his forgotten whistle. Lee snatched it, shoved the door wide open, and chucked the whistle outside.

"Close it! Close the door!" a woman cried from behind him. Lee withdrew from the exit and let the door slam shut, caging them in again.

Lee's chest swelled as he leaned against the wall and pressed his palms to his face. He grunted, then swallowed his urge to scream. Caleb touched Lee's shoulder.

"It doesn't mean he's dead, Lee. We just haven't found him yet," he signed.

Lee forced a weak nod for his brother. He gestured back.

'But what are we gonna do now?'

CHAPTER 12

REN

R en paused next to Pop at the top of the stairs outside the control room, squeezing the inner lining of her raincoat pockets. They were going to see the captain.

"Remember…" Pop began.

"I know, I know. Let you do the talking."

"Right. And try to look appreciative."

Ren smiled, tilted her head downward, and blinked up at him. "This good?"

"I should have left you in the galley."

"I'll be fine. Just knock."

Pop side-eyed her and rapped twice on the door. Through the window, Ren saw the captain standing over a table. He glared at them, pushing his knuckles into his papers. There was no one else there to send them away, so he waved them inside.

"*Kon'nichiwa.*" Pop gave a formal bow.

Ren did the same as they both took off their dripping rain

hoods.

"Uh, *watashi wa* Jim and Ren." Pop was getting a bit better at introductions.

"Sato," said the captain, touching his chest. He gave a half-bow in return.

"Sato-san, *arigato*," Pop replied, reminding Ren how much Pop loved sushi restaurants.

"*Doitashimashite*," Sato replied.

"What are you saying?" Ren whispered through her fixed smile.

"I just said 'hello' and 'thank you.' I have no idea what he said." Pop had reached the limit of his Japanese. Where would they go from here?

Thankfully, a map was spread out on the table.

"May I see?" Pop stepped toward it.

The captain agreed, gesturing them forward.

"Uh…Where are we?" Pop motioned over the wide image of the Pacific.

Sato placed his finger on the map, much further west than Ren had hoped, maybe five hundred miles from the U.S. coastline. She noticed a compass resting above Alaska. They were heading east.

Heading home.

Pop touched the spot the captain indicated and traced a line from there to Seattle.

"Can we go here?" he asked.

Sato seemed to understand. He shook his head. "Ie…uh…no."

"We will pay you." Pop tried to mime payment.

"Uh...*yen?*"

"No," Sato repeated with a sharper tone.

Then, the captain pointed to the Oregon coast.

"*Koko,*" he said, "yes."

"Oregon? You'll take us to Oregon?" Ren asked. She had to restrain herself from jumping up and down. "Arigaro! Erm...*arigato!*" she blurted. They'd be hundreds of miles from home, but Oregon was close enough for her. Sato released an *almost* lukewarm smile at her excitement.

"Radio? Rajio? Can we use your *rajio?*" Ren stepped toward the illuminated box radio beside the control panel. She could almost hear her mother's voice at the other end of it.

But Captain Sato went rigid again, moving to block her from the device.

"No! No *rajio!*"

"But why not?" Ren pressed. She meant to sound pleading, but her tone came out argumentative.

It was not well-received.

"No!" He shot back and pointed to the door.

"Ren, stop. He doesn't want us to use it now." Pop tugged her arm. A cheerful guard slid the door open, then snapped to attention at seeing the Captain's demeanor.

"*Karerawo soto e tsurete iku,*" Sato ordered.

"*Hai,*" the guard obeyed. He opened the door and motioned for Pop and Ren to come out.

Well, I guess the meeting's over.

CHAPTER 13

PETER

A week had passed on the fishing boat. The work was getting easier for Peter as he regained his strength. He'd been enjoying the time alone with Pop. It seemed like Ren had captured most of Pop's attention for the past two years, so Peter liked having Pop to himself all day.

Kenji managed to return Pop's compass, which gave them regular reassurance that they were heading home. Occasionally, the boat would change direction, heading north or south far off course. They would right themselves eventually, but it added more and more days to the journey. Pop tried to casually ask fellow workers for an explanation, but no one *seemed* to understand.

———

At sunset, Peter, Pop, and Ren helped Kenji secure the deck before bed. Kenji and Peter were teaching each other simple words to pass the time.

"*Sakana*," said Peter, pointing to a catch.

"Uh…Fish," Kenji replied.

Peter pointed to Lizzie practicing her knots. "*Rōpu?*"

"*Rōpu, hai.* Uh...Rope." Kenji said, then stretched out his arms sideways. "Boat!"

"*Bōto!*" Peter said, mimicking his enthusiasm.

When finished, Peter leaned against the gunwale, elbows propped up on the ledge. He looked out at the peach and crimson streaks through the clouds and thought about how much Mom would have loved this view.

She must be going crazy right now, worrying about us.

Ren walked up next to him...*on purpose.* This never happened. They had just been stuck on a tiny life raft together for three weeks and had still managed to avoid each other.

This is awkward.

Peter was about to meander away, but then she spoke.

"I want to try and sneak into the bridge," Ren murmured. "I need your help convincing Pop."

"What? Ren, that's nuts. You're gonna tick them off again. They're taking us home."

"Peter, we keep going way off course. At first, Pop guessed it was to follow fish or avoid bad weather, but now he's not so sure. This morning, Pop's compass went missing. I think someone took it."

Peter turned, glancing up at the bridge. He looked back at Ren and crossed his arms.

"Okay, it's weird. So, what? Do you think they're smugglers or something?"

Ren glanced around again. One of the riflemen was sliding out from the galley door, but he didn't look their way.

"Maybe. It would explain the armed guards and their refusal to let us use the radio. They're trying to avoid other boats."

"Why do you care as long as we're still going toward home?"

"Peter, what if they get caught and use us as hostages? What if they're traffickers or plan to ransom our release? I mean, who knows?" Ren insisted.

His very relevant and crucial questions seemed to annoy her.

Peter stiffened.

"Okay, Ren. Don't freak out. Look, they've been taking care of us. We'd be dead by now if it weren't for them. What does Pop say?"

"He said that too and doesn't *think* they mean us harm, but I can tell he's worried. Will you help me convince him?"

Peter couldn't remember the last time Ren asked him for help or even *spoke* to him this much.

But she kind of had a point.

"Yeah, okay," he relented.

"Great..." She relaxed and turned around to study the bridge.

"Are you *positive* you can work this radio?" Peter pressed.

"Yes, I'm sure."

Really? Then why do you look so totally unsure?

But he kept that to himself.

CHAPTER 14

REN

R en and Peter found it easier to convince Pop than she had
   imagined. He must have been more concerned than he'd let
on. Seeing Ren and Peter on the same side for once might also
have helped. Now that they were really going through with it,
Ren was terrified.

*I'm trying to deceive possible drug smugglers. I must be
insane.*

After dinner, Ren snuck onto the deck and hid among the
fishing nets, still mucky from the day's catch. With the clouds
covering the moonlight, it was especially dark that night. Only
one of the armed guards was patrolling. He was perched on the
portside bow, out of view of the stairs to the bridge. Ren just
hoped he stayed over there.

The shift change happened at midnight. The plan was for Pop
and Peter to keep Ito, the relief guard, distracted below, maybe
with one of Pop's card tricks, until the on-duty guy came to look
for him. At 12:05, Ren heard the bridge door shut and the guard
grumbling to himself as he clomped down the stairs.

Ren touched the gold pendant now fixed around her neck.

When the galley door slammed shut, she leaped from her hiding spot and slinked up the starboard side toward the bridge. Ren flipped off her shoes at the bottom of the metal stairs. The sharp safety ridges dug into her feet as she tiptoed up. The ocean was quiet that night. Hardly any waves to buffer the noise.

Ren rustled the door open and shut it behind her. Moving in silence was taking longer than she'd expected, and she was already behind schedule. She slipped over to the radio and flipped the power knob.

Nothing.

No lights or hum—completely dead. She searched around the box, hoping for another switch to get the thing going, clicking every button. When she tilted it to check the bottom, the top cover slipped off in her hands, almost causing her to drop the whole device. She carefully pulled off the plastic shell to find the machine empty—completely stripped. All of the electronic guts that made the radio work had been removed.

NO!

She quickly put the cover back in place and rummaged for some other solution that could possibly help them, but found nothing. She had to get out of there.

As Ren opened the door, she heard the guard talking to Ito on the starboard side. Time had run out. They were going to catch her. There was nowhere to hide in that small control room, and even if there were, she would eventually need to come out. This whole plan had been a bust, and now Sato would be furious.

She heard Ito ascend the stairs, one, two, three steps up. She didn't know what to do or where to go. She tried to come up with a reasonable excuse, but how could she even tell them a lie?

An excuse won't work if they don't speak English, dummy! It's just me, hiding somewhere I'm definitely not supposed to be for no reason other than mutiny. Not good. Not good. Not good...

Just as she was ready to give herself up, her grandfather's voice called out from below.

"Ito! There's something out there! Come see!"

Ito's footsteps paused, then receded down the steps to the deck.

"On the portside! It's back here!" Pop and Peter both called, just loud enough for Ren to know the coast was clear. She flew back down the stairs, much less concerned about the noise now, then grabbed her shoes and dashed into the galley. She heard a cabin door opening just as she slid back into their bunk room. Peeking through the crack in the door, she saw Sato emerge.

Sato climbed up to the deck and stayed out there for what felt like an hour before he, Pop, and Peter came back in.

"I'm sorry. So sorry," Pop said repeatedly to the captain.

"Okay," Sato said with a yawn as he shuffled down the hall.

They had made it. Unfortunately, it was all for nothing. Pop opened the door and found Ren sitting on the bottom bunk.

"What happened? Did you reach anyone?" Pop asked.

Ren shook her head.

"All the radio parts had been pulled out. Someone disabled it on purpose. We're on our own."

CHAPTER 15

REN

October 16th, 2027 - 200 miles south of Seattle.
42 days after.

S ix weeks had passed since the *Bethie* capsized, and still no
contact with shore. Everyone on board seemed more on
edge as the boat continued eastward.

That morning, the crew roused the family two hours before
sunrise.

Ren tied her hair in a braid as Lizzie ate her rice breakfast.
They were both listening to Peter play his word game with Kenji
at the galley table. Peter rested his hand on Lizzie's head.

"Sister," he said.

"Sister," Kenji repeated. Then he put his hand up to pause
the game. Kenji retrieved a wallet from his pocket. He pulled out
a photograph and showed it to Peter. There was a Japanese
woman in her twenties with a white man and a baby. They were
standing in front of a lovely white house with a porch.

"*Imōto*," he said, pointing to the woman, "sister."

"This is your sister?" asked Lizzie.

"*Hai, imōto*…sister," he said again. "Oregon."

"What did he say?" Ren asked. "His sister is in Oregon?"

"I think so," Peter answered.

Kenji spread out a napkin on the left-hand side of the table and another on the right-hand side. Then, he grabbed a small, empty bowl to rest between them.

"Boat," he said as he pointed to it.

"No, that's a bowl," Lizzie corrected.

"No, boat," he insisted, pushing the bowl along the table with a shushing sound. Then he touched a spot on the edge of the left napkin.

"Japan."

He pointed to the right-side napkin in the same way.

"Oregon."

"Oh, it's a map," Peter said. "The bowl is our boat."

Kenji put the picture on the white napkin representing the U.S. He pushed the boat across the table to the picture, put the picture in the bowl, and then pushed it back to the napkin meant to be Asia.

"Sister...to Japan," he said.

"He's taking his sister back to Japan? On this boat?" Ren was confused. By the look of their house, the family could surely afford to fly.

"*Hai*," Kenji said, seeming to understand perfectly. He pointed to Riku standing in the kitchen. "Riku, boy...Sato...uh...Daughter...boat to Japan...Iko, Haruto, Akira family to Japan."

Pop leaned in. "They're all bringing family members back to Japan? On this boat?"

"Why? Peter, does he know that word?" Ren asked. Kenji spoke to Riku briefly in Japanese. Riku seemed uncomfortable with the conversation. Kenji looked at Ren, then Peter.

"Birds…uh…bad…Bad birds."

At that moment, one of the men came in to summon Riku and Kenji to the deck. The two jumped from the table and darted up the steps without a word. Ren and her family followed. When Ren got outside and looked at the horizon, she couldn't believe her eyes.

Land.

"Pop! We're at the coast."

Instantly, Kenji grabbed her arm and put his finger to his lips. As the others came out, he quieted them as well. Kenji led Ren to the portside deck. The whole crew stood silent on their darkened vessel, staring at a coast guard boat near a small harbor far in the distance. Its lights gleamed against the blackened shoreline.

After everything Ren and her family had been through, they could finally contact Mom. Finally, go home. English-speaking authorities were so close.

But Sato signaled to the bridge, and the boat started turning around.

Oh, no. They're taking us away!

The captain was standing right in front of Ren with his back to her. She stared at his pistol strapped to his hip. Should she grab his gun? A shot would get the Coast Guard's attention. This might be her best chance to escape if their shipmates were dangerous.

But something held her back.

Sato turned and caught Ren looking at his holster. They locked eyes, and she braced for a guard's arrest or at least a reprimand. But instead, he offered her his binoculars and pointed out to the distant seacraft she was so desperate to reach.

Ren blinked at him, confused. He pressed the binoculars to her again, and this time she accepted. She held them up and angled them toward the harbor until she found the men on the patrol boat.

They weren't Coast Guard officials, but heavily armed men in plain clothes. They were horsing around and laughing so audaciously that it seemed almost menacing. She watched as one of them threw an empty bottle from the boat and shot it, spraying bits of glass into the water. The act started an argument on board. They shouted and pushed each other until a fistfight broke out. One man hit another in the face with his rifle, and he fell in a heap on the deck.

Sato took the binoculars back and glared at her.

"Danger," he said.

Ren believed him.

But where are the police?

Sato directed the boat southward, away from the harbor. Ren didn't even know what questions to ask. She walked back to her family and looked at Pop.

"Something's wrong," she said.

"What did you see? Was it the Coast Guard?"

Ren shook her head.

———

A quarter mile south, the fishing boat stopped just beyond a private dock, and the crane lowered the *Bethie's* lifeboat into the water. Kenji and one of the guards helped Peter, Lizzie, and Pop climb down to it. Sato murmured to Riku, who then produced a cooler full of iced fish for the family to take with them.

Ren was zipping up her jacket as Sato pulled the pistol from his belt and handed it to her. She didn't want to take it. She'd never even held a gun before. Sato took her hand and wrapped it around the handle, then guided her arm to place it in her jacket pocket. Ren searched his grave expression.

What's happening out there?

"*Arigato*, Sato-san," was all she could utter.

Sato braced her arms and nodded.

"Goodbye, Ren," he said, then motioned her onto the ladder.

Ren climbed over the gunwale and regarded Sato as she descended. Now, she didn't want to leave this man she'd only ever resented and feared. He had saved them, protected them. And now she and her family had to go on alone toward an unknown threat.

Peter, Kenji, Pop, and the guard paddled them quietly to the dock. Before they got out, Kenji grabbed Ren's hand and put it on Lizzie's. Then he put Peter's hand on Lizzie, too.

"*Otagai no chikaku ni ite kudasai.*"

"Peter, what is he saying?" Ren asked.

"I don't know."

Ren felt a shiver up her spine.

She and the others climbed out of the raft. They waved to the men as the winch reeled them back to the boat, racing them away from shore as if afraid of it.

Ren grasped Lizzie's hand and gazed up at the tall cliff before them. Pop and Peter started carrying the cooler up the steep steps to the house at the top. Ren and Lizzie followed close behind as light peeked over the horizon.

CHAPTER 16

REN

B y the time Ren knocked on the door of the cliff-side house, the sun had nearly risen. When no one responded, Peter rang the bell—once, twice, again. Ren peered through a window and found no lights or movement.

"Maybe they're still asleep," she said.

Lizzie pointed to a note that had fallen from the door.

At market. Back by 10.

The four of them headed to the road and kept walking with the cooler in tow. Ren searched sidewalks and into house windows for a glimmer of life, anxious for an end to their prolonged isolation.

At last, she heard American voices in the distance.

Finally, English-speaking people. Hallelujah!

At that moment, Ren didn't care about what she saw at the harbor. They were so close to salvation. She quickened her pace, practically dragging Lizzie down the road as Pop and Peter hurried behind. She had so many questions, and the answers were steps away.

More than anything, Ren couldn't wait to call Mom.

Ren, Pop, Peter, and Lizzie rounded the corner onto Main Street to find a bustling market just four blocks down. Pop laughed.

"We made it!" he said.

The family strode down the hill with renewed energy and excitement. Lizzie was practically skipping. Ren smiled along with them, but her stomach was in knots.

The market swarmed with townspeople bustling between the vendor stands that lined either side of the street. The crowd was immense, maybe ten thousand people rushing to fill their bags and carts. It was frenzied and intense. Everyone seemed haggard, and many were just plain dirty. Definitely not a typical produce market with cheerful shoppers and hippy artisan stands. This was chaotic and huge.

Ren noticed something extremely peculiar. Every person there was tethered to someone else by a strap or a rope, maybe four to eight feet long. Ren, Peter, and Pop looked at each other, unsettled, as Ren gripped Lizzie's hand tighter.

Have we stumbled on some kind of cult?

They lugged the cooler up to the first table they came across and waited to speak to an older man, maybe in his seventies, selling potatoes. A woman, probably his wife, stood beside him. The vendor's current customer was towering—about 6'5. He was brawny, scarred, and ragged—maybe late twenties, with a hawk tattooed on his forearm. The man was tied to a skinny and scraggly-looking man of similar age with a mullet. Their hands and clothes were filthy, and both reeked of sweat and campfire smoke.

"You sold me these same taters for half that two weeks ago, Sanders," the larger patron argued, leaning over the table. The smaller one looked on, smirking at the disturbance his buddy was causing.

"Last time, I let you have a discount just to be neighborly. I told you that, Fitz," the old man's voice faltered.

"You didn't say anything like that, old man. Did he, Kenny?"

"Sure didn't. He's lyin' through his teeth."

Ren looked around them. Others were noticing the blatant harassment but kept walking.

Ren wanted to tell Pop to move to the next stand. The potato argument was escalating, and she just wanted to find a phone and get home.

The customer pounded his tattooed arm on the table and slung the pile of spuds onto the road right at Ren's feet.

"Please, Fitz, these are all we have, and we can't sell 'em so cheap. You and Kenny go trade elsewhere," Mr. Sanders beseeched. He was nearly shouting his pleas across the market, arms outstretched as he scanned the indifferent crowd. Nobody approached. Sanders removed his glasses to wipe the sweat from his eyes. He met Fitz's gaze and flinched.

Fitz smirked and snatched hold of the man's ear, then yanked his plump head over the table. Sanders cried out in pain as his wife begged for them to stop.

"We ain't leavin' 'til we get our due."

Ren and Pop looked around in disbelief.

85

Why was no one helping?

Ren reached down to pick up two of the fallen vegetables. Fitz released Sanders and turned to her.

"Those are mine, 'lil girl. You, give 'em here."

Ren dug her nails into the potatoes and glared at the man, unblinking. She had survived a boat wreck, a shark attack, weeks on a life raft, and hard labor on a fishing boat. She wasn't about to give in to some greasy thieving bully.

Ren handed the potatoes back to the vendor. Mr. Sanders returned a shaky nod, then started squirreling all his produce from the table to the wagon behind it. His wife collected what she could from the ground. Fitz muttered a vile insult, but Ren had learned how to ignore that noise a while ago.

"Let's go to the next one," Pop said, pulling Ren back over to the cooler. They picked it up and pivoted to the next produce stall.

Fitz and his accomplice went right back to tormenting Sanders, now grabbing the man's shirt and helping themselves to the potatoes the wife couldn't get to.

"Leave it, Ren," Pop insisted. "We need to find help." He directed her attention to the stand in front of them.

At this stall, they found a younger guy, maybe nineteen or twenty, wearing a thin green jacket. His table display had a variety of vegetables, fresh eggs, smoked ham, jams, coils of rope, and more. He was tall, with an average build and sandy-brown hair. In her former life, Ren may have found him good-looking, but his demeanor seemed rigid and cold. He was tied to another, much older man, who was burly, shorter, and currently bartering with a Vietnamese couple. The younger one seemed to ignore Ren, instead glancing over her shoulder at the potato stand argument. He muttered something and shook his head. Then, he clicked his pen and went back to writing on his clipboard.

Ren narrowed her gaze. This guy could easily have done something to help the potato seller until the authorities arrived, but chose not to bother. Ren immediately disliked him.

As the clipboard guy turned to speak to his partner, Ren spotted a pistol tucked in the back of his pants. It reminded her of the gun she, too, was carrying in her pocket. The weapon now weighed more heavily on her left side.

"Excuse me," Pop said to him.

"G'day, how ya goin'?" He had a thick Australian-sounding accent and a thin leather band around his wrist. He looked up and nodded to Pop. He noticed Ren for the first time and continued staring at her for longer than she was used to. Heat rose up the back of her neck. The young man cleared his throat and looked back at Pop.

"We need some help," Pop said.

"Reckon we could all use help nowadays, eh? I haven't seen you two before." He swept the knit hats left by the previous couple into a sack under the table.

"We're from Seattle," Pop said.

"Well, welcome to Gladys." His tone sounded almost sarcastic. "I'm Hank, and that there's Marty. Whatcha got for tradin'?" He nodded to the cooler.

Pop opened it.

"Uh, we have some halibut and tuna. Please, have you got a phone we could use?"

Hank froze, then looked at the cooler full of deep-sea fish. He reached over, slammed the lid shut, and ricocheted his gaze around the crowd.

"Look mate, I don't know where ya got that, but you can't show it to anyone 'round here," he said sternly.

"What do you mean?" Ren probed. "Why not? What's going on? We've been at sea for almost two months, and we…"

Hank snatched her wrist.

"Shhhh! Gal, you gotta keep your voice down!" he warned.

Hank released her and looked around again. He seemed to scrutinize the two men, Fitz and Kenny, who were now done with the potato argument and loitering a few yards away.

"Look, I swear I'll help ya get somewhere safe in exchange for your catch. Just cool it here, and keep quiet while we get set to leave," Hank directed as he quickly began to pack up.

Frustrated, Ren bit her inner cheek and complied. Then, a sign across the street caught her eye.

Tethering Enforced
by the City of Gladys
Stay safe.
Stay together.
Stay tethered.

"Pop, look at…"

But Pop was rigid and laser-eyed, scanning the crowd. He turned to her.

"Ren, where are Peter and Lizzie?"

"They were right behind me...weren't they?" Ren couldn't remember the last time she saw them. Peter was always so attentive to Lizzie that Ren didn't check on her as much when he was around.

They must be together, but where would they go?

Ren and Pop looked through the sea of marketgoers, irritated that Peter didn't know better than to wander off. She spotted another table nearby with several children around it, hoping to see her sister's blond head. Two of the children were tied to their young mother, watching her hunt through used clothing and shoes. As Ren approached, the woman looked down at her kids and panicked.

"Jacob! Where's Jacob?" she demanded of her other kids. Their expressions were blank. She called out above the crowd. "Jacob! Where are you?"

Ren flinched at the instant alarm in the woman's voice. She saw Ren looking at her and approached.

"Have you seen a little boy? He's three with brown hair and a green shirt. He's alone!"

"Uh...no, I haven't," Ren said.

The woman began to cry, dragging her young ones as she darted around, calling his name and begging others for help.

"What's happening?" Pop asked.

"This woman lost her three-year-old. No sign of Lizzie?"

Pop shook his head. She was about to go off on Peter's lack of responsibility when Ren noticed a lone toddler up the hill, just beyond the far side of the market, petting a cat.

"Ma'am, is that him?" Ren called out to the mom and pointed toward him. "Just past the sign for Missy's apples.

Beyond the crowd."

Suddenly, a sharp screech ripped over the market.

CHAPTER 17

REN

The crowd erupted in screams. Ren and Pop searched the skies for whatever made the bloodcurdling sound. Around them, people were trampling each other, jockeying to get out of the street.

Jacob's mother yanked off the rope that connected her to her other kids. With trembling hands, she gave the tether to the clothes vendor.

"Keep them safe," she said, then she dashed into the crowd.

"Hannah, no!" the man shouted after her. Hannah ignored him, tearing through the horde toward Jacob as her other kids cried for her to come back.

The mysterious and terrifying shrieks grew louder and more continuous, now coming from all directions.

"Marty!" Hank yelled at his partner. The two of them jumped over their table, pushed past Ren, and chased after Hannah as she clawed her way through the crowd.

Ren righted herself as Peter ran over, out of breath.

"Peter! Where's Lizzie?"

"She didn't come back here? I can't find her!" he panted.

Ren's heart seized in her chest.

"*You lost her*? Why would you even leave us?"

"She ran off because she wanted an apple, and I chased after her! *You* didn't even notice she was gone!"

That stung. He was right.

Pop, Ren, and Peter yelled for her over the swarm, but the uproar from the road and screeches from above drowned out their cries.

Gusts of howling wind blared overhead, hurtling northward toward Jacob. Lizzie's disappearance stabbed at Ren's gut. She felt dizzy and disoriented, nearly losing Pop and Peter in the frenzy. She spotted Jacob's mother breaking through the last of the herd, scrambling in her fight to reach her son.

"There she is!" Peter pointed to the apple stand on the market's far edge. Lizzy was there, clutching her ears and crying for Peter.

Just beyond Lizzy, little Jacob stood alone in the empty street, his eyes on the sky, covering his ears just as Lizzy was. The furious wind and shrieks from above came down upon the small boy like a tight-barreled tornado, knocking him off his feet.

But his body never hit the ground.

He just vanished in the whirlwind of dust.

Swallowed. By...nothing.

Something had devoured Jacob, leaving no trace that he'd ever been there.

Oh my God.

"Lizzie!" Ren screamed, but she wasn't sure if she was even yelling out loud anymore. Nothing felt real. Moving toward her sister without sense or focus, Ren felt as if she were floating through a nightmare.

Hank and Marty were still pushing their way toward Hannah, who had now fallen to her knees where her youngest child once stood, her face in her hands.

"Hannah! Come back!" Hank bellowed.

Hannah didn't move. She just looked up, mournfully succumbing to the cyclone and whistling echoes surrounding her. Her long, wavy hair fanned and twisted above her, caught in the screeching vortex.

Ren watched what looked like an invisible cloak being wrapped around her—a wave of non-existence washing over her body. It was impossible to tell if her cries were from the loss of her son, the fear, or the pain.

And then she was gone.

At the edge of the market, Lizzie was the closest witness to the horrible scene. She stood there, alone and paralyzed, as the crowd scrambled further away from the site…and further away from her.

"Lizzie!" Ren screamed again, so loud her voice ruptured. This time, some heard and turned to her, but no one tried to help.

Ren, Peter, and Pop fought through the current of people. Ren and Pop got caught in a tether and fell beneath the stampede.

Ren was kicked and stomped. Peter yanked her up just as Lizzie's blond hair started swirling above her in the approaching windstorm.

"No!!" she screamed.

Suddenly, a large man descended on Lizzie, completely enclosing her in his arms. Within seconds, the wind subsided, and the sky went quiet, leaving only the sound of hushed whimpering.

"I got her," the man called out. "She's okay."

Lizzie's head peeked over the man's shoulder. Her arms wrapped around his neck as he stood.

Ren nearly collapsed with shock and relief.

Families began collecting abandoned items while comforting their children. Lizzie's savior navigated through at a steady pace. He stood taller than most and wore a red ball cap and a brown utility jacket. He was holding the back of Lizzie's head, trying to comfort her.

Peter reached them first, and the man handed Lizzie to him. Now safe with her big brother, Lizzie's sobbing erupted.

Ren and Pop rushed up from behind.

"The crying's a good sign. She's getting over the shock," the man said. His tone was warm and calm.

"Thank you," Pop stammered.

Ren rubbed Lizzie's quivering back.

"Are you...okay?" Ren murmured, her voice shattered from the screaming.

"Peter! I'm sorry I left. I should have stayed with you." Lizzie could barely get the words out. "I was all alone..."

"I'm right here now. I've got you," Peter soothed. "It's okay."

Ren stared at Lizzie's rescuer, speechless.

Up close, Ren could see he was only a year or two older than she was, though he carried himself more like a dad.

Ren was too confused to show gratitude.

What did he save her from? What is happening?!

Trying to stifle a meltdown, all Ren could do was silently open and close her mouth.

"Thank you," Pop repeated.

"You're welcome," the guy replied. "Glad I was close enough to help."

The stranger walked them back to Hank, who was still catching his breath.

"Lee, well done, mate. She's ruddy lucky you were there." Hank pointed to the detached tether dangling from Lee's waist. "Ya got someone here with you? Where's Caleb?"

"Yes, I'm fine. Cut myself loose to move faster, that's all."

"Good one." Hank reached out and shook his hand.

Marty approached, leading Hannah's other two children, their little cheeks raw and damp.

"What about them?" Lee asked.

"I'll bring them up to Minna. She'll look after 'em," Hank replied. "I'll see you tomorrow, okay?"

"Yep, tomorrow."

Lee nodded with a half-smile at Ren and Pop, then walked back into the crowd.

As Hank returned to packing up, he shot Ren an icy glare.

"We're leavin' now. You need to keep better track of your family."

"I didn't know…Please, what's...?" She remembered Hank's warning and silenced herself, choking down all her fear and confusion.

Hank swiped some ropes off his table and tossed them to her. "Tether up and stop drawing so much bloody attention to yourselves."

Hands shaking, Ren tied her rope to Lizzie's belt loop.

She noticed Fitz sneering at her from across the street, seemingly amused by her helplessness. Ren never felt more vulnerable or ignorant. She sensed his eyes boring into her until the market was well behind them.

CHAPTER 18

REN

The uphill walk to wherever they were headed seemed endless. Ren and Pop pushed Hank's two-wheeled cart carrying the day's traded and unsold goods as Hank and Marty pulled. Hannah's children, a boy and a girl, neither older than six, huddled together among the sacks of flour. Peter carried Lizzie, who hadn't spoken since they'd left the market.

An hour and a half later, the small road ended at a barbed wire fence on a wooded hill. There were two armed guards, a stout man and a woman who looked like Ren's old math teacher. They waved to Hank, then opened the gate for the weary trekkers. Hank gave them a nod as they passed.

A towering lighthouse emerged above the hill, the eye at the top sparkling in the morning sun.

"Almost there, gang," Hank huffed.

The road opened to a cliffside field with a large white house perched at the end of the drive. It had three stories with blue shutters and double front doors. The wraparound porch sloped downward from age, though the railings and woodwork looked recently restored. There was a red barn with fenced-in pigs, goats, and a mobile chicken coop. Adjacent to the barn sprawled a large vegetable garden tended by tethered adults and children, who looked up to gawk at the passing newcomers.

From the porch, an older woman of about sixty was watching over the gardeners. She waved at Hank and Marty and descended a few steps from the porch. She was robust and weathered, with a no-nonsense quality to her. She wore a pair of men's trousers, cinched with a thick belt, a canvas coat, and rubber boots. A large sun hat covered her gray hair, tied in a bun.

"Well, hallo there, lads," she said with a Scottish lilt. "What have ye brought us today from the market?"

"A bit more than usual, Minna," Hank replied heavily.

As Marty pulled the two children down from the cart, the woman raised her eyebrows with a searching frown.

Hank returned it with a shake of his head.

Minna bent down to the two tear-stained faces before her.

"Well, if it isn't George and April. I'm so very glad yer here, loves. Yer safe now with old Aunt Minna."

Hank gestured back toward Ren, Pop, Peter, and Lizzie.

"Also, this family needs a place to stay for the night. They've brought ya some tuna and halibut."

"Really?" She reached out to lead them up the porch. "Then ye probably have quite a tale to go with it. Please, come inside out of the chill."

Minna traded her muddy boots for loafers at the door, reminding Ren to wipe her shoes well on the mat. Ren gestured behind her for Lizzie and Peter to do the same.

A young red-haired woman in her thirties, wearing a farm dress and a tight apron, came to receive them, taking their jackets to hang on the racks in the foyer. She gave Marty a quick kiss and a hug.

"Sally, do ye know George and April? They'll be staying up here with us for the time being." Minna said this with a cheerful tone, at odds with the somber look she gave Sally.

Sally nodded and reached down to the youngsters, smiling.

"Oh, yes. We're great friends from Sunday school, aren't we?" She slid the boy's coat off his little arms. "Oh, George, you've got popsicles for fingers! Come and have some stew."

George leaned in for a tearful snuggle. Sally lifted April to hug her, too, then looked at Lizzie and Peter.

"And what about the two of you? Would you like something warm as well?"

"Yes, they would, thank you," Pop said, nudging them to follow her. Ren could smell savory meat and vegetables wafting from the kitchen. She was starving, but couldn't eat a bite now.

Marty went with the kids to the kitchen, hauling the cooler full of fish.

"We'll get some of this cooked up for supper," he said over his shoulder. "Sally can fry a mean halibut."

Minna removed her garden gloves and extended her hand to Pop and Ren. Her fingers were knobby and warm.

"She can indeed. I'm Minerva Christy. You can call me Minna."

Minerva—like the asteroid with two moons.

"I'm Jim Haley, and this is my granddaughter, Ren," Pop said.

"Erm...nice to meet you," Ren stuttered, still breathless from the hike and everything before. The pleasantries seemed absurd after what they'd just seen.

"Please come sit down by the fire. You must be tired and cold."

"Um, thank you," Ren uttered and followed Pop to the parlor. It was formal but cozy, decorated with ornate antiques, china, family portraits, and paintings of old ships. A hot pot of tea sat on a polished silver tray.

Ren felt too unhinged to be sitting in a room like this, as if she might rip down the curtains or start smashing dishes. Instead, she sat in silence on the sofa next to Pop.

———

Ren listened as her grandfather unloaded the whole saga of what they'd been through—the wreck, the shark, the rescue, and the market. The story seemed to captivate Minna, while Hank just watched from against the wall. Ren was fixated on the figurine creamer on the table—a serene milkmaid holding a pitcher.

"...And that's how we ended up here," Pop finished. He looked at Ren as if checking to make sure he remembered everything.

"Gracious, ye survived out there that long? Yer a tough bunch, I'd say," Minna remarked.

"We thought it was a tsunami or a rogue wave, but—"

Ren jumped to her feet. Her confusion, frustration, fear, *everything* just exploded onto the coffee table.

"Pop, what does it matter what caused the wreck? Is everyone insane? What happened at the market?? We just walked an hour in *forced* silence after Lizzie almost got...I mean...I just want someone to finally tell us what's going on!" Her damaged voice ached with each word.

"Oh, I'm sorry if respecting the loss of those two orphaned children doesn't suit you," Hank shot back. "And jabberin' on like you were in that crowd was putting us all in danger."

"But how were we supposed to know?" she rasped. "I mean… I'm sorry… I just…"

"Ren." Pop took her hand and pulled her back down to the couch.

"Nice gratitude," Hank scoffed. "Perhaps ya should try finding some other fool to take you in, eh? There's the door, and good luck to you."

Minna raised her hand.

"Alright, Hank. Now, that's enough. The good Lord put me in charge of this inn, and I'll decide who stays. We were all just as shocked as she was at the start of it."

Hank hushed and recrossed his arms.

Ren tried to calm herself.

"We're so thankful for your help, ma'am. But what happened to that little boy and his mother? They just disappeared."

"I promise we'll answer yer questions, child. Here, have a bit of tea."

Ren accepted with shaking hands and took a sip. The hot liquid felt good on her sore throat.

Minna began. "The wave that hit ye was from a terrible meteor shower. On September 3rd, the planet was hit by thousands, perhaps hundreds of thousands of meteors. We don't know exactly how many. The information we have came from a few emergency broadcasts—before the radios went dead, that is."

At this moment, after so much time, Ren finally remembered the meteors. She recalled standing on the deck of the *Bethie,* watching them soar above her, and then the impact.

That's what caused the wave. How could she have forgotten?

"They ranged in size from marbles to small houses," Minna continued. "Many people died, and we've had no power and little communication since. Cell towers, powerlines, it's all been destroyed. I'm sure you'll be wanting to call your family, but ye won't be able to from here, I'm afraid."

"Pop, what about Mom?" Ren whispered. This entire time, Ren had been fretting about how worried Mom must be, never imagining she might be in danger, too—or worse.

"My daughter-in-law, their mother, is on Cape George, just north of Seattle," Pop said. "What's happening there? Have you heard anything?"

"We've had some folks come through from Seattle," Minna answered. "It was bad there, from what we've heard, but we don't have many specifics. We do have a wave radio we check on. Perhaps we'll know more soon."

Minna rose to stoke the dying fire.

"Why didn't someone see them coming? Why didn't anyone warn us?" Pop asked.

Minna rehung the poker and sat back in the chair.

"That's another question we have no answer to."

"But what was that sound? *What happened at the market?*" Ren insisted. Both hands were wrapped around her porcelain teacup, holding onto it for dear life.

Minna looked over at Hank.

"The meteors brought some kind of extra-terrestrial species with them," Hank said, his eyes fastened on Ren.

Ren stared back, hoping for a flinch of uncertainty, but he didn't blink.

"A predatory and very dangerous species," Hank continued. He moved in front of them. "A few days after impact, folks started reporting pets missing. Within a week, the beasts began taking kids. Any child outside and apart from other people would be attacked, swallowed up whole. We lost dozens in a day. By the time the authorities confirmed what was happening, the town was already on lockdown."

Ren felt weak. She wanted to take another gulp of tea, but she knew she'd spill it.

"But has anyone ever seen one?" she asked.

"Their camouflage capability is absolute," Hank said. "At first, they seemed to only prowl on foot, and we could spot their tracks in the dirt. But they attack from the air now and can move bloody quick.

"Sometimes you can see their movement, like ripples in the landscape, but it's hard to know where to look. They're also more aggressive, growing in number, and seem to be bigger in size. They have no trouble going after adults. It took us a bit to work out how to protect ourselves. Now we know they'll attack anyone standing more than eight feet away from someone else, sometimes less."

"So that's why everyone…with the ropes?" Pop asked.

"Aye, the mayor mandated a tethering law," Minna inserted. "Everyone outside must stay tied to someone else."

"It's kind of like a seatbelt law," Hank added. "There's no guard around to enforce it anymore, but people get riled if you don't. If we keep feedin' 'em, it'll just get worse around here."

With her head reeling, Ren put her cup down, rattling it against the table. Minna reached out to hold her hands.

"Do hear us, lass. Outside, they are everywhere, all around us, always watching. Ye must keep close to each other at all times."

"Step too far away, and they'll come for ya. There's not always time like you saw today. They can snatch you in seconds without a sound, leaving nothin' but your footprints," Hank warned. "You're lucky you all made it to the market today, untethered as you were."

An icy feeling shot up Ren's spine. What if Pop and Peter hadn't been carrying the cooler? What if she hadn't been holding Lizzie's hand?

"This can't be happening," Ren whispered. The tick of the mantle clock sounded deafening. She couldn't concentrate. Ren looked to Pop for some assurance that none of this was real.

But Pop seemed more alarmed than she had ever seen before.

"But how…what else do you know about them?" Pop stuttered.

"We call 'em banshees because of the noise they make," Hank went on. "They fly, like I said, but not far, maybe a hundred feet or so. We reckon they can't—or won't—swim. When folks figured out they were safer at sea, they began fighting over the few boats not wrecked by the meteors."

"Have ye told anyone else that you were on a boat?" Minna asked.

"No, we haven't," Pop assured.

"Are you absolutely certain?" Hank pressed, eyeballing Ren. "None of you said a word to *anyone*?"

"*Yes*, we're *sure*," Ren pushed back.

Minna rubbed Ren's arm.

"Of course, we believe you," she said. "I apologize for Hank's abruptness. Unfortunately, the desperate and cruel will do near anythin' for a boat. Even good folks will overrun a craft tryin' to get on board. Hank here just means to keep us safe."

"There's a dangerous group of men floating just off the harbor," Hank added. "They steal boats and trade 'em or use 'em to go after more. They're not the only ones who'd hurt ya trying to get one. You must understand that. Do *not* tell anyone you were just at sea under any circumstances."

Ren remembered the scene she witnessed through the binoculars.

"We saw those men on the way here," she croaked through her hoarse voice. "They're on a Coast Guard boat."

"That's them," he confirmed. "You're lucky they didn't see you. If they had, you'd not be here now."

Ren thought of the fishermen who rescued them. No radio, winding route, armed guards—Sato was trying to *protect* the boat and everyone on board.

"What about the armed forces?" Pop asked. "What are they doing?"

Minna shrugged and shook her head.

"We don't know exactly. But I'm certain they're doing their best."

Hank rested his hand on the back of Minna's armchair.

"It's tough to fight something you can't see. Even if they have figured out how to kill the buggers, now there are so many, it's like exterminating a million rodents with a fly swatter."

Ren looked at her grandfather. "Pop, we have to get back to Mom. She's alone."

Pop turned to Hank. "How can we get to Seattle? Can anyone drive us?"

Hank shook his head. "We have lots of vehicles but no gas."

Ren began to crumble. She couldn't catch her breath.

Minna patted Ren's arm. "If yer mother has remained inside with the windows shut tight, she should be safe."

"Stayed inside? We've been gone for almost two months. If she hasn't been able to leave the house, she could be completely out of food by now. Or what if she's hurt and can't get help?" At that moment, Ren had never felt farther away from her mother.

"The authorities are checkin' in on people," Hank offered. "She's probably been retrieved."

"But the house is hidden from the road. What if they passed her by?"

"We'll do our best to help ye get home," Minna promised. "In the meantime, yer welcome to stay with us. It's safe here."

"Thank you," Pop replied. He turned to Ren. "It'll be ok, Lauren. We'll figure something out."

CHAPTER 19

LEE

L ee, Caleb, Fitz, and Kenny walked up Lee's quiet street, carrying their bags from the market. The neighborhood seemed abandoned now, without lights or movement. People didn't linger outside anymore.

Fitz's boasting and Kenny's cackling shattered the silence. Lee didn't find anything Fitz said funny at all, but he humored his brother by chuckling occasionally. As was typical, Caleb seemed happy to ignore him. He'd turned off Hutch's vibrate alert an hour ago.

"I grabbed that stingy badger so fast I thought he'd wet his pants," Fitz went on.

"He probably did a little!" Kenny added, slapping Fitz on the back.

"Yer right. Either way, I got my taters, didn't I?" He held up his full bag. "Hopefully, Mae won't burn 'em this time."

Lee and Caleb climbed up the porch steps. As Lee unlocked the door, he called back over his shoulder.

"I'll go in and send Mae out so you can get home. I'm sure you're eager to cook up supper."

"Aww, I think we got a few minutes, don't we, Kenny?" Fitz answered, following Lee in.

Kenny agreed, as usual. Kenny Dugart had dropped out of high school at seventeen. He'd been working odd jobs around town and lived with his ailing grandma. He had a mousy mullet, a pockmarked face, and a missing side tooth from tripping off a curb near the bar. Most of his shirts were pit-stained, and his pants hung too low on his hips. But it was Kenny's behavior and hyena laugh that was most unappealing.

Kenny had been a misfit in high school and never had many friends. For Fitz's camaraderie, he was more than happy to play follower. Lee never liked him. Kenny brought out the worst in his brother. Had Fitz not been showing off for him, he may have just paid for those potatoes without much fuss.

As Lee, Caleb, and Fitz took off their jackets and shoes at the door, Kenny tromped the grime from the market through to the kitchen. Fitz and Lee followed, but Caleb found an excuse to be elsewhere.

"Say, Lee. How's Penny doing?" Fitz asked as he sat down.

"Just fine, thanks." Lee averted his eyes to the bag he was unpacking. "Yep, she's good. You know, I think I'd better get dinner goin'."

"Come have a seat with me for a sec," Fitz said, patting the table. Lee filled three glasses of water from the tap, handed one to Kenny, who was standing by the fridge, and sat with the other two. Fitz took a few big gulps, then removed his cap and rested it on the table. His hair was matted and slick.

"Now, I hear that Penny's *not* doing so good. How could she, being just holed up in that basement so much? Mae feels bad leaving her alone down there sometimes, but she just can't take it with her claustrophobia."

"I bring Penny upstairs when I'm home, Fitz."

"So, what is that—five hours out of twenty-four? Not much, is it?" Fitz's gaze burned into Lee. "With Dad gone, I gotta do everything I can to keep the rest of you safe until he gets back. And I'm telling you, she ain't well."

'Until he gets back.' It's been months now with no sign that he's still alive.

Lee swallowed hard, chasing the thought from his mind. "Look, I'm doing the best I can," Lee said. "The basement is the safest place we got. Karen was taken from her crib inside the house, and she's not the only one, you know. Those things will slip in through a doorway open for just a minute. And how long until they start breaking through windows? Fitz, we can't be too careful with this. Hey, look what happened at the market today!"

"No need to explain to me, Lee. You know I understand. We've just suffered terrible tragedies, and I know you've felt it more than anyone. I can't imagine having to see Ozzie and Will get taken off that beach, and you unable to save them."

Lee's gut twisted. He looked down and rubbed his hands over the cracked table laminate, wishing he could block the image from his mind.

"But this situation can't go on, Lee. That's why…" Fitz glanced briefly at Kenny. "We need to leave here and get Penny to real safety."

"What do you mean? How?"

Fitz leaned in closer. The smell of his brother had

changed. He'd long run out of cigarettes and bar soap; now, he just smelled dirty. "You know that new family at the market today? You risked your life to save their youngest from a banshee."

"Yeah, what about them?"

"Well, Kenny and I heard 'em talkin' 'bout just gettin' in from a long time at sea. They were trading some huge tuna with Hank, somethin' I'm sure he put a high value on."

"So?"

"If we really wanna keep our family from harm, then we need to get on a boat. I think they got one. It wouldn't be too hard to take it from an ol' man and some kids."

Lee hardened, furious at Fitz for the person he had become. The old Fitz would have never considered this. Kenny's conspiring smirk made Lee despise him now more than ever.

"We're not gonna steal their boat, Fitz." Lee stood to end the conversation.

"I know how you feel, Lee, but they'll be just fine," Fitz went on. "Hank took 'em all up to the lighthouse, and that's where they'll stay if they're smart. Heck, I'd stay there myself if that old bat, Minna, would let us. Lee, we need this boat more than they do. Me and Mae are out of things to trade for food, and I know you are, too. Having to beg and scavenge like this. It's shameful. We'll end up starving to death if those things don't get us first."

Now Fitz stood as well, closing in on Lee's uncertainties.

"Out there, we'll be able to catch plenty to eat and trade so that we'll never go hungry. Out there, Penny can play in the sun and look at the stars without worrying about

what's gonna come eat her.   We   can go   find Dad.   I
believe he's still alive. We'll get him, then sail to a place those
monsters ain't got to."

Lee's face fell.

Picturing Penny and Dad safe on a boat weakened his
conviction. He cleared his throat. "Maybe, but I don't..."

"You don't need to decide now," Fitz cut in. "Next time you
and Caleb are up at the lighthouse, just listen in on
what they're saying. See if you can find out if their boat's still
nearby. Heck, they may even invite you to come see it. Okay?"
Fitz put his hand on Lee's shoulder. "Then we can think about it
and decide together."

Caleb walked back into the kitchen. He paused, studying the
situation. Without Hutch on his arm, he signed to Lee.

'What's going on?'

'I'll tell you later,' Lee signed back, then turned to Fitz.
"Caleb needs my help getting firewood."

Fitz sighed and nodded to Kenny.

"Oh, I near forgot," Fitz said, then he opened the basement
door and called down. "Hey! Is there a lil' munchkin down there
who might like a surprise?"

Lee and Fitz stood at the top of the stairs, looking down as
Penny tiptoed up to meet them. She was now lean and pale,
resembling a flimsy paper doll. She shielded her eyes from the
light. Fitz squatted down to her at the top of the steps.

"Hey, Fitz," she said.

Fitz handed her a small paper bag.

"Hey, lil' bit. Why don't you look through there to see what
you can find?"

The nine-year-old peeked in the sack and found the prize resting on top. She pulled out the paper bag labeled 'dried pears.'

"Yummy!" Penny squealed and gave Fitz a hug around the neck.

"I want you to eat 'em all up for me. Okay, sugar?" Fitz said.

"I will," she promised.

"Atta girl."

Fitz looked up at Lee and winked.

"Fitz," Lee said with a lump in his throat. "Thank you. She really loves those. Seriously, man."

"Aww, don't mention it. Mae told me she hasn't been eating much. Thought she might like 'em." Fitz rubbed Penny's head just as Mae plodded up the stairs.

"Man, took y'all long enough. I'm starvin'!" she said.

"Sorry about that, Mae. We'll see you tomorrow, right?" Lee asked her.

She sighed and nodded. Fitz followed her and Kenny out the door.

"Think about what I said," Fitz called back to Lee, then wedged the door closed.

Caleb asked again, '*What did Fitz want?*'

'*I'll tell you later,*' Lee repeated.

Lee lifted Penny into a gentle hug. In his arms, she felt as fragile as a sparrow.

"Hi. I missed you, lil' girl," Lee said.

"Me too," she hummed. Lee sat her down on his lap at the table as she opened the bag of dried fruit. "I love these."

"And these ones are especially delicious, so you better eat them up before I do!"

She reached in, nibbled on one pear slice, then held it out to give Lee a bite.

"No, thank you, Lucky. Those are all for you."

Penny's appetite had gotten steadily worse. Lee had been racking his brain, trying to find something she'd want. To his disappointment, she only ate two and a half pear slices before closing the sack.

"What's the matter? Don't you like them?"

"I do. I'm just not hungry, is all. Besides, I want to save 'em."

"You don't have to save them, Penny. Me and Fitz will get you as many as you want. Won't you have a bit more?"

"Maybe later," she murmured, then nestled her head under his chin. He could feel her heart flutter against his chest. "What did you see today?"

Lee shared a troubled glance with Caleb.

"Nothing as pretty as you, that's for sure. Just same old boring stuff."

"Did you see any kids?"

"Nope," he said, rubbing her hair from her forehead. "All the kids are stayin' inside where it's safe."

CHAPTER 20

FITZ

Fitz, Mae, and Kenny walked home tethered together as Fitz told Mae all about the scene at the market.

"That stuck-up lil' princess thought she was some kinda tough stuff 'til the critters almost got her sister. Served her right," Fitz said.

Kenny snickered. "Hey, and guess what else?"

A rustling in the leaves froze Fitz in his boots.

"Shh…!"

Fitz clenched and stepped back toward the other two.

"Fitz…" Kenny said again.

"Shut up, Kenny! I heard something. I think it was one of them."

Fitz stared hard into the trees, straining to find any ripples or disturbance. He knew it was banshees. He could sense them always lurking everywhere, always watching, like the Devil waiting to snatch him down to Hades. It kept him awake at night, sweating in his sheets, wondering what it would feel like to get eaten. Every cell in his body incinerated, painfully erased.

"It was just a squirrel, Fitz, fer Pete's sake!" Mae grumbled.

She seemed to be treating him with more and more disdain. The disrespect grated on him more than the nicotine withdrawal. After all, it was up to Fitz to protect the family, so why shouldn't he be fearful and aware? She'd forgotten herself, treating him like a coward in front of his friend.

Before she could speak again, Fitz glared at her with a fisted hand. She shut her mouth and looked at the ground.

"You really think those folks got a boat, Fitz?" Kenny asked.

Fitz rubbed his thumb against the inside of his fingers, over and over, flicking a phantom cigarette.

"They got something. I just know it. And if I have to gut each one of 'em like a fish, I'm gonna get it."

CHAPTER 21

REN

B y nightfall, Ren and her family were completely overwrought. Minna offered them a cottage up by the lighthouse. The thought of a warm, full-sized bed made Ren nearly melt with gratitude. Hank handed her a flashlight and led the tethered group up the cliffside pathway toward its peak. The lighthouse beam pierced through the pitch-black of the shoreline. Ren followed the spotlight as it rotated over the woods. She peered at the shadowy trees.

Did she hear something? Did something move? Ren clutched Lizzie's hand tighter and trudged on, just a step behind Hank.

"How do you power the lighthouse?" she called over the wind.

"What was that?" Hank asked. He stopped and turned to her, and Ren suddenly felt silly. Her question wasn't worth holding everyone up.

"Umm...the light? How do you keep it on?"

"Oh," Hank seemed thrown by the observation. "It's been solar-powered for years. The Inn, too, though most of that charge goes to the fridge and freezer. We hoped to connect an electrified fence to the lighthouse source, but it's a big project, and we need more materials."

"What about the cottages?" Peter asked with a hopeful look.

"Sorry to disappoint, mate. Those buildings never had power."

The family arrived at the little stone house. They watched as Hank fiddled with the key and unlocked the door. Upon entering, he lit a kerosene lamp and started making a fire. There was a small living room with a couch, chair, a table, and a kitchenette. One back bedroom had a queen bed. By the time they had finished looking around, Hank had a little blaze going and was dusting the ash off his pants.

"The fire will heat the place quickly. Ya got sheets and towels in the closet. There's no hot water, I'm afraid. Pete, why don't ya help me with the pull-out?"

Peter and Hank tossed the cushions to the floor and pulled the folded bed from the sofa. When opened, it filled the tiny room.

"Right. So, you're safe inside, but leave the windows closed. Breakfast at seven."

No one said anything. Hank ambled around the couch toward the door. As he tried to slip between Ren and the wall, she lost her balance, tipping over the mattress. Hank caught her waist and arm and let out a whistle through his teeth. Then, he gave her an "I gotcha" head bob.

It seemed unintentionally playful, as if a bit of his former, pre-survival-mode self had leaked out. Almost charming.

Holy moly.

Of all that happened that day, the excitement, then confusion, then anger, then terror, then disbelief, then pure exhaustion—and now this moment, with this guy's hand grazing a sliver of bare skin by her belt, felt like a breaking point. Stimulation overload. She swallowed the stress vomit brewing in the back of her throat as Hank leaned back and awkwardly released her.

"Well, I guess that's it." He opened the door to leave, and Ren snapped to her senses.

"Wait! You can't go out there alone. How will you get back to the house?"

"A couple of lads and I bunk in the cottage next door—just a leap across the path. I'll be fine. Besides, we've hardly ever heard those things up here."

"Why not?"

Hank shrugged.

"We're not really sure. Some wonder if the light scares 'em off." Then he furrowed his brow and raised a finger at Ren. "But don't you be careless about staying together. Just because the banshees aren't squawking doesn't mean they're not about."

It sounded like lecturing, but somehow, less condescending than before.

Maybe he's just getting tired.

"No. We'll be careful," Ren promised.

"Good, I'll see you tomorrow then."

"Hank?" Ren said as he opened the door.

"Yeah?"

"Thank you for bringing us here."

He gave her a final nod and left.

———

Ren tucked Lizzie into the covers the second they got the sheets on the bed. The eight-year-old had barely spoken all afternoon, and Ren didn't know how to console her. As tough as Lizzie had been through everything, Ren wondered if this would just be too much for her sister to handle.

Ren nestled next to Lizzie until she fell asleep, then snuck out of the room.

In the den, she found Peter trying to loosen the half-raised window. She darted over.

"Peter, what are you doing?!" she scolded through her raspy voice. "Didn't you just hear him say to stay away from open windows?"

"Ren, I know. I was just..."

Ren gripped the windowsill and pushed down hard, but the wooden frame wouldn't budge.

"*Just what*? It's like dealing with a child," she said as she jostled and tugged at it. A splinter pierced her finger, and she pulled away.

"Ow! Curse it!"

"Ren, enough!" Pop intervened. "I asked Peter to go over and close that window. He was working on it."

She winced and bit her lip, but couldn't apologize.

"Fine, okay. I was just scared or nervous or whatever." Her change of tone to annoyance was the best she could do. She reached up to try again, but Peter blocked her.

He palm punched the frame's corners and slammed the window shut so forcefully that it may have shattered.

Ren grabbed his arm.

"Peter, stop."

"Just doing what I'm told, boss," he replied, shaking her off, then pushed past her to the bathroom.

Ren threw her hands up and looked at Pop.

He shook his head.

"You've got to do better, Lauren."

Ren sighed and withdrew.

"I know." She looked away and started opening the folded sheets.

"Tomorrow, try to smooth it over," Pop urged. "We just need to stick together, and we'll be alright."

"Will we, though? I mean, will any of us ever be alright? Look what we've come home to." Ren punched a pillow into a fresh case and tossed it on the bed. "Peter's hated me for a while now, and nothing I say tomorrow will change that."

"He doesn't hate you."

"Yes, he does. He and Mom both blame me for Dad. I mean, why wouldn't they?"

"*No one* blames you, Lauren. It's just your anger and stubborn self-punishment that's pushing everyone away. I've let you wallow for too long, but I can't allow it anymore, Ren. You have to let it go now, *please*. All that matters is this family and getting back to your mom."

"You don't understand. You don't see how they look at me."

"Oh, yes, I do. I know your mom loves you. She is trying to hold onto you with all she's got. Nothing could have kept her from coming on our sailing trip. So, what happened? Why did she change her mind at the last minute?"

Ren stared at Pop, remembering the last thing she'd said to Mom.

"I'd rather drown than be on that boat with you."

Ren dug her fingernails into her palms, and her eyes welled. She didn't need to admit it for Pop to know what happened.

Pop softened.

"Whatever happened between you two, your mom knows you love her."

"But what if I never get to see her again? What if it's too late?" The thought of it felt like a lead weight on her chest.

"The cellar and pantry were stocked when we left," Pop insisted. "I'm sure she's had enough to last this long. We'll figure out a way home, and the two of you can start over."

Ren nodded, but her breath was wavering. Pop held her shoulders.

"Look, I really need your help getting us all through this. It's not going to work if you and Pete keep fighting. Despite everything, he and Lizzie still look up to you. I know it. They need their big sister."

Her grandfather pulled her into a hug. Her tears spilled into the comfort of his sweater.

"I love you, kiddo. We'll make it. We'll be okay," he promised.

Ren wished she believed him.

CHAPTER 22

PETER

T he following morning, Peter walked down to breakfast tied to Lizzie, several lengths ahead of Pop and Ren. He and Ren hadn't said a word to each other since the window incident.

After a hard night, Peter was thrilled to get a real meal in the main house—flapjacks, scrambled eggs, hash browns, biscuits, and jam. He actually felt full for the first time in months. It was exactly what he needed to calm his nerves and recharge.

Sally invited Peter and Lizzie to join her and Marty in the garden. They were harvesting vegetables and planting for the next season. The husband and wife looked like a perfect pair in their matching overalls and garden gloves. Sally handed Marty a ball cap, and he gave her better shears—both smiling as if this was just another Saturday in the yard.

"Hey, squirt. Why don't you show them how well you tie knots?" Peter suggested as they attached their tethers on the porch. Lizzie eagerly snatched the ropes. She looped and pulled two perfect slip knots, tying herself to Sally and Peter to Marty.

"How wonderful! I've lived in a fishing town my whole life, and I can't do a slip knot so nicely," Sally gushed.

"Pop taught me. I can almost do the Eldridge knot," Lizzie added.

"Isn't that something!"

"Yeah, if you tie up a person with an Eldridge, they'd never be able to get free," she added with a grin.

Peter cringed as Sally's eyes went wide.

"Okay…neat," she said. "Well, you seem like a tough little cookie. Here, take these gloves, and we'll get going."

Sally donned an umbrella-sized sunhat and led them out to the garden, which spanned nearly half an acre. She kneeled between rows of raised soil and budding plants and set to work pulling weeds. Sally demonstrated to Lizzie what to do, and Marty did the same for Peter.

It felt awkward for Peter to work at the end of a leash. He kept getting tangled up or tripping over it.

"I know it's a pain," Marty admitted as Peter unlooped his ankle. "But you'll get used to it."

"See, right now, we're harvesting our fall vegetables," Sally instructed. "Here's the kale, turnips, broccoli, and Brussels sprouts. Over there, you'll find cabbages and carrots."

Lizzie grimaced.

"Yeah, Lizzie's not a big fan of veggies," Peter chuckled, dropping a handful of weeds in the basket.

"Hey! I eat vegetables, I just like fruit more," Lizzie said.

"I prefer fruit, too," Sally agreed. "But it's too cold for them now. We'll get strawberries, blueberries, and tayberries come spring and summer."

Lizzie tilted her head. "What are tayberries?"

"Tayberries are my favorite. They come all the way from

123

Scotland, like my mum. We cook with them almost every day. It makes the whole property smell delicious."

"What do they taste like?"

"Hmm…like raspberries, only sweeter. I have some frozen that I'm going to make into jam today. You can help me."

Sally pulled some leafy kale from the ground and brushed the dirt off.

"As for the vegetables, our recipes are the tastiest in all of Oregon."

Lizzie frowned and cocked an eyebrow. Sally laughed.

"Believe me, you'll work up such an appetite that by dinnertime, you'll think it's the best meal you've ever tasted!"

CHAPTER 23

REN

R en walked the perimeter of the property with Minna, inspecting the fences. From across the field, she spotted Lizzie laughing with Sally in the garden, astounded by her little sister's resilience.

Meanwhile, I want to curl up and hide under the bed.

Ren and Minna waded through the tall, blowing grass along the cliffside. The repetitive sound and feel of the reeds against her jeans calmed her, as did Minna's confident presence. Ren felt like she was catching her breath for the first time in days, her chest filling then exhaling the cool sea air.

"Lizzie seems to be doing better," Minna observed. "She's a good little helper."

"Yeah, she's always been mature for her age. She seemed to grow up fast after our dad died."

"Well, she's not alone in that up here, love. All of these kids have lost one or both of their parents."

Ren tucked loose strands of hair behind her ear.

"They all seem like they're doing ok, though."

"Children are tougher than most people think, and keeping

busy sure helps. They need the distraction to take their minds off o' things." Minna said.

Ren noticed a woman helping George and April feed the chickens.

"I would have thought people would just keep their kids inside. Wouldn't that be safer?"

"We did at first, but who knows how long this will last? They can't be kept from sunshine forever. Nay, the best place for these kids is close by."

Minna trudged on through the brush and over rocks with the agility of a teenager. Ren had to work to keep the tether between them slackened.

The steep drop of the cliffs protected much of the property from intruders, and a barbed fence enclosed the rest of it. Minna seemed unafraid when she checked on the fences up against the ledge.

Ren glanced over the precipice. The steep drop was breathtaking.

Ren leaned just a bit further to see the waves smashing into the rocks, wondering how long it would take to fall. The wind whipped hard against her back, upsetting her balance. She caught herself but was glad to be anchored to Minna, who was gripping the fence post.

"Mind your step, lass. Many a careless folk have tumbled to an early death off these cliffs. And since I'm the one tied to ye, I'll thank ye to step back a bit," she quipped with a side-eye.

Ren edged away from the ledge as Minna gestured them further along the waterfront.

"Did ye notice the meteor on the beach?" Minna asked.

"Actually, it's a meteorite now that it's hit the Earth," Ren said, but more to herself. It's something her Dad had corrected her on a few times.

"What was that?"

"Nothing. There's one down there? On the beach below us?"

"Down a ways, but yes. The thing must be nine feet tall. Hank can take you for a closer look, if ye like. There doesn't seem to be any more danger nearer to them than anywhere else. Folks were climbing all over it when we first found it."

"What? No one came to rope it off?"

"The sheriff put up a notice to stay off it eventually, for all the good it did."

Seeing a meteorite that size would have been a dream come true for Ren a few years ago. She and her dad would have driven for days to see something like that.

"It doesn't make sense," Ren said. "Most meteors will burn up completely when they enter our atmosphere. If there's anything left by the time it hits Earth, it's usually no bigger than your fist. If the meteorite on the beach is that size, that means it was enormous in space. The government should have seen it way before it got here and warned us. Why didn't we know?"

"Well, maybe t'was all a big cover-up? Didn't want to start a panic, perhaps," Minna offered.

"There are a million telescopes pointed at the sky all over the world. Someone would have seen them coming and told the media."

"Well, just add it to the pile 'o questions we've got built up so far."

Ren wasn't satisfied, but let it go.

The chill was biting that morning, but it was a brilliant sunny day. The greens of the grasses and blues of the sea shone rich and vibrant. The few white clouds cast patterns of moving shadows across the field.

"This property is so beautiful. How long have you been up here?"

"Sally and I used to live in town. My late husband, rest his soul, was the reverend. After he passed, Sally and I bought the lightkeeper's house and land, fixed it up, and opened the inn. The lighthouse is a historic landmark and draws a good lot of tourists, so the rooms stay full. Especially now, with so many needing help."

I can relate. Where would we be now if they hadn't taken us in?

"Sally is such a wonderful cook," Minna continued, "that she was keen to start planting a garden and rearing the livestock as soon as we moved in. Had she not, we'd be in a dire fix now, and I mean not just the folks ye see here."

"Livestock…" Ren pondered. "The banshees don't eat your animals?"

"Nope. As Hank said, they went after pets at first. But once they started taking people, they seemed to leave animals alone. Anyway, what we produce is helping many hungry souls in town," Minna tightened the drawstring on her hat.

"That's nice of you to help everyone."

"Ha, nice nothing. My James would be givin' away twice as much. 'Minna,' he'd say, 'turning our backs on those in need is like turning away from God. Then He'd have a sure, easy time kicking us in the arse, wouldn't He?"

Minna stared out at the choppy water, and Ren followed her gaze. Just days before, the endless ocean was the only view Ren had.

Minna snapped a tall grass reed and began tying it in knots.

"James was always good fun and the most selfless soul I ever knew. Was the kind of man who made everyone feel special and loved."

"My dad was like that."

"Ah, then they'll have each other's good company up where they are."

Ren shivered and pulled the jacket collar up around her neck.

"You know," Minna continued, "they say faithful people shouldn't mourn when their loved ones are called up. We should be celebrating his reunion with the Almighty. I think that's a load of shite. When my husband died, I was furious about it, and I let God know that I was. Would have made sailors blush with the language I used tellin' Him off. But God was patient with me, and I've done my best to make up for it. Besides, my James is still with me."

Walking over the hill, Ren could see the road and the entrance gate in the distance. Hank was there, talking with the posted guards, directing men twice his age.

Minna nodded in his direction.

"I'm sorry Hank was so hard on ye yesterday. He's a good lad, to be sure, but he can be gruff and a bit impatient. He reminds me of a grouchy old dog we used to have. He looked after our family with the grace of an angel but was a bloody arsehole to everyone else."

Ren chuckled. "How long have you known him?"

"Hank? He's a marine biology student from Sydney, Australia. Came here with a whale study group a few months ago. Some of them were guests at the inn when the meteors fell. They never heard from their ship's crew again."

Minna pulled another reed to fiddle with.

"One of his friends was taken by a banshee, and the other two went off to find family. Now Hank's stuck with us, and he practically runs the place. He was the one who set up all our security. I don't know what we'd have done without him."

Ren watched Hank examining the latch on the barn door with another worker.

"Doesn't he want to go home?" '

"Oh, yes. I'm sure Hank misses his da, but rarely speaks of him. He's not really one to burden others with his troubles."

"Well, I don't think he likes me much," Ren muttered, pinning her hair back again.

"Ahh, I wouldn't fret about that. If he gets crabby about yer safety, it probably means just the opposite. I trust Hank with our lives, Ren. So should you."

Ren flushed at the thought of Hank caring about her. She stuffed her hands in her pockets.

"He mentioned last night that you've never heard those things up here. He says they maybe stay away because of the lighthouse. Do you think that's true?"

"No, I don't, really," Minna said.

"Why do you think then?"

"Would it be too predictable for me to say God is keeping them away? Maybe because of our faith or how much good we're doing for others, I can feel Him up here on this cliffside more than ever before. These things go after those by themselves. If Heavenly Father is always with us up here, what better protection can we have?

"I like to think of it like Daniel in the lion's den. Daniel had strength in knowing he wasn't alone so long as God was with him. And the lions, they stayed. What do you think of that?" Minna asked as they neared the southern fence.

"I don't know. I'm not really religious." Ren tried to remember the last time her family went to church.

"Tell me this. Have you thought about what your family has survived? It's a right miracle, is it not? God chose to save you for a reason. He's with you and your family, and I know there's a purpose to it."

Ren turned toward the ocean and closed her eyes to a strong gust of wind off the water. Minna chuckled.

"I'm making you uncomfortable, aren't I?"

Ren looked back and squinted at Minna. She shrugged.

"Yeah, but it's okay. It's nice of you to say those things."

"I'm only speaking my mind, lass. Well, let's finish with this fence. I'm starved and can smell Sally's tayberry sauce from here."

CHAPTER 24

REN

At lunch, Ren helped by putting out plates and filling Minna's hodgepodge of water glasses. Pop had Sally's maps spread out on the dining table, but folded them up as two dozen hungry people poured in for lunch—root vegetables and gravy with leftover pancakes. At mealtime, everyone filed through the kitchen, and Sally served them like a cheerful cafeteria lady. It was a very pleasant way to control rations.

"How's it coming?" Ren asked him.

"Good. I'll tell you about it after lunch, but I think I've found us a way home. Can you tell Liz and Pete to come and eat?"

Lizzie was already warming up in the kitchen, but Ren hadn't seen Peter since breakfast.

Ren stepped out onto the porch. There was a sign tacked up that read: 'Do not leave the porch without a tethered buddy.' If Ren hadn't seen it, she might have forgotten and kept walking. She blocked the glaring sun with her hand, searching for her brother.

Hank came around the house with April and George riding piggyback. Whatever he was saying was making them laugh. The three stomped up the porch steps, then Hank groaned as he swung the little boy off his shoulders.

"Here, can you hold my backpack for me?" Hank asked and surprised Ren by handing George to her. "It's extremely heavy today, and I can't figure out why."

The two children giggled as Ren awkwardly accepted George into her arms. He felt incredibly light compared to Lizzie, whom she could barely hold anymore. This whole charade felt so familiar. Hank looked at her, seemingly waiting for her to continue the game as he untied George's tether.

"Yes," Ren agreed. "It feels like your pack's chock full of potatoes. We should bring them to Sally to stick in the pantry."

George giggled again.

"That's a good idea," Hank exclaimed. "C'mon, April, let's go find Sally!"

Hank untied George's tether and tugged it off him, the fibers brushing along Ren's arms and chest as it slipped free. Hank grasped George's hands, lifted him down to the porch, then led them both to the door. As Hank wiped his shoes on the mat, Ren turned to him.

"Hank? Minna said you might be able to take me to see the meteorite on the beach. Would you mind?"

"Ya wanna see it? Most folks won't go near it now." He pushed the door open for the kids, then shut it behind them.

"Minna said it's ok."

"Well, we haven't heard about it being especially dangerous near it, but I'd still keep my distance. I'll walk ya down where you'll be able to see it from a little ways away. That good?"

133

"Um…," Ren hesitated. "Yeah, that's good."

"Something wrong?"

"I was really hoping to get closer to see what the surface is like. I used to be into astronomy and physics and stuff." As Ren said this, she felt uncomfortable. It was the same way she always felt answering a question in front of her science classes. Nobody seemed to expect or welcome her knowing so much about this stuff. It dawned on her that indulging her scientific curiosity wouldn't be Hank's top priority right now.

He raised his eyebrows and gave a half-smile. The sun caught his eyes, and, for the first time, Ren noticed they were a deep greyish green, kind of like wet moss.

"Really? Yeah, sure. I'd love to hear your take on it, but I'm still not keen to go near the big one. I found a smaller rock on the cliff a while back. I wrapped it up and stowed it in the lighthouse. Would that suit you?"

"Yeah, that'd be great."

"I'll bring it to you later," he offered. "Ya know, they're still coming down."

"More meteors?"

"Yeah, haven't you noticed all the falling stars we've had lately? They're harder to see in the daytime, but they're all over the sky. I imagine by now, they've hit every corner of the earth. Keep an eye up after dark, and you'll spot a hundred."

"Actually, little meteors enter our atmosphere all the time, like multitudes daily."

"Nah, this is different. They're ruddy constant and all over. I can't believe you haven't noticed it. Wait a sec," Hank said, scanning the sky behind Ren.

"What is it?"

"There, look there." He pointed over her shoulder. Ren turned and squinted at the bright sky. Hank grasped her shoulder to line her up with his outstretched arm, his sweater sleeve brushing her cheek. He smelled like fresh hay. Ren fidgeted, then focused her sight on a cluster of light streaks in the sky. The curved lines lingered for a few moments, then burned out.

"Do they all look like that? Moving slow like that, I mean?" she asked.

"Yeah, I guess. I dunno."

"Ok, well yeah. Maybe you're right. I don't think…" Ren stopped herself. She didn't like to make statements without being sure. Hank glanced at the sky, then back at her, as if waiting for her to continue.

"Uh, have you seen my brother?" Ren asked, changing the subject.

"Yeah, he's over there helping cut firewood. Over that way."

He pointed toward the barn. Ren spotted Peter swinging an enormous axe down on a hefty cut of wood. Incredible—he split the log in two on the first try. He looked more like a man than the little brother she knew. Peter smiled as the other two workers slapped him on the back. He was *actually* smiling and laughing, the way he used to after a winning baseball game. Ren hadn't seen that look in a long time, and it made her happy.

In that moment, she really missed him.

Then Ren recognized one of the men Peter was with, the bigger of the two with the old ball cap. It was the guy from the market who saved Lizzie. Ren strained to think of his name.

Did I even ask him? Did I even speak to him?

The whole terrifying experience was a blur.

Maybe Larry? No...Lee? Yeah, it was Lee.

"Hey, Peter! Peter!" Ren called.

He didn't look in her direction.

"Peter! Lunch is out. Come on and eat," she beckoned, trying not to sound irritated by his ignoring her.

Lee nudged Peter in her direction, taking the axe from Peter's grasp. Then Lee led the three of them across the yard, his long strides keeping him effortlessly in the lead. On the porch, they began untying their tethers. Ren walked over just as Peter freed himself. She smiled at him.

But Peter pushed past her, allowing the screen door to slam behind him.

It stung.

I guess I probably deserved that.

Ren turned to the others.

"Um, Lee, is it?" She really hoped she'd gotten it right. "I don't know if you remember me, but you saved my sister at the market yesterday."

"Sure, of course. How's Lizzie doing?" he asked.

"Seems to be much better, thanks. I'm Ren."

Ren put her hand out. Lee wiped his palm on his pant leg and accepted it. Dad had taught her to have a firm handshake, but his massive grasp completely swallowed hers.

"I'm Lee, and this is my brother, Caleb."

"It's good to meet you," she said to Caleb. She then noticed the digital sleeve on Caleb's arm scrolling words across his forearm.

Caleb made quick gestures, and the device spoke.

"It's nice to meet you, too," it said. Caleb stretched out his hand.

"Oh…um…Hi," she stammered and gave him an awkward half-wave.

Lee chuckled and pointed to Caleb's arm. "It's okay. Caleb is deaf, but Hutch here keeps him up to speed. You can just talk."

"Oh, alright. Sorry, I've just never met a deaf person before." She cringed.

Oh, no, that sounded awful. Is 'deaf' even the polite term to use?

Lee put up his hand and shook his head.

"Really, it's fine. You didn't do anything wrong," he assured her.

"You're good," Hutch confirmed.

Ren sighed and smiled.

"Ok, good. Anyway, I just wanted to say thanks for helping Lizzie. If you hadn't been there, I'm not sure what would have happened. Those things were all around her."

Lee shoved his hands in his pockets. "It was nothing really."

"No, it was really brave of you," Ren insisted. "You ran off on your own to get Lizzie. The banshees could have gotten you, too. No one else did that."

He shrugged. "Well, I've got a kid sister, too."

"Okay, I just felt bad for just standing there when you gave her back, not saying 'thank you' or anything. We were just in shock."

Lee glanced at Caleb, who was reading Hutch's translation,

then back at Ren.

"Had you not seen any banshees before? Where are you all from?" Lee asked.

"Oh, we…uh…" Ren realized she'd said too much.

The screen door slammed, and Lizzie came out and grabbed Ren's hand.

"Ren, come and taste the tayberry jam I made with Sally." She tugged on Ren's arm.

"Ok, I'm coming. Did you say 'hello' to Lee? Do you remember him?"

Lizzie looked up at Lee and froze. Then, she lunged forward and hugged him around his waist. When she pulled away, her cheeks were rosy.

"Sorry," Lizzie said.

"Don't be sorry! I love a good hug, and *that* was a good hug."

"Show me your jam, Liz," Ren said and nudged Lizzie toward the door. She smiled at Lee and Caleb once more and followed Lizzie back inside.

———

That night, Ren found Hank's meteorite in a plastic bag at the cottage. Next to it was a note.

Here's the rock. Let me know what you think. - Hank

Ren picked up the bag and held it up to the firelight. It was a beautiful crimson-colored stone, about the size of a baseball, and relatively lightweight.

"What's that?" Pop asked as he put more wood on the fire. "Is it a meteorite?"

"Yes, Hank found it."

"It's red," Lizzie noted as she took out her braid.

"Yeah, I've never seen one like this before," said Ren.

Ren put the rock down, eager for bed after a long day.

Lizzie was asleep in seconds. Ren lay next to her, thinking about how surreal her reality had become. It was hard to remember life before all this, even harder to remember the happier days with Dad. Ren pulled at the pendant on her neck.

She thought about the meteors, the wreck, the lifeboat, the shark. Ren leaned out of bed to twist off the lantern, her hand casting a large shadow on the far wall.

Ren lay back down, staring at the moonlit shadows across the ceiling. She thought of Kenji, wondering if he had ever found his sister and if they were safe. She wondered if Japan was handling all this better than the U.S.

A moment later, Ren shot out of bed.

She crept back to the table and stared at the meteorite again. Ren took it out of the bag, rolled it in her fingertips as she crossed the room, then tossed the rock into the fireplace. She used the poker to push it deep into the coals.

She had to test her theory.

Almost instantly, the fire started popping and whistling. The logs pulsed and began to crumble.

Oh, man! This was stupid. What if it explodes?

Before Ren could react, a fork darted from the nearby table into the fire. Quickly, she grabbed the tongs to pull the rock out, but the meteorite rolled from the fire on its own to meet the iron tool. She couldn't believe her eyes. In seconds, it had grown to the size of a bowling ball. It continued to hiss and steam, then gave a last gurgle and was quiet. The fork handle stuck out of its

139

side, the teeth buried in the hard mass.

Ren examined the transformed object for nearly an hour. Finally, she put it outside on the doorstep, just in case, and got back in bed.

Ren's thoughts swirled around her discovery, keeping her awake most of the night.

By sunrise the next morning, everything made sense.

CHAPTER 25

REN

R en shook Pop awake just as the first rays of sunlight streaked
through the windows.

"Pop? Pop, wake up."

He grunted and rolled over.

"Do you have a route for us to take home yet? On foot, I
mean?" she asked.

Pop wiped the sleep from his eyes.

"Just about," he grunted.

"Great. I have to tell you something."

———

After breakfast, Ren and Pop sat at the round porch table with
Hank and Minna. Pop spread out the state maps for Oregon and
Washington on the old teak table and weighed them down with
coffee mugs.

Then Pop began presenting his planned route back home.
Pop made special note of avoiding major roads and towns. He'd
chosen their campsite locations and marked freshwater sources.
It all seemed very thorough and realistic. As Pop explained, Ren

focused on Hank's stoic expression.

"I think we can make it in about ten to eleven days, taking into account Lizzie's pace, finding food, setting up camp, weather, and rough terrain. We just need some supplies," Pop finished.

Hank shook his head. "No, Jim. It won't work. You'll never make it that far."

"We can. We've survived so much already, and we're experienced hikers. We can handle it," Pop insisted.

Pop was a very seasoned outdoorsman, but Ren tried to remember the last time they camped or hiked as a family. It had been years, maybe three, and Lizzie had only camped out once overnight.

"I'm telling ya, it's too dangerous," Hank said firmly. "If ya come upon the wrong sort, you could all be killed. A lot of folks are starvin' and desperate out there. They'd take Lizzie just to throw her at a banshee as a diversion."

Ren had expected this kind of rebuttal, but still winced at the thought of it.

No, our plan will work. Don't back down.

"We can't just stay here," Ren said, leaning in. "We have to get to my mom. If she's been alone in that house this whole time, she must be out of food."

"I understand, I truly do. But do you think your mum would want you to risk your lives like this? She may not even be there anymore. You're lucky to have found this place, and you'd be a nutcase to leave, especially this time of year. You'll be seeing freezing temps at night soon, and you don't have the right gear."

Ren frowned.

Did he just call me a nutcase?

"Besides, those things are getting more aggressive," Hank piled on. "We have no idea what they'll be like ten days from now or if a tent will be enough to stop them from attacking you in your sleep."

"We can test it here before we go," Ren countered. "Pop and I will sleep in a tent outside overnight. You and Peter can stand watch."

"I already told ya, we don't hear them up here, Ren! It won't be the same." Hank's voice was elevating, and he sat forward now, too—as if he was about to challenge Ren to arm wrestle.

"Then we'll sleep on the beach!" Ren doubled down. The corners of the map were flipping up in the wind. Minna sat back, drinking her coffee, watching the two have it out.

"Oh great, yeah. Just cozy on up to the meteorite while you're out there."

"If that's what it takes to convince you we're going home, then I guess I will."

It now felt like she and Hank were the only ones at that table.

"Look, Ren, even if your little test works, even if you think you have everything planned out, just the two of you can't take those kids that far on your own. What if one of you falls, breaks a leg, or gets hurt some other way? Have you thought about that?"

Ren quieted and looked at Pop. They both turned to Hank.

"Actually, we *have* thought about that," Pop said to him. "We were hoping you would take us."

Hank burst into an incredulous laugh.

"Thanks for the invite, but I think I'll pass. How would I even get back here on my own?"

"You wouldn't come back," Ren said.

"What? What d'ya mean?"

"I have another boat, Hank," Pop said. "We're going to sail west as soon as we get Ren's mom. We'll bring you back to Australia."

Hank went silent, staring at Ren, then Pop. He set both hands squarely on the table and scanned over the map.

We've got him now...

But after a few moments, he looked up and shook his head again.

"Your boat is either a shipwreck or stolen by now. There's no way it's still there."

"No, it's in a storage building on my property at Diamond Point. It's on the Miller Peninsula," Pop said. "No one else knows it's there. There's only wilderness on either side of the Salish Sea, all the way to the ocean. If we leave at night, no one would see us. I'm sure we can make it. Hank, we can get you home."

"You'd sail all the way to Sydney just to drop me off? That makes no sense."

Pop looked at Ren, but she froze, second-guessing her theory. What if she was wrong? She wasn't sure why, but keeping Hank's respect mattered a lot to her.

"Go on. Tell him," Pop urged.

Ren girded her confidence and looked Hank in the eye.

"The fishermen who saved us were coming back here to pick up family—all their families—and bring them back to Japan," Ren said. "I think it's because there are no banshees there."

"What? How do you reckon that?"

"The meteors hit here at night, right? Around 9 pm?"

"Yeah," Hank confirmed.

"And you said you heard that Europe was hit, too?"

"Aye," Minna replied. "We heard it on the radio."

"At 9 pm our time, it would have been 6 am Paris time. Probably just before sunrise. So, if that radio report was right, it would mean the meteors struck the planet's full dark side and maybe a bit farther east or west, depending on how long the shower lasted. Usually, no more than a few hours." Ren was gesturing around an invisible globe in her arms.

"I suppose that's right," Minna agreed.

"That *should* mean the other half of the Earth, where it was daytime, would have been facing away from the meteor stream, right? That whole side of the planet should have been safe from the impact," Ren added.

Hank gestured to the sky.

"Ren, the meteors are still comin' down today. You saw it yourself."

"No, what you're seeing aren't meteors...well, they might be, but not the ones we care about. Not these."

Ren reached under her chair and pulled Hank's transformed meteorite out of a satchel. She dropped the 9-inch-diameter rock onto the table, jostling the uneven table legs. Minna uttered a swear and jerked backward.

"Crikey! Where'd ya find that?" Hank demanded. "It's huge. You shouldn't have it near the house."

"This is the meteorite you gave me last night. After a few

145

seconds of heating it in our fireplace, it grew to this size," Ren explained. "That's why we were never warned the meteors were coming. That's why no one saw them or cared enough to report it. In space, each of these rocks was exponentially smaller. It was the heat from the atmospheric friction that caused them to expand to the huge boulders like the one on the beach."

"Wait, love, you're losing me now," Minna cut in. Her gaze shot back and forth from Ren to the meteorite.

"When an object hits our atmosphere from space, it's exposed to temperatures above three thousand degrees Fahrenheit. Because of that, almost everything burns to dust long before hitting the ground. But instead of disintegrating, blazing temps made these things grow at an incredible rate."

As Ren spoke, Hank crossed his arms and leaned back in the chair. The creases in his forehead seemed to be keeping count of every point he was planning to argue.

"What? How?" Minna asked.

"Most substances get bigger when heated up to a certain point. It's called thermal expansion," Ren went on. "But usually, it's like a few inches of growth on a one-hundred-foot bridge. Nothing like this. No solid matter that *I know* of has ever behaved this way."

Ren set her gloved hand on the protruding fork handle.

"Not only that, but heat also causes these things to develop a strong magnetic field. So strong that this fork flew off our table into the fire. The meteors' magnetism would have mostly steered them toward solid ground and away from water. Unfortunately, it also means they were basically targeting cities and power grid structures when they hit."

Hank scrutinized the meteorite. He put on his leather glove and touched the fork, then the rock's surface.

"Hank, the meteors landed right where they would cause the most damage and where all the people, or food, are," Ren continued. "They're like some kind of crazy, heat-activated eggs. I mean, from an evolutionary perspective, these things are pretty brilliant. Their eggs are virtually indestructible and can position themselves where the organisms will best thrive after 'hatching.'" Ren made a quote sign with her fingers.

"So, then, what's with the meteors we saw yesterday? What are they, if not this?" Hank asked.

Ren shrugged. "My guess would be our own space junk. Even though these things were small, there were so many of them that our own structures, like satellites and space stations, were most likely damaged, breaking off bits of shrapnel. What would be *really* bad is if it set off a destructive chain reaction."

Minna blinked up at Ren. "Whaddya mean?" she asked.

"See, right now, there are over twenty-five thousand satellites and large pieces of tech in Earth's orbit, more than nine thousand metric tons of stuff. When a piece of shrapnel breaks off, the orbital current keeps that chunk of metal whizzing around the Earth ten times faster than a bullet, pummeling and breaking other machinery in its way. That creates even more shrapnel, damaging more machinery, producing an infinite stream of broken-metal missiles until we end up with an asteroid field of our own junk circling the planet. Nothing functional would remain, and it would make space exploration much more dangerous. If that's what's happening, it means we won't be able to get our space tech working anytime soon, if ever.

"These meteors or eggs or whatever wouldn't look like what you showed me yesterday in the sky. They'd be coming at incredible speeds, growing larger and larger, leaving a clear path to where they would eventually hit.

"So, no, I think the egg meteors probably came down on the first night and only for a few hours, impacting only the exposed side of the planet," Ren finished.

"Ok, maybe that's all true," Hank argued. "But banshees spread and multiply like bloody locusts. They must be everywhere by now."

"Not everywhere. If they can only fly a hundred feet and can't swim, they wouldn't be able to migrate over water, right? The fishermen were bringing their families back to Japan because it was safe there and completely free from banshees. And, since Australia basically shares the same longitude as Japan, there shouldn't be any creatures there, either. We just need to get my mom and go."

Ren waited for Hank to smile or at least ease up a bit at this incredible news that his home country was probably safe. But he just stood up and stepped away from the table. He squinted out at the field with his arms crossed. Ren's knee started bouncing under the table as she waited for his response.

A freezing gust of wind blew in from the sea, rattling the house. Hank whipped around at the clatter as if worried the shutters would rip from their hinges and fall on Minna. Minna pulled her jacket closed with a shiver. She looked up at him, seemingly with the same impatience, for an answer.

Hank exhaled and shook his head.

148

"This sounds like a blasted pipe dream, and we could all be killed within a day on the road."

"Hank...." Pop started.

"No! You're a pair of crackin' lunatics grasping at straws. I'm staying right here. If ya had any sense, you'd do the same for Peter and Lizzie's sake, if nothing else. You don't seem to understand or care what could happen to them out there."

Ren recoiled. "Hey! That's completely unfair. I'd give up a lung for Lizzie. We've planned the safest possible route, and we'll move fast. I can't just forget about my mom. She's alone and trapped in that house for who knows how long and probably starving by now.

"You talk about not caring. This is a chance for all of us to get somewhere truly safe—for you to get to your Dad, and you're passing on it because it's easier to stay here as Lord of the lighthouse?"

"Don't you talk about my father! Your plan is just too bloody risky, Ren. It's a nightmare out there and getting worse by the day—swarmin', bloodthirsty banshees, armed bands of people, freezin' cold weather, treacherous wilderness. If, by some miracle, we make it to your boat, we'll be picked off by pirates before we lose sight of the land. And this is all based on a theory that sounds like a lot of flimsy guesswork."

"No. You're wrong!"

Hank rolled his eyes. "And hear me on this, if ya think about tellin' anyone else you have a boat, you'll put your whole family in danger."

"Hank, wait," Pop called out as Hank stormed off and into the house.

"Pop, just let him go," Ren muttered.

He relented, and the two of them turned to Minna.

"What do you think? What should we do?" Ren asked her.

Minna regarded them both with sympathy. "I'm sorry, but I must agree with Hank. Ren's theory is incredible, but the odds are against you all getting there alive. Ye don't understand how dangerous it is, and the banshees would be hunting yer every step. If Hank won't go with ye, then ye mustn't go."

"We can't just give up because he's too scared. Aside from that, think of yourselves," Ren pressed. "You've been too generous already. We can't just stay here, draining your resources when we have somewhere else we can go. More people will need your help when winter sets in. If we wait until the rations get too low, the extreme cold will have us trapped here, and my mom will be dead. The sooner we go, the better."

"You know it's true, Minna," Pop pressed, searching Minna's face for acceptance.

Minna just stared back with regret and no argument. The hardship they'd be facing this winter was an unavoidable certainty.

Ren sighed, racking her brain for any other options.

"What about someone else? Do you think Lee would do it?" she asked.

CHAPTER 26

LEE

L ee held his breath and listened for Minna's response.

When Lee had seen Ren, Jim, Minna, and Hank talking over a table full of maps and notes, he didn't want to eavesdrop. He liked the Haleys and wanted Fitz to forget his whole scheme. But the smell of Sally's stew gave Lee a painful reminder that he'd barely eaten in days. It was his hunger that led him to the side of the house, within earshot of Jim's voice. Lee had convinced himself that Ren's family didn't have a boat or anything else worth taking. But the feeling of his stomach eating itself for twenty hours forced him to find out for sure.

But Lee had been wrong.

The Haleys *did* have a boat. Fitz had been right all along.

And if Ren was correct, there were safe places with no banshees they could sail to.

'*What's going on?*' Caleb signed. Lee had already reached over and switched Hutch off.

'*Nothing. Hang on a sec,*' Lee signed back.

Caleb crossed his arms but remained hidden as Ren went on.

"We'd take Lee and his brother wherever they want to go if

they'd just get us to Diamond Point," Ren said.

Please, please, yes. Lee closed his eyes and held his breath, praying for Minna to send them this chance.

But she didn't.

"Ren, Lee is a truly good lad who has suffered more loss than anyone. I would love to say you can trust him for both of yer sakes. He'd leap at the chance to get Caleb and his sister, Penny, on yer boat.

"But Lee has dishonest and violent people in his life, people he'd never leave behind. If they learned about yer boat, they'd be after it. They may even harm you to get it or tell those murderin' pirates about it. No, ye cannot tell Lee. Best just to stay here with us where it's safe."

"But, for how long?" Ren implored.

"I don't know, love."

Pop sighed.

"I think she's right, Ren. It's too dangerous to go on our own. We'll just have to pray your mom's been found. In the meantime, Minna, we'll do all we can to help you prepare for what's to come."

Lee stood frozen until he heard Ren, Jim, and Minna go inside. As soon as the door shut behind them, he groaned and cursed. Then he charged off to the barn with Caleb trailing a few paces behind.

Caleb tried to ask what happened, but Lee ignored him. He stomped all the way to the wood chopping stump, the red anger burning his eyes. Lee seized the ax and started swinging. He split five logs without a word, replaying the conversation in his head. Lee could have had a chance to get Penny on that boat and far away, where they would have been safe. The opportunity was his, and he knew he deserved it, especially after he had risked himself for Lizzie. It was *he*, not Hank, who dropped his cord to rescue her, but Hank was the one they'd asked. Hank, who'd probably had a perfect childhood. Hank, who got handed a fancy education, his dream job, and nice clothes he probably never had to work to pay for. Hank had surely never suffered like Lee had. He never had to sacrifice himself for others like Lee had.

What good was it to always show up for people if they never gave you a break in return? What had it gotten him, always putting himself last? Finally, a glimpse of a chance. After so much sacrifice, so many sleepless nights, and starving days, he could have gotten a future for the people he loved.

But Minna snatched it away.

Minna always seemed to care so much about them. Now, she betrayed them. And after how much Lee had worried about protecting Ren and her family from Fitz, what had they done? They let Minna convince them to turn their backs on him so easily.

Wood chips sprayed as Lee came down harder and harder on the stump. Each impact sent sharp vibrations up his spine. His hands were numb from his locked grip, squeezing the blood up his wrists. He swung and hammered that ax, swung and hammered, over and over until there were no more logs to chop.

Lee dropped the ax on the ground, his arms quaking and his head pounding like a jackhammer.

He looked at Caleb. His brother's forehead was lined with concern. Caleb closed his right hand, extended his pinky and thumb, then tapped the knuckles to his chin twice.

'What's wrong?'

Lee felt ashamed. He knew if he told Caleb what he was angry about, Caleb would be disappointed in him. And Caleb would be right.

Lee couldn't be angry at those kids or Minna. After all, she was right. It was Fitz. Fitz was Lee's family. Lee owed his life to him and could never leave him behind.

But Fitz couldn't be trusted.

CHAPTER 27

REN

October 26th, 2027 - Gladys, Oregon. 220 miles south of Diamond Point, WA.
52 days after.

Despite Ren's initial resistance, Pop convinced her they had no option but to stay put. Peter and Lizzie were devastated when Pop told them they couldn't go home. Pop tried to reassure them that Mom was probably safe. Peter didn't buy it, but Lizzie seemed a bit more at ease.

On Minna's compound, it was easy to stay busy. They could almost forget about the horrifying invisible creatures surrounding them. If it weren't for the tethers, Ren may have thought the scene at the market was merely a nightmare. Maybe she had imagined it. Perhaps the lasting effects of her concussion made her see and hear things that didn't really happen. To her, that seemed just as likely as the truth. But then the tugging rope connecting her to Sally, Pop, or Lizzie always confirmed this was all very real.

Peter still wasn't speaking beyond monosyllables to Ren, but he was great at keeping Lizzie's spirits up, and the laborious farm work seemed to be good for him. After just a week on the farm, Peter looked as strong and able as he had ever been as a star athlete. Only now, he was older and bigger—nearly a man. Meanwhile, Lizzie loved tending to the chickens and cooking with Sally. Her favorite thing to make was tayberry jam.

Ren helped in any way she could. She cleaned dishes and clothes, worked in the garden, jarred produce, served meals, and fed the pigs. She thought of when her mom had asked for help at home, and she'd refused. Why had she been such a pain? Even if everyone was miserable, why wouldn't she cook a crummy dinner when Mom had to work late? Now, with every chore she did for Minna, she was trying to scrub away the guilt of how she'd been at home.

———

On the ninth afternoon since their arrival, Ren was seated at the kitchen table, jarring dozens of cucumbers for pickling. The pungent vinegar made her eyes water, but at least she had the room to herself for a bit. When she'd gotten half finished, Pop came in with Marty and Hank, all of them thirsty and out of breath.

"Hey, kiddo." Pop kissed her on the head. Ren felt the cold on his jacket.

"What are you guys doing?" she asked.

"Well, this morning, I fixed a leaking faucet upstairs, and now Marty, Hank, and I are working on the fence."

"What are you doing to the fence?"

"Raising it," Hank inserted after a big gulp of water, "and adding more wire and tin can alarms. Any idiot could still break in, but it's the best we can do for now."

Marty examined the calluses on his palms.

"My gloves are shot. Jim, will you come with me to grab another pair?"

"Sure," Pop said. "Let's go."

Pop and Marty shuffled out the back door, Pop patting Ren on the shoulder as he left. In the awkward silence that followed, Hank refilled his water glass at the sink, while Ren kept chopping. He squeaked the faucet off.

Ren hoped he would find a quick excuse to leave. The two of them hadn't spoken since the porch meeting, and that was fine by Ren. Hank had made it clear that he found her selfish and ungrateful, so what was the point of being friendly? She kept hacking and jarring her cucumbers, impatiently waiting for him to finish his glass of water and go, already.

"You're doin' a good job," Hank said.

"What?"

Hank gestured to the table.

"On the cucumbers. You've gotten heaps done."

"Uh…thanks."

"What I mean is, you've all been workin' hard around here. There's a lot to do before winter, and the extra hands have helped."

"It's not like we have anything else to do." Ren didn't mean to sound so bitter. She gnawed on her lip and recrossed her legs under the table. Hank leaned against the countertop, resting the glass against his chest.

"Look, I know you're keen to leave, but right now, you're doin' right by your family and Minna by staying

157

and chippin' in with us. What we do up here supports the whole town."

Ren put down her knife and looked him in the eye.

"I know that, Hank. We'd have been in a ditch somewhere without Minna. It was the least we could do." She intentionally left him out of the acknowledgment.

He shifted. "Yeah, well. I might have been buggered, myself, if I hadn't been staying here. Anyway, now that the weather's gone cold and food's gettin' scarce, Minna will get a lot more people up here, and not all of 'em welcome. With all she's got stored now, the inn's a great target to anyone keen to take it by force. I'm just trying to make certain that doesn't happen."

"So that's why you're raising the fence?"

"Yeah, among other things."

"Like what?"

"We're teaching everyone thirteen and up how to shoot. Jim says he's good, but that you and Pete need to learn. He said you've already got a gun."

"Yeah, the fishermen gave us a pistol."

"Good," Hank put the glass down, pushed off the counter, and put his hat back on. "So, I'm gonna finish something up for Minna, and then we'll get to it."

"What? Now?"

"Yeah. Pickles are pretty crucial, but I reckon you can take a quick break."

At this, Hank smirked and cocked an eyebrow. Then he walked out of the kitchen. Ren just stared at the swinging door.

Did Hank just make a joke?

Ren took a breath, bagged up the remaining fresh cucumbers,

and stuck them in the fridge. She sealed the last jar, then stacked the dozen she'd completed in a box to take down to the cellar. Ren shifted the container to one arm and balanced it against her hip to open the cellar door, then flipped on the light switch. Of course, like the rest of the house, no lights.

Ren grunted, then snatched a flashlight from the counter and clicked the button—nothing. She whacked it against her thigh, and the box nearly wobbled from her grasp. Ren dropped the light and kicked her knee up to brace it. Underneath, she could feel the jars pushing their way through the bottom.

"No, no, no…"

She rushed to put the box on the table. When she looked up, she found Lee staring at her.

"Sorry. I spent the past hour jarring pickles and almost just broke them all," Ren said.

"No problem. Can I help you there?" Lee offered.

"Do you know where Minna keeps the duct tape?"

Lee retrieved tape from the cabinet to his right. Ren emptied the box's contents as he tore off strips with his teeth and secured the bottom. Then they both repositioned the jars inside. His movements seemed precise and quick, as if he did this for a job. She noticed Lee's jacket said 'Big John Fish' and felt the urge to mention her time on the fishing boat, but bit her tongue.

"There you go," he said at last. "That should hold."

"Thanks."

"Sure. Are you bringing that downstairs?"

"Yeah."

"No way. I'll take it." Lee took the container from her. "Just hold the flashlight for me, k? I almost broke my neck twice trying to take these stairs in the dark."

Lee hoisted the box, and Ren shone her light down the steps for him. He was back upstairs in moments and closed the door behind him.

"All set," he said.

"Thanks."

Ren smiled once more as she moved toward the dining room, but Lee raised a hand to stop her. He shifted a few times, eyes fixed on the floor, and rubbed at the light stubble dusting his jawline.

"Uh...Ren, can I ask you a question?"

"Yeah, sure."

He looked up.

"Well... see..." Lee stammered. He pulled his ball cap from his head and began turning it in his hands. "I was just wondering where you all were headed after you leave here. I mean, did you need any help getting there?"

"Well, we, uh..." The question threw her. How did he even guess they had plans to leave? Did Peter tell him? Ren flinched, wondering what else Lee knew.

"We don't know our plan yet," she answered.

"Okay."

Lee parted his lips to say more, but didn't. He seemed so gentle and good. Ren wanted to trust him and ask him to join them. He had saved Lizzie, after all. She was sure Lee could help get them home safely.

But Minna's warning held her back.

Ren stepped around him to leave, and Lee spoke up again.

"You see, Caleb and I would sure like to help you. The two

of us can take you wherever you need to go. We wouldn't need to tell anybody else about it, either."

Ren furrowed her brow. She hadn't told Peter the part about why they shouldn't tell Lee. Now, she felt uncomfortable.

"Um...I think we're ok."

"Look," Lee pressed, "I really need to get my little sister somewhere safer. Penny is sick, and we're not... I mean..."

Ren stood, holding her arms, rubbing her scar with her thumb. She watched Lee strangle his worn-out hat, nearly ripping it apart. Minna said he'd lost more than most. What did that mean? Who had he lost?

How can I just stand here and not say anything?

Hank's voice carried through the door, and Ren cleared her throat.

"Thank you, Lee, but we're good for now. We're just going to stay here."

The kitchen door swung open, almost hitting Lee in the back. Hank stopped short, looking at the two of them.

"Hey, Lee. I think Caleb's looking for ya, mate. Ren, let's get to it so we can be done before supper," he said.

"Okay. I'm sorry, I gotta go," Ren said. "Thanks again for the help with the box."

She clenched as she strode past Hank. She felt ill. She barely knew Lee, but she knew enough. He was a good person, and he was *offering* to help. Help them get to Mom, who nobody else seemed to care about. He just wanted to protect what was left of his family, same as Ren. Hank didn't understand. Why would *he* take the risk when no one he loved was in danger? After all, *his* dad was safe, far away from all of this.

161

Ren resolved to talk to Pop again about asking Lee to take them.

Hank caught up to her on the porch and began tying his rope to hers.

"I know what you're thinking," he said.

CHAPTER 28

REN

"You did the right thing, Ren," Hank said. He gave a quick tug to check the knot, dropped the slack, and looked at her. His gaze was steady, as usual, never a hint of doubt.

Ren blinked and looked away. This was the second time in ten minutes that someone seemed to read her mind. She chuffed and tromped down the porch steps. Hank followed with the same purposeful stride he always used.

"I disagree," Ren replied, her eyes fixed on the path ahead. "Not that it's really your business anymore, but I'm not ready to give up on getting home. I think you're wrong about Lee."

"Oh, yeah?" Hank scoffed. "Do you remember that guy, Fitz, from the market? The slimy ruffian, stealin' that old man's potatoes?"

Ren saw a flash of Fitz's chilling stare. She walked faster.

"Well, Fitz is Lee's big brother, and how I hear it, Lee is deeply loyal to him," Hank went on, matching her pace with ease. "If you tell Lee, he'll tell Fitz, and they *will* take your boat if they get the chance."

Hank grasped her elbow and turned her to face him.

"Look, Lee's a good bloke," Hank stressed. "But he wouldn't leave his family behind. I'm certain he'll tell Fitz, but even if I wasn't, would you really wanna chance it? You saw what he's like. And his mates are bad news, too."

He withdrew his hold and put his hands in his pockets.

"You gotta promise me you won't say anything to Lee or anyone else. Can you please do that?" His expression and tone had shifted. This time, he wasn't ordering; he was asking. Almost pleading.

"Yes, I promise," Ren sighed.

"Good." Hank nodded, then motioned them on.

———

"Steady your   stance. You're missing 'cause you're   too shaky," Hank critiqued at the shooting range. Ren squinted at the cans resting on the fence post forty feet away. Hank stood behind her, scrutinizing her performance with his arms crossed.

"I'm missing because the target is too far away. Why would I shoot someone way over there?"

"Because they'd be able to shoot *you* from way over there. Now give it another go. This time steadier."

Ren raised the pistol, balanced her weight, tightened her body, and locked her arms. She didn't really like shooting. The gunfire was a lot louder than she anticipated. The sound and the force of the shot rattled through her body each time she fired. She also didn't expect the acrid smell, like rotten eggs. Ren winced, held her breath, and squeezed the trigger.

A chunk of wood flew off the fence post.

"There. I got him in the leg," she said with satisfaction.

"Bit better. You're meant to be hittin' the body, though," Hank contested.

"The leg is the body."

"You know what I mean. Center mass. The *torso*, k? The bit with all the organs." He made a sweeping gesture over his chest and abdomen.

"Right." She dropped both hands to her side. "Can't I just use the rifle? It's impossible to aim this thing."

At that, Hank pulled his pistol from the back of his jeans and shot with one arm. One of the cans skipped sideways off the railing.

"Your gun can do it. Stop ya grumblin' and try once more."

Did he use the word 'grumblin'?

Ren suppressed a smile and turned back toward the target.

"This is a waste of bullets," Ren chided, with a shake of her head.

"If you'd hit the thing, we'd be done by now. You're just not lining up properly." Hank turned his navy ballcap backward and approached. "Do you mind?"

She nodded, not sure what she was agreeing to.

Hank moved up behind her. Ren felt his hands search beneath the back of her utility jacket. He found and grasped her hips; his left ring finger hooked through her belt loop. His thumbs and forefingers rested just beneath her untucked t-shirt on her waistline. His hands were warm despite the frigid day. He pivoted her body with a push and quick jostle, and her jeans slid beneath his palms. Hank had touched her several times since she'd been there. She could still feel all the places on her body where he had pressed or brushed against her. Before now,

165

Ren hadn't experienced contact from a guy beyond a handshake, and Hank's touch left a particularly jarring sensation. He seemed so calm, so self-assured and experienced with it all. Ren couldn't help but wonder how many girlfriends he'd had in the past. She thought of him being with a fit Australian girl with blond hair and a perfect figure. Ren's heartbeat rumbled through her chest, up to her ears. She blinked her eyes tightly to push the thought away.

"Square up, aim with your whole body," he said and pressed his left palm between her shoulder blades. "Straighten your posture and hold with your core." Then he leaned his chest into her back and put his right hand under her elbow. He smelled like barnwood and stewed apples today.

"Brace your arms, and don't let the kick throw you off."

Now Hank's breath was on her cheek. Her whole body was hot now, and she could feel sweat sprouting on her forehead.

Lauren, get a grip.

Determined not to miss this one, she pursed her lips and narrowed her focus. The gun fired, and a can popped off the fence. Ren beamed and bit her lip. She'd done it.

"There, see?" Hank said as he withdrew. "Well done. You wanna try a few more times?"

He put his hands in his jacket pockets, and Ren immediately missed them. The skin he'd been touching felt too exposed now. A chill drifted across her waist and up her back.

"No, I think I'm good now," she answered.

"Okay. Let's put the safety on, and we can head in."

Ren held out the black 9mm. Hank positioned Ren's thumb to the safety switch. She flipped it and put the pistol back in her jacket pocket.

"Righto," he said with a smile of approval. Ren noticed he had two dimples on his left cheek. "Well done. Let's head in."

Hank nodded them back down the hillside. Ren was suddenly aware of how separated they were from everyone else, and her chest fluttered.

"How did you learn to shoot?" She asked as they took the turn around the lighthouse.

"My dad is a Lieutenant General in the ADF, the Australian army. Preparedness, self-defense, and the like are really important to him, so he had me training from a young age. I learned how to shoot by the time I was Lizzie's age."

"Wow. And your mom didn't mind?" Ren thought about how adamant her mother was against guns, having seen too many accidents in the ER. She didn't even like shooting video games.

"Nah, she left when I was about two years old. She just wasn't cut out to be a mum, I s'pose. It was always just Dad and me."

Hank kicked at some gravel on the path.

"So, how come you know so much about space?" he asked.

"Oh, my dad was an astrophysics professor at the University of Washington. He taught me a lot of stuff, and we used to go to rocket launches, museums, and things like that. We even tracked UFO sightings, which have actually become a lot more frequent lately."

"Really?"

"Yeah, maybe these creatures are some kind of bioweapon they're using to wipe us out before they invade," Ren said with a chuckle, but Hank's brow furrowed. "I'm only joking," she

167

insisted.

"Seriously, do ya think that's possible?"

"Well, who knows? But I doubt it," Ren said with a shrug. "More likely, these meteors or eggs or whatever were just flying through space and happened to land here."

A light drizzle rolled over the field, sparkling in the western sun. Droplets speckled Ren's cheeks and the shoulders of Hank's jacket.

"What d'ya reckon the odds are they'd hit our planet?" he asked, his palm outstretched to the rain.

"Pretty slim, but more likely than usual at the time they hit. Here, I'll show you." Ren snagged three rocks from the path and handed the largest to Hank. "Hold this up. That's the sun. This is Jupiter, and this is Earth," she gestured to the two smaller ones she had. Ren positioned Earth at the center and Jupiter to the right of Earth, angled so that it was on a different plane from the Earth and Sun. "Usually, Jupiter's mass and gravity protect Earth by pulling away anything that might be on track to hit us." Then Ren orbited the medium rock around Hank's sun to sit on its left side. She held Earth up to the sun's right, all three in a straight line. "But, in September, we were positioned with Earth and Jupiter at exactly opposite sides of the sun. So, anything pulled toward the sun from our side would have direct impact with the Earth first."

Ren felt Hank looking at her, but didn't return his gaze. She just took his rock and tossed all three of them into the grass, then wiped her hand on her jeans. "This situation happens every so often in our orbit, and there's always more buzz about how vulnerable we are when it does. It was just bad timing. In fact, the last time we were alone like that, facing this direction in space was over a decade ago. And, no, I don't think there are any intelligent beings strategically weaponizing the banshees, but I guess there's no way to know for sure."

"Crikey, let's hope not, or we'll really be in trouble," he nudged her arm and pointed to the right. Ren turned to see the arc of a faint spectrum above the cliff just as the drizzle started to let up. She smiled at him.

"If ya don't mind my asking," Hank went on, "Where is your Dad now? It's just, you only talk about wanting to get to your mum."

"He died a few years ago," she said, but nothing more.

"Oh, I'm sorry."

They kept walking in heavy silence. When they were at the house, Hank tapped her arm.

"Look, Ren, I know I kinda acted like a jerk when you told me your theory. It's not that I don't believe ya. What you said makes sense, and it's really somethin' that you were able to put it together."

He scaled the first few steps of the porch, but Ren stopped at the bottom, tightening the strap between them. Hank turned.

"But you still won't come with us," she persisted. "Why aren't you willing to try? You said yourself that food will become an issue here soon. We have somewhere safe we can go before things get bad."

He just looked at her, without answering.

Marty came out the front door and started putting on his boots. Ren conceded and followed Hank the rest of the way up toward the door.

"Hey, Hank, can you come gimme a hand with something?" Marty asked.

"Sure, mate."

Hank stepped to Ren and fumbled with the knot around her waist, lightly tugging her toward him. Her eyes rested on the top of his shoulder. She looked at a bit of his hair that had curled out from under his cap, just over his ear. Hank exhaled when the knot came loose and glanced up at her. His green eyes held hers just a moment, then he turned and walked away.

CHAPTER 29

LEE

Lee, Fitz, and Mae sat at the kitchen table as Caleb and Kenny hovered by the pantry. Caleb had positioned himself to watch Fitz's lips move, but Fitz had gotten good at talking fast, covering his mouth, and mumbling when he wanted to keep Caleb out of the conversation.

"Those folks have been there now almost two weeks. Are you tellin' me you haven't heard nothin' 'bout their boat?" Fitz asked.

Lee rotated his mug on the table.

"Well, Hank's been doing a good job of keeping them away from us."

Kenny kicked the wall behind him with his boot heel.

"That Crocodile Dundee turd snake! Just wants their boat for his self."

Lee tensed, hoping Kenny's outburst hadn't woken Penny.

"Well, like I said, Minna has helped us a lot this past year, so I really don't want to cause trouble. Especially now with how much we need the work up there," Lee added.

Fitz grunted.

"Yeah, but what about us? She don't give two dead rats 'bout me and Mae and Kenny."

"Fitz, we're happy to give you all half of what we're getting from her. You know we are," Lee insisted.

Fitz glared back. The dark shadows accentuated how gaunt his face was becoming. His skin seemed more damaged, his sunken eyes more desperate and severe.

"Lee, is that what you think of me? Did ya think I would take food off of Penny's plate? She's near starvin' as it is. I'm supposed to be lookin' after you, dang it, not the other way 'round. I don't need a handout from my little brother."

"Fitz, it's not a handout when it's family," Lee stressed. "You've always looked after us, and we have a chance to help you now."

Fitz rested his arms on the table and pulled on the cuff of his jacket.

"Yeah, well, if I start moochin' off you, it'd crush the last scrap of pride I got left. You understand what I'm sayin'? This whole town treats me like I'm nothin'. Looks like you're startin' to agree with 'em."

Lee's chest dropped.

"No, Fitz. That's not true." He wanted to say more. Like how lots of folks still respected him, how he and Caleb still looked up to him, or how well Fitz had always taken care of them. None of it was true, though, and he was a lousy liar. There was a long silence from all the things Lee wanted to say but couldn't.

"Well, if you and Caleb are givin' up, then we'll take care of it ourselves," Fitz declared, nodding to his crew.

"That's right," Kenny sneered.

"What? What do you mean?" Lee demanded.

"Tonight we're goin' up there. I know that ol' man's got a boat. I can feel it in my bones, and Kenny and I can get him to talk." As Fitz said this, he placed his pistol on the table. Then, he reached over and put his hand on Lee's shoulder. His grip had become sharp and wiry. "This is our chance to get outta here, all of us, before it's too late. Before those banshees figure out they can take us just as easy tied together as standin' apart. Lee, you just gotta trust me. If they give us what we're after, no harm will come to 'em, and they can stay safe and sound at Minna's. Works out for everyone."

Lee stared at the gun. Then he shook his head.

"Fitz, I want no part of this. If you wanna go up there and take that family's boat by force, me and Caleb aren't gonna help." Lee cringed and pinched his arm beneath the table.

Dang it.

Fitz leaned back in his chair, his disappointment burning a hole in Lee's temple.

"So, they *do* have a boat. I knew it. And you didn't tell us."

"You ungrateful lyin' little snot!" Kenny snapped.

"And did they offer to take you, Caleb, and Penny, out to sea with 'em?" Fitz asked. "After you risked your neck to save their lil' girl, did they try to save you and yours?"

"No."

"Of course not. Why would they? They didn't because they don't care a lick 'bout you. People are only lookin' after their own now, but you don't seem to get that, or you're just too good to get your hands dirty even when it means savin' your family. Think about what Daddy did. He'd never shot a man before that night. But our lives were at stake, so he didn't hesitate. Because that's what a real man does for his kin. And how do you repay him? How do you repay *me*? By lettin' us all die so you can sleep better at night. I'm just glad Dad ain't here to watch you betray us." Fitz stood and put the pistol back in his pocket. He looked at Mae and Kenny.

"Let's go."

The other two followed at once. No one would be reigning Fitz in up there. Lee stood and grabbed his arm.

"Fitz, don't do this," he protested, but Fitz pulled away.

"If you don't help us now, you won't be welcome when we come back for Penny. You and Caleb will be on your own."

The thought of Fitz leaving with Penny was a cannonball to the gut. Lee wanted to protest, but knew it was useless. The only person who'd be able to stop Fitz now would have been Dad. But Dad wasn't there.

Then Fitz turned and left. On her way out, Mae stepped to Lee and hugged him.

"Take care of that girl, ya hear? If you change your mind and wanna catch up to us, I know my folks'll take her 'til we get back," she said.

"Mae. Let's go," Fitz beckoned from the door, and she obeyed.

As the door slammed closed, Lee looked at Caleb.

'Am I doin' the right thing?' Lee signed.

'Yes. We'll be okay.'

Before Lee could respond, Penny's coughing fit rattled up from the basement. Lee crossed to the cupboard and pulled out the cough syrup. He emptied the last of it into the measuring cup,

174

only a half dose. And the pharmacy shelves were still bare.

Lee took a breath, shuffled down the steps, and found Penny curled up on her cot. She rolled over to look at him, her fine sandy hair fanned out on her pillow.

"Hi, Lee," she said with scratchy breath. She rubbed her eye with a small fist.

"Hey, Pen. You want some more cough syrup?"

Penny sat up to drink it. Then Lee reached for her pink water bottle.

"Here you go," he said, and she drank a few sips. "Is that better?"

Penny nodded and lay back down. Lee grabbed the blanket from his cot to wrap over her.

"It's pretty cold down here tonight. Let's get this quilt on you, okay? You know, I think I'll be able to board up all the windows after all. Then we can sleep in the den with the fireplace starting tomorrow. How does that sound?"

"I thought you didn't have enough wood to cover the windows," she said, pulling the blanket up to her chin.

"I figured we could take apart the fence. I'll do that first thing in the morning with Caleb. You'll be much more comfortable, and we'll get rid of that cold."

"Mae will be glad. She doesn't like it down here either."

Lee realized he had no idea how things would work without Mae. Who would stay with Penny during the day?

"You know, you'll even be able to peek outside. Keep an eye on things for me," he said.

"Think I'll see people, too? Think I'll see any of my friends?" Penny asked.

Lee clenched. Now, she would see other kids and want to go outside, too. She'd hate him for keeping her in.

"Maybe…Hey, what do I love most in the world?" Lee asked as he tucked the covers around her.

"A lucky penny."

"That's right, a lucky penny. Now, how about you get back to sleep?"

Lee looked at the bowl of soup he had made for her on the tray next to the bed. She'd barely touched it. He pulled his cot over right next to hers. As he lay down, she reached over to hold his hand. Her skin felt too warm. He held his breath and touched her forehead.

She had a fever.

CHAPTER 30

LEE

11 years old
December 4th, 2020 - Gladys, Oregon
7 years until.

"Momma said we gotta stop for milk," Lee signed to Caleb after they pulled their bikes into the Quick 'n Save parking lot. Mom never liked them being out after dark, especially in such cold weather, but Lee had to stay late for detention. Too many tardies.

They leaned the bikes against the lone light pole and walked toward the gas station. The lights were unusually dim inside, and the sign in the window was flipped to 'closed'. Lee looked through the door. It was early, and maybe Kevin was still around. Their family practically kept this store in business with how often they went there. Kevin would open up for them.

But Lee didn't see any movement. Caleb tapped Lee's shoulder and pointed to a note taped to the door.

Closed early for funeral.

Lee frowned and signed to Caleb.

'Now Mom will be really mad we're late. She needs milk for dinner tonight.'

'You need to stop missing the bus, lazy bones," Caleb scolded with a grin.

'Easy for you to say. I share a room with someone who snores like an old man." Lee gave Caleb a little shove as they turned back toward the pumps.

An old red Chevy rumbled under the lit overhang directly between the boys and their bikes. Lee's chest tightened.

Oh no.

Then Bull Jamison opened the driver's door.

No one was sorrier than Lee when Bull didn't get into college. Daddy said Bull had been betting on a football ride until Coach replaced him as QB with his star freshman, Fitz Keller. Bull made such a stink about it that Coach had him sitting the bench his whole senior year.

Now, Bull had made a sport of terrorizing Fitz, Lee, and Caleb. Fitz had cautioned the boys not to provoke him and to keep their distance. But when Lee saw Bull's truck parked outside the diner that morning, he hadn't been able to resist scratching his house key through its new paint job, from the driver's door to the taillight.

Lee tugged Caleb's shirt to a hard left. He wanted plenty of distance between them and that truck.

"What's this now, boys? Kevin close up shop early?" Bull slurred as he tossed a beer can from the window. The dark beard he'd grown this year made him look older and somehow meaner. His knit skull cap hooded his eyes, and his thick coat made him seem even more enormous.

Lee walked faster.

"Hey, I'm talking to you. I know at least one of you runts can hear me," Bull barked as he strode after them. "Unless being dumb is contagious now." Lee clenched his fists so hard his knuckles cracked.

"Hey, Lee. I saw what you did to my truck," Bull sneered.

"I…I didn't touch your truck. It wasn't me," Lee stammered. How could he have been so stupid? Why hadn't he made sure it was safe?

Lee quickened his pace, eyes fixed on the bikes, assuming Caleb would keep up. But his little brother was unaware of Lee's guilt. He didn't understand the real danger they were in.

So Caleb did something he'd seen Lee do a hundred times when Bull's back was turned.

He turned and shot double birds *to Bull's face.*

Lee snatched his brother and ran.

"You slimy little…" Bull growled as he burst from his truck and bounded after them. The boys yanked their bikes from the light pole and angled them toward the road. Lee had almost thrown his leg over the seat when he heard Caleb's bike smash on its side and his brother scream.

Lee looked back to see Caleb flailing and kicking in Bull's meaty grasp.

"Let him go!" Lee charged at Bull with fists flying, but the brute was too tall for him to land a good punch. Bull responded with a powerful backhand across Lee's skull, knocking him to the pavement. Pain seared from Lee's head down through his nerves and muscles. Lee's left eyelid sagged under an oozing wound. His heartbeat pounded against his temple, and his vision was blurry.

But Caleb's screams snapped his senses into focus.

With quivering hands, he pushed himself up to his feet.

Bull had his brother's arm twisted behind his back.

"You better 'pologize, boy, or I'll break your brother's arm."

Lee glared at Bull's monstrous frame, four times the size of his own. But Lee's burning hatred overpowered his fear.

Ever since Daddy killed the hornet's nest in the shed, Lee had kept this emergency weapon in his backpack, just in case. With Caleb's howls ringing in his ears, Lee swung the canvas bag off his shoulder, ripped open the zipper, and grabbed the half can of wasp spray.

"Bull!" Lee shouted. Bull looked up as Lee crushed the plastic button with both thumbs and soaked Bull's head with the poisonous foam. He gargled and staggered back, grunting and cursing as he tried to wipe his face with his sleeves.

Lee's eyes and nose sizzled in the toxic mist, and the fumes were making him gag. He squinted, held his breath, and dragged Caleb to his feet. Bull's hand hooked the back of Lee's coat, but Lee shimmied it off and yanked his brother onward.

The two boys grabbed their handlebars and jumped on the seats, Lee still sore and half-blind from the blood and wasp killer.

The country road to their ranch was nearly pitch black, icy, and riddled with potholes and dead branches. There had been a terrible storm two days before, and debris still littered the way. Fitz would have cleared it, but he and Dad had been away looking at colleges.

Every few yards, Lee's bike skidded as the tires lost their grip, barely missing an obstacle or sliding into the gully. Injuries from a fall wouldn't be nearly as harmful as the precious minutes they'd lose. They had to get home before Bull caught up to them.

Lee just prayed Mom was home.

With how mad and drunk Bull is, would she even be able to stop him?

The frigid wind cut through Lee's worn-out t-shirt like knives. He wanted to wipe his eyes, but didn't dare let go of a handlebar. Ahead, he could just make out the porch lights to his house through the trees. He could hear a horse neighing in the barn.

We can make it…

The truck's motor rumbled with an ominous rev followed by a blaring car horn. Bull was coming, and he wanted Lee to know it.

*Faster, faster…*Crouched over the seat, Lee's thighs burned as they drove his feet harder and harder against the pedals.

Caleb always matched Lee's pace despite their age difference. They often raced each other down this same road, but never in the dark and *never* over ice.

The truck's approaching headlights reflected off the snowy trees like warning signs, and the boys' shadows grew more defined on the road before them. Lee's arms rattled as the horn blew again, louder and longer. He looked over his shoulder at Caleb and saw the red Chevy closing in from behind. The house was still too far away, and they'd never beat him on the road. Bull would hit them by accident, driving at that speed.

Or on purpose.

As the sound of the engine roared through his chest, Lee shot up his right arm and pointed to the gully, leading his brother off the road. They dumped the bikes just as the truck tires raced by them, spraying Lee's Levi's with slush.

Lee and Caleb darted into the woods toward the house. The lit windows shone bright through the woods.

Momma's there. We can still make it.

The two shivered, sloshing and tripping through the frozen trees as Lee tried to stay sharp. His legs were raw from his sopping pants. His fingers and ears were numb, and the breath in his lungs burned. He couldn't stay out here much longer, with or without Bull chasing them.

The truck door slammed like a clap of thunder.

"I can see you, Lee!" Bull bellowed. "You're really gonna be sorry when I getcha."

Bull barreled through the brush after them. Though clumsy when drunk, he still had the speed and stamina of an athlete.

Just keep going.

The branches were thick, and the roots lay hidden under the snow and shadows, jolting the brothers as they stumbled and sank into divots. Bull continued to gain, but their house was in focus now—just a hundred yards away.

Caleb grunted and panted behind Lee.

Don't slow down. We're almost there.

Lee surged his pace just as his toe caught a root. He landed on the side of his ankle, heard a grinding snap, then plummeted headfirst into a pine.

Lee heard Bull slow to a stride. He could feel the grin spreading across their enemy's face as his flashlight hit their shoes.

"You two are dead meat." He grabbed Caleb by his shirt.

"Can you read my lips, dummy? DEAD MEAT."

"Bull! Don't!" Lee knew his pleas were pointless. He tried to stand, but his ankle was limp and throbbing. He couldn't move his toes.

"I'm gonna make you both real sorry!"

Bull stripped the coat off Caleb and yanked the belt from his jeans. It flew above his head and snapped down across Caleb's back. Caleb's high-pitched cry echoed with each clap of the leather on his skin. Lee screamed apologies as his brother thrashed like a fish on a hook. There would be no restraint. No mercy for either of them.

Lee crawled forward, gripped Bull around the leg, and bit into his calf. He ground his teeth around the mouthful of flesh, nearly tearing through the denim. Bull cursed, releasing Caleb from his grasp. He grabbed Lee's hair and pulled so hard it felt like his scalp would rip from his skull. He threw Lee to the dirt, then kicked Lee's busted ankle. Lee screamed and nearly passed out from the pain.

Caleb tried to scamper away, but Bull snatched his elbow.

"We're not done."

A rifle shot echoed through the woods, and the tree trunk behind Bull sprayed bark on his jacket.

"What the...Who's there?!" Bull demanded.

"Let him go, Bull! Right now!"

Fitz! He'd come home!

At seeing his brother, Lee almost wept with relief. Fitz was there. He'd save them.

"Hey, Fitz! Big quarterback hero. Hear you're getting a full ride to UW, you rotten little pissant."

"I said let 'em go, *now*. I'll pop you one, I mean it." Fitz's sites were locked. He was too close to miss.

"You don't have the guts to do anything with that rifle," Bull scoffed.

Fitz fired again, scraping Bull's sleeve. Lee's ears whistled from the shot as he dragged himself toward his big brother.

"Now let go of Caleb and get off our land. Momma already called the sheriff," Fitz warned, steady as a boulder.

In the distance, Lee could see Dad's car pulling up the driveway. Two flashlight beams came bouncing from his Ford toward the woods.

Dad heard the gunshots. He's on his way with more help.

Lee knew it wasn't over yet, though. Bull was way past reason and would want his revenge while it was still in arm's reach.

Bull grabbed Caleb around his torso and held him up like a trophy.

"Put him down, Bull!" Fitz yelled.

Bull hurled Caleb at Fitz, forcing Fitz to drop his aim. By the time Caleb hit the ground and Fitz pulled up, Bull's powerful arms were on top of the rifle.

"Boys...get away!" Fitz grunted as he wrestled Bull against the trees and rough roots. Fitz was big for seventeen, but Bull had the size and brute strength of a man now, with years of fighting experience.

Within moments, Bull had the gun.

But he didn't shoot. He didn't have to.

Bull beat Fitz with it for an endless thirty seconds.

Fitz had been Lee's hero his whole life. It was because of

Fitz that none of the other kids teased Caleb. Because of him, Lee hadn't failed out of school. Fitz taught them to swim, throw, hunt, and ride a horse.

Now, with Fitz's blood sprayed across their clothes, Lee and Caleb were too beaten and exhausted to do anything to save him. Just a couple of toothpicks for Bull to knock out of the way. All they could do was scream.

Dad didn't give Bull a warning. He fired and took Bull off his feet in one shot. Bull curled up in the mud, rolling and clutching the wound in his side.

Lee trembled as he stared at what remained of his brother. Fitz's body lay in a broken heap, his right arm and leg grotesquely twisted in the snow.

———

An hour later, Lee and Dad sat in the ER waiting room. Lee's broken foot was in a cast, and Dad's eyes were bloodshot and puffy. The fluorescent lights hummed and twitched, grating on Lee's remorse.

Dad reached out and took his hand.

"It wasn't your fault, Lee. Fitz saved you 'cause you and Caleb needed him. He knows there's nothin' more important than bein' there for family. Now, we need to be there for him, okay? Promise me you'll always look after each other."

"I promise, Dad."

CHAPTER 31

FITZ

October 30th, 2027 - Gladys, Oregon. 220 miles south of Diamond Point, WA.
56 days after.

U p at the lighthouse, Fitz, Mae, and Kenny cut their way through Hank's fence next to a pile of tin can alarms yet to be strung up. They slipped behind the quiet barn while the two guards took their break on the porch.

"Minna would be keepin' all them kids in the big house with her and Sally. I'd bet our family is over yonder in one of the cottages by the lighthouse," Fitz murmured.

"No way we'd get up there without those two seein' us," Mae stressed. "That light passes right over the field goin' up there."

"Alright, let's bring 'em this way then." Fitz looked around, then focused on the chicken coop. "We can let the hens out."

The three crept to the bird cage and flipped the latch. The flock was timid, so Kenny and Fitz crept in and grabbed two at a time, tossing them out toward the field. Kenny gave them a few kicks to get them squawking and scurrying. Then they all slinked behind the house.

They didn't have to wait more than a minute before the noise attracted the guards, who hurried down the porch steps to catch them, leaving their rifles leaning against the barn.

"Dang, these idiots sure do make it easy," chuckled Kenny as they continued on through the shadows.

Fitz spotted Hank through the back window with Minna and Marty. He smiled to himself. Hank was a college brat who had swooped into his town and started playing the hero, a title that Fitz had once held. Making Hank look like a fool was just icing on the cake.

"Quickly now," he said. The crashing ocean more than drowned out their footfalls through the stony grass.

Ten minutes later, Fitz stood over Ren and her little sister, sleeping in the cottage. It would be a cinch getting the old man and the boy under control. They'd barely put up a fight. The girl, Ren, might be feisty. Braver. Dumber.

Lying there, Ren looked a lot like Fitz's high school sweetheart. She had the same light freckles, long auburn hair, fit body, and delicate curves. His girl was captain of the cheerleaders, and the only person Fitz had ever truly loved. He'd wanted to marry her, but she'd dumped him just a week after he lost his scholarship—*humiliated* him just like *this* girl had done in the market.

Fitz leaned over Ren, grasped her wrists together, and pressed his hand on her mouth. Her eyes went wide, and she grunted and squirmed. Fitz laid his forearms on her chest and leaned in, breathing slow and deep. Ren smelled like lavender.

Minna's fancy tourist soap. She's been plenty pampered up

here in this palace on the sea, while me and Mae have been rationin' dish soap for shampoo.

He tightened his grip around her hands. Her wrists were small. He could break one if he tried.

"Remember me?" he murmured.

She stared back with contempt and fury. Not enough fear. She kicked under the blanket, and he pressed down harder—just like breaking a new mare at the ranch.

She was starting to sweat. "You need to settle now, Ren."

Ren's veins in her forehead throbbed as the last of her air slipped out of her nose. She gagged into his palm, then blinked her eyes in forfeit. Fitz lightened the pressure, allowing her to take a full breath.

"Now, last time we met, we got off to a bad start. Things are about to get a whole lot better between us...or a whole lot worse. Now, first, I'm gonna take my hand away from yer mouth so you can wake your lil' sister. There's no point in yelling. No one besides yer brother and yer Grandad can hear you, and they can't help ya. If you give me a hard time, it won't be good for any of you. You understand? Can I take my hand away?"

Ren nodded.

"Good," Fitz pulled his hand away and slowly rose. Ren gasped a breath and jerked her body against the headboard. She seemed frightened but not tame.

"Get her up," Fitz instructed.

Ren crawled to her sister.

"Lizzie...Lizzie, wake up." Ren rubbed Lizzie's forearm as she stirred and turned her head, seeing Fitz for the first time.

"Who are you?" she asked.

"I'm Fitz," he replied. "You and your big sis gotta get up now."

As Ren guided her out of bed, Lizzie wiped her eyes. She reminded Fitz of Penny, only stronger and with more color in her cheeks. Lizzie was clearly having an easier time of it than Penny. Fitz hated keeping his little sister locked inside, watching her wither away without play or sunshine.

Now these people come and let their girl run loose in the market, and it's Lee who has to risk himself to save her. It ain't fair.

"Ren, what's going on? What is he doing here?" Lizzie asked.

"I don't know, but just do as he says."

Ren shifted them both to the edge of the bed. Fitz grabbed her arm and brought them into the den; Mae and Kenny had rifles on the boy and the old man.

"Mae, I want the little one over here with Granddad," Fitz directed. Lizzie quickly went to stand between her grandfather and brother. Fitz kept his pistol on Ren.

"Whatever you want, you can have it. Just please don't hurt my grandkids," the old man said. He was in sweatpants and a T-shirt, his white hair going every which way. He had no tattoos or scars. Probably never worked a day of hard labor in his life.

"What's your name, old man?" Fitz asked.

"Jim."

"Well, Jim, that's the right attitude 'cause that's just what will happen," Fitz said. "You cooperate, and no one gets hurt."

"So, what is it? What do you want?" Jim asked. His tone was even, neither submissive nor threatening.

"Your boat," Fitz replied.

"We don't have a boat," Jim said. His eyes flitted to Ren, then back to Fitz.

"Now, you see, that's not what we heard. We heard you *do* have a boat, a real nice one. Why should we believe otherwise after you showed up at the market with a cooler fulla tuna?" Fitz shook his head with a *tsk*. "Ya can't get tuna fishin' off a pier."

"Okay, we *were* on a boat," Jim said. "But it's complicated..."

CHAPTER 32

REN

R en listened as Pop told Fitz the whole true story of what had happened to them. Fitz watched him, eyes piercing, and mouth pinched tight, scrutinizing every word, as if trying to catch Pop in a lie. His grip on Ren's arm tightened, his thumb now digging into a nerve. Ren glanced up at the shelf next to the door—the shelf where they kept the gun. Peter was just steps away, looking at her as if waiting for a signal.

But how many bullets were in it?

Ren looked at Pop, wondering what he would have them do.

Would he want Peter to reach for it? Should they try to fight?

Pop would want to cooperate and calmly talk their way out of this, but Fitz kept demanding more information. As his insistence grew angrier and more aggressive, Ren remembered the potatoes. This man won't give up until he gets what he's after. Ren couldn't allow these people to know the location of their boat, their only hope of getting somewhere safe. It would also lead them to Mom. What would they do to Mom if they found her?

The woman, Mae, had lowered her weapon as she listened. Peter kept looking to Ren, his eyebrows twitching. She knew he was waiting for her direction, but she couldn't decide what to do. It seemed too dangerous, but it might also be their only chance. Peter's brow furrowed as he glared at her, his fingers fidgeting at his sides. Ren couldn't think straight. She could still taste the sweat from Fitz's palm on her lips.

Suddenly, Peter lunged for the bookshelf and reached for the pistol.

"Kid's gettin' somethin'!" Fitz hollered, and before Peter could bring his arm down, Kenny had wrestled him against the wall. The gun fell to the wood floor, knocking a gunshot, then it bounced under the table. Ren tried to dive for it, but Fitz snatched her up with the force of a gorilla. She kicked and scratched, but Fitz barely flinched. Then his giant hand came down on her head like a wrecking ball. She staggered and went limp in his grip. White stars and blotches clouded her vision as pain ran down her spine to the tips of her fingers and toes. She collapsed on the floor in a pulsing heap. Ren had never been struck before, not even spanked as a child. Having a grown man hit her with this much malice filled her with terror, humiliation, and weakness as she had never felt before. Her cheek and jawbone ached. She never wanted to get up again.

"That was a real silly move, girl." Fitz wasn't even out of breath. "You still think yer better and smarter than me, don't cha? All high and mighty with them potatoes. Now look at cha!"

Fitz grabbed at Ren, but she rolled to her side and kicked him hard in the knee. Fitz stumbled back and cursed, then heeled her in the stomach. Ren could feel the kick through to her back as all of her air exploded from her chest. Her lungs convulsed. She couldn't catch her breath. Fitz raised his foot again.

"Stop it!" Pop yelled.

Pop pushed off of Mae and tackled Fitz from behind, both falling to the ground. Ren tried to get up, pulling her way up the armchair. She could hear the scuffling and the grunting blows behind her.

"Watch your knife!" Kenny yelled.

Ren heard Lizzie and Peter plead for them to stop. With her wobbly legs below her, Ren turned and saw Mae and Kenny first. They were calm. Kenny was even smiling.

"Pop..." Ren coughed out. She turned just as Fitz laid Pop on the ground, limp and clutching his side. The fight was over. Fitz dragged her grandfather across the floor by his shirt collar and propped him up against the wall. Red lines started spreading across Pop's shirt.

"No!" Ren shouted and crawled across the floor to him.

Fitz picked up a soiled dagger from the rug. He stood there, shaking, his breath heavy. He stared in silence at the blood on his knife and hand, then at her grandfather on the floor.

"Fitz?" Kenny muttered.

"Yeah," Fitz grunted, then he pulled Ren up by the arm again and threw her into the chair.

"This is your fault! Look what you made me do. I didn't wanna do that."

"Please let me help him," Ren begged.

"Ren, I'm okay. It's not bad. Just do as he says," Pop panted.

"Where's the boat?!" Fitz bellowed. "I know you have

one. You've been tellin' folks all about it. Stop lyin' to me!"

Ren pictured Mom defenseless at the house and didn't know what to do.

"Tell me!"

"Ok, ok! We have a boat," Peter shouted. "But it's not here. It's on the coast near Seattle. It's hundreds of miles from here if it hasn't been stolen yet, so we can't just give it to you! That's the truth. Now, please let us go."

Fitz turned to Mae and Kenny.

"Now, what?" Kenny asked. Fitz wiped his mouth with the back of his sleeve, then looked down at Ren.

"Ok, then, you'll take us there," he ordered Ren. "You and the little one will lead us to it. The boy and the old man will stay here."

"What?" Ren whispered.

"Peter!" Lizzie cried as Mae held her back from her brother.

CHAPTER 33

REN

R en's mind reeled. Her fingers gripped the armchair as if trying to anchor herself to it.

I can't let them take us.

"So now we're going all the way to Seattle?" Mae asked. "With these girls?"

"I told ya, I'm seein' this through," he shot back.

"No," Pop pleaded as he tried to stand. "Don't take them. I'll bring you to it."

"You're in no shape to travel, old man," Kenny scoffed as he pushed him back down the wall.

"That's right, it works better just takin' the girls," Fitz said. Then he turned to Ren. "Get up and get yer stuff." He grabbed her sleeve, and she yanked free.

"I'll only lead you if you just take me and if you let me help my grandfather now. Otherwise, I'll fight you every step of the way," Ren said with her last bit of defiance.

"Nah, I think havin' lil' sister with us is the only way to get you to behave," Fitz sniped. "How about this? Until you agree to do as we say, we're gonna take your brother here and toss him out to play with the banshees."

Fitz nodded to Kenny, who then grabbed Peter and dragged him to the door. Lizzie shrieked and thrashed as Mae gripped her tighter.

All of Ren's fight drained from her body.

"No! Don't do that! I'll take you. Please. We'll go!"

"I don't think you really mean that yet. Throw him, Kenny!" Fitz ordered.

"Ren!" Peter shouted as Kenny shoved him out of the door and slammed it shut. Peter banged on it from the outside as the family pleaded with them to let him in. Ren prayed those things wouldn't be out there.

Please let the spotlight keep them away...

But within seconds, the sound came. One horrible shriek and then another, louder and closer. Peter pounded his fists on the door while Ren screamed for her brother, swearing she'd do whatever Fitz said.

Fitz laughed.

"Alright, alright, now I believe her. Kenny, let him in."

Something skittered atop the roof, heading toward the front door.

"Let him in!" Ren cried.

Kenny swung open the door.

"Get inside, boy," he said.

But Peter wasn't there. Only a dark, empty field stretched before them—no sound except breaking waves.

"He's gone," Kenny called over his shoulder.

Ren's chest heaved. Vomit congealed in the back of her throat.

"Peter!" she gagged as she tried to free herself from Fitz's grasp, straining to look beyond the door. Numbness took over. Everything was muted around her. Just like it had been the night of the accident, she couldn't even feel Fitz twisting her arm to hold her back.

"Let me go! He could still be out there!"

"Make sure," Fitz said to Kenny.

Kenny took a cautious step beyond the threshold. He called out again.

"Hey, kid!"

Suddenly, Kenny flew from the doorway and out of sight.

"Kenny!" Fitz yelled.

"My God…They got him, too," Mae whispered.

Fitz and Mae stared at one another.

"I'm here," Kenny replied as he rounded into the doorframe with a pistol held at his back. Hank and Marty were right behind him.

"Lizzie, get down!" Ren commanded. As Mae fumbled to point her weapon, Lizzie wriggled free and jumped to the other side of the sofa bed. Ren lunged from her chair to her pistol under the table. Fitz made a reach for her, but she managed to kick him away, grab the handle of her gun, and turn it on him. Pressing her back against the wall, she slid shakily to her feet.

"Ha, you're not gonna use that thing," Fitz snarked at her as he raised his hands.

Ren straightened and steadied her aim.

Yes, I will.

Hank shoved Kenny into Marty's line of fire and put his gun on Fitz.

"If she doesn't, you know I will," Hank swore. "Now untie your tether and toss it to me."

Fitz calmly complied.

"Turn around, hands behind you. Ren, shoot him if he moves."

Hank tied Fitz's hands and then sat him down at the table. When Hank had his gun back up, Ren scanned the room for Lizzie. She was in the corner, hugging Peter.

"Peter!" Ren could barely get the words out. "You're alive…"

"We thought those things got you," Lizzie said.

"No, Hank and Marty got to me first. I'm okay."

"Jim? You alright, mate?" Hank asked.

"Yep, still breathing," Pop panted. Ren was already at his side, compressing the slice she found around his waist.

"I don't think it's deep, but it's a long cut," Ren said, struggling to cover the whole thing. Peter grabbed a towel from the closet and tossed it to her.

"We gotta get you to the big house," Hank said.

Pop grunted.

"Sounds good."

"Pete, go grab some scissors, hand towels, a bed sheet, and the comforter," Hank directed. "Okay, Marty, get their tethers and tie up the other two."

"Whatcha gonna do now, Hank?" Fitz taunted. "Turn us over to the cops? They're long gone, ain't they?"

Marty got to work binding Mae and Kenny while Peter came out with the needed items.

"Peter, cut a long, thick strip that can wrap around Jim's

stomach twice. Ren, use it to tie the fresh towels to the wound," Hank ordered. Peter and Ren quickly obeyed.

"Naw, yer gonna have to let us go at some point," Fitz continued. "And the second you do, we'll just come right back again."

"Pete," Hank said, still ignoring Fitz, "cut some handholds around the edges of the comforter. We'll carry him down on that."

"The truth is," Fitz went on, "My buddies from the harbor might be the next ones to come. They may burn this whole place to the ground. They got real excited when I told 'em what you got here."

Ren tried to block out Fitz's voice as she wrapped the bandage around Pop's waist.

"I could just kill you now," Hank hissed.

"You could, but you won't. You can't kill someone in cold blood," Fitz said with a smirk. "So, unless you wanna put Minna's whole place at risk, it's best to just let us take the girls and go. How about this? I promise to sail 'em both back here once we have the boat, safe and sound. We don't wanna hurt 'em. We just want that boat. C'mon, what are these people to you?"

Marty over up at Fitz, but Fitz didn't flinch.

"Not gonna happen."

"I bandaged him, but he's still bleeding through. We gotta go," Ren stressed.

Hank gestured for Peter to hurry with the comforter.

"Let's get him on the blanket."

"Hey, Renny," Fitz gibed. "The next group is a lot meaner than we are. You'd be much safer leadin' us than that crew, believe me. Who knows what they'd do to you all?"

"Shut your slimy mouth!" Hank screamed. "Marty, let's quick tie 'em to the pipe in the bathroom. Then we gotta get Jim to Minna."

By the time they got Pop off the floor, he was as white as a sheet.

CHAPTER 34

HANK

H ank, Marty, and Peter carried Pop down the winding path to the house while Ren and Lizzie ran ahead to get help. Hank's mind raced.

How much longer does Jim have? What if Fitz's mates are on their way? How am I gonna protect this place?

By the time they walked up the porch, Jim had stopped moving. Hank nodded to Marty and Peter to set him down on the floor in the foyer as Minna and Sally rushed in. The bandages and comforter were soaked through with blood.

Marty grabbed Hank's arm.

"What if Fitz was telling the truth, Hank? If he brings those pirates up here next time, we won't be able to stop them. Jim and the kids can't stay here."

"I reckon he's bluffin'," Hank uttered.

"Yeah, but how sure are you?"

Hank was silent. He wasn't sure enough.

"Hank!" Marty persisted.

"Martin, take Lizzie into the kitchen, please," Sally insisted as she pulled out her first aid kit.

Marty picked up Lizzie, but she reached for her brother.

"Peter, come with me," Lizzie pleaded.

"Liz, I gotta stay here and help Pop," said Peter.

Hank grasped his shoulder. "Listen, mate, the best way for you to help is to keep your sis away from all this."

"Peter, go with Lizzie," Jim rasped. His breath was quick and shallow. "They've just gotta stitch me up. I'll be okay."

Peter nodded and followed Marty out. Ren was whispering something to her grandfather. It sounded like plans for when they'd get back home.

Sally cut the bandage and pulled it free to examine the wound, a long, straight cut around his left waist, still seeping down his side. "Ren, put your hand here and press," Sally instructed. "How long has he been bleeding?"

"Um, I don't know. Twenty minutes? Maybe thirty? But it's not bad, right? We've been trying to keep it closed." Ren wavered.

"This may sting," Sally said as she dabbed the wound with antiseptic. Jim made little reaction. He either couldn't feel it or had no strength left to move.

"Mum, find my needle and thread quickly," Sally ordered. Minna dug into the medical bag, retrieved the items, and threaded the needle as fast as she could in the dim light. Sally's hands shook as she took them from her.

"Ren, you need to gently hold the wound closed for me."

Ren blinked and pressed the loose skin together. Jim's blood leaked over her fingers.

Hank took a bottle of whiskey from the dining cabinet, knelt, and poured it into Jim's mouth.

"Hank, I can't see. Hold the flashlight," Sally said. Her gloves were staining red, and when she pushed the hair back from her face, the color smeared across her forehead.

"He's really cold, Sally," Ren said. "Can we put the blanket on him?"

Sally just kept sewing. Hank pulled the soiled comforter over Jim's legs, though he knew it wouldn't help.

"Ren," Jim murmured.

"Shh, Pop, don't talk now," Ren said. "Can't you go faster, Sally? What else can I do?"

"Ren…" Jim choked on his words. "You're not safe here anymore. You gotta take the kids and go without me."

"We're not going anywhere."

"You have to leave. I'll slow you down. More people could be coming."

Jim placed his hand on Ren's forearm.

"Pop, stop it! We're not leaving you," Ren insisted. "Sally, are you done yet?"

Sally put in the last stitch and clipped the thread. She pressed two fingers to Jim's wrist and started counting under her breath. Her eyes narrowed as the counting trailed. Then Sally yanked out her stethoscope and pressed it to Jim's bare chest. The room was silent.

Sally pulled the device from her ears. She looked up at Hank, as if searching his face for something more she could do. Her bottom lip quivered.

"Take Peter and Lizzie, and go find your mom," Jim whispered. His stare was low and vacant. Ren pulled his limp hand to her cheek.

"I can't go without you. I don't know the way or what to do. As soon as you're better, we'll all go."

"You're grown, and you're smart. You can get them home, kiddo. I love ya."

He let out one last ragged breath and went still; his eyelids fell. His skin was gray and sunken.

"What's going on? He's not breathing!" Ren frantically tried to wake him. "Sally, help me!"

"Ren, we did all we could. He just lost too much blood. He's gone," Sally said heavily. "I'm so very sorry."

"He's with God now, love," Minna promised as she tried to reach for Ren's hand.

"No!" Ren jerked away and collapsed onto her grandfather's body.

Hank stood above her. He didn't know what to say or do. Would she even want him to comfort her? He looked at Sally, and she nodded encouragement.

Hank reached out and pressed his hand to Ren's back.

"We…we have to go," he said.

"I can't…," she whispered.

"C'mon," Hank grasped her shoulders and pulled her away. He helped her to her feet and turned her to him. Ren flung her arms around his shoulders and just hung on, weeping.

Hank held her up and let her cry, shaking like a leaf in his arms. His chest hurt, and he couldn't think straight; he wanted to shield her from all of this. Hank braced the back of her head, her brown hair falling through his fingers. He didn't want to let go of her, this brave and fiery person who had been through so much.

Hank looked at Minna and exhaled, accepting the truth. It was no longer safe at the Inn for any of them.

"It's okay, Ren," Hank said. "I'm gonna get you home. We'll leave tonight and go find your mum."

Ren quieted, pulled back, and looked at him. She was exhausted, and it seemed her tears had run out. The road to get here had been awful, and it wasn't about to get easier. Hank wanted to carry her load for as long as she needed. For now, he just had to get them out of there.

"You'll need a big head start," said Minna.

An hour later, packed with food and extra warm clothes, Minna led Hank to the shed behind the barn and unlocked the latch.

"We've been keepin' these here for an emergency. I think this is it," she said.

Minna opened the door to reveal dozens of tourist bikes.

"They'll get you down the road and out of town fast. Go as far as you can until daybreak, then hide them and stay off the road."

Hank swelled with gratitude. They'd really have a chance now.

"Thank you, Minna."

"It's nothin' to what ye have done for us," she said, hugging him. "I'll keep Fitz's lot tied up as long as I can. You get these kids home safe to their mum and then sail away from all this. I pray God watches over yer journey."

CHAPTER 35

LEE

L ee emerged from the basement with Penny's uneaten soup. Caleb was rinsing dishes. Lee placed the bowl on the counter and tapped his brother's shoulder.

'She's got a fever, Caleb. I don't know what to do,' he signed.

They stared at each other. Caleb didn't seem to have any advice this time.

Lee stormed out the back door in a sudden rage. He could hear Caleb rushing after him, but Lee didn't wait for him. Lee grabbed his crowbar and started ripping the fence posts apart, cracking and splintering them as he went. Caleb inched closer behind him, but Lee threw the wood backward to keep his brother away. He didn't want comfort, reason, or protection. Lee just wanted to destroy something.

Over the creaking and slamming of the wood, a shriek rang out. Then a haunting chorus of banshee trills blew in on a wind from the north. The sky from that direction looked like a pool of disturbed water, blurring the stars and rooftops as the swarm washed in front of them. A white oak tree just beyond the yard shook and swayed as the gale descended into its boughs. Several branches drooped lower, twigs snapped, and leaves twirled to the grass below as the calls quieted to a few chirps and clicks. There they perched, waiting. Waiting for Lee to take just a few steps farther away from Caleb.

Lee wanted them to come. He wanted to hit one with his crowbar and beat it to death. His fingernails dug into his hand, gripping the cold iron as he leaned toward the hole he'd just created in the fence.

"I dare you to try it! Come get me!" he screamed all around him into the night. The banshees replied with shrill howls, as the flock quaked and shifted in the tree.

Lee scanned the yard for a sign of one advancing. But he only saw Will and Ozzie's lonely bicycles and Karen's red wagon that her brothers loved to pull her in. He choked on his breath and dropped the bar.

Caleb grabbed Lee by the shirt and dragged him back into the house.

Once inside, Lee shook free. Caleb tried to reach for him again, but was pushed away. Lee hunched over the sink and rubbed a few drops of water on his face and neck. He stared out the window into the darkness.

"Lee?" Caleb said.

Lee turned around.

'I don't see any other way. We're going to help Fitz steal the boat and get out of here,' he signed.

'No, we don't have to, Lee. We can just move up to the lighthouse once Fitz is gone. Minna would help us take care of Penny, and we could stay up there together,' Caleb pleaded.

207

'Don't you get it?! It's not safe up there. It's not safe anywhere. And if Fitz goes through with his plan, Minna will never trust us again. I have to get Penny on that boat. It's our only chance.'

'Please, Lee. It isn't right.'

'I'm doin' it, and if you care at all about me or Penny, you'll help,' Lee signed. *'Dad told us to stick together. Will you help me? Please?'*

Caleb let out a slow sigh of defeat and dropped his hands to his sides. He nodded.

———

An hour later, Caleb was banging on Big John's front door. John and his wife, Camille, had a small townhouse near the harbor. Camille's sister's family lived right next door. Of what Lee knew, they were all decent people.

Penny slept in Lee's arms on the front stoop. His eyes darting at the slightest sound, he counted the seconds until he could get her back inside.

Come on...

From behind the door, a lantern lit the frosted window.

"Who's there?" a man's voice called out.

"Big John, it's Lee Keller. Please let us in."

The door swung open to reveal their boat captain in pajama pants and a t-shirt. He'd lost twenty pounds since that day the meteors hit, and his skin hung loose on his face, making him look much older. He was holding a shotgun.

"Lee and Caleb? What are you doing here?" John asked, waving them inside. "What's goin' on?"

Camille peeked out from the kitchen, wrapped tight in a bathrobe, illuminated by the candle she was carrying.

"John? Who's here?" She said as she hurried toward them.

"Hi, Camille," Hutch said from Caleb's arm.

"Thank you for letting us in. Is there somewhere I can lay Penny?" Lee asked.

"Sure, right in here." Camille led Lee to the spare bedroom down the hall and helped him put Penny in the bed. As she tucked Penny under the covers, Lee wished he had gotten to know Camille better before all of this.

Lee gave Penny one last long kiss on her forehead, still warm from the fever. He felt lead filling his chest, anchoring him to her. He rubbed the top of her little hand once more and stood. Then Lee motioned for Camille to follow him back to the hall.

"John, Camille, I need you to look after Penny for me," Lee said. "Just for a couple of weeks, and then I'll come back for her."

Big John rubbed the back of his head and raised his eyebrows to his wife.

"Lee, you know we would, but you have to understand. We don't have much food as it is," he said.

"I'll try to bring you more when we come back. I really need you, John. She has nowhere else to go."

Camille squeezed Lee's arm.

"Of course, we'll keep her, Lee," she insisted. "But where are you going?"

"Just on a little trip with Mae and Fitz. It's important. Please keep her inside and safe for me. Never leave her alone."

Lee had never imposed on anyone like this before, but the only thing that mattered was Penny.

"I understand. Dale and Georgette will help," she assured him.

"She has a fever," Lee said. "Do you have any medicine for it?"

"She's sick?" John asked. Camille took his hand.

"I have some Advil I can dilute, about half a bottle. I promise we'll take care of her."

"Thank you so much." Lee embraced both of them. "I'll be back for her as soon as I can. If anything goes wrong, you can always take her up to the lighthouse. No matter what's happened, Minna wouldn't turn Penny away."

"What do you mean?" Camille pressed. "Where's Mae?"

Lee didn't answer and opened the door to leave.

Penny emerged from the bedroom, her eyes wide and frightened. She rushed down the hall.

"Lee! Don't go. Don't leave me."

Lee scooped her up and held her, breathing in her smell one last time.

"Penny, I promise I won't be gone long. You'll barely have time to miss me. Aunt Mae's parents are going to take care of you."

She cried as he pried her weak arms from his neck and handed her to Camille.

"I love you, Lucky. I'll see you real soon."

Then he and Caleb walked out. Penny's pleas for them to stay burned through Lee's ears, behind his eyes and down his throat. He swallowed the pain and kept going without looking back.

———

When Lee and Caleb appeared in the doorway to the lighthouse cottage, Fitz looked up and smiled. Lee ignored it. He just bent down to cut their bindings and helped them all to their feet. Fitz wrapped his arm around Lee's shoulders.

"I knew you'd come, brother. I just knew it."

———

After taking control of the main house, Lee had Mae and Caleb pillage food and ammo from the cellar. In the den, Fitz and Lee stood above Minna and Sally, who were seated on the couch. Marty lay tied up on the floor. Several children looked down from the stairwell and banister, having been warned by Lee not to come down.

"Where'd they go?" Lee asked Minna.

She returned his steely glare. "Lee, what are ye doing'? This isn't you at all. Please, don't take it any further," she implored.

"Minna, just tell us where they went, and we'll leave you alone," Lee pressed.

Minna shook her head. "Did Fitz tell you what he did to their grandfather? He killed Jim, Lee. How can ye be helping them?"

"He's dead...?" Fitz murmured.

Lee looked at Fitz for a sign that this wasn't true.

"Uh...the old man went after Mae, hittin' her and tryin' to get her gun. I tried to get him off, and he snatched my dagger from my belt. We scuffled, and he was wounded, but he was alive when I last saw him, I swear. We didn't mean for that to happen."

"Lee, ye can't possibly believe that," Minna protested.

211

"Quiet, ya old bat!" Fitz barked at her. "She's just tryin' to mess with you, Lee."

"Alright, stop it!" Lee bellowed.

"You're scaring the children," pleaded Sally, clutching her chest as if holding one of them.

"We have a scared child, too, Sally," Lee replied. "We're all scared, aren't we? I don't want anyone else gettin' hurt, so just tell us where they went. *Now*."

Minna sighed.

"Back home. They left hours ago," she answered.

Fitz threw up his hands. "We know that! What road are they takin'? Where in Seattle?"

"We don't know where exactly. They talked about a house on the water, but that's all I know," Minna said.

Caleb and Mae were now coming back from the kitchen. Caleb was carrying an extra rifle, and Mae had two satchels full of goods.

"Hun, I got us a buncha that tayberry jam you like," Mae boasted to Fitz. "These greedy high-mucks been hoarding loads of food, while the rest of us are starvin' in town."

Lee recalled something more from the conversation he overheard.

"Diamond Point. That's where the house is. Right, Minna?" he said.

She didn't answer, and that was all the confirmation Lee needed.

"Diamond Point? I know that area," Mae piped up. "My uncle did construction work there. It ain't that big.
If that's where they are, we'll be able to find 'em for sure."

Lee nodded, lifting one of the supply packs. "Then let's go."

CHAPTER 36

REN

R en, Hank, Peter, and Lizzie flew down the serpentine roads of Gladys, heading north on their bicycles. Hank shared a tandem bike with Lizzie while Ren and Peter rode with a tether between them, paying close attention to each other's pace, turns, and obstacles. They each wore a school bookbag from Sally, filled with food.

Hank was right. It was *much* colder at night. The frigid air chafed Ren's face, scraping away any moisture from her cheeks.

The speed felt surreal and invigorating—like flying. Ren peddled and glided, peddled and glided. She always loved her bike when she was younger. She and Peter biked all around the neighborhood when they were around Lizzie's age. Now, she couldn't remember the last time she'd been on one.

Ren kept her eyes fixed on Hank's shoulders in front of her. It was too dark to see much further.

She remembered clinging to him at the house, wishing all of this had been a bad dream.

But when she opened her eyes, her grandfather was still dead—murdered by villains.

Ren wanted to go faster, racing away from all of it. Had Minna not given them bicycles, Ren would have been sprinting.

Hank looked around street corners, leading them through the darkest shadows to ensure they weren't seen. Soon, the four had reached the Gladys town limit, with only woods on either side of the road. It looked like they were alone, but Ren knew better.

The banshees were out there, watching them, waiting for someone to fall behind. Could she outrun them on a bike? How fast were they? If a bear or wolf could outpace a cyclist, surely these things could. Every time a tree swayed or leaves rustled, Ren braced herself for that horrible shriek. But the sound never came.

After three long hours, Lizzie begged for a break. The road was a flat stretch now with just a few mild slopes. Ren was also tired and surprised her little sister had gone this long, even on the tandem bike. Hank allowed them a few minutes of rest, then made the team push on until dawn. They approached a mile marker for the next town just as the sun threaded through the trees. Ren could see much farther in every direction, which meant someone—or *something*—could spot their group just as easily. They were too exposed.

"We're almost there, guys. Pedal faster," Hank urged. Ren didn't know they had a destination, but learning they were almost *somewhere* gave her a last rush of energy.

Finally, Hank motioned for them to pull in front of a small outpost along the highway. The sign read "Mitchell's Patio Furniture." They walked the bikes deep into the woods and covered them with branches, then Hank led the group through the smashed glass front door. Ren's legs ached so much she could barely step over the door frame. Her endurance had waned since her days as a runner.

Hank barricaded the entry and looked around. The dark room was filled with outdoor seating and tables. All the colors and patterns of a carefree summer were dulled by a thick layer of dust.

"Okay, we'll rest here for a few hours. Just find a spot in the back where you can't be seen from the street. I'll wake you in a bit."

Lizzie and Peter flipped the cushions on two patio couches and threw themselves down without a word. Ren uncovered a chaise lounge, and Hank fell into a hammock tied between fake trees. As soon as Ren heard Lizzie sleeping, she sat up.

"Hank?" she whispered.

"Yeah?" he was lying on his back, his arm draped over his eyes.

"Do you think they'll come after us?"

"Don't think about that now. Ya gotta sleep."

"But do you think so?"

He looked at her. "Yeah. Those bindings wouldn't have kept them for long, and since they know what direction we're headed, I reckon they're already coming."

———

Five hours later, Ren woke to the sound of clunking and sliding from the back of the store. Lizzie and Peter were still sleeping, but Hank was gone. Ren rolled off the chair, wandered under the 'Employees Only' sign, and peered down the hall.

"Hank?" she called.

"Yeah, back here."

She followed his voice into a big storage room. The wall-to-wall shelves and bins were packed with outdoor sporting equipment. By the light of three camping lanterns, Hank was dumping out containers and sifting through piles of hiking, camping, and ski gear strewn all over the floor.

"Why is all this stuff here? I thought this was a patio store," Ren said.

"Marty sent me here. The owner's his mate. He had told Marty that he was worried about going under since no one buys yard stuff in cold weather. Marty convinced him to sell rec gear through fall and winter. It was just lucky for us that the world fell to pieces before he put it on the shelves or swapped out that sign."

He pointed to a sign leaning against the wall: "Mitchell's Outdoor Recreation Supply Store."

"Anyway, we can take this big tent here, better coats, packs, and sleeping bags. I found ammo for my rifle and your pistol, but I can't find any guns. We just gotta work out how much we can carry on foot. Lizzie's gonna have a time keeping up as it is."

"She's stronger than she looks. She'll be fine carrying a small pack and sleeping bag, and I think we can handle the rest."

Hank continued sorting, pulling out maps, canteens, travel towels, and more.

Ren started rooting through a box labeled 'travel hygiene.'

"I guess you were right about that guy, Fitz."

"Yeah—I told you not to tell anyone else about your boat," Hank chided. "I *told* you it was dangerous."

"I didn't. I swear I didn't."

"Well, he found out somehow," he grumbled.

217

Ren angled her back to him. Her breath grew tight as she clattered through the miniature toothpastes, soaps, and wet wipes. She found a mesh drawstring bag and started shoving fistfuls of stuff into it.

When she turned, Hank was standing behind her with his hand propped up on his belt. His accusing glare was gone. He inhaled, searching for whatever he wanted to say next. Ren stepped back against the shelf, clutching her toiletries to her chest.

"Hey. Ren, I…" He paused. His gaze dropped to her bundle of items. "Erm…that's a good idea—soap, and all."

He reached above her to retrieve a mess kit and turned away.

Ren scrunched her forehead at the back of his head. She turned and grabbed a small can of bug spray, a handful of garbage bags, and two bandanas. She started dropping her stuff in one of Hank's open packs.

"Do you think it was Lee? Do you think he's with them?" she asked.

Hank was zipping matches and lighters in a pouch.

"Lee may have found out about it," Hank guessed as he zipped matchboxes and lighters in a pouch. "He spent a lot of time with Pete. It's possible Lee could have put things together and spilled the beans to Fitz. I just can't believe he's involved in what those three are doing now."

"Minna told me he lost some of his family to the banshees," Ren said.

"Yeah, two brothers and a sister, all younger than Lizzie. He has one more sister, but I've never seen her. Lee keeps her in the house always. I don't really blame him. It's a wonder he's been able to get through it at all."

Ren could only visualize Lee's face and wringing hands when he spoke to her in the kitchen. She winced.

"I was so thankful he was there…when he saved Lizzie," she said.

Hank handed her a box of granola bars.

"Lee saved my life once, too," he said.

"What? How?"

"A couple of weeks after the meteors hit, some thieves got into the barn, probably after the hens. I was in there alone, and they got the jump on me. I was nearly done for when Lee and Caleb drove 'em off and carried me to the house. I was bedridden for days, but Min and Sal took care of me. As soon as I was healed, I got going on defending the place. Reckon they'll be adding a lot more security measures after last night."

Ren forgot what she was looking for next.

"Ren, I'm sorry about Jim. He was a good guy, and I wish we had gotten there sooner."

Her eyes welled. She swiped a fingertip above her cheek.

"Well, you got there in time to save Peter and the rest of us." She pulled a solar-powered flashlight from its box. Pop would have loved getting something like it for Christmas. Ren's face was still sore from where Fitz had struck her. Gripping that heavy metal flashlight had her yearning to pound Fitz's smug face with it. She took a breath and clipped it to the backpack at her feet.

"Oh, here we go!" Hank exclaimed as he flipped open a jumbo box labeled 'Apparel'. He pulled out a light blue knit hat and tossed it at Ren. "How'd ya fancy a new wardrobe?"

There were eight more boxes just like it.

219

CHAPTER 37

PETER

P eter, Lizzie, Ren, and Hank ate Sally's packed sandwiches and some pears before leaving the store. Lizzie seemed a little recharged in her new outfit, coat, hat, and boots. Peter was proud of how much she agreed to carry after so little sleep. He had found some energy drinks, and now he was borderline manic from the caffeinated fatigue.

Hank insisted it was too risky to bike on the road, so the four of them tethered together and headed on foot northwest through the woods.

———

By late afternoon, the path opened to a field stretching toward the shoreline. The Pacific air blew colder there, and walking through the tall grass returned Peter to the previous night—the grass they rushed through, carrying Pop as he was bleeding out. He could still feel the weight of the comforter in his hands.

Peter felt haggard, disoriented, and really ticked off. Angry at those scumbags who attacked them, angry at himself for dropping the gun, and angry at Ren. When Pop was dying, Peter had to leave to comfort Lizzie. Lizzie wanted Peter because he's the one who's *always* there for her, not Ren. And because of that, Peter didn't get to say 'goodbye' to his grandfather.

Ren walked in front of him, staring out at the water. She was totally tuned out from the rest of them. It knotted his stomach. He wanted to shout at her and bring her back to reality—make her feel guilty for stealing Pop's final moments. But he yanked a handful of grass from the field and tore it to shreds instead. As he scattered the pieces, a waffling shriek blew overhead.

"Stop. I heard something," Peter called out.

Hank whipped around.

"What? What did ya hear?"

Ren and Lizzie turned to look at him, too.

"Was it one of those things?" Lizzie asked, clutching her rope.

"I don't know. I'm not sure," Peter answered, but that was a lie. He was sure he heard a banshee.

"Well, let's just hang here a sec," said Hank.

They waited in silence for two minutes, looking across the horizon. Lizzie took Ren's hand. Nothing came.

"Sorry. The sound's gone now," said Peter.

"No worries," Hank said. "It can be tricky out here on the shoreline. If you did hear one, we'll be fine if we keep together. Let's go."

Peter strained to make out something more as they walked on, but heard only the waves.

"Ren, I'm freezing," Lizzie said after a few minutes.

Ren didn't respond. She didn't even look down.

"Ren," Lizzie asked again. "Can we stop and rest here?"

Peter watched Ren keep walking, gritting his teeth. In a surge of frustration, he strode forward and pulled Lizzie to him.

"Hey, you doin' okay?" he asked her.

Lizzie leaned her head against him. "I'm tired."

"Lizzie needs to stop now!... Ren, stop!" Peter shouted.

This seemed to break her trance. Ren turned and blinked at him.

"What?"

"*Lizzie*, Ren! She's cold and tired. Didn't you hear her?"

"No...I'm sorry."

"Yeah, let's take a quick break," Hank offered as he dropped his pack and pulled out his canteen.

Peter squatted down next to Lizzie. He blew warm air on her hands and rubbed the chill from her fingertips.

Ren passed around her water, and Lizzie guzzled two mouthfuls. Peter recapped and returned it without drinking any or looking at her.

After a few more minutes, Hank stretched to his feet and climbed up on a rock bordering the path. He scanned the rolling field, then locked his gaze northward. A smile spread across his face, and he blew a little whistle.

"Hey, guys, come get a look at this."

CHAPTER 38

REN

P eter lifted Lizzie and placed her on the slanted rock next to Hank.

"I don't see anything," she said.

Hank put Lizzie's arm around his shoulder and lifted her onto his hip.

"It's over that way," he said as he gestured beyond the grassy hill. "Can you spot 'em?"

Lizzie's eyes lit up.

"Yes, I do now."

"Spot what?" Ren asked, looking that way on her tiptoes.

"You'll see," Hank taunted with a grin as he and Lizzie hopped down from the rock and led the other two over the ridge. Ren quickened her pace through the reeds, stretching her view higher with each bound.

When Ren reached the top of the hill, she marveled at the incredible sight.

"Birds," she exclaimed. There were hundreds of them, maybe a thousand.

The throng of beautiful white gulls puttering in the grass

below them was the most enormous flock Ren had ever seen. They looked perfectly content—completely unaware of how much the world had changed.

"Reckon they look a bit bored," he said to Lizzie with a wink.

"Bored?" she asked.

"Yeah, they're just setting up there with nothing to do," he said. "How about we give 'em a jump?"

Lizzie smiled—her first real smile since leaving Minna's.

"Okay, super," said Hank. "Ren, Pete, are you guys ready?"

The two nodded. Ren felt a flutter in her chest. She secured the front latches on her backpack and grasped Lizzie's hand.

"We all go on the count of three," Hank directed.

"No yelling, though," Ren added.

"Righto. No yelling," he agreed. "One…two…three!"

The four raced toward the birds, waving and flailing their arms as if trying to fly themselves. The seagulls exploded from the field in a frenzy, darting this way and that in the sky, weaving between each other with such speed it was impossible to keep track of just one.

Then, the flock calmed, each bird gliding together to form a synchronized, fluid ensemble, churning, twirling, and flowing in unison. The gulls turned into the wind coming over the cliffside. They hovered there above the ledge with their wings out wide like peaceful kites on a string.

The group was entranced by it. Peter looked awestruck—his shoulders rising and falling with deeper breaths. Lizzie was aglow. Seeing her sister's happiness eased every ache in Ren's body. She looked at Hank.

"Thank you," she said under her breath.

He waved a 'no worries' with a half-smirk.

They stood in that spot until the birds flew away to the rocky beach below. Ren pulled off her cap and gave it to Lizzie.

"Here you go, bug. I think my hat's warmer than yours is."

Lizzie put it on.

"Thanks," she said and put her arms up. Ren kneeled and hugged her. They held each other until Hank said it was time to go.

———

The group set up camp near a forest trail just before dark. Lizzie and Peter worked on the fire while Ren and Hank set up the new tent—no small task while tethered with a seven-foot rope. Worse yet, the small print instructions were confusing and difficult to read in the fading light. After thirty minutes at it, Hank and his stomach were both grumbling.

Staring at the little booklet, he extended one arm to Ren.

"Here, pass me that pole."

"That one's not long enough for this part," she answered.

"No, I'm sure that pole's meant to go on this side. The longer one goes over there."

"This is the longer one," Ren corrected.

"No, it can't be. The longer ones are blue, like this one."

"That one's green," said Ren.

"No, it's not."

"Yes, it is. It's hunter green."

Hank furrowed his brow, examining the labeled diagram. He exhaled what sounded like the start of a swearword.

"Hold on, we're getting this all jumbled up. Just hand me the one you've got. Then come back over here and hold this, and I'll get it sorted. Geez, by the time we get this tent up, it will be morning."

Ren passed the pole to Hank. He paused as he compared the tent pieces to each other.

"Oh, yeah, that one is green." Hank ripped the plastic bag off the new pole. "Why the heck would they make the colors so similar? I can't read this. Pete, pass me the flashlight." Then Hank began muttering to himself. "I've thrown up dozens of tents, I don't know why this one is such a blasted pain…"

Peter handed him the light. The fire was now burning strong, so Peter and Lizzie could just watch and enjoy the entertainment.

"Crikey, could they have made this print any smaller?… Okay, wait. You're right. It does go there. Ugh, come back this way. For the love of Mike…I gotta take this apart."

Ren sauntered around the tent, giving Lizzie a wink and a smile.

"Ok, now I gotta extend this one," Hank growled and picked up another folded rod, "and lock…it...together."

The rod refused to snap into place. Hank braced one end against a pine tree and pushed harder. The tree bark chipped off, the rod flew into the brush, Hank lost his balance, and kicked the sack of remaining pieces into a bush.

"Blasted son of a cross-eyed jackal lunatic imbecile who made this bloody tent!"

Ren, Peter, and Lizzie burst out laughing.

———

For dinner, they ate black beans with smoked ham. As the last morsels were scraped from their mugs, Hank pulled a jar of tayberry jam from his pack and smeared it on a piece of bread.

"You brought Sally's jam?" Lizzie chirped.

"Yep, three little jars of it. I figured it would be worth it for a morale booster." Hank took a big bite. Then he moaned and sighed in a big show of how scrumptious it was.

Lizzie scooted next to Hank and reached for the treat.

"I want some!"

"Mmm, me too," Ren chimed in.

"Oh no, this stuff is too good. It's all for me," Hank declared, pulling the jar to his chest.

"What? You're not gonna share at all? Just a little?" Lizzie pleaded.

"Nope, not a bite."

"Seriously, dude?" Peter scoffed. "You're really not gonna give us any?"

"Absolutely not."

Lizzie dropped her hands on her knees in a huff.

"That's total rubbish!"

"Ha," Hank chuckled. "Look who's talking like an Aussie, now." He held up his prized jar of preserves.

"Okay, you three," he announced. "I could be persuaded to share Sally's mouth-watering tayberry jam with you if you'll all repeat the following sentence: 'Hank, you are the best tent setter-upper in the world. Thank you for stickin' with it to make us a hardy shelter for the night. You're the best.' —Okay, go on."

The group begrudgingly repeated Hank's forced praise.

"Good enough! Here you go." He passed the crackers and jam around the fire. "Just one a piece, though. If we ration, these jars should last us the trip."

———

Later that night, the four of them easily fit in the tent with room to spare. They huddled together, stuffed into their line of sleeping bags, warm and cozy after a long day, but no one could sleep.

"Ren?" Lizzie whispered.

"Yeah?"

"Are we really safe in here?"

Ren heard Hank suck in a breath.

"Sure. Remember, they won't bother us if we're together, right? We'll just stay snuggled up like this all night and be fine."

As Lizzie settled, Ren examined the thin nylon fabric stretched tight above her. Will this really be enough to keep those things out?

God, please keep us alive until morning.

CHAPTER 39

REN

R en woke to the sound of a banshee call in the distance. She bolted upright to find Hank and Lizzie already awake. He was helping her roll up her sleeping bag.

"Did you hear that?" Ren asked.

"Yeah, it sounded like the thing was just passing by. We're alright," Hank said. "Bad dreams?"

"What?"

"You were tossin' over there like you were having a nightmare."

"Oh, I don't remember." Ren rubbed her eyes and then reached for her pack. "Did it rain last night?"

"Sure did. Lizzie, go on and wake up Sleeping Beauty. It's time we get going."

Lizzie inched over to Peter's sack and rubbed the tuft of hair sticking out the top.

"Peter? It's time to get up," she hummed. "The early bird gets the worm."

The lumpy bag grunted and rolled over. "But the second mouse gets the cheese," he muttered.

They ate a quick breakfast of nuts and jam on crackers, then started hiking just before sunrise. The dampness in the air cut through to Ren's bones. Lizzie started the day out chatty, but as the rocky hills and muddy trails became more challenging, she grew quiet like the rest of them. They were all saving their breath to keep up with Hank's pace.

Between the heavy clouds and the thick tree canopy, the forest was especially dark and gloomy. Pop's absence felt even more painful now that Ren had had time to really miss him. He would have been spouting cheesy words of encouragement and facts about plants to keep their spirits up.

Every hour or so, Ren heard movement and soft, shrill calls in the trees.

In front, Hank was holding his rifle in case they came across something for dinner. He stopped to look overhead, and Ren came up next to him.

"What do you hope to find out here?" Ren asked. "Squirrels? Or rabbits, maybe?"

"Anything, really. Mind you, we're making a decent racket through this bush. We're probably scaring everything off."

"Oh, sorry." Ren tried to lighten her steps.

Hank smirked and shook his head.

"It's okay. I used to be a noisy hunter as a kid. My dad got real peeved at me, but we never came home empty-handed."

"Are you and your dad close?" Ren asked. She squeezed her shoulder straps.

"Yeah…well, we *were*. He was disappointed when I told him I wanted to go to school for marine biology instead of the military. Ever since we started losing the reef to ocean warming, Australians have been panicked about the depleted fish and loss of tourism. That, paired with the wildfires and droughts, has made for a rough go of it the past few years. I wanted to work on engineering new heat-resistant corals. He didn't understand. We were barely talking when I had to leave with this whale study group."

Hank held up an overhanging branch for Ren.

"I'm sure he misses you," Ren said, then cringed at how cliche and phony it sounded.

"Yeah, I know he does. I miss him, too. He's a good dad, just strict and pretty conservative. It drove me mad when Dad always said there are a lot worse things to worry about than climate change. Ha, I doubt he ever imagined something like what we've got now, though." Hank glanced behind them at Peter and Lizzie. "Anyway, that's why he pushed this army training on me since I was a kid. It grew to be a real pain, but I guess I was able to help Minna a lot more because of it."

Ren focused on the butt of Hank's rifle sticking out behind his jacket sleeve. He wore the weapon with the same ease as his backpack.

Ren wondered if a bullet could kill a banshee.

"Your dad sounds tough," she said after a moment. "At least you don't need to worry about him being alone over there."

"Well, if your theory's right, he's in a safer spot than we are, right?"

"Yes, that's right."

Hank stepped up and over a large fallen log.

"I just hope your boat's still there." He turned to look at her. "It's a long way to Sydney. How good a sailor are ya?" His tone carried a hint of skepticism as he reached out to help her over the log.

"Pretty good," Ren replied. She ignored his hand and leaped over it in one bound. "If you get us to the boat and my mother, I'll get us to Sydney."

"Good. It's a deal," Hank agreed.

Even if I have to paddle us half the way, we are going to make it.

———

The travelers continued through an old-growth forest full of cedar, spruce, and Douglas fir trees, towering at two hundred feet or more. The sun had come out, casting columns of light through the canopy and golden pools all around them. Huge soft ferns blanketed the ground, and the air smelled crisp and clean.

The three siblings would occasionally stop to enjoy the beauty of their surroundings, but Hank pushed them to keep moving. They'd gone   so   far   now   that Ren couldn't believe Fitz or his gang would ever catch them. But Hank wouldn't let up. He kept their breaks short and their days long. No one complained, though. By this point, they were all used to hard work and discomfort. Hank seemed impressed by their grit.

Ren was proud of them, too.

———

By noon on the fourth day, their trail came to a black two-lane highway cutting through dense pines. Ren and Hank edged to the tree line to check that the coast was clear.

"Ok, we're gonna go across quickly. Keep close and quiet," Hank directed.

"The road is completely empty, Hank. I think we're okay," Peter gibed.

"Look, we've had an easy time so far..." Hank began.

Lizze scoffed.

"You think it's been *easy*?"

"*But* we're still in danger," Hank insisted. "There are heaps of nasty folks out here besides Fitz, and it's best they don't see us. We're closer to people now than we've been before. We gotta be careful, got it?"

Ren nodded.

"Yeah," Peter sighed, "I got it."

"Okay, let's go," said Hank.

The four hustled out from the trees and toward the road. Ren felt relief when her foot hit the solid asphalt after days of uneven trails.

Before she took another step, she heard it. The piercing sounds of banshees rang out from down the road, heading right for them.

"Get back! Everyone, back to the trees!" Hank ordered. The family rushed back to the cover of the woods. The horde's shrieking grew louder—so loud Ren could barely hear the car that was speeding around the far bend. She hadn't seen a driving car in months.

It was a little red Camry, probably ten years old, with a

busted headlight. As the car raced toward them, a screeching tornado flew just above it. Based on the sound and wind, there may have been fifty of them or more, shaking the trees on both sides of the road.

Ren, Hank, Peter, and Lizzie covered their ears and crouched together in the nook of two trees. Ren craned her neck around a bush to see a woman, maybe in her late twenties, driving alone. She was sobbing at the wheel, swerving this way and that, as the banshees swarmed around her like a pulsing mirage, obscuring the trees and the car. Ren turned away from the blast of dried leaves from the road.

Ren looked back just as a loud whomp punched the car's hood, leaving a dent the size of a washbin. The vehicle jerked left on the asphalt and careened into a tree a hundred feet down the road.

Hank and Ren stared at each other.

What do we do?

Ren could barely think over the sound of the woman's screams, the banshee howls, the wind, and the hammering of metal. Windows shattered as the beasts crushed the frame, one impact at a time.

Hank seemed transfixed as if he hadn't seen this kind of power from the banshees before—or what a swarm that size could do.

If they can destroy a whole car, what would possibly keep them from coming for us?

The four of them were just a few lambs against a murder of flying wolves. Who cares if they were standing close together? Why should that stop a pack this size?

234

And then the screaming stopped.

The woman was gone, vanished, devoured. Ren braced herself, praying their group wasn't next. She waited for the pack to turn towards them.

Instead, the wind dispersed through the woods and further down the road.

When it was quiet, the four looked at each other in shock, relief...and guilt. They were okay, yes, but could they have done something?

Ren was glad to see Peter had shielded Lizzie's eyes.

At least she hadn't watched.

They lumbered to the street. In the middle of the road, Ren stopped. She stared at the glass lying on the pavement and the mangled car. Her heart started pounding. She stepped toward the wreckage, and the rope around her waist tightened.

At once, a shrill call swooped just above her. Peter snapped at Ren's tether and grabbed her arm. They both fell back to the ground. Ren and her brother looked at each other for the first time since they'd left the lighthouse.

She wanted to thank him, but she couldn't catch her breath. Peter stood up and turned away.

CHAPTER 40

PETER

The following day, Peter woke to sunshine and slightly warmer temperatures. He tied his jacket to his pack, eager to let his swampy armpits breathe for a while.

Sally's apple cider-baking soda deodorant just isn't cutting it. I smell like B.O. flavored salad dressing.

Hank had snared a raccoon overnight, which was served up for breakfast. Peter scarfed it with a smear of jam and thought of how awesome a cold glass of milk would taste with it.

"If we can bag more of these guys, that's less food we'll have to scavenge later from stores or vacant houses," Hank had said. "I'm not keen to get close to people, but I reckon we'll have to."

Sure enough, by mid-afternoon, they came upon a bit of civilization, a vast train yard with a dozen parallel tracks slicing through the field before them. There must have been a hundred old freight cars lined up in rows.

"Looks abandoned," Peter said.

"Yeah, that's what we thought about the road," Ren cautioned. "Should we go around? Hank, what do you think?"

Hank checked his watch, then scanned the length of the

yard.

"Naw, going around is a long route. If we're gonna make it to the next camp spot before nightfall, we gotta pass through it."

Lizzie held up her pointer fingers in absolute agreement.

"Yes, shorter is better."

Peter gave her a low-five.

"I'm with Liz. Let's cross."

Hank led them, silently weaving through the staggered freight cars. They hopped over gravel patches to stay on the quieter grass and wood. Peter was hoping to find food, but all the boxcars seemed empty or locked. They kept a good pace, and before they knew it, just a few rows remained to clear the field.

A nearby voice froze Peter in his tracks. He tugged on Ren's rope, then waved the group closer to an old black engine. From what Peter could hear, three adults stood between them and the woods.

It was difficult to make out what the strangers were saying, but Peter could tell from their tone and laughter that these were not like Minna's people.

They sound like the tool bag bullies from school who used to mess with Ren.

Peter got down on his hands and knees to look under the red boxcar behind the engine. He watched three sets of booted legs walk across the gravel, kicking rocks as they went. A cigarette flicked between them, and a shotgun barrel hung below one set of knees. The three stopped on the other side of the boxcar, and their voices became clear.

"There's a few more open ones that way," one said.

"Any that don't smell like a toilet?"

"Probably not, but they smell better than you."

"Shhh," said the third person, a woman. "I thought I heard something."

Peter held his breath.

"Like what?" said the first.

"I don't know, just something."

"Can we please just find an open car now? If those things are here, I don't want to be outside."

"Yeah, okay, let's cross through here," the woman agreed.

The trio slid into the space between the red boxcar Peter stood next to and the blue one behind it. Peter quickly waved Ren, Hank, and Lizzie into the gap between their side of the boxcar and the engine.

Peter could hear the clang of metal as the others maneuvered over the connector hitches, one at a time.

Hank had everyone untethered. He lifted Lizzie above the iron clamps, then she and Ren navigated the web of obstacles, careful not to rattle the dangling chains. Their dull thumps were masked well enough by the racket the other group was making.

Hank went through next, but his foot caught a cable. It snapped back with a clang, and he stumbled onto the gravel. Peter froze as the movement near the blue car hushed.

"Hey, did you hear it *that* time?" the woman argued.

"Yeah, I did."

Hank looked at Peter and motioned for him to crawl below the hardware. Peter passed Hank his pack, then slid his body beneath the hitches, the rocks digging into his hands and knees.

"It's coming from this way," the woman said. "Check by that engine up there."

Ren and Lizzie hid behind the engine, and Hank stepped up on the red boxcar ladder. Once Peter was through, Hank yanked him up the ladder just as the woman passed from the red boxcar to the engine, followed closely by the other two.

"Check under there," the woman ordered. A man grunted and dropped onto all fours. Peter watched Ren grip Lizzie tighter, holding her perfectly still behind the train's rear wheels. The man paused for what seemed like ages, then let out a wheezing sigh as he stood.

"Nothin'."

"Alright, let's move around the engine and check the other side," the woman said.

Ren looked up at Peter and Hank for a plan. There was no way the four of them could move without being heard.

The three sets of footsteps shuffled to the gap between the train car and engine—the one Peter had just passed through. Peter tapped Hank.

"Should we run?" he mouthed.

"Hey, Pam! Look over there," one of the men said from behind her. "That open car over there. It's got stuff in it."

The footsteps retreated, stopping several car lengths away.

"Looks like food boxes," the man exclaimed.

Peter gritted his teeth.

Aw, man. We coulda gotten more food.

"Well, hop up there and see," Pam said.

Hank softly snapped his fingers at Peter and the girls, then pointed toward the woods.

The sound of the man banging and thumping on the car was enough to mask their escape.

They were just a few yards into the woods when an explosion of shrieks and pounding metal came from behind them.

"They're in here!" a man cried. "Help me out! Help me…"

Then his voice was gone. Banshee screeches rumbled from the steel nest into the air as the other two people screamed and fled for cover.

Peter gulped.

That could've been me.

The family stayed motionless as the train yard quieted.

A sudden chorus of chirps and growls sounded above them. The attack had disturbed another large flock of banshees resting in the trees that surrounded Peter and the others. The branches creaked and bobbed under the shifting of the stirred flock. Ren braced Lizzie as Peter scanned the canopy. He spotted a rippling blur hop from one limb to another, then vanish. Within moments, they were silent again.

Oh man. Those sneaky gremlins are everywhere.

———

Set on avoiding people for the rest of the day, they kept to the forest.

Lizzie's silence hung over all of them like a storm cloud. For hours, her knit-covered head drooped over her chest. Her steps dragged through the icy leaves, and her hands hung limp. At times, her breath quickened, and Peter knew she was remembering something awful. But there had been too many awful somethings for him to guess which one.

Peter squeezed his shoulder straps. This new reality was taking a big toll on his little sister. And Peter couldn't protect her

240

from it. He couldn't tell her it would get better. He could only tie on her tether and lead her from one scary ordeal to another.

What could I possibly say or do to make her feel better?

Wait...

A wry smile spread across his face.

"Hey, Lizzie," he said with an exaggerated sigh. "I'm getting really bugged driving up this same old strip. I *gotta* find a new place where the kids are hip."

Lizzie paused and looked up, then kept walking.

Ren peeked over her shoulder at them with a smirk.

"My buddies and me are getting real well-known. Yeah, the bad guys know us, and they leave us alone," Ren sang softly, taunting Lizzie to take over.

Lizzie stopped again, this time letting Peter walk up next to her. She looked up with a glint in her eye and bit her bottom lip.

"Whatcha think?" Peter asked.

"I get around," Lizzie started singing. *"From town to town..."*

Peter and Ren echoed in the *"Get around, 'round, 'round, I get around"* backup, imitating the various octaves of The Beach Boys. And when Peter hit Brian Wilson's girlish pitch, Lizzie leaked a giggle.

Peter's chest warmed as Lizzie's voice grew stronger, singing one classic song after another to the beat of her livened footsteps. Hank joined in when he *thought* he knew the lyrics—usually, though, he was way off. But that seemed to make Lizzie even happier.

That's my girl.

After the musical therapy, Lizzie switched to comedy.

"Hey Hank, why was the mushroom the life of the party?" Lizzie called up to him.

"Why?"

"Because he..."

"Hey, out there!" A powerful man's voice bellowed from ahead of them. "I can see you!"

Peter's spine locked.

Oh, no.

CHAPTER 41

HANK

H ank heard the shout come from the log cabin just ahead, barely visible behind a thick patch of bushes. He cursed himself for not noticing it sooner.

Just looking at the butterflies and daisies, dummy.

"Hello? Please answer. I need your help!" the man yelled.

"Run. Everyone, run!" Hank charged, and the four dashed westward away from the house and trail, stumbling through thorny brambles. A loud gunshot rang out above them, and Hank yanked Ren and Peter down by their jackets. They ducked for cover behind dense shrubs. From there, Hank could see a tall and burly, dark-haired man standing on the front porch. The stranger looked around thirty, and his left arm was in a sling.

"Please! I'm not going to shoot you. I just fired so you'd stop," the man called out. "We need help."

"Stay down," Hank whispered to the lot. Then he yelled toward the house, "We can't help ya, mate. Please just let us pass, and we won't be a bother. Shoot at us again, and we will return fire."

"My name is Sergeant Robert Martinez. I'm here with my five-year-old son. We need to get to McChord Air Force Base just south of Tacoma. You're headed in that direction. Please, let us come with you."

Hank peeked around the tree. The man stood next to a little boy, still holding his ears from the shot.

"Look, if we pass by the base, we'll send someone back for ya!" Hank answered, hoping this would appease him.

"No one's been by in weeks. We have very little food left, and my arm is broken. It's too dangerous for me to take my son on alone. You look like good people, and I see you have kids with you. Please, can we join you?"

Hank looked at the others.

"What d'ya reckon?"

Lizzie put her hand up.

"I think we should help them."

"Why?" Peter asked.

"I dunno. They seem nice to me," she replied.

"*Nice?* Kinda trigger happy, don't you think?" he scoffed.

Lizzie shrugged.

Hank nudged Ren. "What do you want to do? We don't have a lot of food to spare."

"I think the bigger our group, the safer we'll be from banshees and whatever else," she said. "He's got a little boy. They look okay to me."

"*And*," pressed Lizzie, "since we've been rescued like six times since the boat wreck, I kinda feel like we should help someone else now, right?"

"Yeah." Peter tugged Lizzie's braid. "I guess so."

244

"Great, okay then," Hank agreed, then called above the bushes. "Take the clip out of your weapon, mate, and toss it with the gun off the porch."

Robert seemed eager to comply and held up his one good hand. Hank stood with his rifle raised next to Ren, and the two approached the porch. Hank retrieved the pistol and cartridge and stuffed both in his pocket. The boy was clutching his father's pant leg, wide-eyed and jittery. He wore a navy jacket and camo pants.

"Thank you all *so* much," Robert insisted. "I'm not sure how much longer we would have lasted."

Hank frisked Robert, then looked through his green canvas bag. Ren watched him with her pistol drawn.

Hank wondered if she could actually shoot this guy if it came to it.

"I have another knife in there and some more bullets, but that's my only gun," Robert said.

Hank found the knife, a military-grade folding blade, and handed it to Ren.

"I'm sorry again for the shot. I just…"

"Hang on, mate," Hank cut him off, then bent down to the boy. "Hey, what's your name, fella?"

"Zack," he said.

"And who's this big guy?" Hank asked, pointing to Robert.

"My dad," he said.

"What does your dad do for work, pal?"

"Um…he flies jets and helicopters and stuff," Zack answered, rubbing his nose.

"That's pretty cool. It's quiet out here. Is there anyone else with you?"

"No. It's just me and Daddy."

Hank was pleased that Zack wasn't looking up to Robert before answering.

"You're doing great. Just one more question. Your daddy looks really strong. Do ya think he could pick you up and put you on his shoulders for us? Could he do that?"

Zack shook his head.

"Um…no, he can't right now. He hurt his arm. He needs me to help him do stuff," Zack said, puffing up a bit. He was proud of himself.

"Good one, big man." Hank nodded to Ren. "That's all I got."

Ren smiled and put her pistol and the knife away. She crouched beside Zack. "Hi, my name is Ren. Would you like to come with us?"

Zack nodded as Robert rubbed his son's shoulder.

Ren pointed to the others. "This is my brother, Peter, and my sister, Lizzie."

Hank helped Robert put his backpack on over his injured arm, noting how light it was.

They really were out of food.

"Are you hungry, Zack? Do you like jam?" Ren asked. She dropped her pack at her feet.

Zack nodded. Ren pulled out the tayberry jam and spread some on a rice cracker.

"This is a special treat we get every night. Tell me what you think."

He scarfed it in one bite and grinned. "It's yummy."

246

"You bet your bottom it's yummy!" said Lizzie as she and Peter walked up to meet them.

"You can keep the rest of this jar. We have more," Ren offered.

Zack smiled as she put the lid back on and stuck it in his dinosaur bag.

"Here's some granola, too. It will hold you over until dinner." Hank handed him the small ziplock bag. Zack held it out for his dad.

"You eat that, lil' man," Robert said. "I'm okay."

"Can I tie their knots?" Lizzie scampered up the steps to fasten their tethers.

Hank had her tie Robert to his tether, and they got moving.

"So, Robert, where ya been before this?" he asked.

"When the meteors hit, we were on vacation down the coast. Our car got wrecked that first night, so we've been making our way back to my base on foot. We've gotten a few rides and shelter from nice folks, but it's been tough."

"Just the two of you traveling all this way?"

Robert glanced over his shoulder. He lowered his voice. "No, my wife was with us. The creatures took her not too far south from here."

"I'm sorry, mate."

"We came upon this cabin, found some stored food, and decided to stay until it was safe to move again."

"How did you hurt your arm?" Hank noticed the bandaging job wasn't great, and the sling was just a cut-up undershirt.

"When I heard that noise they make, I wrapped my arm around my wife's rope to pull her closer. She was just a few feet away, but they took her before I could grab her arm. When they yanked her off the tether, it snapped my wrist."

Hank stopped him. "What? It took her when she was next to you? Both you and Zack?"

Robert nodded.

"Yeah. I didn't want to chance traveling alone with him after that, particularly with my injury. I'm hoping that with a bigger group, we'll be safe. I gotta get Zack back to the fort."

"McChord is on our way. We can get you there," Hank, but his chest was clenching with alarm.

They're getting more aggressive. How long 'til keepin' close doesn't work anymore?

CHAPTER 42

REN

Throughout that day, Ren kept passing Zack more to eat. He looked like skin and bones. Ren thought of Mom and how thin she must be, praying she was still hanging on. She tried to remember how much food was at Pop's house when they'd left months ago. Had Mom gone to the store since then, or had she been making do with cereal like she often did? What if they were already too late?

Despite this reminder, Ren was pleased to have Robert and Zack with them. The two brought new life to the group, and Robert turned out to be a skilled trapper. The food he caught far outweighed what he and Zack were eating. They soon learned that despite his massive physique, Robert was just a big teddy bear. His boisterous laugh lightened everyone's spirits, even after the most dismal days. And Robert and Zack shared a bond that reminded Ren of her dad. Lizzie seemed happy to have a fresh audience for her jokes as well as a new playmate.

Zack rode on Peter's shoulders, playing the tenth round of the animal guessing game.

"I'm thinking of an animal that's really strong, and it has a

249

horn on its head."

"A rhinoceros!" guessed Lizzie.

"Nope! It's a narwhal!" he blurted. "I win!"

"What? We weren't finished guessing!" objected Lizzie.

Peter chuckled.

"A *narwhal*? Who is this kid?"

"Peter, you know what a narwhal is," Lizzie said.

"Yeah, but I don't think I did when I was his age."

As Ren listened, she remembered going with Peter to the aquarium when he was five, and she was seven. He pulled her from one exhibit to the next, announcing fun facts about each animal.

Ren looked up and caught Hank staring at her. She flushed as his gaze stayed fixed, completely at ease and unapologetic. They just kept walking, looking at each other for a long, peaceful minute.

"Hank, look," Robert said. Hank blinked and turned to follow Robert's eyeline.

"Ok, my turn," Lizzie continued. "I'm thinking of an animal that's gray, and it's really, really big…"

Lizzie stopped just before running into Peter. The group stared in awe at the vast, crushed path of trees where a huge meteor had mowed through them. It rested deep in the earth, maybe seventy-five yards away. It was enormous—the size of a two-story house. Ren imagined how many creatures had hatched from it and shuddered.

Where did they come from? How will we ever defeat them all?

She felt Lizzie grasp her hand.

250

Then they fell back in line and walked on.

———

That night, Ren could barely sleep. The tent had gotten snug with the two new campers, and she couldn't get comfortable. Ren rolled to her side, curling her arms under the covers. The lyrics to a song popped into her head.

"I know I love you. And you love the sea..." she murmured. It was the last song she'd heard with her dad at the concert that night. Her fingertips brushed the scar on her arm, tracing over it again and again. She squeezed her eyes tight.

There was a sudden screech, then the thumps of something landing near their campsite.

Two closer shrills came again, and Ren's heart sped. She wanted to wake the others but was too scared to whisper or move. Scratching and growling circled the tent. Faint, undefined, moonlit shadows bobbed around the vinyl over rustling leaves. The sound of a breathy whistle accompanied an inward bulge on the tent wall.

Lizzie rolled over and nuzzled against Ren, exhaling into her shoulder. Ren hugged her sister and held her breath.

The growling stopped, and the figures swept away into the woods. All was quiet again.

Trembling, Ren kissed Lizzie's head. She reached over and grabbed the back of Peter's shirt. She squeezed the handful of fabric until her knuckles went white.

Then Ren released her grip and let her hand rest beside him, her pinky just touching his sleeping bag as she fell asleep.

CHAPTER 43

REN

**November 7th, 2027 - 35 miles south of McChord Air Base.
64 days after.**

R en walked beside Robert as they ascended a steep, wooded
hill in mid-afternoon. Robert carried Zack in his good
arm, huffing and puffing.

"Daddy, stop breathing so hard," Zack insisted.

"Stop breathing hard!" Robert scoffed. "Easy for you to say.
Your dad's not in as great shape as he used to be, kid."

"Maybe you need to exercise more," the five-year-old
suggested.

"Oh, yeah? That's a good idea. In the meantime, how about
we switch places, and you carry me for a bit?"

Zack shook his head. "That's silly."

Hank and Ren looked at each other and laughed.

"Yes, very silly," Robert panted.

At the top of the hill, the group came to another two-lane
highway and a sign that read, "Welcome to Garner Falls."

Below them, about a thousand homes and a town square sat
in the basin of a valley. The distance to go north across

it wasn't too far, but the town stretched wide to the east and west.

"What do you reckon?" Hank asked Ren and Robert.

"I think we should take the eastern route around it. The terrain is trickier, and the route is a bit longer, but there won't be as much risk of people being over there," Robert said.

Hank studied the landscape. "Nah, I think that will keep us elevated and exposed near town for too long. Someone could see us. I say cut through just inside the western edge, where the homes are mostly damaged. It's a shorter distance, there won't be as many people, and it'll be easier to stay hidden. We'll also have a better chance of finding food. Ren, what do you think?"

Ren was pretty beat, so the choice was easy. "I say we take the west side," she said.

"Okay, looks like we're going west," Robert said.

Hank turned to the rest of the group. "Alright, let's take a quick breather, then we'll head down. We'll have to move through town quickly and quietly, so be ready to hustle."

Ren stared at the homes below her. They reminded her of where Grandma used to live. Ren remembered the last time she heard Mom talk about her while making one of Grandma's cookie recipes.

"I miss your grandma a lot...but she's always with me. She's with you, too, ya know? Just like me and Dad, Pop and Pete, and Lizzie. That's the great thing about having people who love you. You're never alone."

Peter came up beside Ren to look at the view.

"Peter, do you remember Grandma's old house? With all those crazy wind sculptures in the backyard?" Ren asked.

"Yeah, kinda." Peter's tone was actually lukewarm.

"We watched those things for hours together."

Peter squinted his eyes over the town in a daze, as if searching for a clear memory of that backyard.

Ren fiddled with her braid.

"Peter, I wanted to say…"

"Alright, guys, let's go," Hank announced. "I'll lead. Robert, you bring up the rear."

Ren swallowed her words as the group rose, all swinging their packs back on their shoulders. Peter helped Robert put his arm through his straps, and Robert fastened the waist buckle with his fingertips.

"Can you clasp the chest buckle for me? Can't get an angle on it," Robert asked.

Peter nodded and snapped it in place.

———

Slipping through the empty neighborhoods, the group came across one house with a garage apartment in the back, barely visible from the street. The door had been left open, and the inside was dusty and abandoned.

Hank found the pantry.

"Oodellahlee, lookie here!" he exclaimed in a whisper.

There was canned soup, pears, peas, carrots, and some assorted dry goods, including rice, crackers, and oatmeal. He began pulling things out in armfuls. Ren had never seen Hank so jubilant.

He must really be sick of campfire squirrel.

They found some clean clothes, and everyone took a quick

cold shower. The crew split their haul evenly between bags and left in high spirits just thirty minutes later.

The route led them to an industrial area. Some construction vehicles were left open around the property between the handful of vacant warehouses.

A narrow pass between two brick buildings and a dirt yard beyond it was all that stood between the group and the woods. Single file, the six crossed through the alley, stepping around piles of broken glass and garbage.

"Gonna eat well tonight," Hank said with a grin. "Must be our lucky day."

Before Ren could answer, she felt a sharp yank on her tether as Robert and Zack screamed behind her.

CHAPTER 44

REN

R en whipped around to find Robert on the ground, wrestling and exchanging blows with two men. They were medium-sized, maybe in their thirties. One was bearded, with red hair and ripped jeans, and the other wore a tattered IBM jacket. A third fair-haired man with a black eye had Robert's gun pointed at the rest of them before Hank could raise his rifle. He had on mismatched hiking boots.

"Hold it right there. *Right* there! Put your guns on the ground," he shouted.

Hank squeezed a fist, then slowly obeyed. Ren cursed herself for leaving her pistol in her pack.

Out of reach again!

Peter grabbed and untethered Zack, who had been pulled through the dirt by his strap to Robert.

"Look, mate, please just let our friend go, and we'll give ya whatever you want," Hank said, raising his hands and inching forward.

"Move any closer, and we'll stab your buddy," the blond one warned. "We just want the gear."

Ren felt powerless as Robert took another swift punch to the back of the neck. The memory of getting beaten by Fitz inflamed Ren's face and gut. Robert could only land a few blows before the men had him secured from behind, tugging him by his backpack further and further away from the group. He tried kicking and squirming out of their grasp, but his resistance was met with more jabs until he was limp.

"The belt! Unlatch the belt!" The armed man barked, his gun still fixed on Hank. The other two unbuckled the waist strap and yanked again, now putting more pressure on his broken arm as they continued to drag him further away. Robert was now nearly unconscious. The chest buckle caught against his neck. Peter held Zack, still crying for his dad, and shielded Lizzie behind him. She had her head buried in Peter's jacket.

"It's not comin', Jay!" the redhead hollered.

By this point, they had Robert fifty feet away and were still going.

"Look," Hank tried again, taking a step, "you can have the pack and gun, but just let us come get our guy, okay? Just don't leave him alone out there, alright?"

"Don't come any closer!" Jay snapped. "Eddie, get the chest latch!"

The redhead pulled a blade from a belt harness and cut through the last strap. The pack came loose.

"Wait! Please, don't leave him," Hank yelled.

"Stay back!"

The men peeled the pack off of Robert's shoulders as he groaned in pain.

He's too far away. They're going to leave him!

Ren looked at Hank, and he nodded to her, then dropped his bag. She pulled off the slip knot connecting her to Lizzie and set her pack down as well. Zack's cries vibrated Ren's fingers as she tried to focus. She crouched slightly, tilted forward, and planted the ball of her right foot a step behind her.

"Let's go!" Jay yelled as the IBM man slung Robert's duffel bag on his back.

"Stop! Ya can't leave him alone out there," pleaded Hank.

Robert grabbed at Jay's foot, tripping him to the ground. The gun fired and shot Eddie in the calf. The redhead screamed and fell, now bleeding through his pant leg. Jay kicked a boot into Robert's chest to free himself, then staggered out of reach. Hank took three strides closer, but Jay jerked his rifle around and shot at Hank's feet.

"Get back!"

The IBM man threw Eddie's arm over his shoulder and started hauling him away.

Ren pinched her pendant, then cocked her arm in front of her.

Robert's alone! He's all alone!

Ren's whole body twitched, aching to spring forward.

The shriek of a banshee echoed overhead, and dust from the yard swirled up behind them. Jay recoiled at the screech. He turned to flee with the other two.

Hank's voice fired like a race gun.

"Now!"

Ren sprinted.

She stretched, pushed, and swung her body, matching Hank stride for stride with the cyclone just behind them. Another shriek

258

rang in her ears, taunting her as the girls had during her last race so long ago, but Ren didn't falter.

Hank slid through the loose dirt alongside Robert as Ren lunged on top of him, shielding him from the piercing tornado. Ren's hair thrashed above her. She buried her face from the gritty windstorm as Hank slung his arm across her back.

Finally, the yard quieted, and the wind receded.

Hank's breathing stayed heavy against Ren's forehead until he withdrew his arm. Ren sat up and wiped the dirt off her face with her sleeve.

Robert groaned.

"Ya okay, mate?" Hank asked.

Robert's face wounds were starting to swell. He also had a split lip and a bloody nose.

"Super. Except my head is exploding. I can't see from this eye. Arg...and I may have a cracked rib." He coughed then grunted in pain. "Next time, I get to pick the route, okay?"

"Deal," Hank agreed.

"Daddy!" Zack cried from Peter's arms.

"I'm okay, pal! Daddy's okay."

Ren pulled a bandana from her pocket to dab Robert's nose while Hank looked over at Zack, still wailing for his dad. Hank seemed transfixed, his breath wavering.

Ren reached out to calm him, lightly touching his knee.

"Hank?"

Hank snatched her hand up and kissed her palm. He pressed it to his cheek, exhaling onto her wrist.

"Thank you," he murmured.

CHAPTER 45

PETER

That night, Peter tended the campfire. He was next to Robert, who lay flat on the ground like a pummeled log. Every movement seemed agonizing for him.

"How're you doing?" Peter asked.

"I'll live. I think they really jacked up my arm, though," he said. "Your sister did a great job rewrapping it. She said she's bandaged you up a time or two."

Peter glanced down at his left wrist.

"Yeah. I used to get hurt a lot on my skateboard before Mom finally made me quit." He flinched at the thought of his mom. It had been so long since he'd seen her, and a lifetime since she forbade him from skateboarding.

"You're my only Peter," she'd say. *"I don't have any backups."*

Robert repositioned his broken arm on his chest. He caught Peter staring at him.

"Something bothering you, Pete?"

"No. I mean,...um...can I ask you a question?

You don't have to answer," Peter stammered.

"Sure, pal. What's up?"

"Why do you think those things attacked your wife, even though you were together? I mean... Sorry, I just..." Peter quieted as Hank came over to check the hare he had cooking on the fire. Peter didn't really want to include others in this talk, but Robert didn't seem to mind.

"No, it's okay. You know, I've been thinking about that every night since it happened."

"Since what happened?" Hank asked.

"Pete's asking about my wife, Tracy—why she was taken."

Hank shifted and poked at the rabbit.

"All I can say is," Robert continued, "after we had Zack, my wife got something called the 'baby blues.' It's when new moms get some degree of depression. It's a common thing, but it usually passes. Hers never did. We tried getting her help, but it just got worse. Then she started getting sick. Couldn't sleep. Lost her appetite. Her therapist told us her state of mind was affecting her whole body. Her condition was poisoning her, essentially."

Now, Peter felt *really* uncomfortable. He had no idea Robert was going to talk about his late wife's mental health. It felt super intrusive. Peter picked up a stick and started making circles in the dirt while Hank opened a can of stew.

Hank is probably sorry he came over here.

Robert went on. "Have you ever heard about how certain animals, like wolves, can smell fear or vulnerability? Well, I wondered if it's not just being physically detached that sets them off, but also feeling alone, you know? Feeling isolated—vulnerable."

"Do you really think that?" Peter asked. He recalled seeing viral videos of dogs that knew when people were about to have a seizure or heart attack.

"I'm not a scientist, but maybe these things can sense inner turmoil and weakness, and they go after it. Unfortunately for us, the more loved ones they take, the more loss and suffering they inflict, the more damaged we all feel." Robert took a deep breath and looked up at the tree canopy. "I'm sorry, I don't have a better answer for you, Pete. Right now, the best you can do is keep close to your family. Be grateful for the people you have, right?"

Peter nodded. Then he glanced across the fire at Ren. She was scratching Lizzie's back, fixated on the fire. The shadows flickered across her pensive expression.

Peter remembered the last time Ren had wrapped his arm. He was eleven, and she was fourteen. He'd fallen at the skate park, showing off for his friends. Bret had laughed and called him a loser. He was nearly crying by the time he got home and told Ren. She wiped his face and called Bret a skunk buzzard. Then she bandaged him up, put his arm in a sling, and helped him get comfortable on the couch. They ate cookies and watched a scary movie until Mom got home.

"Love you, dude," she'd said.

He hadn't heard that from Ren in a long time.

CHAPTER 46

REN

R en blinked as Hank crossed in front of her view of the fire. He placed the pot in the coals and handed her a slice of cooked rabbit. By the time she accepted it, she couldn't remember what she'd been thinking about.

The two of them hadn't spoken since he'd kissed her hand. Her pulse quickened.

"Thanks. Looks good," Ren said, averting her eyes. She focused on the tender meat, dampening and singeing her fingertips. She blew on it a few times.

"Yeah, came out okay," Hank agreed. He waited for her reaction.

Oh, no. Please don't watch me eat.

Ren tried to look polite as she bit off pieces of the barbecue now dripping down her hands. She was sure a sliver or meat had landed in her hair. She decided to wait and check after he'd left.

But instead of leaving, he sat down and leaned next to her against the log.

Great.

Ren brushed her hair back over her shoulder with her pinky.

"Thanks again for comin' with me to get Robert. You're pretty quick—for a gal." Hank winked.

"'*For a gal*'?" Ren bantered. "Well, I used to run track."

She swallowed the last bite, then propped up her soiled fingers, searching for a way to clean them.

"Why d'ya stop?" Hank asked. He held his canteen over her hands and dribbled a bit of water over them. She flicked the drops off and wiped her hands on her jeans.

"Er...when my dad died, and I just didn't wanna do it anymore. So, I quit."

"And now?" Hank recapped the canteen and set it beside him. When he leaned back again, his jacket sleeve rested against hers.

"What do you mean?" Ren asked.

"What were your plans for college? Ya must've been startin' senior year before all this happened."

Ren fiddled with her zipper, wishing she could change the subject. What could she say that wouldn't sound pathetic? Right before all this happened, she hadn't been any better. In fact, she'd been even more directionless, unmotivated, and distant.

Like a moody zombie.

Mom begged her to start looking at schools, but Ren hadn't bothered. She even blew off her SAT.

It seemed the collapse of the world was the only cure for the coma she'd been in.

Now, here was Hank, who had the requisite skills for the military but the passion to pursue marine biology. And what had she done? She'd given up on school, sports, and even her best friend, Annie.

"I don't know. I never figured out what I really wanted to do after high school," she said finally.

"Ren, you're a genius. All that stuff you figured out with the meteors? It's amazing. Ya coulda gotten an astrophysics degree with your eyes shut. Ya still could if the world ever goes back to normal. They'll need folks like you more than ever."

Ren's cheeks felt warm. She'd never thought of herself like that. All the stuff she and her father had talked about usually made her feel like a geek. It certainly wasn't something she'd broadcast to guys.

"Tell me something," Hank went on. "Tell me something cool about the stars that only a brainiac like you would know."

"Umm…"

"Like the North Star up there." He pointed up to the bright pinprick in the sky. "Tell me about it."

"Well, that one is actually *not* the North Star," she said. "It's Venus. Didn't you learn about navigational astronomy in marine biology? You're on boats all the time."

"Yeah, well, guess I should have." He smirked. Then he reached toward her face.

What's he doing? Oh, man—Is he going to kiss me?

She tensed as his fingers brushed tangled leaves from her hair. The outside of his thumb dusted her cheekbone.

"Sorry, ya still got leaves on ya," he murmured. He pulled up one knee and rested his elbow on it. "Go on. What were you saying?"

Wait…What was I saying?

"Um, thanks." Ren went on. "So, the brightest object in the

sky, besides the sun and the moon, is Venus. Three billion years ago, Venus was a lot like Earth. It was temperate, with land, oceans, and probably life."

"Really? So, what happened to poor Venus?"

"It absorbed too much radiation from the sun. Eventually, the oceans began to evaporate. The greenhouse effect from water vapor is worse than CO_2, methane, or any other gas. Now, it's an inhospitable pressure cooker covered in dense reflective clouds. That's why it's so bright."

"Huh, so is this where we're headed, you s'pose? I've protested against fossil fuels, but I never worried about water vapor."

"Well, the one good thing about the apocalypse is that now the world's carbon footprint is basically nil."

"Well, that's a relief." Hank chuckled as he sat up to stir the pot.

Ren stared at the fire again. After a few moments, her mind wandered back to her days on the track team and the last time she had raced.

It was on that day. The day of the concert.

The day of the accident.

CHAPTER 47

REN

15 years old
March 7th, 2025 - Seattle, Washington
2 years until.

R en pinched the pendant on her necklace. She crouched and
tilted forward, planting her right foot in a lunge behind her,
twisting the ball of her foot into the clay. She spread her fingers
behind the starting line and raised her eyeline to the horizon.

This is it.

The crack of the gunshot ripped through Ren like a current.

Her muscles, joints, and bones ignited. She sprinted like a
machine with synchronized propellers—digging, stretching,
pumping, rotating, then again. Her brown ponytail whipped
through the wind behind her. All Ren could hear was the rhythm
of her breath and the crunch of the track beneath her cleats. Her
form was perfect, her energy like a jet engine.

Ren was about to be the only freshman ever to make the
Cyprus High varsity relay team. They were State Champs
and practically high school royalty. The exhilaration of the sure
win tugged at the corners of her mouth. She had to suppress it. A

smile wasn't best for breathing.

Another marker passed as Ren charged around the track. She glanced left, searching for her one opponent, Chrissy Brates.

The demon Barbie doll.

But Chrissy wasn't even in her periphery. Ren was kicking her mean, plastic, perfectly made-up face—and it felt amazing.

And when Ren made the team, all the other relay girls, girls she idolized, would be nicer to her. More accepting. Maybe even friendly.

Stay focused. Push harder.

Peter's voice cut across the field from the stands.

"C'mon, Ren! You got this!" He'd left baseball practice to watch her. Ren was glad he'd be the first to know she'd made it. She just had to keep this pace.

Then, alongside the track, the voices of her would-be teammates rose above Peter's, screaming for Chrissy.

"Go, Chris! Push it, girl!"

"Don't let her beat you! Faster, Chrissy!"

She glanced left again. Chrissy was still a few lengths behind.

Emily, the team anchor, cut across the track, out of the coach's earshot. As Ren flew toward her, she glanced at Emily for some sign of support, but her face was pursed in disgust.

"We don't want you on our team, Lauren!" she hissed as Ren blew by. "Chrissy, crush that dirty hag. Move it!"

Ren tried to ignore, maintaining her fighting lead. She rounded the second turn, hurtling toward the line of onlookers at the finish line. But the repulsed expressions of the other two teammates were all she could see. Then Sherry mouthed a word at her, and Ren's heart turned to lead.

Moisture whisked from the side of one eye. Her breath lost its rhythm.

Then…Ren started to slow.

"Don't let up, Ren!" shouted Peter. "Finish strong! Run!"

Ren's chest deflated, and her gaze dropped. She didn't want to look at her brother for this.

In the final leg, Ren let Chrissy brush past her and win.

Ren hunched over, panting, pressing her palms on her knees. Chrissy recovered beside her, hands on her hips. It was her big moment to brag, but she took the victory without a word.

She knows I had her beat. The last thing she wants is a rematch.

As Chrissy walked to her fans, Peter hopped down from the stands and jogged over to her. He handed Ren her water bottle.

"You were flying, Ren. Forget relay. You'll own the hundred this season."

Then he reached out for a low-five.

"Gotta get back to practice," he said. "See you at home."

———

Ren walked up the steps to her front door, hair dripping from the gym shower. She dumped her bags by the stairs, flipped off her shoes, and went up to her mother's studio.

"Mom?" she said as she leaned through the door frame. Ren's mom was under headphones. Paint speckled her hands, smock, and hair. She wore faded nursing scrubs and the house shoes with dingy lining. Hobbes, their golden retriever, lay in Ren's favorite armchair. Seeing Ren, he lifted his head and whapped his tail on the cushion.

Ren stroked his head until he settled, then wrapped her arm around her mother's shoulders.

"You're home!" Mom said with a start. "How was your day? Did you make relay?"

"No, Chrissy beat me."

"Oh, sorry, sweetheart. I know you wanted it. Next year, maybe, ok?" She rubbed Ren's arm and gave it a squeeze.

"Yeah, maybe..." Red nodded toward the painting. "Hey, you're almost done."

Mom beamed at her accomplishment. "I am. It needs one more thing, though..." She handed Ren the brush.

Ren bit her lip and grinned. She wet the brush with a flaky gold paint and added three light touches to the canvas.

"Now, it's done," Mom declared, then took the brush and plunked it in the water jar.

Peter wandered in from the hall, his hair and clothes caked in sweaty clay.

"Hey," Mom said. "How was baseball?"

"Dominated. Coach wanted me to remind you about Allstars."

Mom sighed.

"Allstars...sooo much driving. But if you want to, we'll do it. We'll have lots more time to talk about responsible dating and adolescent development and..."

Peter's eyes widened.

"I'm sure Dad can take me," he broke in.

"Well, if that's what you want," she said with a playful shrug.

Mom's phone pinged. She read it and stood.

"Yikes, I gotta motor!" Mom dashed out and down the hall. She called over her shoulder. "Peter, please take a shower. I love you, but you're polluting the house!"

"Wait, you're going out tonight?" Ren yelled after her. She knew what that meant for her—babysitting duty.

Not if I can help it. It's fright night at Annie's house.

A few minutes later, Ren snuggled Lizzie on the couch with a Waldo book. She had a perfect view of the front door and her case ready for when her dad walked in. Ren knew Miss Bee could probably still babysit. Sure, she charged more and cleaned up less, but Ren couldn't be expected to sit three weekends in a row.

"Hello, family!" Dad bellowed as he burst through the door and swung it closed behind him. He strutted into the den as if greeting his fans.

Dr. Nick Haley wasn't exceptionally handsome, just an average-looking guy in his early forties with a receding hairline, ears that stuck out, and an off-kilter fashion sense with too many Hawaiian shirts. But he had the presence of a rock star.

Mom gave him a kiss as she flitted through the room, and Ren saw her chance. She stood to block his escape.

"Dad…"

"Hey, there she is," Dad gushed, wrapping his arm around Ren's shoulder. "The sweetest, most considerate daughter in the world, who never minds watching her two younger siblings when she knows her parents need an evening out…."

"Dad…"

He extended his other hand with dramatic flair.

"And when people ask me how I was lucky enough to have such a daughter, I tell them heavenly angels delivered her on a carriage made of sunshine. The absolute light of my life..."

Ren stifled her smile.

"Thanks, but it won't work. Annie and I were gonna hang out. Can you please just call Miss Bee?"

"Oh, but your siblings need you," Dad implored. "They love and adore you more than anything. Don't you, Lizzie?"

"Yes!" Lizzie chirped.

Ren grimaced and crossed her arms.

"Sorry, Ren, your mom and I are planning a wild night out, aren't we, hon?"

"That's right!" Mom chimed from the kitchen.

"In fact, if we're arrested, you may need some cash for bail." He feigned searching for his wallet.

The doorbell rang.

"I'll get that," he said and crossed to the foyer.

"Dad, this isn't fair. I...." Ren began but stopped when her dad returned with Annie, both of them grinning.

Dad handed Ren his phone, lit up with an e-ticket.

Lunar Eclipse Soul and Shine Concert.

Mural Amphitheater. General Admission.

"Remember when you begged me to buy tickets to this, and I said 'no'?" her dad asked, hands on his hips. "That's because I had already bought them! Happy early birthday!"

"What?! AHHH!" Ren hugged him, then stumbled around the couch to hug her mom.

"We're leaving in ten minutes," her dad announced as the two girls squealed and skipped up the stairs.

—

By the time they arrived at The Mural, the beautiful green field under the Space Needle was already packed with people. The four of them miraculously found a free spot when someone moved elsewhere.

Ren stared up at the surreal, rust-colored moon. They'd seen several lunar eclipses over the years, but somehow, this one felt the most vivid. The most spectacular.

A few clouds rolled over the park, and it started drizzling, but Ren didn't mind. It was invigorating. She held up her palms as the band came out to the roar of the crowd.

For Ren, nothing compared to the thrill of a live show, the energy of the crowd, the spectacle of the musicians, the sound resonating in her chest. Ever since her parents took her to her first concert, Ren was determined to be a music junkie just like them. The light rain twinkled in the spotlights all around them, making the setting even more magical.

Ren and Annie sang along perfectly to the songs they knew and guessed the lyrics for the others. Ren turned to find her parents hanging back a few steps, nestled together. Mom smiled and held up rocker horns with a fierce head bob. Dad bit his bottom lip and did air guitar.

Ren laughed.

My parents are awesome.

This may have been the greatest night of her life.

—

After the show, Mom and Annie frolicked ahead down the

sidewalk, while Ren strolled arm in arm with Dad. She loved the warmth of his shirt in the cool air.

It had just started raining again.

"Did you have fun?" he asked.

Ren scoffed.

"Dad, are you kidding? It was terrible. So boring. Why did you drag me here?"

"Haha, I had fun, too. Your mom sure had a blast," Dad remarked. Then he glanced down at Ren. "You know, she mentioned you didn't make relay today. Were you going to tell me?"

"It wasn't a secret. No big deal."

Dad paused and turned to look at her, but Ren averted her eyes. It seemed to be all the confirmation he needed to know she'd thrown the race. Her father sighed and kept walking. Shame climbed up the back of Ren's throat, and her breath wavered.

Her dad would never have given up like that. No one ever intimidated him.

"I really dislike those snotty little Jell-O heads on that team," he said. "And I don't feel good about what you did, but...I understand why you did it."

"I just couldn't deal with their garbage all season. I'll be happier doing the hundred."

Dad nodded and wiped droplets from the top of Ren's head, smoothing down her hair.

"Ah, but wouldn't it have been better to smoke Chrissy at the race and then tell the coach, 'No, thanks'?"

Ren shrugged. "Yeah, maybe..." Ren envisioned how great

it would have felt to reject *them*.

Arg, why didn't I think of that?

"Hold your ground, Ren. Don't let 'em scare you." Dad squeezed her shoulder. "Because we don't suffer jerk-face bullies, do we? Do we, Lauren?"

Ren rolled her eyes up and smirked. "No, we don't suffer jerk-face bullies."

"Good.   Listen, whether   or   not you   win   on that racetrack, your mom and I love and believe in you all the way. Just remember that and run like hell, okay? Show 'em the rocket."

"Okay." Ren leaned her head into his shoulder, and he kissed her head. No one understood her like her dad did.

"Yep, Ren the Rocket…On the bright side for me, at least I won't have to sit next to their tool bag fathers at the meets."

Across the street, a man waved to them from a blue Honda.

"Hey, there's our Uber. Come on, ladies! Hurry to the crosswalk," he called to the others. He nudged Ren to zip in front of him.

Suddenly, the sky opened to a downpour. The distant crosswalk seemed silly when the shelter of the car was just steps away. Besides, the street was empty.

"Dad, we're getting drenched!" Ren shouted and stepped off the curb.

"Careful, Lauren!" Dad called after her, as Mom and Annie followed Ren's lead.

Dad ushered the girls across, and Mom ran around to shotgun. Annie threw open the rear driver's side door and dove across the back. Dad helped Ren hop in behind her.

"That was crazy." Ren laughed, wiping her face. She held out her new smartphone to take a selfie with Annie.

Dad smiled and waited. Ren never took pics of herself.

"Okay, now push over," he said, hunching toward the back seat.

Ren's phone slipped from her fingers and bounced out onto the pavement.

"Dad, I dropped it!" she said, leaning out. "Do you see it?"

He gestured her back in, then bent down to search beneath the car.

"Yeah." Dad got down on all fours. The rain came harder as he lowered his shoulder to stretch under the Honda.

"You got it?" Ren asked.

Dad grunted, then slowly rose with the phone in his fingertips. He wiped the screen on his jeans and examined it.

"It's cracked!" he yelled over the pounding rain.

"Get in, quick! You're getting soaked." Ren reached out for the phone.

"*Getting* soaked!?" Dad laughed and handed it to her. "Scoot over."

But the swelling beam of headlights had already flooded Dad's body.

A blaring horn.

Shrieking tires.

He turned just as the speeding car hit him.

The sideswipe smashed the Honda in an explosion of broken glass and twisted metal. The open door ripped off the frame, impaling Ren's arm as it swung across her seat. Her elbow cracked, and glass slashed through her forearm.

But she felt nothing.

She didn't hear Mom's screams.

She couldn't see Annie trying to help her.

Everything was blurry and muted. A moment ago, Ren's father was laughing and alive, inches away from her. Now, he was lying far away, in the middle of the cold, wet street—alone and lifeless.

CHAPTER 48

JAY

November 8th, 2027 - 33 miles south of McChord Air Base. 65 days after.

The day after their run-in with the big group in town, Jay and Gavin sat around their campfire. Gavin was searching through the backpack they stole from the big guy with the broken arm, cursing that there wasn't any more food in it. Jay gripped the pistol, impatiently waiting for Gavin to find something more.

Another disappointment was that there were fewer bullets in the gun than Jay had hoped for, but he had no intention of telling the others that. Jay thought this guy would be the perfect target. He had the weapon, the backpack, and the injured arm, and he was positioned at the end of the group.

After all that hassle, we barely got enough for a decent supper. At least I got the gun.

Eddie was still asleep. They had cut his jeans to bandage the gunshot wound as best they could, but blood was soaking through the wrapping. He had remnants of berry jam and crackers still mushed into his beard from the night before.

"Dang it!" Gavin cursed. "Eddie ate all the rest of that jam! The only thing left in here are these stale crackers. That greedy little sneak."

Gavin tossed the empty jar labeled 'Sally's Tayberry Preserves' and kicked the backpack away. Jay sat, evaluating their circumstances.

He kept eyeing Eddie's leg.

"Hey," he murmured to Gavin. "We gotta leave, Eddie."

"What d'ya mean, leave him?"

"I mean, his mangled leg. Those monsters have been stalking Eddie since yesterday as if he were a lame deer. You've heard them, too. They're drooling for him."

Gavin hesitated.

"I dunno, man. You were the one who shot him. Leavin' him here doesn't feel right."

"Look, I'm sorry about that, but it wasn't my fault. That ape pulled me down. We gotta look at the situation as it is. Besides those creatures at our heels, he's slowing us down too much. We'll never make it to the next town before starving out here. That leg's probably already infected. Eddie won't last another day, whether he's with us or not."

"You don't think we can get him some medicine?"

"From where? Even if we could get him to a pharmacy, all the shelves have been cleaned out."

Gavin poked the ground with a stick, then looked at their wounded companion.

"So, you with me?" Jay pressed.

"Yeah, I guess so," Gavin sighed. He tossed the stick and stood, then zipped into his old IBM jacket.

The two men collected only the useful items, leaving their garbage behind.

Jay heard people coming through the woods and froze. He peeked out from a boulder blocking the pathway.

"Aww, man! It's that group we took the pack from. I told you we were moving too slow! Let's go," he ordered.

The two of them quickly fled the campsite without a glance at Eddie, who still hadn't stirred. They darted east through the trees toward the river.

It wasn't even a few moments before banshees howled from the sky. Jay heard Eddie's screams and cringed, trying to ignore them. Gavin paused, but Jay grabbed his arm and pulled him on.

It's too late anyway.

As Jay ran faster down the hill, he thought about how disappointed his wife would be if she'd lived to see him now.

CHAPTER 49

HANK

From the winding trail, Hank heard the banshee attack and the abrupt end to a man's screams. He signaled for everyone to huddle and duck behind shrubbery. After a few minutes of quiet, he motioned for Peter to join him around the trees to make sure it was safe.

"Okay, guys. It's clear! You can come up," Hank called to the others.

The group circled the site. There were smoking embers from a dying fire and remnants from Robert's backpack scattered about the clearing.

"Hey, my stuff," Robert exclaimed. He groaned from his injuries as he picked up the empty jelly jar. "Well, what's left, anyway." He tossed it aside, scanning the other discards. "Guess we know who's been here."

Ren peered around the forest.

"We need to be careful not to catch up to them." She reached in her pocket to grip the pistol.

"We'll keep an eye out ahead," said Hank. "But I bet they left in a hurry when they heard us comin'. I doubt we could catch 'em if we tried. And based on what we just heard, they're at least one man down."

Several hideous squawks came from the woods, followed by the sound of something, or *somethings,* falling heavy through branches to the ground.

The group stared at each other.

"Uh…what was that?" Peter asked.

"It must have been banshees, but I've never heard them make a sound like that before—like they were in pain," Hank replied.

Peter peeked around a boulder into the trees.

"Hank, come here and look," he beckoned, and the two walked off, leaving the others behind.

Hank spotted the things just a few yards downhill under a maple tree—four dead banshees among the fallen leaves. He and Peter cautiously circled them.

The creatures' camouflage had dissolved, revealing translucent, smooth grey skin. Their bodies looked like heaps of murky gel. The smallest two were the size of raccoons, while the largest was maybe 150 kilos, like a fully grown bear.

I wouldn't want that gooey giant coming for me. Crikey.

The figures had oblong bodies with no distinct heads. No eyes or mouths. Just long slits on either side of where a head should be. There were no visible arms, just massive, manta ray-like wings flopped on either side of two of them. The other two banshees had mounds protruding from their bodies where their wings would be. Their legs looked powerful and agile, with

282

three razor-sharp claws from each foot.

"They look sorta like liquid metal from Terminator Two," Peter said. "But, like, more see-through."

"Yeah, they do." Hank nudged the one closest with his rifle, then pushed it over. "Never seen a dead one before."

Peter squatted for a closer look.

"What do you think did it? What killed all of them at once?"

"I dunno. They don't seem to be injured. We should take the smaller two with us to the base." Hank dropped his pack. "I have a garbage bag we can stuff 'em in."

"They don't have any mouths. How do they eat?" Peter asked.

Hank studied the corpses.

"Well, I'd guess these things must *absorb* their prey. Certain worms, parasites, and sponge-like creatures consume nutrients through their skin. These guys can eat through tissue instantaneously. And not just meat, but clothes, too. Those slits probably help them smell and vocalize. I'm just guessing, of course, but that's what it looks like to me." Hank unsnapped the top of his bag and pulled out a garbage bag.

Peter was mesmerized.

"Freakin' bizarro."

CHAPTER 50

REN

A t the thieves' campsite, Robert and Zack sipped water while Lizzie and Ren held their hands over the fizzling ashes.

"Daddy, I have to go," Zack declared, crossing one leg over the other.

"All right, let's go right around this rock, okay?" Robert held Zack's hand, and the two stepped out of sight beyond the tree line.

Ren squatted next to Lizzie, who started drawing a picture of a cat in the dirt with a stick.

"That's pretty good," Ren said and spotted another drawing stick. As she reached for it, the edge of her scar peeked out from her sleeve. She stared at the raised purple streak on her skin. Ren's breath quickened, and she squeezed her right hand around the mark, then pulled the sleeve down.

A missile of screeching wind rocked Ren off her feet as a banshee swooped past her. She scrambled to Lizzie as another sounded from above.

"Ren!" Lizzie yelped and grabbed Ren around the waist.

"This way." Ren pulled her back between two boulders

bordering the site. "Stay close to me."

"I am! Why won't they go away?" Lizzie turned her head away from the flying leaves and held tighter.

A growling noise started advancing through the woods. Ren spun around to face it, straining to see through the debris. She could just make out a massive figure blurring the pines.

"Hank, help!" Ren screamed, tucking Lizzie further behind her as the screeching grew louder.

"We're here!" Hank shouted as he and Peter rushed back. They huddled around the girls until the banshees dispersed. Robert and Zack also returned and quickly tied their tethers to the rest of the group.

Lizzie was gasping, almost hyperventilating. Hank stooped down to calm her.

"Deep breaths, gal," he soothed.

"It all happened so fast," Ren stammered. "I don't know what…"

Peter cut her off.

"Ren! What did you do to provoke them?" he raged, his gaze razor sharp. "Did you walk away from Lizzie? Did you leave her?!"

Peter's whole face was aflame. His neck muscles were rigid and bulging. Ren had never seen him so mad.

Ren's voice caught. She grabbed her rope and held it out to him.

"No! She was right here, tied to me the whole time."

Peter snatched the tether from her and yanked on both ends, each firmly attached to a sister, then threw it back at Ren.

"This stupid rope isn't enough to keep her safe, Lauren!"

285

"I know! I had her right with me, Peter!" Ren insisted.

"Yeah, right, sure you did. You're so selfish. So wrapped up in yourself to care what happens to any of the rest of us. I should have known better than to leave Lizzie alone with you."

"Peter, I'm…I'm sorry, okay?"

"Oh yeah? Sorry for what?" he demanded.

"I'm…" Ren glanced around at the group, her face sunken and flushed. She could barely meet Peter's gaze. "I'm sorry about Dad. The accident was all my fault, and I can't make up for it. Please…can't you forgive me?" Ren started breathing harder to dry her eyes.

"*Are you kidding*?" Peter shot back. "This has nothing to do with the accident. It's about *afterward*. We all needed you, and you bailed. You were the only one who could have really helped Mom, but instead, you abandoned all of us. Lizzie and I just didn't exist to you anymore. I was twelve years old, trying to hold it together and keep things normal for Lizzie, while Mom worked double shifts and cried herself to sleep every night."

"Peter…" Ren whispered.

"And where were you? Locked in your room. As if yours was the only pain that mattered," he hissed. Peter's eyes were glassy, but he didn't flinch. "Hey, if you're done with us, if you wanna just give up—*then go*." With that, Peter yanked Lizzie's tether from her waist, picked her up, and turned away. Lizzie clung to him, burying her head in his shoulder.

"Hey, Pete," Hank said, but Peter ignored him.

When Lizzie had calmed down, Peter put her down, tied her strap to his belt, and latched them both onto Robert while the rest of the group watched in silence. Then Peter swung his pack on his back and wiped his face on his sleeve.

Robert put his hand on Peter's shoulder.

"She's gonna end up just like your wife," Peter said to him just loud enough for Ren to hear.

Robert's wife? What's she got to do with this?

Peter pulled his tethered group down the trail as Hank tied his rope to Ren.

Ren couldn't look at him. She wanted the ground to swallow her up so she'd never cause any more grief. As Hank's hands shifted and turned with the tether, it felt like something was twisting and pulling her insides. Hank yanked the final knot tight, then paused and looked up at her. Ren could only stare at the ground.

"Ren, he was just scared," Hank murmured to her forehead. "He didn't mean…"

"Let's just go," Ren uttered. Two tears fell on the toe of her boot.

CHAPTER 51

HANK

H ank and the group hiked in silence for the rest of the day. Zack's occasional commentary was all that broke the tension. Robert seemed especially protective, staying within just a few steps of his son at all times.

Hank noticed Peter occasionally wincing, kicking rocks, snapping twigs, and muttering under his breath. Hank knew the feeling. He'd felt it every time he'd fought with his dad—every time he'd said something he'd regretted.

Ren trudged onward, a few strides ahead of Hank. After all that had happened, she wasn't beaten, and she wouldn't stop. He wanted her to lean on him, but she'd barely look over. Her determination had strengthened, and her pace had quickened. She was going to get to the end, no matter what. He just hoped she'd find some peace when it was over, when they made it to her mum.

But even then, it won't really be over, will it? Reckon 'better' is all we can bloody hope for.

Hank remembered the feeling of her hand's cool skin against his lips. He flinched, unsettled by how emotional he got after saving Robert.

But all Hank could think about was how heartbroken Dad had been for years after Mum had left. Some days, he had trouble getting out of bed.

As bad as that was, Robert's loss was much worse. He and his son had to watch his wife get devoured by beasts just steps away from them, like something from a horror movie.

The only person Hank ever really loved was his father. When he saw Zack frantic to get back to Robert, he recalled how scared and insecure he felt as a child when Dad wasn't around. There had been a long period when he'd have horrible crying fits at school—always fearful that his dad would leave, too. Then, Dad would have to come pick him up, and they'd spend the rest of the day fixing things around the house, cleaning, or reading.

When Robert was attacked that day, and Zack almost lost his father, Hank had only been able to get to Robert because of Ren. So Hank was thankful—immensely thankful for her heart, courage, and speed. She was selfless and brilliant, and he never wanted to let go of her hand.

Hank exhaled, shaking his head.

Think about somethin' else, ya dope, before you start bawlin' like a bloomin' infant.

———

At sunset, the group reached a mountain summit just above the tree line. They stopped to wonder at the incredible view. Hank's eyes passed over the blue-tipped clouds with reds, pinks, and oranges shooting from the descending sun. The warm colors spilled across the crystal lake in the valley below. It was this kind of scene that had made him want to fight for the delicate natural world around them. He had chosen that path because nothing the army or government could build would ever be this beautiful.

Hank stood in the back of the group, with Ren just a few feet in front of him. She hadn't spoken in hours. He stepped up behind her, almost touching her back, and started to reach out—but stopped himself. He lowered his arms and balled his fists at his sides.

A moment later, Ren took a half-step back into him. She let her head and shoulders lean lightly against his chest, and they both inhaled. He gently grasped her arms.

"You're strong," he said to her. "Strong and brave, and you're gonna make it."

She looked over her shoulder at him. Her expression was beautiful and searching. Hank regarded her hazel eyes, her mouth, her glowing sun-speckled skin—memorizing her face because he knew she'd soon look away.

When she turned, Hank brushed his hands down her forearms and wove his fingers through hers. Staring back at the idyllic sunset, he could feel her heartbeat on his chest, beating in the same rhythm as his own.

CHAPTER 52

LEE

**November 8th, 2027 - 35 miles south of McChord Air Base.
65 days after.**

L ee, Caleb, Mae, Kenny, and Fitz had made it another day at
 an unyielding pace. Lee's legs and shoulders were sore, his
shins raw from short-cutting through brambles, and his face felt
like cracked leather. Worrying about Penny had made
sleep nearly impossible. Every time he'd close his eyes, all he
could see was her face pleading with him to stay.
Twice, he'd considered turning back.

Everyone was struggling now.

When Mae wasn't complaining, Kenny was, and the tension
between Fitz and Caleb only grew in the constant close proximity.
Just before sunset, they came upon a deserted industrial area in a
small valley town. Lee suggested they stop there to rest.

The group found an unlocked warehouse where they could at
least escape the cold. They entered quietly, finding no sign of
other occupants. The smell of urine and rotten food would keep
anyone from living there, but it was tolerable for a short break.

"Sweet mercy!" Kenny exclaimed when they came upon a cluster of swivel chairs on the factory floor. Lee collapsed on the nearest seat, melting into the cushion, lumbar support, and armrests. Chairs were a luxury they hadn't experienced all week.

"Think there's any food here? My stomach has been chewin' on itself since yesterday," Mae remarked after a few precious moments of peace.

"Woman, can I just rest for a millisecond before you start yer gripin'?" Fitz grouched from his headrest.

"Yeah, just zip it for once," Kenny added.

"Well, if you lazy mules won't check around, then I will. And see if I share any of it." Mae dropped her tether and turned to leave.

Lee sat forward.

"Hold it, Mae," Lee inserted. "You can't go by yourself through here. Caleb and I will look with you."

Mae sauntered behind Fitz, resting her hands on the back of his chair.

"What a nice gentlemanly thing to do, Lee. I don't get much of that nowadays. Hope you don't mind watchin' me relieve myself if I find a decent toilet."

Fitz grunted, then rolled his eyes.

"Alright, alright. I'll go with you." Fitz hauled himself from the chair and slung his rifle over his shoulder. He shuffled off behind Mae toward the far side of the room and down a hallway.

Kenny began spinning himself in the chair like a child. Caleb switched off Hutch, then patted Lee's leg.

'This is pointless. How are we ever going to find them? They could have already sailed away by now,' he signed.

Lee sighed, removed his cap, and brushed his hair back with his fingers.

'I know. Let me figure out how to convince Fitz to head back. Just don't do anything yet.'

Lee felt a sense of peace wash over him. He'd made up his mind, and now he'll get back to Penny so much sooner. They would figure something out for the winter. If Fitz and Mae wouldn't come back with them, maybe Camille would help take care of Penny.

A gunshot and a loud crash, followed by Mae's screaming, echoed through the room.

"Hey! Put 'em down!" Fitz shouted. Lee, Caleb, and Kenny jumped from the chairs and chased the noise through the propped door labeled 'Administration.'

In a room with dozens of cubicles, they found Fitz holding two men at gunpoint. Mae was rubbing her arm beside him. Lee snatched up a pistol from the floor.

"Fitz! What's going on?" Lee asked.

"These two skunks tried to attack Mae," Fitz snarled. "Then that one took a shot at me!"

"Look, we're sorry," the light-haired one said. He had on a Soundgarden sweatshirt and mismatched boots. His hands were above his head. "You guys just surprised us, is all. I wasn't really aiming for you. We were just trying to scare you away, I swear."

His Italian-looking companion nodded in agreement. He was wearing a company jacket that looked like he'd been in a fight.

"Liar! You heard us comin' and were waitin' to jump us," Fitz barked as he shifted his rifle back and forth between the two of them. "Kenny, search these two before they try somethin' else."

Kenny slapped his hands down each of them, front and back, and then shoved them against the wall.

"Okay, Fitz," Lee said calmly. "They're unarmed now. We should just leave. They won't bother us."

"Ha! We can't be sure of that, can we? He might have a shotgun hidden somewhere. They'll just follow and shoot us all," Fitz countered. "We're gonna have to hurt 'em bad enough to slow 'em down."

"We don't have anything else. We swear it," the dark one insisted. "Please, just let us go."

"Wish I could believe you. Down on your knees," Fitz ordered.

Oh, no!

Lee racked his brain for a way to talk him down.

"Fitz, hold it!" Lee shouted, holding his hands out. "Hey, what are your names?"

"I'm Jay. This is Gavin," said the Soundgarden guy.

"Okay, I'm Lee. Have you two been around here long? We're looking for some people, and maybe you've seen 'em. Two brown-haired teens, a girl and a boy, and a little blond girl, traveling with an Australian guy."

"Yes! Yeah, we've seen them," Jay replied. His arms were shaking above his head.

"They're lying to save their butts," Mae shouted. "Fitz, don't listen."

"They came through here this morning! They were with another guy and a kid, but one of them was definitely Australian," Jay added. "We can show you where they went. Just don't hurt us."

Lee put his hand on Fitz's shoulder.

"I believe him, Fitz. Just let them show us, okay?"

"Fitz, hold on," Kenny said in protest. "Don't..."

"Quiet, Ken," Fitz directed. He looked at Lee, then back at the captives. "Okay, you two lead us to where you last saw 'em. Don't try anything, lest you wanna get shot."

———

"Is this it? This pile a trash?" Fitz asked, sweeping his flashlight over the garbage at the site Jay had led them to.

"This was some of their stuff. And it was the last place we saw them," Jay said, his hands still up, eyeing the rifle Kenny kept trained on both of them.

Lee walked around, sifting through the remnants of the campsite. His foot knocked into something hard with a clinking sound. He picked up a dirty glass jar and examined the label.

"Sally's Tayberry Preserves," Lee read aloud. "It's them."

"Well, hot pockets," Fitz hollered. "I told ya we're gettin' close! Kenny, tie these two to that tree."

"What?!" Jay demanded. "We told you the truth! We'll die out here."

"Better that than allowing you to tail us." Fitz nodded at Kenny, who passed Fitz his rifle and started tying the men to a birch. When Gavin tried to resist, Fitz struck him with the butt of his gun. He stumbled, and Kenny dragged him by the shirt collar to the tree.

"Wait, stop," Jay protested. "He's bleedin' now. Those things will come for us for sure. Please, you can't leave us out here."

Lee didn't care. He could barely hear what was going on.

After all of this struggle and doubt, Fitz's plan was working. They were actually getting close now. The boat, Penny's salvation, and finding a safe place to live were all within reach. Adrenaline coursed through him, numbing his aches and steeling his resolve.

"We gotta move faster," Lee directed, ignoring the terrified men. He tossed the jar into the brush. "If we hike through most of the night, we can catch them. Two minutes, then we keep going."

CHAPTER 53

REN

**November 9th, 2027 - 17 miles south of McChord Air Base.
66 days after.**

The next morning, the group woke to frost and light snow. The bitter cold drained Ren's already-waning energy. Lizzie seemed particularly lethargic and didn't eat much for breakfast.

"You okay, bug?" Ren asked as they packed up to leave.

"Yeah. Are we almost there?"

"I think so."

Hank had said they'd get to the base by the end of that day. At least there, they could get some rest, warmth, and a decent meal.

Ren was about to tie the lantern to her pack when Peter came and reached for it.

"That's heavy. I'll carry it today," he said.

"Oh…thanks," Ren sputtered. She handed it to him, trying to think of something more to say, but nothing came.

Then Peter stepped away without another word.

Hank secured the garbage bag with the two dead banshees to

his backpack, and Lizzie tied everyone's slip knot.

They hiked for hours. By midday, Lizzie had slowed even more. Hank took her pack, and Peter carried her. She fell asleep on his shoulder.

By the time Lizzie woke, Ren could hear rushing water ahead. Eager to see the last landmark before the base, Ren and the rest of them quick-marched the rest of the way to the ravine. Reen peered over the ledge to see the mighty Nisqually River far below. Its white waters tumbled and crashed through the steep, winding gorge.

Hank pulled out the map.

"Hang on a second. There's supposed to be a crossing. I reckon it's just around this bend there."

The group followed him along the high cliff until they saw the bridge. The meteors had all but destroyed it. Steel and cement remains of the structure spanned the width of the gorge, but it looked barely stable, just piles of rocks, balancing on cracked support beams.

Ren's heart sank.

"Hank, what do we do?" she asked.

Hank examined the map again.

"Ahh…the next nearest crossing is about eight miles backtracking southwest. And it's in town." He shook his head.

"That's another day, at least," Robert stressed. "McChord base is only seven or eight miles from here in the other direction. "If we cross here, we could be there by dark."

Hank surveyed the mangled bridge.

"I reckon we should try it here. It's been a long time since the meteor shower. The debris should be settled by now," he said. "It's gettin' cold, and we all need rest."

Ren looked at the treacherous pass. The drop to the river may have been forty or fifty feet in the middle.

"Ren?" Hank wanted her vote.

Ren looked down at Lizzie, leaning against Peter. She was pale, shivering, and exhausted. She needed to get to that base by tonight.

"Let's try here," Ren agreed.

"Alright then." Hank put away the map and untied his tether. "Peter, you and I will go first to make sure it's safe, and then we'll come back to help the rest across."

The two dropped their packs, then climbed down to the piles of cement resting atop the tall, arched support columns. They crawled over and slid down the jutting boulders. At the midpoint, the only way forward was along a twenty-foot narrow stretch of cement with a long metal rod running four feet above it. They had to sidestep along the ledge holding the rail, but they managed without much difficulty.

"Okay, we'll go in two groups," Hank said after he and Peter made it safely back. "Peter, you lead, followed by Zack and then Robert. When you three are over, I'll go with Lizzie and Ren."

The group retied their tethers according to Hank's instructions.

Robert and Peter led Zack by the hand to the ravine's edge. The boy looked over the drop and tugged backward.

"I don't want to go."

Robert squatted next to him.

"You got this, Buckaroo," he said and rubbed Zack's little

shoulder.

Zack reluctantly nodded and unplanted his feet, following Peter onto the pummeled bridge.

Lizzie clung to Ren's arm as they watched.

The first group of three steadily made their way until the last twenty feet, when Zack's foot slid down loose pebbles on a flat boulder. He and Lizzie shrieked as Peter scooped Zack up by the arm and lifted him to the next secure foothold.

"Ren..." Lizzie panted.

"It's okay. Peter got him. See? He's almost across."

At last, Robert, Peter, and Zack made it to the far cliffside. Robert dropped to his knees and hugged Zack, then signaled to Hank with a thumbs-up.

Hank turned to Ren and Lizzie.

"Alright, ladies, our turn. We're just gonna take it slow. I'll go first, then Lizzie and Ren in back."

He led the two girls down to the crumbled rocks. From there, the bridge looked higher, the river seemed angrier, and the wind through the canyon felt more powerful than when they were on firm ground. Ren gulped and stepped forward, but Lizzie froze.

"Ren, I'm scared."

"I know, Liz, but we have to do it. The other group made it just fine," Ren soothed.

"Zack almost fell!"

"No, he just slipped a bit, but Peter had him the whole time. Look, we're all tied together. No one is going to fall. Just follow Hank, and I'll be right behind you."

"You can do it, gal," Hank said, reaching out to lead her between two rocks. "I know ya can."

Lizze took his hand and carefully stepped forward. Ren looked down again and shuddered. She never thought she was afraid of heights. But, then again, she'd never been in this much danger of falling before.

Easy to feel safe on an airplane with a movie and a bag of pretzels.

Ren steeled her nerves and continued on, staying just a few steps behind Lizzie.

"That's it, Liz. One foothold, then handhold, at a time. Just keep watching Hank and do what he does," she said.

Ren trained her focus on replicating what they did—step up on this notch with left foot, right leg over, lean on right hand—trying to ignore the terrifying roar of the water below.

When they reached the narrow stretch, Hank turned to them.

"We're just gonna hold onto this pole here and slide across, nice and steady. Just do as I do, and don't look down. We're halfway there."

Only halfway? Holy moly, this is awful. It looked so easy from the cliffside.

Slowly, the three slid down a flat rock sheet to the thin cement ledge. Hank helped Lizzie onto the walkway and placed her hands on the bar above it, next to his.

"The bar is secure. Just keep your eyes on your hands and tiptoe across," Hank said.

Ren grasped the bar behind Lizzie. As she watched her feet find the cracked balance beam, she glimpsed the frightening precipice. Her vision wavered, and she thought she might faint.

Wake up, Ren! Just focus on the bar and follow Lizzie.

Ren dug her fingernails into her palms and inched on.

301

"See, it's not so bad. Just keep coming," Hank urged.

They continued until Hank was almost at the end of the bar.

Then a menacing voice shouted from behind them.

"Well, hello there, gang! Fancy meeting you here!"

Ren spun her head around. On the cliffside, Fitz, Mae, and Kenny stood with their rifles raised.

"Hey, little girl. Remember me?" Fitz taunted with a sickening sneer. "Ya didn't think you'd get away that easy, did'ja?"

CHAPTER 54

HANK

"Fitz, you bloody snake!" Hank growled. His body pulsed with trapped rage.

What do I do?! We're birds on a wire out here.

Robert had his gun up and ready, but Hank already knew it was no use.

"Hands up, over there!" Fitz bellowed across the river at Robert. "We got more guns and more people to shoot 'em."

With Kenny's rifle pointed at Peter and Fitz's at the bridge, Robert put his pistol away.

Hank pressed his forehead into the rock wall in front of him, furious at himself.

How could this have happened? Minna said she was gonna hold 'em for at least a day. How could they have caught us?

He raised his head, ready to hurl another insult, as Lee and Caleb walked out from the tree line.

Oh, no. Lee!

"Okay, we don't want to hurt anyone," Lee said. "We just need the three of you to make your way back to us."

"Lee, what the heck are you doin'?!" Hank demanded. "Ren, don't move."

"This has nothing to do with you, Hank. We have business with this family, and then everyone will walk away fine," Lee said. "First, please drop your rifle."

Hank clung to the support rod. He had nowhere to go and no way to defend any of them. He held on with his left hand, then shimmied the rifle strap down his right arm and let it fall to the water below.

"Good, now please start walking this way to me," Lee instructed. "We're comin' down there to help you."

"Ren, don't!" Hank yelled.

"Talk back again, and I'll shoot ya," Fitz warned. "Then you'll bring these two ladies down with you. Is that whatcha want?"

Lee and Caleb slid down onto the cluster of rocks at the start of the bridge and made their way toward the girls.

"Follow me, Lizzie, okay?" Ren said.

"Are they gonna hurt us?"

Ren didn't answer. She just started inching back the way they came. Hank was ready to pound his fist into the cement. He couldn't figure out what to do. When Lizzie's cord pulled tight around his waist, he still didn't budge.

"He meant now, Hank. Move it!" Fitz barked and fired two shots just below them, hammering off chunks of rock. Hank could feel the vibrations wobble through the rod, and Lizzie screamed.

"Stop! I'm coming!" Hank shouted.

Lee reeled back at Fitz.

"Fitz, hold your fire!"

"He was stallin'. I was just gettin' their attention," Fitz answered.

Hank crept along after Lizzie. By this point, Caleb and Lee had reached the narrow strip. Caleb held out his hand to help Ren up to the more stable pathway.

As Ren stretched for him, the shelf below Lizzie fragmented and fell.

Lizzie shrieked and clung to the rod with nothing below her but the river.

"Lizzie, no!"

Before Ren could take even a step toward her, Lizzie's gloved hands slipped from the bar, and she dropped. The freefall ended with a hard jolt at the end of Hank and Ren's tethers, jerking Lizzie's body from the middle. She wailed for help as she dangled below them.

"I gotcha, Lizzie," Hank yelled. "I won't letcha go!" Hank latched his elbow around the rod and gripped the cord with his hand, praying the knot would hold. His side of the gap was angled downward and covered with loose debris. If he moved too fast, he could slide off.

"Ren, keep coming toward Caleb!" Lee called out. "You can't help her from there. Come to me, and we can pull her up."

Hank edged to the gap, so Ren would have enough slack to get to Caleb. He could hear Peter, Robert, and Zack climbing down the other side of the bridge to rescue him.

"I'm at the end, Ren. I can't take another step," Hank shouted. "You gotta pull hard and reach out for Caleb. When he's gotcha, I'll drop my tie to Lizzie. Pete's comin' for me."

Ren fought the swinging anchor tied around her waist. She had to let go of the rope to switch hands on the rod. Red stretched for Caleb's arm. Lizzie flailed below, trying to stay upright.

Just as Ren touched Caleb's fingers, the ledge below Ren collapsed. She hung from the rod with just her right hand supporting the weight of both girls. Ren screamed, still straining her left hand out for help. Caleb brought his toes to the tip of the ledge and leaned out for her.

Come on, Caleb, just a bit further, mate.

The boulder beneath Caleb shifted. Lee snatched him back just as it rolled and toppled off the bridge.

"No!" Caleb yelled. There was no way for him to reach Ren now.

"I can't hold on!" Ren cried.

Then she lost the bar.

Ren plunged fifteen feet to the end of Lizzie's cord. She and her sister swung like a pendulum below Hank as he strained to hold the rope and the bar. The weight of the two girls yanked him closer to the crumbling ledge. Peter and Robert had almost reached him on the other side, but they were having trouble getting Zack down safely as he cried and resisted.

"Hold on, Hank!" Robert yelled. "Don't let go. We're coming!"

Hank's ledge broke off, falling like sharp bricks around the girls. They both screamed as Hank writhed in the air above them. His left hand gripped the arm that was still hooked over the bar. The tether was digging into his waist, stretching his spine like a rack.

Then he felt it slipping over his hips. Hank quickly dropped his left hand to hold up the rope, but the swinging drag jostled his right elbow off the bar. He caught the rod with his right fist, now his last hold on the bridge. He looked down and saw Lizzie and Ren screaming up at him for help. There was no more he could do.

Peter's voice rang out from above.

"Hang on!"

He and Robert were almost there.

Just hold on a few more seconds, mate. Just…hold…on…

Hank's right hand started cramping around the rod, his fist weakening. He roared with frustration and fear.

Then, his fingers gave out and slipped off the bar.

Ren, Lizzie, and Hank dropped forty feet to the freezing river below.

CHAPTER 55

REN

To Ren, the fall was endless. So long, it felt like flying. Then she smacked the ice-cold water as if plunging through glass.

Ren rolled and tumbled against the riverbed, banging and scraping her back, legs, and forearms. She didn't know which direction was up. The frigid water burned her skin, and it felt as if her lungs were frozen tight. When she finally surfaced, she could barely take a breath before the current pushed her under again.

The tether around Ren's waist jerked her back and forth through the churning whitewater like a fish on a line. She was still attached to Lizzie and Hank, but couldn't find them. She could only see the water spray and the blur of the boulders, bludgeoning her as she surged down the ravine.

Ren stretched and clawed, trying to find a secure hold on a rock, jamming and twisting her fingers until her nails felt like they'd rip off.

She had little strength left, and her vision was dimming. A sharp web of branches stabbed at her chest and legs. The current had run her into a fallen tree. She grappled herself up and took a huge breath, then spat out water and blood.

"Lizzie!" she hacked, but the thunderous river drowned her voice. She yanked on the rope connecting her to her sister and pulled as hard as she could. Ren elevated herself on the branches and searched the water. Lizzie's arm surfaced, then her head.

She wasn't moving.

"Ren!" Hank yelled from a rock downriver. He was still tied to Lizzie on the other end.

"Help me get her!" Ren pleaded.

Hank climbed up on the rock and pulled at the cord, wrapping it around his elbow as he reeled them in. Ren jumped back in the water to swim down to him, pulling Lizzie toward her until she could prop her head above water. Hank dragged the girls to his rock, then ripped Lizzie from the water by her cord. He turned, snatched Ren's hand, and heaved her out next. Ren gasped for breath on the boulder, trying to get a look at her sister, but Hank threw Lizzie over his shoulder before she could. He bounded across the stepping stones to the shallows of the riverbank.

Hank lay her on the pebbly sand and began pressing on her chest.

"One, two, three, four…," he grunted as he pumped. Ren fell to her knees and held Lizzie's hand. Ren's fingers were shaking from the freezing cold, but Lizzie's were still.

"C'mon, Lizzie!" Hank yelled as he lifted her chin and blew into her mouth. Then, he did it again. "C'mon!"

"One, two, three, four…" He pumped on and on with no response, no life, no breath from Lizzie's frozen lips.

Ren remembered holding Pop's hand as Sally tried to save him. She was just as terrified. Just as helpless.

Hank tried again, holding her nose and forcing air into her lungs.

"Lizzie, breathe!" Ren begged. They were so close to home. They had survived so much. She couldn't lose Lizzie now.

"One, two, three, five..." Hank went on, his hands and voice trembling. He kept losing count.

Ren squeezed Lizzie's hand and caressed her face, both still blue and limp. Hank took another deep breath, lifted Lizzie's chin, and blew hard down her throat as if passing his whole life force into her. Hank looked like he was about to pass out before he shook his head clear and started pumping again.

"One, two, three..."

Lizzie stirred.

"She's moving!" Ren cried, grabbing Hank's shirt to stop him. The two rolled Lizzie to her side.

Lizzie wretched and gurgled water from her mouth as Ren pulled her hair from her face.

"Good gal, Lizzie! You're okay," Hank panted. He collapsed into the sand.

Ren rubbed Lizzie's back and cried out with relief, the cloud from her breath falling on Lizzie's cheek.

"I'm so sorry."

CHAPTER 56

PETER

Seventy feet above the Nisqually River, Peter, Robert, and Zack ran along the cliff ledge, trying to find a safe way down to the riverbank.

Peter cursed himself for not getting to Hank sooner. He should have just left Robert and Zack. He could have reached Hank before any banshees would have.

Why didn't I just go? I could have saved them.

Peter kept charging along the ravine until trees and tall rocks blocked his path. Robert came up behind, still carrying Zack.

"Can you see them down there? I can't see them anymore!" Peter shouted, leaning far over the edge. "Robert, we need to try to climb down!"

Robert snatched him back. "No, Pete, we can't. It's too dangerous here."

"We have to!"

"We'll get down another way," Robert insisted. "I promise we'll find them."

Peter fell to his knees and pounded his fists in the dirt, replaying the vision of his two sisters falling. The desperation in Ren's voice. She needed help, and what had he done?

Nothing.

Robert lifted Peter to his feet and yanked him north into the woods. Peter barreled behind him, swearing and gnashing his teeth, his harsh words from the campsite still burning his ears.

If you're done with us, if you wanna just give up, then go. I won't stop you.

Why did he have to be so cruel? All his fury and resentment from the past two years had just spewed from his mouth and clobbered his big sister. He had crushed and humiliated her in front of everyone—even Lizzie. Ren had been doing all she could to keep them alive and make it to Mom. And instead of being there for her, he punched her in the gut.

Please, God, let them be alive.

CHAPTER 57

LEE

Lee, Caleb, Fitz, Kenny, and Mae ran down the south side of the gorge. Lee's heart hammered in shock and remorse.

What have we done?

His eyes could barely focus on the rushing water below them. How could he get down there to help them?

"Alright, hold it," Fitz called, raising his hand to stop them. "Just let 'em go."

"But we gotta catch 'em," Kenny huffed. "Who knows where they'll end up."

"There's no way they're still alive, Kenny," said Mae, catching her breath. "Didja see that fall?"

Her words cut into Lee like a dagger.

Lee turned just as Caleb cannonballed into Lee's ribs, tackling him to the ground. Caleb threw punch after punch at him as Lee blocked, pushed, and shifted away—refusing to fight back. Caleb's fist smashed into Lee's jaw, and the fury behind it jarred Lee more than the blow.

Caleb and Lee had never fought before.

Fitz peeled Caleb off, hooking his forearm around Caleb's

313

throat.

"That's enough, runt," Fitz growled, and Hutch lit up with Fitz's insult.

Caleb couldn't read it. He was gasping and flailing as he struggled to pull Fitz's arm off his windpipe.

"Fitz, let him go," Lee ordered. He rubbed his cheek and got to his feet.

Fitz complied and pushed Caleb away. Lee grasped Caleb's shoulders, but Caleb shook him off.

"Why did you pull me back?" Hutch demanded. *"I could have saved them!"*

'No,' Lee signed back. *'You would have fallen, too.'*

Caleb's gestures sliced and pounded in response.

"You're wrong. I could have," Hutch shot back. *"What are we doing, Lee? What if they're dead? It's all our fault."*

Caleb's look of disdain, rage, and disappointment filled Lee with shame. His brother would have to bear the guilt of this, too, though none of it belonged to him. It belonged to Lee and Fitz— and the bloodthirsty monsters hunting them down.

'I'm trying to get us through this, Caleb,' Lee pleaded. *'I'm trying to save you and Penny.'*

"This is wrong, and it will never work. Please, let's just go home, get Penny back, and figure out something else," Hutch implored. *"Come with me, Lee."*

"Hey!" Fitz cut in. He spoke slow, clear, and loud right into Caleb's face. "Don't you tell Lee what to do. He's staying with me, but you leave if you want to. I sure as heck won't miss you. Yer a burden on us all and you always have been. Mama worked herself ragged caring for you 'til she had no strength left

314

to fight the cancer. I gave up my whole future when I had to save your ungrateful butt from Bull. Now, Dad's all alone in the middle of the ocean, so you can prance around with that stupid gizmo. You're responsible for every bad thing that's happened to this family."

Hutch couldn't keep up with the translation, but it didn't matter. Caleb already knew how Fitz felt.

Fitz rushed at Caleb and ripped Hutch from his arm.

"And I liked you better when I couldn't hear you." Fitz turned and reeled his arm back to throw Hutch in the river as Caleb clawed to get it back.

Lee grabbed Fitz from behind and shoved him to the ground, then snatched Hutch away. "Fitz, that's enough!"

Fitz rolled to his feet, and Lee clenched his fist.

"I was the one who provoked Bull that night," Lee swore. "If you want to blame someone, you lay it on me. But the truth is, Bull didn't mess with us at all before you took his spot on the team. It was you he always hated, not Caleb. From now on, you leave Caleb alone, Fitz, or I'll never speak to you again. I'm dead serious. Me, Caleb, and Penny will be gone from your life for good."

Fitz's eyes sharpened as he spat on the ground between them. He shoved his hands in his pockets and shrugged.

"Whatever you say, Lee. I'm not the one who wants to give up. All I'm tryin' to do is keep this family together like Daddy would want."

Caleb wiped his damp eyes with his sleeve. Lee reached out to him, but he jerked away.

Lee heaved a deep breath. He turned to address the whole

group while signing for Caleb, "Now, we all know we didn't mean for them to fall. It was an accident. The fact is, we have no way of guessing where they'll end up. But if...*when* they get out of the river, they'll be headin' back this way as quick as they can. Meanwhile, Peter is still out there. As soon as he can, he'll be racing toward the boat and his mom. We need to keep moving toward Diamond Point. We gotta stick together. Alright, Fitz?" Lee shot Fitz a glare, and Fitz returned a stiff nod. *'Caleb, that okay?'*

Caleb's arms hung limp in submission. He had nothing else to say.

CHAPTER 58

REN

R en held Lizzie as she followed Hank to retrieve his backpack, which was caught in brambles just downriver. The garbage bag with the banshees was still attached. Hank threw the pack on the riverbank and tore into it.

"Quickly, take off your coat and top, down to your bare skin. Do the same for Lizzie," he said, whipping out another large garbage bag.

"What?" Ren asked through chattering teeth.

"Do it now!"

Ren stripped down to her bra, too scared and freezing to be embarrassed. The cold air felt like knives on her skin. Hank peeled off Lizzie's coat, sweater, and shirt, then placed her back in Ren's arms.

"Now hold her snug in front of you, chest to chest."

Ren braced Lizzie as Hank ripped a hole in the top of the bag. Her sister was only faintly breathing. Hank put the bag over both their heads, then lowered it around them. He pulled off his own coat, wrung out the water as best as he could, then wrapped it around them and zipped it up. Cocooned together inside and out of the wind, Ren felt instant relief. Hank took out his ax and put on his backpack.

"Let's go. We gotta move fast."

He rushed through the woods, hacking loose branches and twigs as he went. With Lizzie in front of her, Ren could barely see her feet. Her arms were restricted beneath the wrap, and she wouldn't be able to catch herself if she fell. But she managed to keep up. Hank stopped and pointed to a rockface with an overhang covering a patch of dry ground.

"There, against that rock," he said.

With a bit of his lighter fluid and a handful of brambles, he threw together a small fire. Ren paced around him, trying to heat the bag with her body. A tingle of warmth was spreading between her chest and Lizzie's, but Ren's hands and feet were still numb.

"Lizzie? You doing better?" she murmured.

Lizzie didn't answer, but her breath was deeper, and the shaking had subsided slightly.

Once the fire was strong enough, Hank pulled out a tarp and laid his sleeping bag upon it alongside the fire. His hands shook violently as he unzipped Ren and Lizzie from the coat.

"Take off the wet pants, and lie down in there," he stuttered. Ren peeled off her soaked bottoms, then nestled Lizzie into the down-and-fleece bed and curled up around her. The sleeping bag had been in its waterproof case and was remarkably dry. Hank covered it with the ripped garbage bag, then his coat, and Ren's. After peeling off his wet shirt and pants, he folded himself into the bag behind Ren, grunting as he zipped them up as much as he could with three occupants. Ren squeezed against Lizzie to make room as Hank wrapped his arms around her. His body felt ten degrees colder than hers. Ren could feel heat passing from her back to his quaking chest. Hank buried his face beneath the cover behind her. His staggered breath blew more warmth through the bag.

The heat from the fire seeped into the fluffy lining and loosened Ren's hair. In her arms, she felt Lizzie's heart beating stronger, and her skin was finally dry.

They lay there exhausted and broken from their battle with the river. As Ren's skin thawed, the pain of her injuries intensified. But having Lizzie snuggled against her and Hank's arms around her was an overwhelming relief.

We all survived. The worst is over.

"Ask her something," Hank uttered, still shivering. "To make sure she's okay."

"Liz?" Ren said, brushing Lizzie's hair back. "Can you tell me where we're going? Do you remember?"

Lizzie took a deep breath and tilted her head up.

"We're going to Mom," she said, just over a whisper. "Where's Peter?"

"I don't know, bug," Ren said. "But I promise we'll find him."

———

At dawn the next morning, Ren woke to find Hank and Lizzie still asleep. Lizzie's body was toasty, and her cheeks had more color.

Hank's arms still enclosed Ren like a heated blanket. She hadn't felt this secure and comfortable in months.

Ren wanted to stay tucked in there forever. She didn't want to get up to another day of freezing, starving, pain, and fatigue. She stayed perfectly still, savoring the moment.

After a short while, Hank groaned awake.

"Are you up?" he murmured.

"Yes."

Ren was happy when he didn't withdraw. For two minutes, they lay there silently pressed together, just breathing in and out. Hank gently reached down Ren's arm to grasp her hand. He rubbed his thumb back and forth over her knuckles.

"How's Lizzie?" he asked, his nose and mouth brushing her bare shoulder.

"She hasn't stirred much, but she's warm. I think she's doing better."

"Good, then it's time to get going," he exhaled. "I'll need my arm back now."

Ren propped herself on her elbow as Hank pulled his arm free, slid out of the sleeping bag, and stood. He retrieved his clothes from beside the fire's ashes. Ren looked away, but blushed when she heard him putting on his t-shirt and pants.

"The clothes are cold, but they're dry. We need to get back to the river for water before we hike."

Hank handed Ren her things, and she dressed beneath the covers. Her body was covered with tender bruises.

"I don't have much food left, but if we ration, we can make it," Hank added. "We'll keep headin' northwest until we hit a landmark and adjust course from there to the base."

Ren started tying up her boots.

"Do you think that's where Peter and Robert went?"

"They may be lookin' for us, but the river dragged us pretty far away. I'm hoping Robert convinced Pete to get to safety, especially with Fitz and his gang about. If they're not to McChord yet, then I bet they will be by the end of the day."

Ren hardened at Fitz's name.

Hank fished some nuts from his pack and handed them to her.

"Hopefully, we'll find food on the way, but it's more important we move fast. The good news is your pistol seems okay. Besides the axe here, it's our only weapon. Good one for zipping it in your coat instead of your pack."

"I forgot that I had." Ren squeezed Lizzie's arm. "Liz, we gotta get up."

Lizzie rolled over, hair matted to her face.

"Hey," Ren kissed her forehead. "How are you feeling?"

"Hungry. My chest is really sore."

Ren thought of Hank pumping Lizzie's lifeless body. She swallowed hard. "Here, let's get you dressed. It's time to go."

———

The three packed up and moved on in weary silence. Conversation took energy that none of them could spare. Hank and Ren took turns giving Lizzie a piggyback when she needed it. There were only a few beaten paths, so they fought through rough and hilly woodlands most of the day. At least the weather was dry and a bit warmer. When the hunger got unbearable, Hank cut into a pine tree and stripped off some fresh bark beneath the surface. He handed a piece to Lizzie.

She frowned. "You want me to eat that?"

321

"Yep, it'll tide you over so we can save the other food for tomorrow. Lil' trick my dad taught me."

Lizzie grimaced and took a bite, then Ren did the same. It tasted like a chewy, dirty car freshener.

"Just force it down, Liz. You need it," Ren insisted, trying not to gag herself.

———

By sunset, they had hunkered down in a small hunting shelter for the night. Lizzie had just a few bits of jerky before she curled up in the sleeping bag and passed out. Ren and Hank sat by the fire, huddled close for warmth.

"You know, you would have probably been okay if you had dropped your tether," Ren said softly.

"What?"

"On the bridge. Peter had almost made it to you. When you saw the ledge was breaking, you must have known your side would go, too. If you had dropped the rope, you could have saved yourself."

Hank smirked at the flames.

"Yeah, well. Letting you go didn't occur to me at the time." He turned slightly and smiled at her. Then his eyebrows furrowed. "I still can't believe Lee was helpin' 'em. I reckon he's not who I thought he was," he sighed.

Ren remembered Lee desperately wringing his hat in the kitchen that day. He needed help for Caleb and his sister, and she had just walked away, even after he had saved Lizzie. She hugged her knees to her chest.

"There's something else that's been bothering me. Do you

remember that fight between Peter and me?" Ren asked.

"Yeah."

"Peter said I was just like Robert's wife. Do you know what he meant?"

"Oh…erm," Hank hesitated. "Well, Rob's wife was taken by banshees, even though she was tethered to Robert and Zack, right? Well, Peter asked Robert why he thought that happened, and Robert had a theory. I guess it worried Pete."

"What was the theory?"

"Robert said that his wife was struggling with depression and loneliness. He thought the banshees could sense that feeling, kinda like dogs can sense those things. And because the creatures thought she was alone or weak, they went after her—vulnerable prey, ya see."

Ren felt the night air seeping down her neck. She pulled her skull cap from her pocket and slid it on her head.

"Do you think that's possible? Scientifically, I mean," Ren asked.

"Biologically speaking, all animals with social structures have different neural and physiological reactions when isolated or wounded. The fear and feelings of unprotected weakness trigger the release of epinephrine, sweat, and things like that. Conversely, when put in closer contact with others in the herd, it's an entirely different internal state. Herd members feel comforted, protected, and stronger against danger. Certain predators sense the chemical changes in their prey and react to them."

Ren thought of Hobbes, their dog. He always seemed to know when someone needed affection. Mom used to joke about

323

it.

"Here comes Dr. Hobbes for a therapy session."

"People are different, though," Hank went on. "We're complex. We feel secure and connected to others even when we're alone." Hank lowered his voice and looked at his hands. "Or we can feel isolated even when surrounded by people who care about us. That mental state of vulnerability affects our body chemistry, and it's possible these creatures can sense it.

"The dead ones we saw didn't seem to have any eyes that I could tell. If they are sightless, then they probably rely more on smell and instinct."

Ren shuddered and crossed her arms.

"Ren, I don't want to frighten you. Peter was just mad and shaken up. He doesn't really think you're like Rob's wife."

"It's okay. Right now, I'm only thinking about finding him and getting us all back to Mom," she said.

"You will. We should try to get some shuteye."

Ren nodded and slipped into the sleeping bag beside Lizzie. Ren thought about Mom, wishing she had Hobbes with her, but they had sent him to a farm for the week before leaving. Ren grieved at the thought she'd never see Hobbes again and wrapped her arms around Lizzie. Hank climbed in behind her and zipped up the bag.

"Hank?" she asked

"Yeah?"

"Will you please stay close to Lizzie tomorrow?"

"I'll keep close to both of you," he promised.

CHAPTER 59

REN

T hunder woke Ren, sweaty from an intensely vivid dream. Her damp skin made the morning chill even more biting. Hank was already awake and packing up.

"A storm is coming. We have to go now," he said.

Ren rolled over to wake Lizzie. Her cheeks looked sunken, her lips dry and cracked. Thankfully, Hank had assured them they would reach the base by the end of the day.

Ren didn't think Lizzie could make it another night.

They hiked through narrow, wooded trails under a light drizzle. The garbage bag carrying the dead banshees gave off a rancid smell. Ren wanted to leave them behind, but Hank insisted they were too important to throw away.

Ren's feet felt like lead as she stumbled on every root and stone. Completely spent and aching, her movements were powered only by foggy adrenaline. Hank and Lizzie seemed just as tired.

The group came upon a small, abandoned trailer park where they found a few Twinkies and a bag of chips. The calories helped, but the junk food gave Ren a headache.

Hours later, the three emerged from the woods above a two-lane highway running along the side of a lake rimmed by a stony beach. Far out in the water, a lone dead fir tree soared nearly two hundred feet in the air. Half of its bare branches had broken off. An abandoned single-axle semi-truck sat near the road, its tires just touching the shallows of the lake.

The drizzle opened up to a downpour. Lightning lit up the sky with the crack of thunder half a minute later.

"We should rest in the cab of that truck until the rain lets up a little," Hank called over the storm.

Ren squeezed Lizzie's hand. They were dying for another break. A steep rockface dropped from where they stood to the road, but it looked easy enough to descend. Ren crouched over the ledge and dropped her feet over. She led the way for Lizzie, checking each foothold on her way down. Hank gave them a good lead and then followed Ren's path.

"Careful, Lizzie. This rock is slick," Ren cautioned. Ren placed Lizzie's foot on a more stable nook.

Ren's feet touched the grass, and she reached to help Lizzie the rest of the way.

Ren looked up to Hank just as he pressed his full weight on that one icy stone.

"Hank, not there—" Ren yelled, but it was too late. Hank slipped on the sharp rock edge. He screamed as it sliced down his right calf. Hank scrambled for another place to grip, but his balance faltered, and he tumbled violently down the eight-foot drop to the highway. Ren rushed him and cradled his head.

"Is he okay? He's not moving!" Lizzie shouted over the storm.

Ren put her head against his chest, then his face.

"He's unconscious. His leg is bleeding pretty badly."

"What do we do?" Lizzie's jaw started to quiver, and her eyes were squinting and blinking in the rain.

Before Ren could reply, a banshee shriek echoed across the lake. Ren spun around, trying to find where it came from. Then, two more followed.

"Ren..." Lizzie gasped.

Oh, no. Not now.

Ren shook Hank by his shoulders.

"Hank! Hank, c'mon! You gotta get up!"

He didn't respond or move. She bit her bottom lip, trying to decide what to do. She looked at the truck across the beach, then turned to Lizzie.

"He's out cold. Okay...you'll have to help me drag him to the truck," Ren said as she wiped the sopping hair from her face and tied it back.

Another shriek sounded. Ren reached into Hank's pack, pulled out her pistol, and stuck it in the back of her pants. She squatted next to Hank and propped him up, then pivoted away from him.

"Lizzie, help me pull him up," she said. Ren pulled his arms over her shoulders and braced his wrists under her chin. She heaved his body up on her back. Lizzie gripped Ren's outstretched hand and helped pull her to a doubled-over standing position. Hank's body lay limp over Ren's back like a two-hundred-pound cloak.

Holy moly, he weighs a ton!

"Okay, now I'm gonna need you to help hold him steady so I can walk," Ren instructed.

Lizzie nodded and braced her hands around Hank's belt.

"Great, now let's move."

The rain pummeled the three of them as Ren and Lizzie hobbled across the two-lane highway. Hank felt like an awkward sandbag, his weight shifting in different directions with every step. Ren's grip couldn't tighten around his thick wrists. Even with Lizzie using all her strength, it didn't help much. She was just too weak. They both were. The banshee cries grew louder.

"Ren! I can see them! Look over there!" Lizzie pointed down the beach to the edge of the far woods. Ren followed her gaze.

She saw them.

The heavy rain running down their bodies revealed their sleek, terrifying forms. A small herd of banshee silhouettes, maybe twenty, emerged from the trees, walking in a tight formation. They looked like two-legged, headless, translucent wolves. Ren couldn't make out wings until three of them stretched massive sails out and attempted to fly. They seemed to struggle and flail in the windy downpour, then fell after just a few feet. The pack continued to advance on foot, calling out in wails and high-pitched growls.

Lightning streaked across the sky, flashing bright reflections off each approaching predator.

"They're coming, Ren! What do we do?"

The truck stood between the girls and the banshees. It was their only hope.

"C'mon, Lizzie! Lift! We have to hurry!"

Ren leaned hard into Hank's arms, straining under each shaky step. His feet dragged behind her as if intentionally resisting. A trail of his blood stained each rock they stepped over. He was so heavy. Ren's legs wobbled below her.

The banshee screeches sounded louder, overpowered only by the thunder.

"There's three of us! Why are they still coming?" Lizzie screamed.

Ren wondered if they could sense Hank's injury—smell his blood. They had to get him to the cab and cover the wound. The girls slipped and stumbled on the icy rocks, barely able to see as rainwater washed down their foreheads. Their ankles twisted into the sharp crevices. Ren tried to focus on the semi-truck. Just beyond it, the beasts crept closer like an ominous wave. Their piercing cries were incessant.

"Ren! They're getting closer!"

Ren tried to move faster, then careened forward, her knees and elbows jamming between the stones. She screamed in pain and frustration as Hank flopped to her side.

"We have to drag him. Grab his arm! Just a few more feet!" she yelled.

Ren could hardly hear herself over the banshees. The girls hooked their elbows around Hank's, then towed his limp body further.

Finally, they reached the cab door.

"Hop up there and help me pull him up!" Lizzie ambled into the driver's seat. She grabbed the back of his jacket and leaned all her weight back as Ren hoisted him from below. Her thigh and back muscles shook and ached. She rocked onto her toes to give Hank a last heave over the front seat. Ren gripped the sidebar and followed him up. She shoved his legs over and slammed the door closed. The stillness of the truck was an instant respite from the nightmare outside.

We made it. Thank you, God.

Ren panted, fighting back her fatigue. Behind the driver's seat was a folding vinyl partition leading to a small bunk space.

"Lizzie, hop back there. Help me get him through and lay him on the bed," she directed. Lizzie obeyed and pulled Hank's arms through while Ren pushed his torso and legs from the rear. The blood from Hank's calf covered her arms.

"Okay, now, look for a towel or a shirt or something. We have to tie it around his leg, or he'll bleed to death."

Lizzie rifled through cubbies and shelves. She pulled out a white undershirt.

"I found this," Lizzie said.

Something slammed against the outside of the truck. The passenger side door crunched inward.

Barely breathing, Ren peeked over the steering wheel through the windows. The banshees were just outside, tightening the pack around the truck, their bodies writhing between each other, scraping their sharp claws against the cab doors.

CHAPTER 60

REN

"They're trying to get in!" Lizzie cried.

"I know! Just hurry and finish his leg. I'll find the keys," Ren tore through the glove box, dashboard, and console. As she searched the floorboards, another monster slammed into the side of the truck.

"There's blood everywhere. I don't know where to wrap it!" Lizzie said, her voice shrill with panic.

Ren shook her head in exasperation. No keys anywhere. She darted back to the bunk and grabbed the cloth from Lizzie, tearing it into strips with her teeth as two more hard impacts rattled the cab. She wrapped the strips around Hank's pant leg, yanked it down in a knot, then did it over again until the whole calf was tightly sealed. She looked up just in time to see a banshee bust through the small bunk window.

Lizzie ducked as claws scratched through the shattered pane. Its talons stretched into the opening, grasping for the girls. Ren slammed the metal window cover down hard on its legs. It shrieked and withdrew.

"Shutter the other window!" Ren ordered, and Lizzie lunged to the opposite side, wrenching the shade down.

331

At that point, Ren didn't know what else to do. Lizzie startled and whimpered with each sickening collision against the cab.

Ren held her little sister and kissed her head.

"I want Mom," Lizzie said into Ren's chest.

"I do, too," Ren answered. The thought of her mother's face flooded her with longing. She held Lizzie tighter.

Ren spotted a cluster of glistening metal under the driver's seat.

The keys!

She snatched up the keychain and flung open the partition. The banshees were pounding against the hood and roof. Ren slid through to the front seat.

"Ren, no, come back!" Lizzie begged.

"Close the curtain and stay there." Ren jammed the keys into the ignition and turned. The engine grunted and sputtered. She tried again and again, with no result but an empty grind.

"Come on! Please!"

She twisted the key again, praying for a miracle. The truck chugged, the gas gauge pulsing on 'Empty.'

It was no use.

A huge banshee rammed into the windshield. A crack splintered across the glass like the lightning above split through the sky. Ren covered her face just as the banshee hit it again.

The windshield shattered.

Water and glass sprayed into the cab, slicing at her arms and hands. At that moment, she didn't hear the banshee cries. She heard her mother's screams after the car wreck.

"Ren, come back!" Lizzie yelled.

As the creature crawled onto the shard-covered dashboard, Ren reached for her pistol and fired, striking the base of its wing. It yelped and limped across the front of the truck, then rolled to the ground. She shot another one off the hood, and two others scattered at the booming thunder.

The driver-side door was now crumpled and hanging on one hinge. The door took one last powerful blow, then dropped into the horde of beasts pacing just below. Ren sprang toward the partition but was jerked back by her waist to the front seat. Then came another forceful yank on her tether, cutting into her abdomen.

They were dragging her out.

Ren tugged at her rope, trying to untie herself, but couldn't find the knot. With one final pull from below, Ren tumbled out of the cab, smacking her tailbone and arms on the wrecked driver's door. Ren dug her heels into the ground and pressed back against the truck, barely able to see through the downpour. She clambered to her feet as a banshee leaped at her from the group. She jerked and shot it down, then shot two more as they tried to fly above her. The three injured creatures writhed and squealed on the rocks.

Another flash of lightning.

The banshees paced in a wary half circle, shrieking and growling as if discussing what to do next. Another banshee lunged. Ren shot twice. One bullet fired. Then an empty click.

NO! NO! NO!

Thunder exploded above, rattling Ren's ribcage. This time, the pack didn't cower.

Ren swung the pistol around her in defense, now just a

threatening prop. Two banshees hopped on the hood over her shoulder, and she darted away from the truck toward the rim of the lake.

What do I do now? What can I do?

Ren stepped back a few paces, then looked down at the water sloshing around her feet. She gazed at the pouring rain, broken glass, and the twisted metal around her. She couldn't breathe. Couldn't think. And the banshees kept inching closer.

Another blinding bolt of lightning.

For the ones without wings, their backs seemed to churn on the surface with pulsing knobs ready to expand.

CRACK. CRACK. BOOM.

The thunder shook Ren's spine and pierced her eardrums. She heard a high whistling as her arm hair lifted off her tingling skin. An acrid burning odor wafted through the air. She looked up at the tree towering over the lake and the flashing storm clouds above it.

The banshees crouched, ready to spring.

Ren turned toward the dark, deep water.

And she ran.

She sprinted over rocks into the freezing waves. The banshees surged forward, splashing through the shallows, howling at Ren's heels. She didn't look back. At the deep water, she plunged and swam further and further away while the beasts reared back at the drop off. They prowled along the ledge, testing the depths for a shallow path forward. They couldn't swim after her, but they wouldn't leave their cornered prey.

Ren didn't want them to.

She raced on until the water was deep enough. Then Ren lifted her head into the pelting rain, took a deep breath, and dove.

Two feet, five feet, eight feet, ten feet down. Ren clawed and kicked her way through the cold, murky water. At the lake floor, she grabbed onto clumps of weeds and pulled her legs below her, anchoring herself. Ren waited, staring up at the rain splattering on the surface. She could see the silhouette of the enormous tree hovering over her view of the sky.

Thunder cracked. The sky went white.

Ren held her breath under that water, thinking of her father. She remembered the two of them watching a thunderstorm through the window at Pop's house. She was nine.

"Dad, when lightning strikes water, how come all the fish don't get electrocuted?"

"Well, what happens is the negatively charged storm clouds draw all the positively charged water particles upward. So, when lightning strikes, it shoots across the surface, and the fish below are safe—if they're deep enough."

"How deep do they have to be?"

Ren couldn't remember Dad's answer. As the fiery current shot down the dead tree and across the lake, Ren just held on.

She felt it.

The peripheral electricity charged through her body. It burned so badly that she was afraid she was dying. She spasmed and gagged in the water, but held firm to the floor.

Finally, the pain subsided. Her muscles relaxed, and her body went limp.

Swim!

Ren wearily bobbed and kicked off from the dirt, climbing up toward the daylight. She broke the surface and gasped for breath. Allowing herself a moment to breathe, she rolled onto her back. A wave sloshed against her face. Ren reeled up and scanned the shoreline.

At first, she couldn't see anything. Just the empty beach and truck. The shrieking had stopped. The only sound was the rain and the crackling of the burning tree, billowing smoke across the sky. The truck was beaten and wrecked, but no creatures were around it. None anywhere. Ren forced her body in motion, struggling to shore.

By the time her feet touched the ground, Ren saw them— dozens of dead banshees floating lifelessly along the shoreline. Their gray translucent bodies bobbed atop the rough water; wings spread around them like hideous lily pads.

Ren slogged through the shallows, her hands still aching and twitchy.

"Lizzie! Lizzie, are you okay?" she cried.

Nothing.

"Lizzie, answer me!"

Then, the metal window shield jerked up. Lizzie held out her hand and waved.

"I'm here! We're okay!" she called back.

Ren breathed a deep sigh, dragging her dead legs toward the cab. The rain had let up to a drizzle. She willed herself into the truck, and Lizzie flung her arms around her.

"I thought you were dead," Lizzie said. "I couldn't hear you anymore, and I thought they had gotten you."

"It's okay. We're fine now," she panted.

But they weren't fine yet. Hank's leg had stopped bleeding, but the injury was serious. Worse yet, he had barely started to regain consciousness. Ren had no idea how they would make it out of there, and it was only a matter of time before more banshees came.

At that moment, the rain slackened, and a new sound overpowered the drizzle—a soft, steady beat.

It grew louder and closer. Coming toward them from above.

"What's that?" Lizzie asked.

Ren stood on the doorframe, gripping the seatbelt, and looked up. A military helicopter circled above the lake like a dark angel.

Ren grabbed the drop string above the steering wheel and pulled down, blaring the semi-truck horn.

"Lizzie, pull on this!"

Lizzie took over as Ren waved and yelled, choking on her relief. The helicopter touched down on the empty highway.

They were saved.

Robert and two others emerged from the chopper and ran to the semi-truck. Robert helped Ren and Lizzie down from the cab. They both hugged him, and Robert held them back with his one good arm.

"Let's get you out of here," he said.

The uniformed men carried Hank away on a stretcher, collected his pack and the garbage bag attached to it, and then pulled another five dead banshees from the water. Robert helped the girls stumble to the helicopter, both speechless with shock. The officers examined their cuts, buckled them in, and then put

337

headphones over their soaked hair.

As they lifted into the air, Ren felt like she was liquifying into the seat, emotionally and physically overwhelmed. She looked across the cabin at Robert and mouthed the words, 'Thank you.'

He nodded and gave her a thumbs-up.

CHAPTER 61

REN

From the helicopter, Ren could see huge crowds of civilians swarming the airbase. They were standing in food lines, building shelters, and waiting to be checked in. Soldiers were collecting weapons at the gate.

"Refugees," the pilot reported through Ren's headphones. "Mostly from Seattle. The city's infrastructure and most buildings were destroyed by the meteors. We've been trying to keep order and distribute resources, but there's never enough. It's starting to get pretty violent down there. You should stay away."

As the craft touched the helipad, Peter burst through the doors. Ren and Lizzie fumbled free from their seatbelts and ran to him under the last turns of the chopper blades. Ren threw her arms around her brother as Lizzie grabbed his waist. With Peter's height and the way he grasped the top of her shoulder, it felt like hugging Dad.

"I'm sorry," he said.

"I'm sorry, too—for everything," Ren replied, squeezing tighter, her heart swelling. The renewed bond with Peter filled Ren's emptiness so much that she felt almost whole. She vowed never to let anything come between her and her family again. Now, she just had to get to Mom.

———

The next morning, Ren sat by Hank's bedside in the crowded overflow medical center. Small cots filled the repurposed plane hangar, accommodating thousands of people. Most cases were due to hardship injuries or malnutrition, but many were routine conditions you'd see in a hospital. The man in the cot next to them had just had his appendix removed. Down the hallway, Ren had passed a young woman in labor.

Hank had fallen back asleep after the doctor stitched up and braced his leg. Peter and Lizzie were off getting food when Hank finally began to stir. Ren placed her hand on his forearm, and he opened his eyes.

"Hey, how are you feeling?" she asked.

"Wrecked," he groaned. "My leg feels like it was put through a lawnmower. My head is killing me, too."

"Yeah, you took a bad fall."

"That's what they told me," Hank said. He examined his leg and the cuts on his arm. "It sounded like you had a rough go of it after I conked out."

That's an understatement.

"Yeah. Well, we made it." Ren handed Hank a water bottle. He downed most of it and dropped it on the cot next to him.

"You might have died tryin' to save me like you did," he said. "They were most likely comin' after my bloody leg, ya know. You'd have been safer if you'd left me."

Ren smirked.

"Well, leaving you didn't occur to me at the time."

She reached to take the bottle back, but Hank grabbed her right hand with his. He slid his grasp up around her forearm, and she held his wrist—the same way they'd held on when he'd saved her from the river.

"Yeah, lucky for me," he murmured. They regarded each other in silence. Ren was mesmerized as warmth filled her chest. Her pains seemed to subside. She couldn't come up with anything to say next. But nothing really needed to be said.

"Look who's awake, lazy bones," Robert announced as he approached Hank's cot.

"Good to see you, mate," Hank greeted.

Robert had buzzed his hair and wore a camouflage airman uniform with 'Martinez' stitched below his right shoulder. A Velcro brace supported his broken forearm.

"I've gotta say, you've looked better, man," Robert chuckled.

"Yeah, but we'd have been *much* worse off if ya hadn't come for us," Hank stressed. "Thanks for that."

"Don't mention it. How's the leg?"

"Not great, I'm afraid," Hank grunted. "But I'm a quick healer. As soon as I can walk well enough, we'll keep movin'."

Robert glanced around, then leaned over the bed.

"Well, luckily for you, you won't have to go any further on foot. I got you a ride," he said with a wink.

"What? What do you mean?" Ren asked.

A ride. Dear God, can this be true?

"My superiors were so thrilled with those dead critters you brought; they offered to give you a lift home. A crew was headed up there anyway to bring them to a research lab."

"When can we leave?" Ren was trying to catch her breath. She couldn't wait to tell Peter and Lizzie. She thought they'd need days to recover before the final trek to the house.

"Probably tomorrow morning. Just gotta get this guy a crutch." Robert nodded toward the patient.

Ren felt lightheaded as her eyes went glassy. She was going to see her mom tomorrow. Their grueling journey was over. Ren flung her arms around Robert's shoulders.

"I can't tell you what this means to us. Thank you so much," Ren insisted with tearful joy.

Hank cleared his throat.

"Yeah, alright, that's enough of that," he cut in. "Remember, I was the one who carried those stinky buggers all the way here."

Ren laughed again as she released Robert, her whole body jittery with excitement.

———

The next morning, the siblings and Hank packed up and said their goodbyes to Robert and Zack.

"Oh, I have some more good news for you," Robert declared as he led the group to the helipad. "You asked me if we had intel on Australia. Last we heard, they're doin' good. No meteors or banshees. They've invited world leaders to Sydney to work on a defense plan."

Hank looked over at Ren with a beaming smile. "You were right, you clever gal."

Ren blushed and exhaled with relief. Peter held his hand up

for a medium five just like he used to.

"Great job, Ren. Dad would be proud of you."

Robert shook Hank's hand and then waved goodbye from the door. The chopper crew escorted Hank, Ren, Peter, and Lizzie the rest of the way and helped them buckle into seats. The three siblings strapped in side by side and put on their headsets. The propellers sprang to life, churning Ren's whole body with anticipation. As the wind streamed through the open cabin, Ren, Lizzie, and Peter grasped hands.

CHAPTER 62

REN

November 13th, 2027 - Diamond Point, WA
70 days after.

R en held her breath as the chopper descended on the field beside her grandfather's dock. Beyond, she could see the quiet Victorian house with the wrap-around porch nestled among the weeping willows. Ren thought of Pop; he'd built that house and often said he wanted to die sitting on the porch swing.

Two armed soldiers escorted Ren, Peter, and Lizzie from the helicopter to the house. Dead leaves covered the porch, and many broken windows were boarded up from the inside. Apart from the occasional shrieks from the woods, all was quiet.

The two men banged on the locked door, calling out 'Claire' with no response. When they kicked it in, the bolt broke through the door frame, but the door would only open a few inches. An armoire had been pushed up against it.

"Mom!" Ren yelled as she squeezed through into the foyer. "Mom, are you here?"

Leaving the two lieutenants behind, she ran through the main floor and into the kitchen as Peter flew up the stairs. The house was freezing.

"Mom! Please answer!" Ren belted out.

Silence.

Mom isn't here. We're too late!

"Mom!" Ren tried to swallow the panic down her throat.

"Mom?" Lizzie called as she ran into the room. "Ren, where is she?"

Ren couldn't look at her. What would she say? Peter's frenzied footsteps stumbled downstairs and into the room behind them.

"Mom?!" he shouted.

Lizzie turned to him.

"Peter, we can't find her. Do you think she was rescued already?" Lizzie asked.

Peter's breath trembled.

"Uh...yeah, probably," he answered. Lizzie took his hand and looked up at him, but Peter wouldn't let her see his face.

Ren scanned around for some sign of what had happened to her, but the room started spinning.

She couldn't have left. The door was blocked from the inside. Those things must have gotten in...

Ren clenched her eyes tight, fighting the image of it—the terror Mom must have felt when they came for her. Ren couldn't breathe.

"I want Mom," Lizzie whimpered behind her. Ren heard the shuffle of Peter picking her up.

"It's okay, Liz," he said.

This can't be true. It's all my fault.

Peter walked up beside Ren, and she turned to him. His gaze was soft and heartbroken—without a glint of blame.

The folding pantry door squeaked open.

"Ren? Ren, is that you?" came a voice so weak Ren barely recognized it.

Mom emerged from her hiding place, pale and wafer-thin. She held Pop's hunting rifle at her side, leaning against it as if it were the only thing holding her up.

The four stood there, staring at each other—overwrought by all they had been through to get to this moment.

Mom collapsed to her knees. She broke down in tearless sobs, reaching out to her children. They rushed to hold her, huddling together on the floor of their grandparents' kitchen. This was where Dad made his crab cakes. Where Mom wrote their Christmas letter. Where Ren built her telescope. Where Peter always won at Monopoly. And where Lizzie took her first steps. They were together—in this safe place where they never knew fear, hunger, or evil before any of this happened. Ren wanted to tell her mom about their ordeal, how sorry she was, and how much she missed her. All that came out were tears. Mom lifted her head and tucked Ren's hair behind her ear. Ren had never loved her more.

The lieutenants pulled Mom from the embrace and led her to the table. They began checking her vital signs, and one handed her a vitamin shake.

"Drink that slowly," he said.

Mom took a sip, then recounted her story.

"After the meteors, the first radio broadcasts told everyone to stock up on supplies and shelter in place. So, thankfully, I bought enough food for all of us, and I stayed here, waiting for you to come home. When they announced a deadly new species, I tried to leave, but the second I stepped off the front porch, those things were everywhere. Since then, they've surrounded the property, just waiting for me to give up and come out. I shot one when it broke through a window. Then I put the boards up and prayed someone would find me. Nana's stock of her jarred fruits and vegetables kept me alive, but the food had just about run out."

The medic raised Mom's sleeve to take her blood pressure. Ren winced at the sight of her bony arm, the skin sunken between her veins and joints.

"I didn't think I'd last the week and nearly lost hope of ever seeing you three again. I'm just so grateful you're okay." She held Ren's hand, then looked around the room. "Is Pop here?"

Ren and Peter told Mom everything, starting with the night of the boat wreck. In Mom's weakened condition, Ren hated to deliver the news about their grandfather's death. Her mother took it with a mournful strength as if waiting to grieve for Pop when the time was right. When Ren had finished, Mom looked at Hank for the first time.

"So, you're Hank?" she asked. "I'm so happy to meet you. Thank you for all you've done for my family."

Mom stood up to hug him, and Hank held her steady.

"They helped me just as much as I helped them, Mrs. Haley," he said.

Ren helped her mom sit back down and grasped her hand.

"We need to leave for Sydney as soon as possible. Is the *Amelia* safe?"

347

"I don't know."

———

Ren led Hank out to Pop's storage hangar, the tether between them so slackened it brushed across the grass.

"Pop and Dad started working on this boat years ago. They'd talked about taking her around the world, someday," Ren said as she pulled the keys from her pocket.

Heart pounding, Ren opened the padlocked chain and pushed aside one of the metal doors.

And there she was.

Pop's 1970s thirty-eight-foot yacht filled the room like a sleeping giant. Even with the downed mast, the *Amelia* was a grand sight with a deep navy hull and mahogany deck.

Ren and Hank looked at each other and laughed out loud.

"She's a beauty!" Hank exclaimed.

"She is. Wait 'til you see her with sails," Ren insisted. "Pop just finished adding solar panels, the mast lowering system, and a water desalination filter. She could be in the bay and ready to go within an hour."

Hank pulled Ren by her tether, enclosing her waist in one arm. His other hand slid under her hair, cupping the back of her neck. He paused, breathing against her cheek.

Then he kissed her. It was soft and lingering as if he was savoring her with each tender touch of his lips against hers.

It was Ren's first kiss.

And she wasn't nervous, shy, or uncomfortable. It felt like a wonderful dream—exhilarating, blissful, and safe. She wrapped her arms over his shoulders and combed her fingers through his hair. After all they'd been through, she'd memorized his every muscle indentation, each pattern of textured skin, every hair curl dusting his neck. Ren belonged in Hank's arms. Kissing him was the easiest thing she had ever done.

"Look at me, Ren," he said. His green eyes were striking and sincere. "I'm only going back because you're comin' with me. I could never leave you behind. No matter what happens, we're in this together, now."

Ren smiled and kissed him again as he lifted her off her feet.

———

After an hour of inspection, they deemed the *Amelia* seaworthy and ready for the journey. As Ren descended the ladder from the boat, Hank pointed to old cans of navy paint stacked against the wall.

"We should paint her sails," he said with a glimmer in his eye. "After dark, she'll be nearly invisible."

Ren smiled and nodded.

The whole family joined in the project of camouflaging the *Amelia* with renewed optimism. With a brush in her hand and paint speckling her clothes and hair, Mom looked just how she had in her art studio. Lizzie and Peter were laughing all morning, practicing Hank's accent before they all journeyed to Australia.

Ren's face was sore from smiling so much.

Something she hadn't experienced in years.

———

Just before sundown, Ren and Hank found Pop's old Chevy truck behind the house. Ren creaked open the driver's door, climbed into the seat, and found the keys in Pop's glove box. She kissed her finger and touched it to the old photo of her grandmother taped to the radio.

"You look right at home in here," Hank said.

Ren rubbed her hands over the steering wheel.

"I learned to drive in this truck."

Hank grinned and tapped the door frame.

"Good one, gal." He nodded toward the ignition. "Okay, now, give her a try."

Ren took a deep breath and turned the key. The rusty old 4x4 groaned to life.

"It works!" she exclaimed, bouncing in her seat. "It even has a full tank of gas."

Hank leaned in to kiss her cheek, and Ren gave the motor a celebratory rev. The loud rumbling echoed across the field and down to the bay.

———

Peter had the great idea to scout the nearby vacant homes for more supplies. He and Hank spent the evening and the following morning scavenging. Ren, Mom, and Lizzie cheered when the guys returned again and again with heaping boxes of food and other goods. Hank seemed to find the fanfare ridiculous, but couldn't keep a straight face when they chanted his name. What the guys found, in addition to the full food containers from the lieutenants, would easily get them through the voyage to Sydney.

By noon, Ren and Lizzie were consolidating bins in the kitchen when Hank and Peter came looking for another load to bring to *the Amelia.*

"You guys have done an incredible job," Ren commended as Hank and Peter came through the back door. "I can't believe all this food was left behind."

Hank still blushed at her praise. "We ready for the next batch?"

"Yes, these five here, please." Ren pointed to a pile by the door.

"Where's Mom?" Peter asked.

"She's upstairs getting more blankets and towels," Ren said.

Peter and Hank each picked up two of the five boxes.

From upstairs, Ren heard Mom calling to her. "Ren? Can you come help me with something?"

"Yeah! Coming!" Ren called back on her way up the stairs.

CHAPTER 63

LEE

November 13th, 2027 - Diamond Point, WA
70 days after.

Lee, Fitz, Mae, Kenny, and Caleb had been searching the wealthy properties across Diamond Point since midday, finding nothing but cold, empty homes. Just before sundown, Lee led the group out to another abandoned dock in hopes of catching some sign of the Haleys down the shoreline. He peered across the glistening water. Nothing.

Kenny plopped onto the pier and started rooting through his pack for some food.

"How're we ever s'posed to find 'em?" he moaned as he swiped a jelly container clean with his fingers and then sucked on them. "Mae, you said this would be easy."

Lee cracked his knuckles and looked away. He was sick of Kenny's disgusting habits and constant whining. He'd have liked to rip the black nails right off Kenny's grimy digits.

"It's bigger than I 'member, Kenny!" Mae bristled. "They musta built up more since my uncle worked out here."

"Quit belly achin', Ken," Fitz grumbled. The arguing continued, but Lee had gotten adept at tuning them out. He stood next to Caleb at the foot of the dock. Caleb didn't acknowledge Lee, but at least he didn't turn away.

Looking out over the bay, Lee spotted a cluster of floating driftwood. He stared at it, remembering that horrible day at the cove when they'd lost Ozzie and Will, then learned they'd lost Karen too.

All three little ones ripped away in an instant.

Lee remembered how his throat was hoarse for days afterward—sore from screaming their names over and over.

The sound of a banshee cry swooped across the dock. The group huddled together as another flew in from the water over their heads, so close it blew Lee's cap from his head. In a panic, Fitz yanked Mae, throwing her between himself and the threatening wind. She fell into Kenny, who caught her and helped her stand. When it was quiet again, Mae turned to her husband.

"You pathetic lil' sissy," she hissed.

"Shut your mouth, Mae!" Fitz's face contorted, and his ears were bright red.

Mae scoffed and shook her head. Fitz bellowed in anger, kicked rocks, then covered his face with his hands.

He took a deep breath and reached out for her.

"Look, I'm sorry, baby. Those flyin' devils are just makin' me crazy. Had I been thinkin' clearly, I'd never have done that." Fitz put his arm around her and his hand on Lee's shoulder. "You are my family. You're all that matters to me. And I swear I'm gonna get us that boat tomorrow so we can get somewhere

353

safe. That's all I want."

Fitz scanned the others' faces, searching for some sign of support. He gently stepped toward Caleb. It looked as though Fitz wanted to sign to him, but couldn't remember how. Fitz reached out his hand.

Caleb recoiled. Even Kenny looked at Fitz with contempt.

Fitz turned to Lee, his eyes wide and imploring.

"Lee, you're still with me, right?" he asked.

Lee just stared back, expressionless.

Fitz hardened his jaw, then snatched Kenny's jar and hurled it at the trees. Lee thought he heard a muffled squawk, but something else caught his attention.

It was a mechanical thrum, subtle and distant.

"*Shhh!* Did you catch that?" Lee ordered.

The group remained silent. Then, the loud grind of an old truck motor rumbled across the bay. Startled birds fled the trees about a mile northwest of them.

"There! Them birds were probably settin' right over it," Mae said, pointing down the shore. "It's gotta be them."

Caleb nudged Lee's arm.

"What is it?" Caleb signed.

"A truck close by. We think we found 'em."

Caleb looked back at Lee with an imploring gaze, but Lee turned away. Only Penny mattered now. He had to get that boat and get back to her.

"Okay, let's pack it up," Lee directed. "We gotta find that house."

———

354

Just after noon the next day, Lee, Caleb, Fitz, Kenny, and Mae spotted Hank as he carried boxes into the hangar and slid the door closed behind him. Lee felt a surge of relief at finding him still alive. He'd been trying to put the river out of his mind for days. The vision of Hank and those girls falling had haunted him every minute since.

If Hank's here, then Ren and Lizzie must have made it too. Thank God they survived.

"We got 'em," Kenny chuckled. He spat into the weeds.

"Okay, the boat's gotta be in that storage house," Fitz said.

"We need to get Hank fixed first. The family will be easy."

Lee snatched Fitz's arm to look him dead in the eye.

"Don't kill anyone, Fitz. We leave *everyone alive*. Swear it to me, right now."

"Lemme go," Fitz said, shaking him off. "I swear I won't kill anyone, okay? You've got my word. You and Caleb just go get that truck over there to pull the boat out."

Lee hesitated, scrutinizing Fitz for some sign of deceit.

"Lee, I know you two don't want to do this part. Just trust me to take care of it as calm and cool as we can. Aside from Hank, none of these folks is a threat. Once he's tied down, the others'll give up."

Fitz was right.

Lee didn't want to have anything to do with subduing Hank or the Haleys. He just had to keep his eye on the ball and get the boat ready to leave. He knew Fitz wouldn't be gentle if Hank resisted.

But he swore to me he wouldn't kill anyone. I have to believe him. It's almost over.

Lee sighed and nodded, then motioned to Caleb to follow him to the truck.

CHAPTER 64

FITZ

A s Fitz led Mae and Kenny to the hangar, he passed his reflection in an outside window. He froze, not recognizing the figure before him. He was gaunt, dirty, and savage-looking. The overgrown hair from his face and neck lay matted on his muddy jacket. His sunken eyes looked maniacal. This person in the glass was feral with the worn look of someone ten years older.

Fitz turned away from it and followed Kenny across the hangar threshold.

And there it was—the most beautiful classic sailboat Fitz had ever seen, pristine and shiny with a hull that looked like it had never touched water. On the floor beside it, boxes of food and supplies were stacked like birthday presents. Fitz stared in awe. Here was the glorious prize he'd fought so hard for. His chest swelled with pride, and his eyes moistened, knowing he'd done it. He'd saved his family. After all the times he'd let them down in the past, this would finally make up for it.

Fitz heard movement from above. The three walked to the bottom of the ladder as someone stomped from the galley onto the deck.

"I'll go get the last few," said that *cocky* Aussie accent.

Hank. Just who we're lookin' for.

Fitz nodded to Mae and Kenny, pressing his finger to his lips. They raised their weapons.

Hank emerged over the edge of the deck, clean hair and clothes, clearly rested and fed. He climbed down the ladder without even checking to see if anyone was around. Just taking his sweet time.

As comfortable as an ole' goat in a pasture.

When Fitz noticed Hank's leg in the brace, he almost giggled out loud.

"Hello there, koala man," Fitz snarled as Hank's foot touched the ground.

Hank whipped his body around, eyes wide with rage and disbelief.

"Fitz…" was all he could manage. His unarmed hands balled into fists. Fitz was amused seeing this arrogant weasel backed into a corner and hoped Hank would try to fight.

Just give me a reason…

"Hands up, now," Kenny said.

As ticked off as Hank looked, he did as he was told.

"How was the swim?" Fitz taunted. He rested his rifle back on his shoulder.

Hank bared his teeth like a dog.

"Ya think that's funny, do ya? Ya coulda killed an 8-year-old gal and her sister. That makes ya feel tough, does it?"

Fitz flinched, then mustered a cool smile and shrugged.

"It's not my fault the bridge collapsed. And if you had just done what we said right away, you all wouldn't have fell. Now, come over this way and…"

A heavy metal object shot from the boat deck and pummeled Fitz on the bridge of his nose. His vision went red as he fell back, delirious.

"Arg! What was that?!"

"A dang soup can!" Kenny shouted.

Thunk. Thunk.

Fitz heard Mae and Kenny holler and moan as they fell to the floor. Fitz fought to stay on his feet as he grappled for his weapon, now dangling at his side by the strap. He still couldn't see. Blood from his nose seeped down into his beard and mouth.

"Peter, get Kenny's gun," Hank shouted. Fitz was doubled over when he heard Hank barreling toward him. Fitz braced his feet and flailed his arms, still struggling for balance. The room was rocking like a channel marker.

Hank sucker punched Fitz and shoved him against a support beam. Fitz's rifle strap tightened, slipping down Fitz's shoulder.

He's grabbin' the gun.

Fitz yanked back on the strap, then hooked his right arm around Hank's collarbone, trapping him from behind in a bear hold. He reached his left hand along Hank's abdomen until he found the cold steel of the barrel. His right hand snatched the other end of the rifle, pinning Hank against him. Fitz yanked the weapon hard into Hank's gut, squeezing him as he grunted and twisted.

Fitz was starting to get some blurred vision back when a sharp boot hammered his knee, nearly knocking the joint inward. He hollered and toppled, bringing Hank down with him. Hank rolled from Fitz's grasp and started jerking the rifle away. Fitz kept his hands locked on it in a loaded tug-of-war.

Only Hank was holding the smart end of the gun.

Fitz reared sideways and slid his grip over the trigger guard. They crashed into a row of bicycles, ramming Fitz's back into a jagged foot pedal. Hank started peeling Fitz's hand off the gun, but Fitz drove a head butt into Hank's cheekbone. Hank released his grasp and fell back. Fitz staggered, cursing and spitting, furious that this wasn't over yet. This pissant was smaller than him. Probably never even been in a real brawl. But now Fitz had hold of the rifle...if he could just get his balance and clear his sight...

From the other side of the room, he could hear Kenny and the boy scuffling and throwing punches.

Where's Mae?

Hank's shoulder rammed into Fitz's ribs. Fitz fell over a supply box, exploding the contents across the floor. Hank dove on top of Fitz's left arm, pinning it down as he reached for the gun in his right. Fitz could finally focus on Hank's face just above him. It was red and pulsing with fury. Fitz kicked and shifted, but couldn't get him off.

Hank had his hand on the rifle, nearly out of Fitz's grasp.

Fitz glanced over his shoulder. He let go of the gun, snatched a cracked jar, and smashed it over Hank's crown.

Fitz's face relaxed to a grin as Hank's fingers loosened, his head bobbed, and then he collapsed on Fitz's chest. Fitz wiped the jam off his hand on the back of Hank's shirt, then pushed him off like a rag doll. He stood to find Peter and Kenny still tussling.

This kid's a tough one.

Fitz approached Peter from behind and pinned his arms back. The kid tried thrusting his elbows and kicking to get free, but Fitz barely flinched.

"Alright, son. Settle down now," Fitz instructed. "Kenny, let's get him tied…"

Kenny strutted over and jabbed Peter twice across the face. Peter went limp in Fitz's arms.

"Aw, Ken. Ya didn't have to do that to the boy."

"That little runt had it comin'," Kenny barked. He touched his palm to his bloody ear and cursed.

Mae remained seated on the floor, holding her head.

"Mae? You alright, hon?" Fitz asked as he laid Peter on the floor next to Hank.

"Yeah," she answered. Kenny reached his hand down to help her up.

"Okay, let's get these two secured," Fitz said, spitting blood from his mouth. He fingered the chipped edge of a front tooth and tried breathing through his nose. It felt like snorting a wasp stinger.

Son of a gun, that hurt.

Fitz lumbered around the space, looking for a way to contain Hank. His eyes landed on two bicycle chains hanging from the tool wall.

CHAPTER 65

HANK

H ank woke with a start as Fitz clicked the metal bike lock around his chest, securing him to a support beam near the wall. Fitz casually stood and turned away as Hank squirmed in vain against his restraints. Hank noticed his clothes were covered with shards of glass, and his hair and chest were soaked with something. He didn't think it was blood. Hank licked his gooey lips. Tayberries.

That ogre hit me with a jar.

His head felt like a beaten, fleshy sandbag. He couldn't lift it. Peter lay on the floor beside him, barely moving.

"Peter," Hank gurgled, then cleared his throat. "Pete, ya okay?"

Kenny's shoes appeared next to Peter. He hunched down and pulled Peter's wilted body from the floor.

"No, wait. Fitz, you can have the blasted boat. Just leave us alone and go," Hank grunted. His focus felt dislodged and fluid. Hank heaved his head up, and it flopped back against the beam. Kenny had Peter over his shoulder. The boat was gone, and the hangar doors were opened wide.

"Don't you worry, Hank. We're fixin' to depart right now. Mae and Kenny wanted to thank you for all the food you packed for us. We'll be sittin' pretty out on the water in this floatin' paradise," Fitz jeered.

"Leave Peter…" Hank implored.

"Now, Lee don't want us to kill nobody. Had me swear to it," Fitz said with mock solemnity. "So, I'm just gonna leave you tied up."

A devilish smile spread across his face as Fitz dangled the tubular bike lock key in front of Hank.

"The key will be safe and sound right…there." Fitz threw the key far into the field weeds.

Rat…turd….mud…dingo!

Hank tried again to wriggle free, angling his torso against the beam to try to slip out. It was no use.

"Hey, Kenny," Fitz went on. "It's a beautiful afternoon. How 'bout we leave this big ole' door open for our buddy?"

"Good idea," Kenny agreed.

"C'mon, let's go," Fitz said. On his way out, Fitz gave Hank a last kick in his busted foot, sending spasms up his leg.

Hank groaned, but wouldn't give Fitz the satisfaction of asking for mercy.

The three walked away without looking back, Peter dangling between them like a deer carcass.

Hank struggled and twisted, pressing his aching body against the chain.

The shrill call of a banshee blew in from the field.

Oh, bugger.

Hank fixated on the enormous entryway. A sharp wind

363

swayed the outside trees, then gusted through the weeds just beyond the threshold. A second one blew in behind the first, both landing with a crunch on the gravel. The pebbles sprayed as they launched back up into the hangar rafters. Two shrieks echoed within the cavernous steel walls.

Hank could make out two rippling mirages gliding past the high window. They circled, landed, then moved from the tool table to the wall, to the small desk beside Hank, and then off again, kicking up papers that floated down around Hank's legs. The room settled as both creatures landed in front of him. He could see impressions of their feet on the gritty floor. Their dust-covered skin took shape in the light from the door.

The closer one growled.

"Right, come on then!" Hank shouted. "Get it over with!"

One set of clawed footprints drew nearer, then scraped off the floor. The wind from its hovering wings blew the hair from Hank's face.

Hank could feel the terrible creature just above him. He could hear it breathing in his wounded scent.

The dust and jelly dripping down Hank's face burned his eyes. Accepting his fate, he closed them.

Hank held his breath and braced for the pain.

The banshee held, billowing before him, sucking forceful breaths in and out. After a last lingering moment, the thing let out a final shriek.

Then both banshees flew away.

Hank exhaled in disbelief and confusion. Why had they left him? He should be dead. At that moment, though, it didn't matter.

Where's Ren?

She and her family were in danger, and he was still stuck under this blasted rusty bike chain.

Hank searched around him for some way to get free. It was impossible to slip through the bonds. He grazed his leg through the fallen papers for a solution, some kind of miracle.

Hank spotted the corner of a blue Bic pen and looked down at the tubular lock again.

Thank you, Lord.

Hank arched his knees and started pulling the papers toward him with the tip of his boot.

CHAPTER 66

REN

R en and Mom were hauling supplies downstairs when a
sinister voice sounded from the front yard.

"Hi-dee-ho in there! Hey, Ren, we got yer brother out here."

Ren froze, dropping her box of clothes.

Fitz?! No, it can't be.

"Ya hear me in there? Come on out now and see!" the voice
said.

"Who is that?" Mom whispered as Ren crossed to the
boarded window and peeked out.

It *was* Fitz and two others from his gang.

And they had Peter.

"Hello in there!" he yelled again.

Ren lunged toward the kitchen to fetch her pistol, then
remembered it was already packed on the boat. She pressed her
hands on her head, trying to figure out what to do.

"Ren!" Mom repeated.

Ren grabbed Mom's arms.

"*Shhh*, don't say a word," she whispered. "It's them. The
people who've been chasing us."

"They've got Peter!"

"I know. I'll get him. You go find Lizzie and hide somewhere," Ren directed. "Hurry!"

Mom hesitated, eyes darting between Ren and the door.

"Go, now," Ren ordered. Her mom nodded, then dashed toward the back. As soon as she was out of sight, Ren flung open the door and stepped out onto the porch.

Mae, Fitz, and Kenny stood just below her like a pack of mangy hyenas. Ren fixated on Peter, praying for any movement.

His leg twitched.

Thank you, God. He's alive!

Ren exhaled and tightened her shoulders, determined not to show fear.

"Give me back my brother," Ren demanded, her tone firm and even.

"Aww, it's good to see you again, too," Fitz sneered. "We don't want to hurt anyone else. We just need the keys to your pretty boat over there, and we'll leave yer brother here with you."

Ren pulled the boat keys from her pocket and held them up by the anchor key chain.

"Good girl," Fitz said. "Now toss 'em over, nice and easy."

Her eyes narrowed.

"And what about Hank? Where is he?"

"Hank's fine. We left him safe and sound in the hangar. Let's stay focused on Pete here, though. You don't want to cause his death like you did your ol' grandpa, do ya? I'm sure you must feel real guilty 'bout that."

Ren's skin burned with rage and loathing.

"How do I know you'll let Peter go?" she seethed.

Fitz cocked his head and winked. "You'll just have to trust me."

What choice did she have? Ren tightened her fist around the keys, the metal teeth digging into her palm. That boat was their salvation. All of their food and supplies were on board.

She looked at Peter, loosened her fingers, and tossed the keys to Fitz.

"Very good. Thanks so much," Fitz said. He swung the keychain into his palm and then squeezed it into his pocket. He and Kenny shared a victorious snicker.

"Now, bring me Peter," Ren pressed.

Fitz helped Kenny set Peter on the grass. They propped his body up against the picket fence twenty feet from the porch. When Fitz pulled a bike chain from his shoulder, Ren shouted, "No! You said you'd give him to me!"

"No, I said I'd *leave* him with you. And I am," he answered. "Now, we're gonna lock him to this fence and walk away. When I say it's okay, you can scurry down here to scare off the beasts. I'm sure they'll be on 'em in a moment if you don't. In fact, I think I hear some of them now."

Ren heard them, too.

A cluster of restless banshees chirped in the weeping willow just beyond the gate. The branches sagged, and the hanging reeds rustled, shaking loose the last of the withering leaves. She gauged the distance to her brother as Fitz, Mae, and Kenny backed away, further and further.

"Okay...*now*," Fitz shouted.

Ren leaped from the porch as the three ran away toward the

dock. Ren took ten sprinting strides to the fence as a shrill wind swooped off the roof and blasted her from behind. She wrapped her arms around her brother and held tight, ducking her head into his chest. The call quieted, and she could hear a creature perch on a tree limb with the others.

Peter's chest swelled with a deep breath.

"Peter?!"

He moaned, still slumped forward. His nose and mouth were bleeding, and his hands were battered and swollen.

Ren tugged on the bike chain, trying to slide it off. The tight metal dragging over Peter's wounds made him cry out in pain. He couldn't slide out. Ren started kicking at the fence post to break it when Mom rushed out to the porch.

"Mom, stop! Stay there!" Ren warned. "Those things are everywhere."

"Lauren, I can't find Lizzie!"

"*What?*"

Ren jumped to her feet. She looked down at Peter and then back to her mom.

"Ok, then, come here to guard Peter. I'll try to find her."

Cautiously, Ren took just a few steps from the fence post to bridge the distance to the house. Mom inched down the porch steps and started sliding her feet onto the path. A shriek rang out.

"Now! Go!" Ren yelled.

The mother and daughter ran toward and past each other, just brushing shoulders as they switched places. The banshees flurried and whistled. Now, the adjacent willow also creaked and swayed under banshees settling on it—both trees bearing more and more invisible weight on their limbs. A few high-pitched,

369

hungry barks from one creature were mimicked by the others surrounding the yard.

Ren raced through the house, looking in all of Lizzie's favorite hiding places, calling her name. She cursed herself for leaving her sister alone in the house. How could they have been so careless? Ren ran back to the front and shouted for her and for Hank, praying they were somehow together. Their names were drowned out by the squawks of the banshees, which only frightened and infuriated Ren more.

"Mom! What do I do?" she yelled in desperation. "She's not here!" Ren screamed once more at the yard and garden. "Lizzie!"

Peter bobbed awake at Ren's cry.

"Mom…." he uttered.

"Peter! We can't find Lizzie!" Mom said, cupping his face in her hands. His swollen lips quivered as he tried to speak.

Peter weakly murmured something in her ear.

CHAPTER 67

REN

N o!" Mom gasped. "Ren, the boat! Lizzie's on *the Amelia*!"

Ren's heart raced as she looked toward the boat ramp one hundred yards away through the field. The stolen craft was already unhitched from the trailer and tied to the dock. Lee and Fitz were securing the *Amelia's* mast, while Mae and Kenny walked alongside her on the dock. They were ready to leave— with Ren's little sister somewhere aboard.

The banshees were now yelping nonstop and flapping up and down in a fever. They burst through the willows' reeds, howling as they advanced and withdrew—inching ever closer as Mom tended to Peter's wounds.

Ren looked at her mother and brother, heart racing. If they couldn't free Peter, Mom couldn't move. How would Ren make it to the boat with no one to run with her? It couldn't be done.

Then, if Ren died trying, the two of them would surely die too, stuck on that fence post. If Hank was still alive, he'd die trapped in the hangar.

But if I let that boat leave the dock, I'll never see Lizzie again.

She grabbed her hair and closed her eyes, wishing she knew what to do. Her dad would be able to figure this out. If only he were here with her. But he was dead and gone—like Pop and Grandma.

Through her heaving breaths, Ren remembered what Mom said about her grandmother.

"She's with you, too, ya know? Just like me and Dad, Pop and Pete, and Lizzie. That's the great thing about having people who love you. You're never alone."

Ren remembered what Hank said to her that night by the campfire.

"...People are more complex. We can feel secure and emotionally connected to others even when we're alone...predators can sense it..."

Then, she recalled Minna's story from that day on the cliffside.

"It's like Daniel in the Lion's den. Daniel had strength in knowing he wasn't alone...And the lions, they stayed."

Ren thought she knew what to do, but was too afraid to try it. She didn't trust herself. As the banshees grew louder and more aggressive, she staggered back toward the house.

The last night with her father flashed across her mind, his arm wrapped around her, walking in the rain, reminding her not to give in for anything. She could still feel the warmth of his shirt, hear the soft reassurance in his voice.

"We love you, and we believe in you all the way. Just remember that and run like hell, okay? Show 'em the rocket."

Ren looked at Mom and Peter, then at the dock. She whispered to herself as she tightened her body like a loaded spring.

"Ren. The. Rocket."

Ren touched her necklace.

Then she ran.

Ignoring the perilous screeches and her mother's pleading, she ran. She thought of Pop hugging her on the *Bethie,* Peter and Lizzie's embrace at the base, Hank kissing her beside the boat, and her mother snuggling with her in the art studio.

Ren kept running.

The banshees exploded from the trees like a hurricane. The monsters swarmed, dove, and swooped around her, shrieking in a horrible, deafening chorus. The violent wind nearly blew her off her feet as she tore through the tall grass. But they didn't attack her. They were letting her pass.

Ren kept running.

"Kenny, shoot her!" Fitz shouted.

From the dock, Kenny raised his rifle and aimed.

"Don't!" Lee hollered just as Kenny fired. But his shot hit two beasts flying in Ren's path. They fell grey, stunned, and squawking on the ground before her. She hurdled them both and kept running.

"Why aren't they gettin' her?!" Mae yelled.

Ren saw Mom and Lizzie nestled with her on the porch swing, Dad beside her at a rocket launch. Her parents dancing and singing in the kitchen. She heard the songs in her head. She felt them with her, the comfort of their arms around her shoulders. She wasn't alone. They were there. All the people she'd ever loved were on that field, protecting her as she ran.

Mae raised her rifle.

"No, Mae! I said stop!" Lee screamed. "Fitz, please!"

"Drop that girl, now!" Fitz bellowed.

Another shot rang out, and Ren braced for the bullet to hit her.

But it was Mae who dropped, shot dead through the chest. Her body rolled off the pier into the icy bay.

"Mae! No!" Fitz cried. "Kenny, get out of there!"

Now alone on the dock, Kenny lunged back toward the boat. But it was too late. He screamed just before he was dragged under a herd of wailing banshees and disappeared.

LEE

Across the field, Lee saw Hank appear from the side of the house, looking up from his rifle.

"It's Hank!" Fitz raged. "I'll kill him!"

Hank answered him with another shot as Fitz crouched behind the deck benches.

"Start the boat, Lee! Go!" he ordered.

In a panicked daze, Lee fumbled for the keys. Fitz was looking through his sights for Hank, but he'd disappeared into the trees. Fitz cursed aloud, then shifted the rifle barrel toward Ren. She was still sprinting toward them, closer and closer, and completely unprotected.

"I gotcha now, girl," Fitz murmured over the loaded barrel.

"No!" Lee shouted again and leaped to stop Fitz, but Caleb emerged from the cabin and got there first. Caleb gripped Fitz's rifle with both hands, face to face with his brother—his enemy— trying to wrestle it away. Fitz growled. He popped his elbow in Caleb's face and flipped him overboard like a discarded catch.

"Caleb!" Lee cried as he ran to the railing, shoving Fitz from his path. Caleb had managed to keep hold of the deck by his fingertips. The two locked eyes as Lee reached for Caleb's weakening grip.

"Leave me! Get the girl!" Caleb said in his broken voice. Then Caleb's fingers slipped, and he fell into the freezing bay.

——

REN

Ren ran on, the shrill calls of the banshees surrounding her. She saw her family at the beach. Biking with Lizzie. Cooking with Mom. Saw Peter beside her, racing her to the dock as they had so many times before. A banshee swooped again, its wing burning her cheek. She didn't falter.

Ren's stride hit the dock, clunking over the uneven boards. The *Amelia* had drifted a dozen feet from the edge. She took a deep breath, envisioning Dad and Pop waiting for her at the end of the pier. As she rushed toward the edge, her toes nearing the last plank of wood, she felt their hands grab her arms and catapult her body to the escaping vessel. Ren flew, pumping her legs through the air. She hit the deck with her midsection, pounding the wind from her lungs. Gasping, she tried to scramble up the ledge. Her toes scrounged for a hold on the polished hull. Her fingers were slipping.

———

LEE

"Caleb, no!" Lee stared at the water with stabbing dread until his brother finally resurfaced.

"The girl!" Caleb yelled again, pointing toward the middle of the boat. Lee spun around.

There, on the cabin steps, was Lizzie, crouched in the shadows. Lee saw her and instantly thought of Penny. He saw his little sister sitting below him on the dim basement steps, looking up with her bright eyes. Lizzie was just as innocent and just as scared as Penny would be if she were here. He couldn't bear it anymore.

At that moment, for Lee, it was over.

Lee crossed toward the galley, but Fitz grabbed the back of his shirt and jerked him around.

"What are you doin'? We have to go!" Fitz yelled.

"We gotta bring the girl back," Lee demanded, pointing at Lizzie.

Fitz stared at their hostage in manic shock. He froze for just a moment, then tightened his grip.

"There's no time!" He growled as he pulled Lee away from her. "They're comin' for us! Do you want this boat, or do you wanna die?"

376

Lee reeled out of Fitz's hold, then punched his older brother across the jaw. Fitz stumbled back, caught himself, and then wobbled forward. Lee hit him again, only harder, as if pummeling all the bad that had spawned in Fitz since that terrible night in the woods. Fitz slumped against the railing.

Lee snatched Lizzie up in his arms just as he had done at the market when they first met. And, like last time, Lizzie didn't resist. Lee cradled her and stepped to the railing, searching for Caleb. Banshees hovered in a clustered blur just above the water, waiting for his brother to surface. Caleb came up for a quick breath, and the creatures swooped down on him like hawks on a fish. Caleb dodged and dove under, just beyond their reach. As the banshees leaped up from the surface, water rushed down silhouettes of their empty claws. Caleb was trapped underwater.

"We gotta jump in. I gotta save Caleb, then I'll take you back, okay?" Lee promised as he grabbed a life vest. "Hold on tight. It's gonna be cold."

Lizzie nodded and clung to him.

Lee stepped to the railing as Fitz raised his gun.

"Stop, Lee! Put the girl down," he ordered.

———

FITZ

Fitz's hands quivered around the rifle now pointed at Lee, his brother, the person he loved most in the world.

"Fitz, it's over now," Lee insisted.

377

Fitz swallowed hard. This betrayal was like a knife in his ribs.

"So that's it?" Fitz asked. "You were gonna just jump in and leave me here to get eaten? After everything we've been through? I mean...you're all I got left."

Fitz heard Caleb splash to the surface, gasp, and gargle a scream as he went back down. The banshees howled and shrilled as the wind blew Lizzie's hair across Lee's chest.

Fitz tried to close his ears to it. "I said, drop the girl," he repeated, but he couldn't steady his voice.

"Please," Lee said, and he put her down behind him with the same care he'd always used with Penny.

Fitz's baby sister.

Lee turned and raised his hands. "They won't let Caleb up to breathe...Fitz, he'll drown."

Fitz looked over the railing at Caleb, struggling below the water. As the freezing north wind coursed through his coat, Fitz remembered that cold night in the woods. When he'd heard Bull attacking his two brothers. Fitz hadn't hesitated to put himself in harm's way to protect them.

Fitz was a hero. He was *their* hero when they needed it most.

Fitz watched Caleb fighting for his life. Only this time, Fitz wasn't the hero. *He was Bull.* A worthless brute, now hurting the ones he once fought to save.

Fitz's chest and knees weakened. He lowered the rifle as his eyes moistened.

"Thank you," Lee said, reaching for the gun.

A crack rang out from the field when Hank let another shot

go. Fitz felt the bullet rip into his shoulder, knocking him against the railing. Lee lunged to cover him as Hank fired another. It caught Lee in the side.

Lee collapsed to the deck, clutching his waist.

"Lee, no!" Fitz howled, and he reached down for him.

"Hold it there!" Ren stood across the stern with Kenny's rifle locked on Fitz. "Back away."

Fitz's insides twisted as he shuffled backward, his arms aching to help his brother.

But Fitz could see it in Ren's eyes—the same anger and resolve Fitz had felt when he held his rifle on Bull. She was ready to shoot him dead if she had to.

"Lizzie, come here to me," Ren said.

Lizzie darted to her sister and clutched the back of her jacket. Beyond the railing, the banshees' screams for Caleb rang in Fitz's ears.

He turned unsteadily and looked into the water as his younger brother gasped a flooded breath, barely sinking in time to escape their clutches. Fitz knew he wouldn't have long before he got too cold to fight.

And it had been Fitz who'd put him there.

Lee had pushed his back against a bench seat, still trying in vain to get up and save Caleb…, but if Lee jumped in that water, neither of them would come out alive.

And they both deserved to live.

"I'm sorry, Lee," Fitz said. He snatched a lifesaver from its hook. Ren fired a shot as Fitz leaped over the railing and into the bay.

The freezing water stung his skin and hardened his lungs.

379

Fitz dove beneath the dark waves and reached for Caleb's arm. Fitz hauled him up to the surface. The banshees scattered above them with raging shrills. Treading water and quaking from the cold, Fitz pulled Caleb's body through the lifesaver. Caleb's cheeks and hands were greyish blue, and he was barely moving.

"C'mon, Caleb. Wake up, brother," Fitz said, rubbing Caleb's shoulder. Then he called up to the boat. "Please, he needs help! Lee, help me."

—

REN

Ren looked down at Lee, hunched on the deck against the benches. He held his side as he reached for the rope to the lifesaver. It shifted on the deck just beyond his fingertips.

Lee lifted his gaze to Ren.

"Please help my brother," he said. "I'm begging you. Please save Caleb."

Ren looked into Lee's eyes, the same eyes that had reassured her after he'd saved Lizzie's life. The same eyes pleading for her help in Minna's kitchen before she'd turned away.

Ren set the rifle down. She grabbed the rope from the railing and propped it over her shoulder. She turned toward the dock, dug her feet in the deck, and pulled.

"Lizzie, help me," she beckoned, wrapping the cord around her hands as she fought for another step. "Put the rope around the port railing and pull it back this way."

Lizzie wrapped the rope through the bars as a pulley, then started tugging it back toward Ren. They could hear the trickling water as some of Caleb's deadweight lifted from the surface, dragging up the starboard hull. Ren grunted and fought the cord slicing into her shoulder muscle, but she inched further. Her feet started slipping.

"Ren," Hank called.

She looked up and was overcome with joy at seeing Hank alive as he ambled toward her.

"It's Caleb," Ren pleaded. Hank nodded and grasped the rope.

Together, the three lifted Caleb over the rail and laid him on the deck.

LEE

"Caleb," Lee rasped.

Oh, God. Please let him be okay.

Lee watched as Hank sat Caleb up and slapped his back hard. His skin was a translucent blue, and his hands quivered on his lap. Hank pounded again, shouting Caleb's name for a response.

At last, foamy water spewed from his mouth, and Caleb reared back for his first deep breath. Lee burst out a short sob of relief.

"That's it, mate," Hank said, propping him up. "Liz, run and get dry blankets. Ren, start the engine, and we'll get the heater goin'.''

Caleb moaned, but kept breathing. His eyes were open now.

In a weary fog, Lee remembered Fitz. He strained to look above the edge of the deck and saw Fitz treading water just below. His big brother smiled back up at him, a last glimmer of peace in his gaze.

Then the banshees returned, and Fitz didn't fight. They pulled him from the water and smothered their phantom wings around him until there was nothing left.

Fitz...

"Lee!" Lizzie's cry was muffled, and her footsteps sounded miles away. She kneeled next to Lee in the expanding red puddle on the deck and pressed her small hands to his side. "Ren, help me!"

Lee bobbed his head to look at Lizzie.

"You remind me of my little sister," he said weakly. "My lucky Penny." He smiled, remembering her face and the way that she laughed. But darkness overcame his vision as Lee went numb.

CHAPTER 68

REN

December 2nd, 2027 - 1,500 nautical miles southwest of Seattle. 90 days after.

Three weeks later, Peter manned the helm as the *Amelia* flew southwest toward Australia, her dark sails nearly invisible against the Pacific blue. Ren sat on the foredeck, watching Hank and Lizzie mend a fishing net. Sidling up next to Hank, Ren noticed a red blotch on the back of his shirt. She scratched her fingers over it.

"This shirt still has tayberry jam on it. Haven't you washed it?" Ren chided.

"Yes, I have. I'm sorry if it offends you, m'lady, but that stuff stains, and it's not like I have a bunch of other shirts to choose from. Right, Liz?"

"Yes, that's right," she agreed.

"So you'll just have to deal with it," he snipped.

"Fair enough." Ren smiled and affectionately tucked his hair behind his ear.

"Hey, Lizzie, look at that blue whale!" Hank announced,

pointing over the starboard side.

"Where?" As Lizzie spun around to scan the water, Hank pulled Ren in for a kiss.

Lizzie turned back and rolled her eyes.

"Next time, just tell me if you're gonna kiss, and I'll look away myself," she said.

Ren laughed and wrapped her arms around Lizzie.

"Hey, Ren, can you get me some scissors, please?" Hank asked.

"Yeah, and can I have a water?" Lizzie added.

"Sure." Ren stretched as she stood.

On the way to the cabin, she called to Peter at the wheel.

"You need a break?" Ren asked.

"Nah, I'm doing good. You could tighten the vang for me, though," Peter said.

Ren gave the pulley connecting the boom to the mast a good tug.

"That's good. Thanks," he said.

As Ren moved toward the steps, she paused to look at him once more.

"You look a lot like Dad right now," she said.

"Yeah?" Peter's chest swelled, and he smiled. "Thanks."

Mom was reorganizing shelves in the cabin as Ren came downstairs.

Ren hugged her from behind.

"You're still in here?"

"Just trying to get this done," Mom sighed.

"Why don't you take a break? Go get some fresh air, and I'll help with this later."

384

"That does sound nice. I think I will." Mom turned and kissed Ren on the head. Then she went up the stairs into the sunlight.

Ren scanned the galley, thinking. Where would Pop have kept the scissors? She rummaged through cabinets and containers. She opened a bottom drawer and found them sitting on top of an old Discman and several battery packs. She picked up the music player and popped open the lid. Inside was a CD with writing on it.

Favorite Mix for Claire, Love Nick.

Ren put the headphones on and pressed play. She smiled and stuffed the scissors in one pocket and the Discman in another. Then, she grabbed two water bottles and headed upstairs.

At the stern, Ren found Lee resting on a bench as Caleb fished off the back of the boat. Mom had insisted on how lucky Lee was that the bullet passed through his side like a needle. He and Caleb were listening as their little sister, Penny, read from one of Lizzie's books. She had already gained some weight and color since they'd picked her up from Gladys. Mom said having Penny there was helping Lee heal faster.

Ren stepped over and handed one of the water bottles to Lee. He reached up to take it and wrapped his hand around hers.

"Thank you," he murmured.

She knew it was for more than the water.

Ren smiled at him and nodded.

CHAPTER 69

ROBERT

**December 2nd, 2027 - Military Research Facility. Seattle, WA
90 days after.**

B ack in Seattle, Staff Sgt. Robert Martinez stood before his commanding officer and two scientists in a sterile, windowless room, his arm now healed.

"After extensive test work on the two alien subjects you brought us, we've found that the toxic substance was some kind of fruit, likely a type of berry it had recently ingested. It may have been eaten by a person they preyed upon," one of the researchers said.

"If we can find out what it is, we'd have a chance at beating these devils. Sergeant, you were at the site where the creatures fell, correct? Do you have any idea what it could have been? These gentlemen have tested countless berries with no luck, and meanwhile, the beasts are getting bigger and more aggressive every day."

Robert stared at the three men, straining to find an answer for them. Sally's jam label flashed across his mind.

"Have you tried tayberries?"

The End

I was born and raised in New Orleans, LA, where I spent my childhood immersed in adventure stories, often cultivating elaborate imaginary worlds in my bedroom and backyard. This early love for "pretend play" naturally evolved into a deep passion for film, creative writing, and theater in high school.

I put my creative passions aside when I attended the University of Georgia and the University of Texas business schools and chose a career as a CPA.

When I had my first child, I left the corporate world to start a photography business and began writing multiple award-winning screenplays. Now a mother of three living in Atlanta, I've decided to fully embrace the pursuit of storytelling, which has been a dream come true. I'm so thankful for my friends, family, and readers for supporting me in this extraordinary journey.

www.ingramcontent.com/pod-product-compliance
Lightning Source LLC
Chambersburg PA
CBHW010513100726
47903CB00009B/2720